OTHER BOOKS IN THIS SERIES

A Suitable Affair
An Improper Encounter (2018)

THE PERFECT
DUCHESS

Erica Taylor

Amberjack Publishing
New York | Idaho

AMBERJACK
PUBLISHING

Amberjack Publishing
1472 E Iron Eagle Dr.
Eagle, ID 83616
http://amberjackpublishing.com

Publisher's Cataloging-in-Publication data
Names: Taylor, Erica, author.
Title: The Perfect duchess / Erica Taylor.
Series: The Macalisters
Description: New York, NY; Eagle, ID: Amberjack Publishing, 2018
Identifiers: ISBN 978-1-944995-57-7 (pbk.) | 978-1-944995-58-4
(ebook) | LCCN 2017948763
Subjects: LCSH Twins--Fiction. | Family--Fiction. | Marriage--
Fiction. | England--Social life and customs--Fiction. | Historical
fiction. | Love stories. | Regency fiction. | BISAC FICTION /
Romance / Historical / Regency
Classification: LCC PS3620.A9432 P47 2018 | DDC 813.6--dc23

Cover Design: Red Couch Creative Inc.

Chapter One

May 11th, 1813
London, England

ndrew Macalister, the Duke of Bradstone, hated his birthday.

And he hated the Macalister Birthday Ball.

Well, perhaps not entirely, as it was difficult to hate something that had been so beloved by his mother. The Macalister Birthday Ball was an annual event carried on in her memory, but hosting five hundred masked members of London society's *haute ton* was the exact opposite of what Andrew wanted to be doing on his twenty-ninth birthday.

Andrew nodded pleasantly at two simpering ladies as they strolled past. Or rather not exactly pleasantly, as he was scowling at the ladies, but they did not seem to notice—or care—and he was fairly certain one winked at him in return.

Repressing an exasperated sigh, his gaze slid to the man standing beside him, eyes narrowing into a glare. His younger brother, Lord Luke Macalister, averted Andrew's hard gaze, his shoulders trembling with suppressed laughter.

"It is not my fault if the ladies of the *ton* are a little more forthcoming this evening," Luke said with a shrug. The top half of his face was hidden behind a black mask, but his lavender eyes twinkled with glee. Andrew wished the masks were better at concealing identities, but he knew hiding from the hordes of society was never truly an option. He was forever known to the masses; he would only ever be the Duke of Bradstone.

His own black half-mask was one of two things that made the evening marginally tolerable. Thankfully, this was not a traditional masked ball, and Andrew was grateful for the absence of elaborate costumes. His older sister Sarah, the widowed Marchioness of Radcliff, had what she claimed was an "ingenious idea:" send a simple black half-mask with every invitation.

"Happy Birthday, your g-g-grace!" a well-wisher tried to say. Andrew turned to regard him, but the poor gentleman lost his nerve. Why he had this effect on people, he had no idea. Twelve years ago, he had just been the plain Lord Andrew Macalister, and in his own mind, he still was. His title had changed, not him, and it irked him that everyone felt his acquisition of a dukedom required a change in how they treated him. It was not that he was not appreciative of his current circumstances, just the conditions that prompted it. One moment he was a lowly second son with little in the way of prospects, and the next, a highly sought after duke who wanted nothing more than to hide in the attic. That hadn't been a possibility at the time, or any time since, and it certainly was not an option now.

So he stood in a foul mood turning darker with each tick of the grandfather clock. The only thing that kept him from running from the room—the only thing, besides the lack of costumes, that had the ability to make this evening tolerable—was the lovely Lady Clara Masson.

Lady Clara was a bright spot on an evening that had the potential to be utterly miserable. He had known Lady Clara since she was a child, and despite their complicated history, it seemed fitting that this particular woman would be the one to catch his eye—again.

The crowd parted a fraction, and Andrew had a clear line of sight to the object of his attention dancing a lively country dance. She was breathtaking, laughing in the arms of her partner, her blonde curls bobbing as a few unruly ones fell rebelliously out of her coiffeur. She was average in height and in possession of elegant curves Andrew could discreetly appreciate.

Lady Clara turned away from her dance partner, separated by the steps in the dance. As she moved along the line, her eyes scanned the crowd and fell onto Andrew's.

For a second Andrew could scarcely breathe. The top half of Clara's face was hidden beneath the damned black domino, but he could see that her dark eyes had an unusual sparkle. They widened a fraction as she focused on him before turning back into the dance with choreographed steps.

The momentary glance had lasted barely a second, but Andrew felt his mouth go dry and his heartbeat increase. It would seem she recognized him as well. It would not do well to be caught staring again. The Duke of Bradstone did not stare. The Duke of Bradstone was never infatuated. And the Duke of Bradstone would most certainly not be interested in *this* particular lady.

Andrew tore his eyes away, lest the *ton* observe his interest. He shuddered to think what would happen if he appeared to be even remotely interested in any young lady, much less this one. His well-crafted barrier managed to keep the marriage-minded females away, and he was usually avoided at most functions, even his own, mainly due to the scowling, brooding expression he plastered on his face. It was not that he was unusually unhappy or perpetually ill-tempered, though everyone thought him so. It was simply difficult to carry on a conversation when people, particularly women, were either too intimidated to utter an intelligible sentence or were drowning him in ridiculous flattery. People only wanted him because he was a duke.

"A very Happy Birthday to you, your grace!" came another well-wisher, and Andrew nodded politely to the gentleman before him. The red-headed man grinned widely, and Andrew scowled, recognizing one of his oldest friends behind the black half-mask, Lord Rheneas Warren, the Earl of Bexley.

Grumbling, Andrew muttered, "Bexley, please, not you as well."

"His graceness is in a mood this evening," Luke warned, and Andrew shot another glare at his brother. "Graceness" was an adaptation of "grace," which his siblings used to poke fun at him. Unfortunately, the teasing name had caught on and was used more and more often.

"It would appear so," Bexley observed.

Glancing at Andrew, Luke noted his disgruntled mood. "You do appear awfully distracted, old man."

Andrew shrugged nonchalantly, and Luke laughed.

"Next year it is your birthday that will be plagued with this dreadful event," Andrew vowed. "It would be reasonable to argue that since this ball is in celebration of all our birthdays, we should share the blessed event. Having it on my actual birthday makes it *my* birthday ball. And I would prefer to *not* have such an event fall on the date of my birth."

"What would you wish instead?" Luke asked, turning his inquisitive eyes onto his elder brother. Andrew stared at him for a moment, aware that Luke's question had an uncharacteristically somber undertone. His brother may have been a rogue and a flirt, but occasionally he carried a remarkably serious current about him. Andrew opened his mouth to reply, to tell his brother to sod off and let him be in his foul mood, but he stopped himself. There was no reason to take his frustrations out on his younger brother. Luke was merely being Luke: poking about where he did not belong and asking the wrong questions.

Andrew shrugged again, turning back to the dancing couples, his eyes searching for a certain blonde dressed in pink. "Something that did not involve the *ton*."

The dance floor was a blur of black, pink, gold, and the ever-present debutante white. Everyone was dressed fashionably and extravagantly, adorned with crystals, sapphires, rubies, ostrich plumes, and delicate beadwork. Each of his guests wore the same simple, black mask, and for a brief moment, Andrew saw the beauty in the simplicity of Sarah's idea. With all the extravagance and elegance, the flaunting of one's wealth and position, on this one fact they were all forced to be the same, equal.

He spotted Lady Clara again, smiling brightly at her dance partner as the last strings of the country dance came to an end. In the past five years, she had been the only one to catch his attention, to demand his notice. His mind wandered, intrigued by the idea that he could just walk up to her and ask her to dance with him. After all, he was the host, and technically, they had already been introduced.

Luke eyed Andrew for a moment more, his perceptive eyes taking in more than just the duke's irritable mood, before breaking out in a brilliant grin. "How can we cheer you up then? It is your birthday, after all."

"There are a number of lovely widows in attendance," Bexley suggested.

"Do not get any ideas," Andrew warned, looking away from the dancing couples, away from Lady Clara. "My only desire is to endure the rest of the evening."

"We are merely suggesting someone to keep you company as you brave the remaining evening hour and, possibly, the early morning as well," Luke replied.

A pair of vaguely familiar girls draped in their debutante whites stepped past the gentlemen, drawing Andrew's attention away from his brother. The room was nearly bursting at its seams, and the occupants were forced to stand almost improperly close to one another. The two girls took advantage of this, pressing a bit too close as they passed, giggling as they mumbled their apologies with heavily-lidded eyes and slow, seductive smiles.

"Happy Birthday, your grace," one young lady purred, and for the life of him Andrew could not remember her name. Not that her name mattered; the debutantes were all the same. They stared at the pair of Macalister brothers like ravenous men before a feast.

Not wanting to give the silly girls any invitation to linger, Andrew nodded, and, luckily, the pair moved to stand a few steps away, sipping their champagne. Andrew breathed a sigh of relief.

Luke raised an eyebrow at him and sighed. "Your loss."

The music was starting again, and Andrew searched the edges of the dance floor for Lady Clara. He spotted her in the corner nearest him. His height gave him a slight advantage over the rest of the ballroom, and he peered at her as discreetly as he could. She seemed to be in conversation with a young woman Andrew recognized as a friend of one of his sisters.

The conversation did not look to be a friendly one. Lady Clara tilted her head up slightly in defense, and he wished he knew what was being said. The unknown lady stood directly in front of her, blocking Lady Clara's only exit from the ballroom. Andrew realized her only other option was to turn completely around, walk back across the dance floor, and leave out a side door. Clara was stuck, forced to endure or interrupt the gathering couples on the dance floor. Her escape seemed impossible.

"Oh look, the trollup is finally being put in her place," said one of the girls to his right, dramatically conspiring with her friend. Andrew glanced at the girls who had passed moments earlier and saw they had also noticed the exchange.

The second girl giggled. "Serves her right for showing

her hussy face here. When will she learn she's not wanted?"

"She's already been ousted from Almack's," the first girl replied. "If I had my vouchers revoked I doubt I'd ever show my face again, much less at such a public event."

"What is Lady Laura saying to her?" the second girl asked, and Andrew looked back at the confrontation.

Ah, Lady Laura. Norah's friend, Andrew remembered.

"As a dear, personal friend to the Macalister family, Lady Laura was horrified she showed her face here," the first girl explained. "I'm sure she felt it was her place to say something to Lady Clara. It is not as though she was invited. I am shocked Lady Clara was not denied at the door."

The girls giggled again, and Andrew stepped away from his brother and friend and the safe haven of a certain exit. He leveled a dark glare at the two girls before striding off towards the corner of the dance floor.

Lady Clara Masson was doing her best not to plant her fist in Lady Laura's pretty blue eye. Realizing their encounter was starting to draw more notice, Lady Laura's voice was steadily growing louder with spite. Clara wanted to escape back to when she was dancing and laughing and no one cared to be rude to her, when no one wanted to acknowledge her presence. She was tolerated because of her beauty and because her brother was the Earl of Morton, although her brother despised her and made no secret of it. The *ton*, it seemed, did not know what to do with her. Her brother had made her a social pariah by refusing to associate with her, but her scandalous reputation was built mostly on rumors. For the most part, people pretended she did not exist. One moment she was sought after and the next she was avoided, though the reason was not a secret. She knew everyone thought she'd been involved in her sister's disappearance, or that she was responsible, and it did not help that her brother treated her like she was an illness. Until this moment, Clara hadn't really minded her position on the edges of society. She was a part of the *beau monde* by birth, but she was not welcome. She had survived without vouchers to Almack's and an abundance of friends doting over her. Clara merely wanted what every other marriageable-aged woman wanted—a means to escape her own family.

Her brother, Lord Jonathan Masson, the Earl of Morton, was not in attendance tonight, though Clara was certain his absence had more to do with their host than her. She glanced about the room again, trying to keep her wounded pride out of her eyes, hoping no one would flat-out tell her to leave. That might be the final crushing blow, and she was not sure how much longer her spirit would hold out.

Sensing Clara's resolve starting to crumble, Lady Laura smirked, fanning her face with her lace fan, her pale blonde curls moving with the breeze.

"Darling Lady Clara, how did you get on the guest list?" she inquired. "I did not realize prostitutes were invited to society functions."

"Only the good ones," Clara replied cheekily with a sweet smile. "Isn't that why you are here?"

Lady Laura's eyes glowed murderously, and her grin thinned to a sneer. "It is so nice to have you returned to London after your adventures on the Continent. Tell me, was it an Italian lord who paid your way? Did you repay him on your back?"

Clara balled her first, her nails digging little crescents into her palm through her white gloves.

Lady Laura tilted her head forward to whisper loudly, "I doubt Bradstone would be happy to see you here making such an inappropriate scene. I imagine you were turned away at the door. Pity you had to sneak in through the servant's entrance." She popped her bottom lip into a pretty pout. "Poor dear, no family who wants her. No friends to speak of. Whatever shall become of you?"

Clara decided she might as well hit the lady and be done with it. It would be quite satisfying. She glanced around at the sea of faces, and it seemed like all were turned towards her. Everyone was watching, waiting for her to take a wrong step, to completely fall from their good graces. Until now, all they had were rumors and false leads, and Clara was not one who was easily chased away, especially when she hadn't done anything wrong. Anyone else would have fled to the country, away from the stares and whispers, and the malice dripping from the polite smiles of the *haute ton*. And even if Clara had wanted to flee, she had nowhere to go.

The mass of people swam before her eyes as fury and tears threatened to spill over, and Clara swallowed down the crushing fear that surfaced when she was reminded of her deplorable options in life. He brother hated her, and her family avoided her for fear of her brother; everyone else was dead.

A face from her past was suddenly clear amongst the blur of the ballroom. He was tall, dark, and deliciously handsome, and he was heading straight towards her.

Clara recognized the Duke of Bradstone at once. His eyes were hard, his stride full of purpose, and for a split second, Clara thought he was coming to throw her out. A very public fall from grace, she knew that was what Lady Laura wanted and what everyone was expecting. Clara braced herself for the end, but then the duke turned his gaze onto her, and his face softened.

"Lady Clara," he said, bowing over her hand, a gentle look in his blue eyes. "I believe this is my dance."

"Yes, of course, your grace," Clara replied smoothly, blinking away her shock as she smiled at Lady Laura. "It was nice to see you again, Lady Laura."

Lady Laura's eyes flamed in outrage, and Clara swallowed down the panic she felt seconds before.

The duke swung her into the waltz that had already begun, and they fell effortlessly into the steps, like they had danced them before. But they never had, despite having known each other since their childhoods. She eyed him expectantly, trying to assess his mood. The Duke of Bradstone was a stranger to her, but she knew Andrew Macalister very well.

"I apologize for my tardiness, my lady," Andrew said. "It is quite difficult to move across the ballroom quickly."

"Yes, well, do not let it happen again," she replied brazenly with a shrug and a smile.

His lips twitched, and she was reminded of how handsome he was. Dark, curly hair, always meticulously cut, coiled behind his ears. His eyes were a deep, bright blue, like the sky reflected in the pools of the Lake District near her country home in Cumberland.

"I am quite pleased to see you," he said. "It has been a long time."

"I am not too afraid to show my face in public, you know," she retorted, a little more venomously than she intended. "If they think they can chase me away, they are severely mistaken."

"I never thought you the type to tuck tail and run," Andrew replied.

"Yes, well, these rumors floating about have me a little on edge," Clara admitted as they moved across the floor in time with the thirty other dancing couples. "You must know the things said about me are not true. I would hate for such things to lower your opinion of me."

"It would take a lot more than some silly rumors for that to happen," Andrew replied. "My opinion of you is not based on the opinions of others."

"I wish the rest of the *ton* had your good sense, your grace," Clara replied. "Regardless, I was given strict orders not to attend this ball. My brother does not know I am here."

"You snuck out?" Andrew chided in mock outrage.

Clara laughed. "Did you really think I was going to miss this? Besides, it was a bit of a rebellion on my part, I will admit. He explicitly said no one was to attend, 'no one,' of course, meaning *me*."

"And you came anyway."

Clara nodded. "Of course I did. When Jonathan issues such an order, it is like an invitation to disobey. It was fun, if not the tiniest bit dangerous."

"Dangerous," Andrew repeated to himself, grinning at her as he twirled the two of them in an unnecessary turn.

"What is the fun in life if there is no danger, no excitement?" she asked, returning his brilliant smile with one of her own, a little dizzy from the turn. "One ends up stodgy and boring and cranky, like my brother, who claims that masked balls are the very epitome of impropriety. If they are so inappropriate, then how is it that so many people flock to them each year?"

"Because people want some excitement and danger in their lives," Andrew replied. "Secretly, of course, this is all done with the presumed anonymity of a mask. Not that these masks are any good at hiding anyone's identity." The music ended, the last strings of the waltz quivering in the air, and he held Clara for one breathless moment longer than necessary.

He looked at her and seemed to be taking in her entire face as if for the first time. An odd glint twinkled in his eyes before they stepped away from each other.

Clara glanced around the ballroom, scanning the sea of faces. Everyone was seemingly uninterested in the dancing couples but obviously desperate to have firsthand knowledge of the night in order to have the best gossip tomorrow. She knew it had been reckless to come tonight, but her Great-Aunt Bridget had goaded her into it, claiming she would be there to chaperone. True to her erratic and eccentric disposition, Great-Aunt Bridget was nowhere to be found. Luckily, another aunt was in attendance and had agreed to act as Clara's chaperone, if only in name, as long as she behaved herself. Aunt Lucinda did not want word of their associating to get back to her brother lest he peg her as an accomplice. Jonathan despised anything 'Macalister' almost as much as he despised Clara.

The music began again, and Andrew swept her into his arms for a second dance.

"Tell me, your grace, what is the most dangerous thing you have ever done?" she asked him, embracing the forwardness she was rumored to possess. She typically was not so presumptuous, but this man seemed to always draw out a side of her she often forgot existed.

"Probably rescuing you from the clutches of Lady Laura," he replied, though she knew it was not the truth.

Clara nodded in agreement. "Yes, that was a most unfortunate encounter."

"I was not certain if I was rescuing you from her or if she was the one in need of the rescue," he commented, glancing down to her. "You looked ready to hit her."

Clara laughed. "I wanted to. But even I am not that brash."

"Other than Lady Laura, are you enjoying your evening?"

"Immensely so," she replied and smiled up at him. "Are you?"

"My evening has taken a turn for the better," he replied. His eyes twinkled again.

"All it takes is dancing to lift your spirits?"

"With the right partner. . ."

"How are you sure that partner is me?" Clara asked coyly. "Are you prone to entertain multiple partners in one evening?"

Andrew swallowed hard, blinking at her in brief amazement. A lovely blush raced up to her face, but she did not look away. She impressed herself with her composure.

"I danced twice earlier this evening," he answered. "Once with one sister, and then again with another."

"Prearranged, of course."

"Of course," he replied.

"Your sisters are very lucky to have you as their brother, your grace," she added, annoyed at the wistfulness in her voice.

"Compared to your brother, I must appear a saint."

"Indeed," she replied.

"Will he be displeased when he discovers you attended tonight?"

Clara nodded. "I had hoped to slip away unnoticed with no hint of anyone discovering I was in attendance." She sighed. "I was foolish to think that I could force society to accept me despite the horrid things said about me. I should have known they would choose my brother and the lies." She watched as the blue of his eyes grew into a dark, stormy tempest. His face hardened, and he looked away.

"Oh dear, I've done it again," she sighed. "My audacity has ruined yet another evening. Please forget I said anything, your grace. I should not want to ruin your birthday celebrations."

"You are not ruining anything," he practically growled at her. "I just—"

Andrew clamped his mouth shut, and Clara took that as an end to the conversation. His behavior was baffling, though she had long given up on understanding him.

As Lord Andrew, he had laughed and teased and enjoyed life. As the Duke of Bradstone, he was cold and hard as stone, hence why the gossip rags dubbed him the "Stone Duke." She had liked Lord Andrew—she did not know what to do with the Stone Duke.

Andrew did not look at her for an entire turn around the room, and she gave up on her attempt at forcing him into conversation. This was the last dance until supper, and she hoped she could make her escape without another incident.

The duke stepped away abruptly and bowed again, the dance set ending. As she dipped into her curtsy, Clara studied his hardened expression, taking in his handsome features. Andrew was a full head taller than her, and she had to tilt her head to meet his eyes. His shoulders were broader than she remembered; they fit perfectly into his flawlessly tailored evening coat. His cravat was expertly tied, and an elegant and expensively jeweled cravat pin winked at her in the candlelight.

Tilting his head to the side, he did not say anything as he studied her, almost as if he were seeing her for the first time. Clara did not want to break his gaze or the magic of that exact moment because she knew the real reason she had snuck out of her brother's London residence was for a chance to see this man again.

Watching the lovely Lady Clara was something Andrew realized he could do for hours. He was mesmerized by the way the flecks of gold in her eyes reflected the candlelight. There was a touch of worry in those eyes, and it annoyed him that she had a reason to be worried. He caught a couple of inquisitive glances from his sisters as he moved Lady Clara off the dance floor. He ignored them, pretending he was not about to cause an uproar among the marriage-minded females in the room. Never had he danced with a woman who was not his sister, at least not in the last five years. The repercussions of his rescuing Clara from the likes of Lady Laura would be unfathomable, but he was choosing to pretend it was nothing.

I will figure this all out tomorrow. Tonight, I will just enjoy it.

The crowd had begun to count down to midnight, led by his brother Luke, half a room away clapping to the countdown, laughing with his cronies around him.

"Five, four, three, two, one!" There was a loud "Huzzah!" rousing laughter and applause as everyone took off their masks. Andrew pulled off his mask, pushing it back over his head as Clara fiddled with her ribbons, her fingers slipping on the knot. His gloved fingers moved over hers, and he untied the knot, the mask sliding to her hands.

Shyly, she trailed her gaze up to meet his, her dark lashes blinking hesitantly. Belatedly, a genuine smile spread across her face.

Gads, he had forgotten how beautiful she was. It nearly stole his breath away.

"I do not believe I have wished you a happy birthday, your grace," she said sweetly, her voice soft and warm. At the sound of the words "Happy Birthday" people around them turned to see who was wishing who a happy birthday. This sparked another round of "Happy Birthday, your grace!" before they realized who had originally spoken the words and pointedly turned away, shooting disapproving glances her way. Clara's eyes darted around the ballroom, and Andrew could see the hurt of rejection on her face, and it angered him. The light that had glittered in her eyes moments earlier had dimmed; the flicker of danger and excitement had faltered. While he was a largely accepted member of society, she was not.

Of course, after all these years it had to be Clara to make him break all his own rules. He chuckled at the absurdity of it, and a few glances darted their way.

"I'd appreciate it if you would not laugh at me, your grace," she said sternly, her voice firm, and he looked down to her eyes practically spitting fire at him.

"I was not laughing at you, Lady Clara, just at the situation."

"I fail to see what is so amusing," she said crossing her arms across her chest, her black domino mask gripped tightly in her hand.

"Just that it was you under your mask and me under mine," he admitted. "Of all the people in this entire ballroom, it was you and I in the end."

"I still don't see the humor," she replied. "Now if you will excuse me—"

"You are not going to join me for supper?" he asked, halting her with his hand on her arm.

She looked down. "I don't think that is such a good idea," she answered, her gaze slowly trailing up to meet his, holding for a moment before glancing to the people surrounding them who were discreetly watching their interaction.

Shrugging, Andrew replied, "We danced the supper dance together, which grants me the courtesy of escorting you to supper. Unless, of course, you are eager to get home."

He knew she was not. He knew she wanted more than anything to stay and be a part of the festivities. That was the problem: he knew Clara Anne Louise Masson, had known her for years. Andrew had once been the boon companion of her older brother, the Earl of Morton. Once, he had dared her to a diving contest at her Lake District home, once he had thrown toads at her and always celebrated when he bested her in a horse race. And once, five years ago, Andrew had been engaged to Clara's twin sister.

Clara eyed him suspiciously as he offered her his arm.

"What harm can it do?" he asked softly.

Hesitantly, she accepted his arm. He looked down at her, drinking in her light. He noted her delicately arched eyebrows, one currently raised in either confusion or amusement. Her nose was a tad too full to be considered perfect, but it suited her face. Her rose-colored lips were pulled to the side as she chewed on the inside of her cheek.

"What has gotten into you this evening?" she wondered.

"I just feel like living a little dangerously tonight," he shrugged.

Clara rolled her eyes in exasperation, and he released a loud bark of laughter for the first time ever as far as the *ton* could remember. It would be the talk of the town the next day, he could see the lines of the gossip rags practically writing themselves.

Before leading her into supper, the usually stoic Stone Duke of B— uncharacteristically danced with, laughed with an unmasked Lady C—, the slightly scandalous twin sister of the woman who had jilted him at the altar five years earlier. Could this indicate the Duke of B— is back on the marriage mart? Faithful reader, we will wait and see . . .

Chapter Two

lara was not exactly sure what had come over her. Her carefully crafted plans to be gone before supper had disappeared swiftly out the window on the late spring breeze. She tried to remain calm and collected and, most of all, composed, but doing so under the Stone Duke's intense gaze was a feat on its own, much less without five hundred or so people watching their every move.

The massive dining hall was lined with countless tables adorned with elaborate candelabras and floral arrangements, with every remaining inch covered with food. Footmen waited with individual platters and assisted guests with plates of cheeses, meats, fruits, and a delectable table of sweets. The crowd swarmed to the tables, flocking to the food.

Clara walked demurely by Andrew's side, her hand never leaving his arm. She was not sure how he managed to keep her by his side or if it was even appropriate she be there. What made it worse was that everyone noticed. She was generally avoided, sitting on the edges of society as everyone watched her flirt with disaster and boldly continue to show her face, knowing she was one misstep from officially falling from their ranks, and yet, somehow, she hadn't. It was like an unspoken currency among the *haute ton*; those with the best, newest, and juiciest first-hand gossip could rule the gossip mill. A good piece of gossip was worth its weight in gold, and Clara was their golden goose. Everyone watched the almost-ruined Lady Clara on the arm of their host—the place of the duchess.

Worse, it was painfully obvious. Andrew smoothly introduced her to numerous people, but no one knew where to look or if they should smile or nod or bow or glare. Everyone knew of her name; the reactions on people's faces left no mystery about that, however, no one knew who she was to the duke. No one wanted to insult his grace, but no one wanted to be friendly to her either. Andrew seemed oblivious, smiling at her much too often, including her in conversation where the topic might have warranted her opinion. Clara had never talked so much at a social event in her life.

While she truly wanted to deny it, she was very aware of the duke. Not because he was a duke or because he had once been engaged to her sister, but he had always had an effect on her, even years ago when she met him as a child, before he could not see past the brilliance of her twin.

Five years earlier, Clara had ruled society at the right hand of her twin sister, Christina. It had been a natural position, being the twin sister of the Belle of the season, and Clara had found it enjoyable, amusing even. It had all been a bit silly, but sometimes the attention was appreciated. She never outshone Christina's radiance, even though they were physically identical. Christina had been a tad more charismatic; people had flocked to her and waited with bated breath to hear what she had to say. Clara, by association, had been pulled into her sister's popularity. People wanted to know her and be friends with her because she was Christina's twin. Andrew had even been struck by her radiant power, so much so that he proposed marriage to Christina soon after one dance at their debutante ball.

In the end, Christina had cried off, leaving Andrew standing at the altar. Clara had been dragged to the country until the scandal of Christina's abdication wore off. A year later, just a month before the start of the new season, her father, the old Earl of Morton, died. Clara was about to reenter society as her own person and not as an extension of her sister, and suddenly that was all gone. Into mourning they went, and Jonathan assumed the title. No season for Clara. And then, almost a year to the day later, they received the news that Christina had died as well, and she was forced back into mourning, another season lost.

Two years of mourning was really quite boring. She had been out of her blacks for just over two years, but this was the first chance she had to return to society. Jonathan had refused to fund her a season, he refused to sponsor her at all. Clara thought her chances thin to ever get an opportunity to make a suitable marital match of her own, but then her Great-Aunt Bridgette had intervened and demanded Jonathan show some sort of familial commitment to his sister, insisting he bring her back to London. Great-Aunt Bridgette had funded her season but warned she would extend such a kindness only once.

Normally Clara never stayed for supper—too confining, too many people to stare and point and whisper. Upon reentering society at the beginning of the season, the whispers seemed to follow her everywhere. No one wanted to believe she had been in mourning all this time, everyone had chosen to create their own details of her life and believe them as truths. Balls and dancing provided activity and entertainment; it was easy to hide behind laughing and flirting and not have to think about what people were saying about you.

"Are you enjoying your meal?" Andrew asked, and she looked up at him, smiling politely.

"It is wonderful, your grace," Clara replied.

"Is it?" he asked. He leaned forward an inch and whispered, "How could you know if you have not even taken a bite?"

Clara glanced down at the fish on the plate in her hand and realized he was correct. Not that she would have eaten it.

"I am afraid you have caught me in my faradiddle, your grace," Clara replied charmingly. "I am actually quite sensitive to fish, in fact, to all meat that comes from the sea."

"Really?" he asked, and looked bothered by this new information. "I did not know."

"I see no reason why you would, your grace," she replied.

He shrugged. "No matter. Now I am aware; I will make certain no fish is served when I know you will be attending one of my events."

He looked down at her just then, and the look vibrating through his eyes set her heart thumping wildly in her chest. Her entire body felt warm under his smoldering gaze. The sounds of the dining room faded away, and, for a brief moment, all she saw was Andrew, the boy she had once fancied as a young girl.

The sound of rambunctious laughter tore his eyes away from hers, and she released a breath she did not realize she had been holding. What he was creating in her, the way he was making her feel . . . it just would not do.

Another party guest again monopolized Andrew's attention, and while he appeared to be interested in what the young lord before him was discussing, it was apparent Andrew was not particularly involved in the topic. The young lord glanced at her curiously as she stood by the duke's side in the middle of the dining room. Andrew glanced her way every now and then, offering a teasing smile before politely looking back to the other guests with feigned interest. She was certain he was not actually interested in the trends of iron exports used for the two wars Britain was currently engaged in, or the proper way to rotate a crop, or how the elections of the next prime minister were going to shape the nation's future, but he pulled off his act as a dutiful host with skillful ease. Then again, she had known him a long time ago. Maybe this was who he had become over the years. Maybe he was no longer the boy she once knew.

Andrew was bored senseless as he listened to Lord Marlow natter on and on about his ingenious crop rotation system. He did not have the heart to cut the man off and tell him his system was a waste of time. As much as he wished otherwise, he needed to be a polite and hospitable host, just as Sarah had drilled him to be for years.

"Your grace," Lady Danbury said dipping into a curtsy.

Quickly swallowing his mouthful of food, Andrew nodded to her. Lady Danbury was a woman well past her youthful prime, but she refused to admit to that fact. He thought she must have been beautiful during her days as a debutante, but her marriage had weathered her in years, as she was surely closer in age to his aunts than his sisters.

Lady Danbury smiled, blinking her long lashes at him before turning her steely gaze onto Clara. "Lady Clara, it was such a pity we did not see your brother in attendance this evening."

Clara swallowed the piece of carrot she had just put into her mouth and smiled sweetly at Lady Danbury.

"He was here for a few minutes," Clara replied, and Andrew knew she was lying.

"I must have missed him," Lady Danbury said.

"How could you know for sure you did not see Lord Morton, Lady Danbury?" Andrew inquired, turning his gaze onto the malicious countess. "Everyone was wearing a mask."

Laughing lightly, Lady Danbury smiled an almost flir-tatious smile at him. "Of course, your grace, how silly of me. But then, Lady Clara—" Lady Danbury looked back at Clara, "you remained without him here. How very . . . *bold* of you."

"I am flattered you think so of me," Clara replied smoothly, a hint of challenge in her tone. "But alas, my brother merely made sure I was properly in the care and chaperonage of my aunt before leaving. He has no fondness for masks."

"You are here with your aunt?" Lady Danbury asked and looked around the room which was still compacted with ball guests. "How unfortunate that you were separated from her."

"I am certain I will find her by the end of the evening," Clara explained. "I, of course, would have come into supper with my relations, but since I danced the supper dance with his grace, he was kind enough to escort me to the dining room."

"How generous of his grace," Lady Danbury said, looking back at him, attempting to pin him with a sultry glance. He tried his best not to blatantly glare at the countess, no matter how rude she was. Noticing his ire, she shrank back.

"Lady Danbury," Andrew began. "I believe I missed Lord Danbury this evening."

Lady Danbury had the decency to blush. "I believe he is still in Devon dealing with estate business. My good friend Mr. Chauncer is fetching me a glass of champagne, and I had to practically beg him to accompany me tonight, as I would not miss your birthday celebration for anything. I wish you a very Happy Birthday, your grace!" she said, raising her empty glass to him which resulted in another chorus of five hundred or so people cheering, "Happy Birthday!" He nodded and drank from his own glass, and Lady Danbury wandered off.

Glancing down at Clara, he watched as she gazed longingly at her plate as it was removed from her fingers by circulating footmen.

"Is the supper over?" she asked, almost wistfully.

"Unfortunately, I think so," Andrew admitted as his own plate was removed. "Would you like something more to eat?"

"Oh, no, your grace, I have had enough," Clara replied, her smile returning. "A perfect midnight snack after a night of dancing."

"We have Gunter's just through here," he said, slipping her hand back into the crook of his arm. He pointed to the doors at the side of the dining room, the same ones they had come through from the ballroom. There were doors all along the wall that opened back into the ballroom. "But we cannot go in until my sister Sarah says we are allowed."

A dark-haired beauty with an annoyed expression on her face came through the crowd at that exact moment, and he could not help but inwardly cringe. Sarah did not look pleased with him.

"Andrew, there you are," Sarah said, trying to stamp down her irritation with an overly affectionate tone. "Gunter is ready if you'd like to proceed."

"Thank you, Sarah," Andrew said. She nodded to him and smiled tersely at Clara before being swallowed back into the crowd. Winking at Clara, who looked bemused by his sister, Andrew pulled her toward the ballroom doors.

"What is your favorite?" he asked, glancing down at Clara.

"Favorite what?"

"Of Gunter's ice flavors," he clarified.

"Oh, um . . ." Clara thought for a moment, her brows pulling together, her lips drawing to one side as she chewed her lip. "I have not been to Gunter's in ages, but I remember enjoying the lemon. What about you, your grace?"

"I enjoy the strawberry," he replied. "Or sometimes the peach."

"I would have thought you an enthusiast of the vanilla," she replied.

He laughed. "I am fond of vanilla," he replied, ignoring the heads that turned again in their direction. "But not in an ice. Something about it as ice cream just isn't quite right on my palate."

"I agree," Clara said. They paused along the wall of doors and accepted a glass of champagne from the footmen. One footman offered Andrew a small fork which he tapped along the side of his glass, the tinkling sound halting all other sounds in the room. All eyes were on him.

"I would like to extend a very gracious thank you on behalf of my siblings and myself. We are all thankful to have such wonderful family and friends to celebrate our birthdays each year. The masked ball was a particular treat, and I would especially like to thank my sister, Lady Radcliff, for her ingenious idea." A round of applause rippled through the crowd with a loud cheer from Luke before everyone looked back at Andrew. "My mother started the tradition of this birthday ball over twenty years ago to celebrate all of her May-born babes, and we continue in her honor each year. Please join me in a toast wishing us all a very happy birthday, and may we see you all again in another year."

Another loud chorus of "Happy Birthday!" and Clara smiled at his nice sentiment before taking a sip of the delicious champagne.

"Let us return to the ballroom where Mr. Gunter has graciously provided a special treat in honor of the occasion," Andrew concluded, and the doors behind them opened into the ballroom.

With Clara on his arm, they led the promenade of guests back into the ballroom. He knew he was making a spectacle of himself, and of Clara by extension. His attention to her would not go unnoticed. But he was amazed to realize that he did not care. He liked having her beside him.

"I thank you, your grace, for a wonderful evening," Clara began, glancing up at him through her long lashes. "But I think I must take my leave. I am sure my aunt and uncle are ready to retire for the evening. Late nights are not typical for them."

"You are welcome to stay without their chaperonage," Andrew offered. "I am certain my sister would be willing to act as your interim chaperone until you are ready to leave." He could see the deliberation going through her mind, and she pulled her lip to the side and chewed the inside of her cheek. It was most endearing, and he was certain she was unaware she was doing it.

With a sigh and a shake of her head it seemed she had made up her mind. "It is a most generous offer, your grace, but I really must be leaving. I will have the wrath of my brother to answer to in the morning, I am sure, and he is easier dealt with on a decent night's sleep."

"You must have an ice first," Andrew insisted, steering her toward the side tables where Gunter and his associates had set up serving stations.

"I really should—" Clara began, but he cut her off.

"I insist, Lady Clara," he said before smiling at her. "It is my birthday after all."

"Is today your actual birthday, or has everyone just forgotten that the purpose of this ball is to celebrate all of the Macalister birthdays and not yours alone?" she inquired.

He smiled more brightly at her. "Today is my actual birthday," he replied. "Or rather, yesterday was, since it is well past midnight. But I proclaim that my birthday will spill over into the next day or until one goes to bed." Gunter dug a square-shaped metal spoon into the ice cream and deposited the dessert into a small porcelain dish. "It is my birthday wish that you enjoy your favorite flavor of ice cream before vanishing out the door."

"It is hard to refuse the birthday wish of a duke," Clara said accepting the dessert from the confectioner. Andrew accepted his own pale pink ice cream and nodded his thanks to Gunter. They stepped away from the serving table as guests swarmed in to receive their own treats.

As Clara had a few small bites of her dessert, Andrew could see the delight the taste brought her. Her eye lids fell slightly as each dollop of frozen cream hit her tongue. She savored each bite, allowing it to melt on her tongue before swallowing it down.

"Lady Clara—" Andrew began, but the arrival of Clara's aunt cut him off.

"Lady Clara, we really must be going," Clara's aunt said.

"Yes, Aunt Lucinda," Clara responded. "Your grace, may I introduce my aunt, Lady Lucinda Yarrow?"

"I do not believe I have had the pleasure," Andrew replied, bowing to the woman who bore more resemblance to Clara's brother than she did Clara.

"Aunt Lucinda, this is our host, his grace the Duke of Bradstone," Clara introduced.

"Your grace," Lady Lucinda said politely as she dipped into a curtsy. "We have enjoyed a splendid evening, but it is time for us to take our leave. And as Lady Clara is under our chaperonage, she really must accompany us." Lady Lucinda threw Clara a hard look making it clear she was not pleased with this association or responsibility.

Nodding to her aunt, Clara murmured a soft, "Of course, Aunt," before handing her barely-eaten ice cream to a passing footman. Smiling at Andrew, she thanked him for the dance and for escorting her into supper.

"My offer still stands, Lady Clara," Andrew said, attempting once more to keep her with him. Lady Lucinda looked slightly taken aback, no doubt assuming the worst of his comment, which indicated she did not think very highly of her niece.

Glancing nervously at her aunt, Clara replied, "Thank you, your grace, but it is not necessary. You have been too generous already."

Clara did not want to leave; Andrew could see the hesitation in her eyes. Reluctantly she took a step away from him, her eyes not dropping from his gaze. Lady Lucinda's eyes narrowed. Clearing her throat, she took Clara by the arm and tugged her towards the doors.

"Goodbye, your grace," Clara said softly before the crowded ballroom swallowed her whole, and she was out of his sight again. Her goodbye sounded as if she thought it was their final one. Andrew shook his head. He would make certain that it was not.

Chapter Three

The late morning sunlight spread into the deep depths of Andrew's study, reflecting off the well-polished mahogany desk and directly into his ducal eye. He held a stack of papers before him effectively blocking the light from hitting his face, though that was all the papers were good for. His morning had come much too quickly, and he wished he could have had the same lie in the morning after the birthday ball that his younger sisters took advantage of. But, unfortunately, he had work to do.

"Might I ask what has come over you?"

Andrew flicked the papers down and regarded his elder sister Sarah.

"Regarding?" he asked evasively.

"Andrew, you know exactly what I am referring to," Sarah replied, her hands planted on her hips in a perfect imitation of their mother. Or perhaps not an imitation but more of a mannerism she had adopted as the eldest female of ten children.

"You could be referring to any number of things, Sarah. You will need to be more specific if you want a more specific answer."

Sarah huffed at him, and he grinned, his smile hidden behind the papers. No matter how old he would get—duke or not—he would always enjoy goading his sister.

"For Heaven's sake, Andrew," she sighed, exasperated. She practically stomped over to the window and pulled the curtains shut, then turned and regarded him again. "Put down the parchments. I am referring to Lady Clara."

"What about her?" he asked, regretfully setting the papers aside.

"I could not help but notice that you were unusually attentive to Lady Clara yesterday evening. Did you forget that you were in a very crowded ballroom? You danced with her. You never dance."

"I dance," he replied with some heat.

"You never dance with someone who isn't your sister," Sarah amended. "And Lady Clara made you smile."

Andrew could not hide the small smile that crept to his lips. "Yes, I daresay she did."

"Well?" Sarah asked. "What does that mean exactly?"

"Exactly?" he asked. "It means . . ." Andrew sighed and ran his hand through his hair. "It means . . . I don't know what it means."

"She made you smile."

"Am I supposed to propose marriage to the first girl to make me smile?"

"You must know what the *ton* is saying," Sarah replied, and he spied a set of newspapers sticking out of the pockets of her dark grey skirts. The morning gossip sheets.

Andrew clenched his jaw. He could predict exactly what the *ton* was saying without needing to read the gossips rags.

"Andrew, you must have some sort of explanation for your behavior."

"I am not required to explain my actions to you or

anyone," he snapped at her. "Now leave me be."

Sarah's brow rose, and she crossed her arms over her chest. "No need to be so defensive, Andrew. I am only looking out for your well-being."

"Last I checked, I was the duke," he replied. "And although you often act the part, you, dearest sister, are not my duchess. I do not require you to look after me."

"You must be quite smitten with the lady for you to be this up in arms up about it," Sarah declared, her eyes narrowing. It was always that way with Sarah. Perhaps it was because they were so close in age. Perhaps it was because together they had assumed the roles of duke and duchess, father and mother to their younger brothers and sisters. Somehow, Sarah always knew him better than he knew himself. "And if you do not require my assistance, then find a wife and have her take up the duties. I can assure you it will be difficult to procure my aid in the future if the gratitude I receive is your foul mood." She quit the room, slamming the study door on her way out.

Damn the meddling females in this family.

Andrew ran his hand through his hair causing it to stick up on end for a moment before falling back into place.

He should not have taken his frustrations out on his sister and knew he should apologize. It was not Sarah he was irritated with but himself. His thoughts were a mess. Lady Clara had him in knots all evening and well into the morning.

He did value Sarah's help with the things that would normally fall to his duchess. She was a marchioness, though a widowed one, and hosting came naturally to her. Sarah was only one year older than him. She had been his companion growing up, his partner in crime.

There were ten Macalister siblings in all. Samuel, the heir, had been strong and responsible. He was everything a duke should have been and everything Andrew had not been at seventeen. Sarah came four years after Sam, and each year after, another Macalister was born. Andrew had been the first of the spares with Bennett and Luke following. Susanna came five years after Luke, then twins Norah and Nick, then Charlie followed two years later. Last was Mara, the very baby of the Macalister clan, arriving four years after Charlie.

Andrew stared absently at his empty study, his thoughts of Sam taking him back to the day he learned of the accident, the day he had been forced to grow up. He had been at Eton.

An argument with a friend had resulted in a brawl outside their dormitory, only to be broken up by their prefect, who had been sent by the headmaster to fetch Andrew.

Worried he was expelled from school for the brawl, Andrew had followed the prefect out of the building, across the lawns, and into an administration building where the headmaster's office was located.

Sitting down in a dark green leather chair, the same chair he had so frequently occupied during his years at Eton, Andrew could not help but wonder what this was all about.

"Am I in trouble, sir?" Andrew hesitantly asked the headmaster. "If this is about the fight, I swear—"

"No, no, you are not in trouble," Headmaster Quick said, his voice sounding weak with age.

"Sir?" Andrew asked as the headmaster sat down and read over a piece of paper. The elderly headmaster handed him the paper, the crease lines still visible where the paper had been folded.

"I'm so sorry, my young lord," Headmaster Quick said.

"For what, sir?" Andrew asked and looked down at the paper.

The words swam before his eyes, tears mixed with shock and disbelief. His tall, proud father, a duke through to his marrow, had died, and his brother, Sam, who Andrew had worshipped from afar, had died with him.

"As the next eldest son, Lord Andrew . . . you are the Duke of Bradstone now," the headmaster told him.

Andrew did not remember the carriage ride home. He had a vague recollection of walking into Bradstone Park in Kent and immediately having his mother's arms around him. The days afterward flew by, and he saw the haunted looks on his brothers' faces and the tears streaking his sisters'. His youngest sister Mara had been barely a year old. At the age of seventeen, Andrew became the tenth Duke of Bradstone.

He knew his life had changed, forever. The things he had thought about doing with his life—his dreams, his desires, his goals—were no more. Everything had shifted. His position in society had changed; he was no longer a second son of a duke, but a very young and very wealthy duke himself. He now had expectations and responsibilities and obligations he hadn't previously had; he had a title he had not been raised to inherit, and he had a very large pack of younger siblings who were all looking to him for guidance and reassurance. He had to be strong; he had to be an unfailingly solid wall for his family in their grief.

In one terrible moment, Andrew lost his father, his brother, and the rest of his life.

His mother had insisted he return to Eton the following fall, and he was treated differently as he stepped back onto campus as a duke. Suddenly everyone wanted to be his friend. Everyone wanted his opinion. Everyone just wanted to be near him. He maintained a few select friends, those who were close to him before he became a duke, but there was one friend who turned the opposite way of everyone else. Instead of wanting his approval, he despised Andrew. Instead of hanging onto his every word and asking for his opinion on every trivial thing, Lord Jonathan Masson, then Viscount Sterling, later the Earl of Morton, hated Andrew's newly ducal guts.

Losing their mother six months later did not help things for any of the Macalister clan.

With so many expectations of him so soon after the deaths of his mother, father, and brother, he had done the only sensible thing: he had given everyone what they wanted.

He had approved Sarah's marriage to the first man who asked, only because Sarah had begged it of him, and then Andrew had been a strong and a solid shoulder for her to cry on after the death of her husband five years later.

He allowed Bennett to run off and join the Royal Navy, later purchasing his commission when it was requested.

He financed Luke's random and lengthy trips out of the country.

He endorsed Susanna in all of her charitable dealings.

He supported Norah as she joined practically every women's club she could manage.

He tried to remain impassive when Nick got into fight after fight, not commenting too much on how prize fighting was not the most respectable pursuit for a gentleman.

He willingly supplied Charlie with whatever obscure scientific instrument he desired.

And Mara . . . well, Mara had been merely one year old when they had lost their father and Sam, so he had taken on the role of a father more to Mara than to any of his other siblings. Mara had him wrapped around her finger, and he did not mind. He knew he spoiled her shamelessly. He could not help it. Mara was his baby sister, and he found it very hard to deny her anything she wanted.

Andrew had put on a brave face, the new face of the Macalister family, and done what the *ton* expected of him. He dutifully sat in the House of Lords, he dutifully hosted a ball each season, he dutifully managed their estates, tenants, properties, investments, and business ventures. He did his duty to the title that ruled his life.

It was that duty which prompted his proposal to Clara's twin sister, Lady Christina Masson. Five years ago, the old Earl of Morton had still been alive and had enthusiastically consented to the marriage of his prized daughter to the *ton's* most eligible bachelor. But Christina Masson had cried off, leaving him standing at the altar on their wedding day as she ran off to Gretna Green with her father's footman. Andrew had chased them all the way to no avail. She had completely disappeared.

Twelve years after inheriting, Andrew had carved a nice place for himself. Though different from what he had dreamed of doing during his days at Eton, he was not dissatisfied with his life. He knew he would have to marry eventually, possibly even soon. It now fell to him to produce an heir and establish the continuation of the Macalister lineage. He certainly was not getting any younger.

A long time ago he had known the sweet and mischievous Lady Clara with braids and warm smiles, back when her eyes did not carry the hurt he had witnessed last night. He saw a fair amount of Clara Masson while he was a welcome friend in the Masson household and later when he was courting and engaged to her sister, but he had not set eyes on her since that day in the church, when Christina had disappeared. Clara had been a beacon of light then, and it bothered him that the light had dimmed. He knew pursuing a relationship with her was not going to be easy. Her brother hated him, and the feeling was mutual. However, there was something between himself and Clara, and after losing happiness once, Andrew was not about to give up if fate was offering him a second chance.

Lady Clara Masson glared at her older brother, biting down hard on her lip to ease the tremble of fear racing through her. Lord Jonathan Masson, the Earl of Morton, was tall and imposing, and cruelty danced behind his dark eyes. In Clara's opinion, he was insufferable, he was mean, and she hated him.

It also did not help that he was kicking her out of his house.

"Jonathan, where do you expect me to go?" she asked,

straining to keep the desperation out of her voice.

"I care not, Clara," he snapped at her. "I am through with you disgracing this family with your wanton ways. Throwing yourself at Bradstone like some two-pence harlot. You disgust me. I will have you in my home no longer."

"You are being absurd, Jonathan," Clara argued. "You cannot do this; you cannot toss me out with the rubbish."

"I should have done it years ago," Jonathan said, turning his nose up at her. "You will not drag my illustrious title through the mud."

"Oh please," Clara huffed and rolled her eyes. "You are not as important as you think yourself."

Jonathan grabbed the plate in front of her and threw it against the wall. Clara jumped as the porcelain shattered, the crash echoing off the walls, and gaped at her brother in shock. He sneered at her, clearly enjoying her discomfort.

"Leave," he said, his voice dangerously low. "I do not care where you go. You were so determined to be at Bradstone's last night, go back there. Go be the duke's whore."

Clara's sudden intake of breath was all the satisfaction she would allow him. He would not see her tears; he would not see her fear.

"I will pack my things then," Clara managed to reply, keeping her voice even before turning and fleeing the breakfast room, taking refuge in her rooms. She tried to ignore his shouts, but they cut into her all the same. He was cutting her off. He was kicking her out; he had disowned her. She was twenty-three years old. She had no dowry, no funds to her name apart from a pitiful inheritance from her mother, which would come to her upon her twenty-fifth birthday. How would she survive for two whole years?

I could stay with Aunt Lucinda, Clara thought. Her father's sister and husband had never approved of Jonathan's treatment of her. The Yarrows were nearly impoverished, not that they would admit to such a disgrace, and Jonathan refused to aid them in any way. They would take her in out of the goodness of their hearts, but it was not a long term solution. Clara knew they could barely afford what they had, and she would hate to be a burden on them. She hated feeling dependent.

The only other person she could possibly turn to was her eccentric Great-Aunt Bridgette, who had basically put her in this position when she had forced Jonathan to bring Clara to London for a season. It had been Great-Aunt Bridgette's hare-brained idea to attend the Macalister Birthday Ball to begin with, only Great-Aunt Bridgette had not attended as she had promised. Luckily Aunt Lucinda had attended the ball, and Clara had been grateful for her presence.

Filling with despair, Clara sank into the chair next to her. Great-Aunt Bridgette, her paternal great uncle's widow, lived in London, though Clara was not sure where. Great-Aunt Bridgette had funded her season this year, with the strict instructions to "Make a good match, for I will not spend another penny on you!"

Clara wiped away a rebellious tear and stood, trying to shake herself into action. She certainly could not stay here, not with Jonathan, not when he was in such a rage. She had never seen him this angry before, and she did not doubt his seriousness. Jonathan had always despised her.

Of the four Masson siblings, Jonathan, Christina, herself, and Patrick, Jonathan had always been their father's favorite. Father tolerated his twin girls with the expectation they make spectacularly advantageous matches. He had seen something different in Christina than he had in Clara, though since they were identical twins, Clara had never understood what it was. Something about Christina had always drawn people to her, and her supposed superior beauty and charm had won Father's favor as well. Patrick was four years her junior and had left three years ago to join the Royal Navy. Jonathan had purchased him a commission earlier that spring. But it was Clara whom Jonathan despised. Jonathan had always kept a special well of cruelty deep within him that he reserved just for her. She had known she would have to face her brother's wrath for attending the Macalister Birthday Ball last night, but she had not expected anger of this magnitude.

Clara hastily pulled dresses out of her wardrobe, stuffing as many as possible into the two traveling trunks she had yanked out from under her bed. The fine gowns and day dresses Great-Aunt Bridgette had purchased for her went into the trunks. They would have to be sold; it was much too humble an end for such nice things. She would find a way to repay Great-Aunt Bridgette for her generosity. Clara wouldn't need nice clothes now.

Tears fell unabashedly down her cheeks as she surveyed the mess of garments scattered around the room. She was not sure how she was going to manage to leave, it all seemed too impossible. Last night had been full of such magic and promise, even if her tall, dark rescuer was the man her sister had jilted at the altar. But he hadn't seemed to mind. He even found it amusing. *Amusing.* The Stone Duke had found something amusing. She had witnessed the cold demeanor the gossip sheets wrote about, but she had seen his laughter and his gentleness, almost as if she was seeing a fleeting glimpse of the long lost Andrew, the boy who had been her first childhood friend. If Andrew was choosing to smile at her, it had to mean something. And now . . . now she would not know what that something was.

She did not know how long she sat there and sobbed into the arm of the chair, crumpled and shattered inside. She did not hear her brother stomp up the stairs, but the crash of the door slamming into the wall jolted her out of her trance.

"Stop your sobbing and get the hell out of my house!" Jonathan roared from the doorway and Clara jumped. He stormed into her room, and slammed the nearest trunk closed as she jumped again.

"Jonathan! what are you doing in here?" Clara cried at him, horrified. "This is my bedchamber!"

"This is my house, Clara, in case you forgot," Jonathan reminded her. "And I want you out. You have five more minutes to get what you are taking with you into those bloody trunks. Whatever does not fit is being burned, so pack accordingly, Clara."

Clara could not stop sobbing. She was exhausted from the night before. Under her brother's hateful watch, she quickly packed a few more things into the remaining open trunk, grabbing the items that were personal to her. It was scarcely two minutes before he started bellowing again and throwing things in a dramatic and terrifying rage.

"Goddammit, Clara, hurry up!" he shouted, throwing a porcelain cat against the wall, the sound causing her to spill her armful of books onto the floor.

"Books?" Jonathan barked at her, boring down on her over his thin nose, so unlike her own. He looked so much like their father that it scared her, with his dark brown hair and angry stone-grey eyes. "What are God-dammed books going to do for you when the men in the streets have had their fill of you?"

Clara did not answer, she merely scooped them up and dumped them into the nearest open trunk.

"You have got to be the most worthless female relation in the history of the world," he snapped at her. "Most sisters can at least be sold off to a husband, but not you!"

"I could get married," she pleaded. Her voice shook with fear and exhaustion as she tried to hold herself together. "Please, Jonathan, I've barely had any time in town to find a husband." She just needed to make it out of the house. She would call for a hackney. If she could just make it out of the house and to Great-Aunt Bridgette's, she would be fine, temporarily. Great-Aunt Bridgette would surely let her stay for at least one night. She would figure everything else out later.

He picked up a vase from a side table and threw it across the room, barely missing Clara.

"Do you think I actually want you to find a husband?"

he asked, with a vicious laugh. "Why would I wish that upon anyone? No one will have you! Clara, I'm doing you a favor. You are not worth the trouble of trying to marry off. I got rid of one sister easily enough, at least you will prove useful payment. You I will dispose of, like trash."

Clara tried to stand up, but her legs gave out. Exhaustion was starting to overtake her—exhaustion combined with terror. She had to get out of the house immediately.

"Where am I supposed to go?" Clara questioned. She could not control her tears and was mortified of them at the same time.

"I don't bloody care!" Jonathan laughed madly. "You and these two trunks are going onto the street, and from there you are no longer my business." Jonathan yanked the hair gathered at the back of Clara's head, hauling her to her feet.

With every ounce of resolve and strength she had remaining, she pulled on the deep recesses of her being and found the strength to plant her legs beneath her. She felt her senses awaken, and she knew he would kill her if she did not fight.

He slapped her across the face with the back of his hand, and dark spots danced before her eyes. Her face throbbed in burning pain. He had actually struck her. He had always been cruel with his words but never with his hands. He raised his hand to assault her again, and she stood her ground, her eyes burning with tears and hate and fear.

The second hit was harder. It knocked her off balance, and her feet gave out beneath her. She hit her head on the side of her bedframe before crumpling to the floor.

Chapter Four

orton House was in chaos.

Having walked the few blocks to Morton House from Bradstone House, Andrew had heard the screams and shouts from the street and found the door to Morton House ajar. So far no one had noticed him standing halfway in the house. The butler was nowhere to be found. There were maids scurrying around and footmen carrying things up and down the stairs. Most looked frantic and terrified; some looked ready to burst in rage.

"Pardon me?" he called, but no one turned to look at him or even acknowledge that they heard him. *I should probably leave*, he realized. This seemed to be a family matter, and he should keep his nose out of it. But he was curious. What could cause such uproar?

He was on the point of walking away when a crash upstairs made him pause. Something did not feel right. Andrew dropped the bouquet of hothouse flowers on the floor and took the stairs two at a time. He heard Clara's sobbing and Morton's yelling. He had been to Morton House before when he and the earl had been friends, so he remembered the basic layout of the house. He went up another flight of stairs, following the sound of Clara's frantic voice. Nearly sliding into the doorframe of what must be Clara's bedroom, Andrew scanned the scene. Dresses were strewn about everywhere, books littered the floor, and pieces of porcelain were scattered across the carpet. A terrified looking maid was huddled in the corner, a footman standing in front of her, protecting her. Morton was standing over Clara's crumpled form on the floor, a pool of blood seeping from a wound on her head.

Andrew threw himself at Morton, grabbed his arm by the wrist, spun him around, and knocked him solidly on the jaw. Morton stumbled backward and regained his balance before lunging at Andrew. The impact threw them both back into the wall, and Morton was able to land a few punches before Andrew threw an elbow into the side of Morton's head. Morton stumbled back, shaking his head to clear his vision, and Andrew took advantage of Morton's momentary distraction, grabbing him by his throat.

"So you've come back for your whore," Morton sneered, struggling against Andrew's grip.

"You've seen what my fists can do to you," Andrew said, his voice cold and hard. Pulling the man closer, he offered a final warning. "If you touch her again, I will kill you."

Morton spat in his face, sneering as Andrew wiped at it with his free hand before releasing him. He planted two punches into Morton's abdomen before landing a final blow to his jaw. Morton spun the impact and fell to the floor.

Andrew was at Clara's side in an instant. She did not move or open her eyes, and her breathing was shallow. He had to get her out of here.

"A towel—something!" Andrew commanded, looking around at the terrified servants. "Something to press to her head. She's bleeding."

The maid hurried to the wash basin and returned seconds later with a plush white towel, still damp from when Clara washed her face that morning.

Pressing the towel to her head, Andrew angled her wound against him, slipping his hands and arms under her limp body, lifting her up. As he stood, he addressed the remaining servants who were peeking into the room from around the doorframe in terror and awe.

"Get me a carriage. Now."

A footman scrambled out of the room, and Andrew followed him, holding Clara carefully in his arms, the towel pressed between her wound and his chest.

"Have all of Lady Clara's things packed and ready," he told a formidable looking woman he assumed was the housekeeper.

"Yes, of course," she said and bobbed a curtsy. "Where shall I send them?"

Andrew thought for a moment. "A carriage will arrive for them. I want eyes blind to the crest upon it. Lady Clara does not need any more scandal than she has already had to endure. But I assure you she will be safe and protected."

The woman curtsied again, and Andrew saw how her eyes misted up before she hurried up the stairs, grabbing two maids with her along the way.

"The carriage, sir," a man who must have been Morton's butler said to him, and Andrew hurried out of the house. He managed to get Clara into the hackney before turning to the butler at his heels.

"I am sorry to leave you all to Morton's wrath," Andrew said. "If any of you find yourself in need of employment, you can present yourself to a Mr. Evans at Evans, Smith and Watson on Piccadilly."

"Very good, sir," the butler replied. "And if we wish to inquire about the lady's health and well-being?"

"I will make sure you are kept informed," Andrew replied.

"Very well, sir," the butler said with the same misty look in his eyes. Andrew nodded and closed the carriage door, rapping his knuckles on the top of the roof. The carriage lurched into motion, and he was thankful to see Morton House fade around the corner.

He looked down at Clara's tear-streaked face, the blood smeared through her blonde hair. *Please let her be okay,* he prayed.

"Where are we headed, good sir?" the driver asked through the hatch, and Andrew answered with the address. He did not live far from Morton House, but far enough that he did not want to be seen carrying Lady Clara's form through the streets of London. It took only a matter of minutes before the carriage was rolling up to his front door.

"Fetch Dr. Lennox on the Mall," Andrew said, getting down from the carriage, still holding Clara in his arms. "There is a ten pound note in it if you can do it quickly, and don't speak of this to anyone."

"Aye, sir," the driver said, tipping his hat, and he was soon rolling out of the Bradstone House gates.

The front door opened before Andrew, and he hurried into the house.

"Sarah!" he cried once he was inside, taking the stairs carefully, not wanting to jostle Clara even further. "Sarah! Now, I need your help!"

He managed to open the door to the first bedchamber he came to, kicking the door wide open and setting Clara gently on the four-poster bed.

"Andrew!" Sarah exclaimed as she came into the room. "What on earth is going on?"

"She's not conscious, Sarah, and she has a head injury," Andrew explained, barking orders for towels and blankets at the few servants who had entered after his sister.

Sarah looked down at the unconscious woman on the bed, and he thought he heard his very proper sister let out a very unladylike swear.

"Sarah, what if . . ." he swallowed, unable to even say the horrible words rattling about in his mind. No, Clara would be all right.

Sarah lay a steadying hand on his arm and told him, "She will be fine, Andrew. Just wait and see. Has the physician been sent for?"

Andrew nodded numbly, his gaze dropping down to his front, realizing blood from her head wound had seeped onto his jacket and shirt. He looked as though he had been shot.

With Sarah's steadying hand on his shoulder, Andrew sat near the bed as blankets and towels were carried into the room, sheets were pulled from chairs, and the curtains were pulled back to allow sunlight to shine through.

Andrew had a hard time putting into words what he had seen or what he was feeling. He recognized the heart-gripping fear at seeing her immobile, unconscious, so distracted in his own worry he never even questioned the depth or reasoning for his distress. He did not see Sarah's knowing glances or question why she was not putting up more of a fuss at his presence inside the bedchamber.

Within ten minutes, Dr. Lennox had arrived, and Andrew told the account of what he had witnessed, ignoring Sarah's shocked gasps and the look of worry increasing on the good doctor's face. He was middle aged, Andrew knew, though time had been kind to him. He had sandy-brown hair and clean, simple attire: brown breeches, brown coat. His gentle eyes made him seem trustworthy even if his methods and remedies were a little unorthodox at times. Some of the medical community thought him eccentric—Andrew thought he was by far the best physician in town.

"Sounds as if she's been through quite an ordeal," Dr. Lennox said and dabbed a wet cloth over Clara's head, examining the wound just beneath her hairline. "I will need to examine her to make sure nothing is broken, so it would be best if you leave, your grace."

Andrew nodded though he did not want to budge. He

spun around meeting Sarah's eyes, and he prayed she saw in them what he was always so careful to hide. He cared for Clara, much more than he was willing to admit aloud, and this realization frightened him. He did not want to leave her alone.

"I will stay with her, Andrew," Sarah said, nodding.

"Thank you," he muttered hoarsely, overcome with relief.

He stepped outside the room and glanced back at Clara's slumped form on the bed before the door closed upon him.

Andrew felt exhausted. He swallowed back the lump in his throat and took a few steps forward, wondering what to do next. He wanted to hit something. He wanted to cause Jonathan Masson pain. Descending the stairs, he hurried down the hall to his study, slamming the door shut before collapsing into the chair nearest the door.

He wanted to murder Jonathan Masson. He wanted to rip him limb from limb. He wanted to go back to Morton House and finish what he should have finished twelve years ago.

But he could not leave Clara. She had been in his life again for less than a day, and she was already deeply entwined in his senses. He ran his hands through his hair, linked his fingers at the back of his head, and leaned back, closing his eyes.

When he'd slid into Clara's doorframe and saw Clara crumpled and bleeding on the floor, Morton standing over her, ready to strike again, he had gone red with rage. Fury had blurred his vision and he had attacked a peer. Brother or not, he would not allow Clara to be bullied and abused by Jonathan Masson ever again. Never mind that Andrew had assaulted the man in his own home and abducted the man's sister . . . he was not going to allow Clara to feel that brand of hatred ever again.

"What the devil has gotten into you?" a voice asked, and Andrew opened his eyes. A grinning red-headed man was hovering over him, and Andrew blinked up at his friend,

Lord Rheneas Warren, Earl of Bexley.

"Seems like everyone wants to know the answer to that question, most of all me," Andrew replied.

"You are acting quite out of character," another of Andrew's friends, Lord Jeremiah Aster, Viscount Halcourt, said as he walked into the study followed by Lord Redley Ralston, Viscount Kensburg, Andrew's maternal cousin.

"Please, by all means, gentlemen, come right in," Andrew drawled at his best friends.

"Oh, we will," Bexley replied. "I say, Andrew, but you are covered in blood."

Andrew glanced down again. "S'not mine," he mumbled.

"Give the man a moment to breathe," Halcourt said. "He's just abducted someone. Allow him to regain his composure." Redley gave him a bewildered look as he tossed his hat onto the chair, followed by his gloves.

"Funny, Halcourt," Andrew said to his dark-haired friend.

Halcourt merely shrugged as he removed his gloves. "I did not say it was funny."

"It really is not like you, old chap," Bexley agreed, tossing his hat and gloves beside Redley's. Redley shook his head and sat down.

Redley was the only man in the room Andrew was actually related to by blood; though, by appearances, one could not tell they were related as Redley's light grey-blue eyes and light blond hair contrasted Andrew's. Despite being cousins, Andrew had not met Redley until later in their teen years, and Redley had never disclosed all the details of his life before that. Andrew only knew their upbringings had been significantly different, and as a result, Redley was a peculiar sort. He rarely ever spoke a word.

The other two men were two of five men whom Andrew would trust with his life. Those five men had stood by him before and after his inheritance of the dukedom, remaining true in their friendship when so many others had been there only for personal gain.

"Honestly, Andrew, you need to be careful who you abduct in broad daylight," Halcourt said.

"What made you do it, Andrew dear?" Bexley asked. "Just trying to thwart Morton? By nabbing his sister?"

"Will you lot please stop?" Andrew sighed and pressed his fingers to his temples. "I don't know what came over me; I don't even know what possessed me to be there. All I know is that he was hitting her, and she was . . . lying on the floor bleeding, and I just lost control. The lot of you would have done the exact same had you been there."

There was a brief moment of silence wherein his three friends regarded him, and he eyed each one of them, silently daring them to continue their chastising.

"Gads, boys, he looks actually torn up about this," Bexley commented with a grin. "I think he might be in love with the chit."

Redley nodded in agreement.

"Can't be in love with her yet, can he?" Halcourt asked. "He just met her yesterday."

"Again," Bexley reminded them. "He technically already knew her."

"I am not in love with her," Andrew grumbled. "And she was the sister of the girl I intended to marry when I saw her last."

"Has she even made her bows?" Bexley asked.

"Don't know if she has, actually," Halcourt replied. "Would the Queen even receive her?"

"With a reputation such as hers?" Bexley asked. "Not likely."

"She made her bows with her twin sister before their father died," Andrew interjected. "Those horrid rumors about her did not start until this season, well after the death of the old earl and Jonathan Masson ascended to their illustrious title."

Bexley snickered. "Illustrious title," he muttered into his

drink. "Who does Jonathan Masson think he is? His title is no more illustrious than the rest of ours, our favorite duke excluded, of course."

Andrew rolled his eyes as his three friends snickered. Jonathan Masson had been a first-born son with a courtesy title when they had all been chums at Eton. He and Andrew had been best friends. Jonathan enjoyed listening to the plans Andrew had for his life, knowing he would never be granted such freedom, since Jonathan's first born status deprived him of a life of entirely his choosing. It was not until Andrew became a duke and Jonathan was still waiting to inherit that their friendship came to an abrupt end. That was when Jonathan's true nature had come out, though Andrew did not know why he hadn't seen it earlier in their acquaintance. Andrew had once been his right-hand man, but he had never noticed the depth of Jonathan's vile nature. With the inheritance tables turned, Andrew became Jonathan's favorite target. He was never openly rude; it would not look good to openly snub the young Duke of Bradstone. Instead he used everyone around him as his weapons. Slowly he poisoned the thoughts of the other boys in school; even some of the faculty began to believe the lies that Jonathan spread about him. And he had done the same thing to Clara. A few not-so-subtle hints, some sly innuendo, and he let the imagination of the *ton* run wild. The stories about Clara were outrageous; some were downright mean. And no one else realized her own brother was the source.

"You don't believe what's been said about her?" Halcourt asked, and Andrew shook his head.

"Not for a second," he replied. "We all know how horrid Morton can be when he sets his mind to it."

"If you believe her, that is all that matters," Halcourt said.

Andrew jumped to his feet and stood nose-to-nose with his dark-haired friend. "I *do* believe her, and that *is* all that matters." Redley stood up as well, placing a hand on Andrew's shoulder, like he had when they were lads brawling in the school yard.

Halcourt's face scrunched up in confusion. "Isn't that what I just said?"

"Calm down, Andrew," Bexley said and handed him a glass of brandy. "Don't hit him before dinner, it is bad form." Redley pushed Andrew down into his chair before retaking his own seat.

Andrew accepted the offer of his own liquor and gulped it down.

"Luckily no one saw you carrying Lady Clara out of Morton House or into Bradstone House," Halcourt began.

"Then how did you know about it?" Andrew asked.

"Bloody man has spies everywhere, I tell you," Bexley replied when Halcourt did not.

"—so there will be no accounts of the event," Halcourt continued as if they hadn't cut him off.

"What about Morton?" Andrew asked. "I half expected you to be the watch called out for my arrest. I did assault him and abduct his sister."

"Actually, he's already left London," Halcourt replied.

"Already?" Andrew repeated. "I was there scarcely an hour ago."

"Apparently he came around shortly after you left with Lady Clara and took off straight away."

"Halcourt, how is it that you know these details?" Andrew asked.

Halcourt merely shrugged and took a sip of his drink.

Andrew's mind was spinning with the information Halcourt had delivered. Morton could not be trusted, and Andrew would not trust him to not go after Clara again. She'd reentered his life for less than a day, and yet, he was unwilling to let her slip away again. Her safety was of the utmost importance. He would do anything to keep her safe.

Andrew eyed the men surrounding him. "You lot would offer unconditional support, should I need it, right?"

"Dare I ask where you are going with this?" Halcourt asked.

"I have an idea," Andrew began. "Granted, it is still half-formed and hare-brained, but Lady Clara needs to be protected. Halcourt, can you do . . . whatever it is you do and find out what you can about Morton? He was in the process of throwing Lady Clara out when I intervened."

"That seems a rather extreme reaction," Halcourt replied. "What did she do?"

Andrew shrugged. "Last I saw her was early this morning, leaving the ball. I cannot imagine she would do anything to warrant such a vicious response from her brother."

Halcourt nodded. "I agree. I will see what I can find out."

"If your idea of protecting the chit is leaning the way I think you are, you are going to need more than unconditional support from just us," Bexley pointed out. "But you have it, regardless."

Redley agreed with a curt nod.

They were interrupted by a knock on the door, and a butler stepped in.

"The doctor has asked for you, your grace."

"Yes, very good," Andrew replied. "Thank you, Howards. Also—please send a carriage around to Morton House. I suspect Lady Clara might be staying with us for some time. I'm sure she'd appreciate some of her own things."

Howards nodded. "Yes, your grace."

"We'll be off, your grace," Halcourt replied.

"We just came by for your brandy, anyway," Bexley said, picking up his hat. Redley downed the rest of his glass before setting it on the side table.

"I take it you will not be at Almack's this evening," Halcourt said, pulling on his gloves. The four of them moved into the main hallway.

"I don't know," Andrew admitted. "But it is doubtful."

"Very good," Halcourt said, making his bow before leaving.

Bexley and Redley rolled their eyes at their always over-ly-formal friend and bowed as well, more of a way to mock

Halcourt than as a sign of respect to the duke.

Andrew did not mind. He always took their jokes in stride.

Andrew turned and hurried up the main stairs two at a time, coming to a halt outside the bedchamber where he had left Clara. Dr. Lennox was just coming out of the room.

"How is she?" Andrew asked.

Dr. Lennox looked pale. "She hasn't regained consciousness, so I surmise she is heavily concussed. I've cleaned and treated the wound and bound it to prevent further bleeding. If she wakes up—"

"*When* she wakes up," Andrew corrected.

The doctor swallowed and nodded. "When she wakes up—and I am very hopeful she will—she will need to rest the first two days, three solid meals each day. But try to keep her in bed." The good doctor had the decency to blush and quickly amended his comment. "Do not let her on her feet while her dizziness remains. Twenty-four hours at least before she should walk unassisted. She's been through an ordeal and will require a good amount of support," the doctor warned. "There is no telling what damage abuse can leave in its wake."

"May I see her now?" Andrew inquired and was relieved when the physician nodded.

"Please send word when she regains consciousness."

"Of course."

Andrew stared at the solid oak door, not knowing what to expect on the other side. It was not that he was afraid, quite the opposite. He was not sure of his feelings. He was fairly certain he was about to make a very rash decision, but he could only hope it was right. He had spent twelve years making sure he had no doubts about anything, and that slip of a girl found a way of getting under his skin in less than a day.

Slipping silently into the room, Andrew nodded to Sarah, who sat beside the bed in a chair. Sarah patted his arm as she passed, silently offering him support, though he knew she was taking in more than just his worry over the injured girl. Her eyes met his, and there was compassion and a hint of amusement in them.

His attachment to Clara shouldn't have been this strong after only having her in his life again for scarcely a day. Years ago, she had been someone important to him regardless of how silly that childhood infatuation had been.

Now she was here, injured no less, and her little mews of tormented sleep were preventing the room and Andrew's temper from calming completely. He moved to sit beside the bed and smoothed his hand over her forehead and cheeks, careful to avoid the bandage wrapped around her head. He hadn't seen the full extent of the injury, but he hoped it would heal without issue.

Clara's distressed breathing calmed under his touch, and it brought him some comfort knowing he could at least offer her something to ease her misery. He could not change her brother or his treatment of her, he could not change how the *ton* treated her and how the rumors flew about her like leaves in the breeze.

Or could he?

Andrew looked away, his mind racing at the possibility of saving this girl, keeping her away from the forked tongues of the *ton*, keeping her safe from the hateful actions of her brother. Was such a thing possible? Could he turn the tide of society's opinion of her? Could he possibly hope to offer her the type of protection she needed?

It was an intriguing idea. *But first thing's first*, Andrew thought. *She has to wake up.*

Chapter Five

Clara's feet twitched slowly, and she was vaguely aware of her surroundings. Definitely not her own bedroom, as she was in a bed and not crumpled on the floor, which was the last thing she remembered. Wherever she was, it was quiet and peaceful, and that was certainly not typical of Morton House.

Her lids fluttered open, her brown eyes trailing the length of the room, from the darkened windows, to the olive-green drapery, the walls with a striped floral wallpaper, the posts of the bed and the bed draping above, and finally to Andrew, standing watch at the foot of her bed like a guardian angel.

Or perhaps a vengeful archangel. His eyes were dark and hard, practically glaring his displeasure.

"Where am I?" she asked, her voice hoarse and dry. She tried to sit, wincing at the pain in her head. Her palm found the bandage wrapped around her.

"Bradstone House," he answered coldly, and his tone

made her want to bury herself down in the blankets. With a nod to her bandages, he added, "A physician has been in to see you. Do you remember what happened?"

Clara frowned, her memory fogging as she tried to recall the details of how she came to be in Bradstone House. "My brother, he was quite angry with me for attending the ball. He . . . he hit me. After that, everything is a bit of a jumble."

"You were bleeding on your bedroom floor," he supplied. "I intervened before your brother could cause you further harm. He will not have another opportunity to harm you, Lady Clara."

"I thank you for the rescue, your grace," Clara said gratefully. Relief rushed through her accompanied by a flood of emotions that were too complicated to untangle and analyze. She broke away from his gaze. "Once I am well, I will be on my way."

"You will not," Andrew stated. "You are not going anywhere."

Clara's eyes snapped back to his face, her brows pinching in confusion.

"It is quite improper for my time in this house to extend beyond what is required for recuperation," Clara replied, not enjoying the dark glare he was sending her way.

"You misunderstand, Lady Clara," he said. "I intend to marry you. Only once you are out of Morton's reach will you be truly safe."

His words hung in the air, and for a very long moment Clara wondered if she had imagined it.

"I beg your pardon?" she asked, incredulously.

"You and I will be married."

"Surely you jest," she said, but there was no trace of humor on his handsome face.

"Far from it."

"You've not even asked me," Clara replied.

"Lady Clara, will you marry me?" he asked gruffly.

"No," she answered. "And you don't want to marry me,

not really."

"You are in need of protecting," he replied. "This is the course that offers the highest level of safety."

"You don't even know me."

"I do know you."

"You knew me when I was a child," she allowed. "I imagine I am not the same person and neither are you."

"Who we are now does not matter," he argued. "What matters is your safety. Under my roof, with my name, you will be protected."

"This is lunacy," she muttered, wondering if she was still asleep in some head trauma-induced hallucination. The words she'd wanted to hear her entire life were coming from the man she'd always dreamed of marrying, but it was all wrong.

"Have you anyone else in the position to offer you the same level of protection as I?" he inquired.

"Well, no, but—"

"Good, we are in agreement."

"We are absolutely *not* in agreement, your grace," she sputtered. "And furthermore, what gives you the right to make such decisions on my behalf? You are not my brother or father or in any position to act so high-handed."

"You are in need of protection," he insisted. "You brother has done a fine job of acting as horridly as possible, leaving you penniless and without a place to go. Do I have those facts correct?"

"Yes, but you needn't be so blunt about it," Clara grumbled. "I might be penniless and destitute, but I am still a lady. I have friends."

Much to Clara's surprise, Andrew's face softened. "Yes, you do. I am your friend. My sisters will be your friends. You have an ally here should you choose to accept it."

His words rang with a painful truth, as much as she wanted to deny him.

"What about my aunt and uncle?" Clara asked, trying to

find any other option than his ridiculous plan. "Or Great-Aunt Bridgette?"

"Would either one of them be willing or able to take you in?" Andrew asked, even though by his tone he knew the answer.

"Well, no," she admitted. "Great-Aunt Bridgette said she would not spend a penny more on me, and my Aunt Lucinda practically disowned me in the carriage last night for coming without a chaperone. It was a lucky twist of events that she was even here. She was not pleased to have Lady Danbury rush over to inquire about her chaperonage of me."

It might have been her imagination, but Clara thought she saw Andrew's lips twitch.

"No, I imagine she did not."

"This cannot be happening," Clara muttered to herself, giving her head a little shake, trying to come up with something, anything else but marriage to the one man she actually wanted to marry. But not like this, not when he did not want to truly marry her. He'd almost married her twin sister, for goodness' sake.

Nothing came to her.

Andrew stood at the foot of the bed, watching as she struggled with herself, trying to find another solution, waiting for her to come to the inevitable conclusion.

"I will agree to marry you," Clara said slowly, not truly meaning the words. "But I will not marry under scandalous circumstances. I've had enough rumors and scandal to last my lifetime. At the very least, I would like the banns to be called." Banns took three weeks to be called in each of their home parishes. Her home parish was near the Scottish border, and would take a messenger at least a week to get there. She'd just bought herself four weeks—four weeks for her brother to be dealt with, four weeks to find another solution than being strapped to someone who truly did not want to marry her.

"I can agree to that," he replied with a nod.

"Fine."

"Fine."

Clara watched him, waiting for him to burst out laughing, claiming the whole thing to be a joke or an elaborate prank but nothing came. Had she actually just become engaged to the Duke of Bradstone? The gentleman she'd held feelings for since . . . forever?

No, she reminded herself. The engagement would not be real, at least not for her. She would take the protection his name offered, even as his fiancée, and find another way to be safe from her brother. Andrew had broken her heart once, she wouldn't allow him to do it again. That left her four weeks to figure her life out.

A soft knock came on the door, and Andrew called for the person to enter. A maid appeared carrying a pitcher and towels.

"Martha," Andrew said to the maid as she came through the door. "Have my sisters dressed for the evening yet?"

Martha set the pitcher and towels down on the table beside the bed. "I do not believe so, your grace," she replied.

"Very good. Could you please ask them to attend me for a moment? And have tea brought up as well."

"Yes, your grace," Martha replied curtsying.

"That is not necessary," Clara said softly. He turned his gaze back to her, and she blinked in surprise. The cool aloofness was gone, his blue eyes had melted into warm pools of light. There was no pity in his eyes as she had feared there would be. There was only concern.

"It is absolutely necessary," he replied, not moving from his post at the end of the bed. "The physician said you need two whole days of rest."

Clara blanched at the prescribed treatment and then winced at the pain in her head. "What am I going to do for two whole days?"

"Read," he suggested. "Rest. Allow your head to heal. You took quite a blow to the face as well."

"What about my brother?" Clara asked. "Does he know I am here?"

"I do not know what your brother knows," Andrew replied. "He's left London."

"Jonathan is gone?" she asked, startled. "How long have I been asleep?"

"A few hours," he replied. "And yes, Morton is nowhere to be found, according to my sources."

"You have sources?"

Andrew nodded. "I've a friend who is rather adept at . . . well, things like this, I suppose."

"Does he fancy himself a spy?" Clara asked in jest, but Andrew did not laugh. "Oh, goodness, is he a spy?"

Andrew shrugged. "I've never asked."

"Will he be able to determine where Jonathan has gone?" Clara asked. "And what happens when he returns?"

"Do not worry about any of that right now," Andrew replied. "Just rest and relax. The doctor said you are not to over-worry yourself."

There came knock on the door, and Andrew called for them to enter. Two familiar-looking women came into the room, followed by a stout woman carrying a tea tray and Martha the maid. Clara recognized them as Lady Susanna and Lady Norah, two of Andrew's sisters. Clara had seen them from afar throughout the season, and briefly when Andrew was engaged to her sister Christina.

Lady Norah Macalister was a beauty of a very rare sort, with dark chocolate hair and twinkling turquoise-blue eyes. Her long dark hair fell in waves around her face, only part of it pulled off her shoulders. She wore a fashionable mint-green day dress, the color highlighting the green tint to her blue eyes perfectly. Clara had a feeling that was the reason she chose the color.

Lady Susanna was equally as lovely, though in a less daz-zling way. Susanna had a warm, round face and smiling blue eyes, the same color as Andrew's. She wore a dusty rose day dress, simple yet elegant, her hair pulled away from her face and off her shoulders in a loose bun.

The casual airs emanating from these two ladies were startling to Clara. She was used to the elegantly formal version of the two Macalister sisters: Lady Norah was impeccably and most fashionably dressed at the balls and soirées, a popular social butterfly who always reminded Clara a little of her society-obsessed twin sister. Lady Susanna was less the regal lady and more approachable and agreeable in such casual attire and airs. Someone, Clara thought, she could be friends with.

Another woman came through the door and Clara recognized Lady Radcliff from the night before, elegant and full of authority. She was carrying a bundle of clothing that she set gingerly on the side of the bed.

"I've brought you something to change into," Sarah offered, patting the folded white nightgown. "Your things have not yet arrived, and I felt you might sleep better not done up all evening."

"Thank you, Lady Radcliff," Clara murmured, trying to sit up, wincing again at the dull throb along her scalp.

"Sarah, Norah, Susanna, I'd like you to officially meet Lady Clara Masson," Andrew said. "Lady Clara, please meet my sisters."

"Pleasure," Norah said, and she and Susanna dipped into a curtsy.

"It is indeed," Clara replied. "I would do the same, but it seems I am to be bedridden, and I think your brother would be quite cross with me if I got out of bed just to curtsy."

"I would," Andrew replied.

"Might I ask what happened to create this situation?" Susanna asked, her gaze raking over Clara's face. Clara knew there was an ugly bruise forming on her cheek. It was tender to the touch now. It would be quite sore in the morning and a horrid purple color.

"My brother, the Earl of Morton," Clara admitted with

a sigh, a little embarrassed to be admitting all of this to Andrew's wonderfully elegant sisters.

"That is repugnant," Sarah said, clearly appalled.

"I survived," Clara said with a shrug. "If not for your brother coming to my rescue . . ."

She looked at Andrew, and for a moment felt the other occupants of the room fade away until it was just Andrew staring intently at her with his bright eyes melting into hers.

The sound of tea cups clinking brought them both out of the spell, and Clara quickly looked away. Sarah was pouring tea, seemingly unaware anything had transpired between them.

"Lady Clara, how do you like your tea prepared?" Sarah asked.

"Two sugars and a splash of milk, please," Clara replied. "And please just call me Clara. Since you are all present at my pathetic sick bed, I would appreciate you all using my Christian name. This is all less embarrassing that way."

"Quite right," Andrew said and turned to address the taller of the two maids. "Martha, could you possibly have Beverell find me another chair, please? I am certain to break the ones in this room."

"Yes, your grace," Martha replied, curtsying, and left the room. Clara realized there was no fear on the maid's face, no terror, no recoil. Andrew spoke to his servants with respect. He used their names, correctly she was certain, and he was polite. He said *please*. Jonathan was never so mannerly.

A moment later a burly footman came in bearing a larger chair, more suitable for his grace's tall frame.

"Ah, much better," Andrew said and settled himself into the chair. "Thank you, Beverell."

"Is there an explanation for Clara's appearance in our home?" Norah asked.

"Yes," Andrew replied. "Clara has agreed to become my wife."

A stunned silence swept through the room, pierced only

by the sounds of porcelain tinkling together as Lady Radcliff sipped her tea and set her cup down.

"That is rather . . ." Susanna began.

"Unexpected," Norah finished.

"Indeed," Sarah added. "Though perhaps not so." A strange look passed between Sarah and her brother, and Clara looked away.

"It seems this was his best solution to offer his protection," Clara added.

Norah frowned. "Truly there was no other way?"

"There was not," Andrew replied with finality.

"Andrew, you cannot possibly expect the *ton* to accept this?" Norah asked, with a guilty glance to Clara. "With absolutely no offense intended, Lady Clara, I am sure you are a lovely person. It is simply—"

"I know what is said about me," Clara interjected defensively. True, she was not the most popular person, and wild rumors flew about her activities the past five years, but she was still the daughter of an earl. That had to count for something.

"The *ton* will accept this engagement," Andrew stated gruffly.

Clara shot him a look in warning. "I assure you, this was not something I intended to happen when I woke up this morning," Clara stated, returning her gaze to Andrew's befuddled sisters. "Far from it. But we are here in the end, it would seem. None of this was my idea, and I tried to deny him. Your brother seems to be a rather stubborn individual, though I am sure this you already know."

Norah and Susanna glanced at each other in bewilderment, though Clara did not quite understand their confusion.

"You told him no?" Susanna asked.

"Twice," Andrew replied.

"Possibly more," Clara added.

"Then why . . ." Susanna began, but her voice faltered.

"Clara will have my name and title to offer protection

from her brother," Andrew continued. "I would appreciate the support of each of you."

The three sisters exchanged a glance, something passing between them that Clara did not understand, and as each turned to regard her again, she saw a strength and determination she had not expected.

"It seems we are to welcome Clara to the family," Sarah said. "Whatever you need from us, Andrew, we will do our best to provide."

Andrew looked at Clara expectantly. It was strange to suddenly have allies, especially the darlings of the *ton*. In society's eyes, the Macalisters could do no wrong. Any slight misstep was shrugged off with a condescending laugh. Not that any of them ever did anything to warrant a scandal. Having these people as her champion might improve the *ton's* opinion of her. Maybe.

"A friendly face at a ball would be nice," Clara admitted.

"I cannot promise we will become the best of friends," Norah replied. "But you will have my support."

Norah's declaration was not surprising. The fashionable Lady Norah was friends with a much different group of people than Clara associated with, though truthfully there were few people who would associate with her when not wearing a mask at a ball. No one would ever think Lady Norah Macalister, the queen bee of the season, would lower herself to be friends with Clara. Lady Susanna, however, was a different story. She was sweeter than her sister, at least in society's eyes, and she maintained a much different set of friends, and they seemed to set their own rules within ranks of the *haute ton*.

"Ignore her," Susanna said with a wink. "You and I will be the best of friends in the end. Just you wait and see."

Clara took comfort in Susanna's prediction and determination, appreciating the rebellious streak in this prim and proper lady. The stiffness of her posture was just a prop, Clara realized, and she felt a softening towards her newly-acquired friend, almost as though she were recognizing a kindred spirit of sorts.

"You are certainly braver than I expected, daring to take on my brother as your husband," Sarah said. "You will find unconditional support beneath this roof, but we cannot control the *ton*."

Andrew snorted. "I can."

"That is a bit conceited of you, your graceness," Norah said to him, though they all knew it was true.

Chuckling, Andrew set his tea cup down, waving Sarah off as she went to pour him a second. "Perhaps not alone. But between myself, Connolly, Bexley, Halcourt, and Redley, of course." Turning towards Sarah, he asked, "Can we count on the other Marchioness of Radcliff as well?"

Sarah nodded.

"There is another one?" Clara asked confused.

"My late husband's older brother died without a son," Sarah explained, "and the title passed to my husband, who also died without a son. My sister-in-law is also a good friend of mine since our debut, and we became the widowed Marchionesses of Radcliff."

"You are quite the formidable pair," Norah added and Sarah laughed.

"Also Luke," Susanna added. "No one ever doubts a word Luke says even if he's seen as a rogue."

"We have rumor on our side," Norah added looking at Clara. "There is already enough assumption about you. The speculation over this engagement will sweep the town like a firestorm. People are going to want answers."

"People tend to believe the lies over the truth anyway," Clara said with a shrug. "I'd rather they not know about my brother."

It was decided that the Macalister siblings would keep their evening plans and attend Almack's; it was Wednesday night after all. They would each spread their story, making the excuse for Clara that she was indisposed with a headache and ignoring the fact that she was not welcome at Almack's anyway. By the morning, the entire town would be buzzing.

Clara was grateful for their help, and she told them so. But she was also feeling exhaustion creep in, and she fought to keep her eyes open. Andrew noticed first and shooed his sisters out to dress for the evening. He appointed Martha to be Clara's lady's maid and told Clara that if she needed anything she was to ask. Clara nodded and thanked him, feeling sleep overpower her.

It was dark when she woke again. It took her a moment to recognize her surroundings, and she sat up slowly, looking around the darkened room, waiting for her eyes to adjust to the dimness. It was then she realized there was someone else in the room with her. It was a man, sitting in the large wing-backed chair Andrew had occupied earlier in the day. Fear tore at her throat, and she scurried backward up the bed as the figure leaned towards her. It was Jonathan, she knew. He had come to hurt her or snatch her back or—

"Clara, calm down, it is only me," Andrew's strong, low voice said in the darkness, and his face was a blaze of momentary light as he lit the candle on the bedside table.

"You-you-you scared me." Clara fought to regain control of her breathing but was failing, pain shooting through her temples, white spots dancing before her eyes. "I thought . . . I don't know w-what I th-th-thought."

"You thought I was your brother come to harm you," Andrew supplied, and she nodded. He stood up, stepped forward, and sat on the edge of the mattress. "Clara, listen to me, and listen well. I am not going to let Morton hurt you again. He will not come back for you; he will not be allowed near you. I promise you. You are quite safe in Bradstone House. You are safe from him."

Clara nodded and felt the tears well up in her eyes, from fear, from pain. She felt her composure start to crumple, terror and panic subsiding, but the events of the day—her brother, Andrew's rescue, her engagement—it was all just too much. Tears spilled from her eyes, and she choked on a sob.

Scooping Clara into his arms, Andrew cradled her in his lap while she cried onto his black evening jacket. Rubbing his hand over her back in relaxing circles, he cooed soothing nothings into her ear, holding her as the gasping sobs overtook her, her chest tightening in anguish, and she fought to breathe properly.

She could not catch her breath, and she could not stop crying, could not stop the tightening feeling that was crushing her chest, cutting off her airway. She was going to die. Jonathan would have his way in the end.

"Shhh, Clara, calm down," Andrew cooed at her. "Breathe, Clara, focus on my breathing and focus on making your breathing match mine. Think about my breathing . . . that is it, calm down and just breathe."

In and out, breathe in and out, she told herself. She focused on his words, focused on just breathing, simply making her chest rise and fall with his. His arms around her offered a level of comfort she had not felt in years. The tension and the fear seeped out of her as her breathing began to match his, his broad chest rising with hers as his warmth calmed her pulse. He held her, for many long minutes, more than she wanted to count, but soon she could feel her lungs filling, unrestricted, with air. The loosening of the deadly crush against her chest melted away and within a few minutes she was calm and could breathe normally again.

"Better?" he asked gently, and she nodded into his chest. Carefully, he tucked her back into the blankets and pillows, mindful to not jostle her head any further.

"Thank you," she whispered, not willing to trust her voice just yet.

"Of course," Andrew replied. "My brother Charlie always had breathing problems as a child. I learned to calm him. Don't feel ashamed or embarrassed by your tears, Clara. You went through an ordeal, and it was quite traumatizing."

"I know," Clara acknowledged. "I'm usually much more

composed than this. I hate feeling like I'm coming apart at the seams."

"It may seem like that now, but give it a couple days. Things will look better. *You* will feel better."

Clara sighed and looked up at him. "You know, your eyes look almost grey in the candlelight."

Andrew chucked. "And the gold specks in yours make your eyes sparkle."

"Really?" she asked and he nodded. "I've never noticed before. Thank you, your grace, that was most kind of you to say."

"You are welcome," Andrew replied. "And there is no need to address me as 'your grace'. We dropped the formalities yesterday, remember?"

"Was it yesterday?"

"Oh yes. It is nearly three in the morning. The girls arrived home an hour or so ago and I've just returned myself. The girls are no doubt already asleep."

"Was Almack's as wonderful as ever?" Clara asked wistfully, but she regretted it immediately. She hated the longing in her voice, tinged with envy. She hated that she was not accepted there, and that there was nothing she could do about it. She hated it more that it even bothered her to begin with. Perhaps there was more Christina in her than she thought.

Andrew made a disgusted face. "Almack's wonderful? Certainly not. Bad lemonade and a stuffy ballroom. I left the girls in the competent hands of my brother Luke and left as soon as I could. I went to Brook's and spread the news of our engagement, called upon a friend who is working to locate your brother, and then I came home."

"And snuck into my room to watch me sleep," she finished. "You know this is highly improper."

"I wanted to see for myself that you were well," he explained, shrugging. "You are quite adorable when you sleep."

Clara blushed and looked away, hoping the color rising

in her cheeks was not apparent under the light of a single candle.

"Was there any information?" she inquired, not looking back at him. "About my brother?"

"None so far," Andrew replied. "He hasn't been seen at any of his nearer estates, and there have been representatives sent out to the farther ones."

Glancing back to him, her brows pulled together. "Representatives?" Clara asked. "He sounds rather like a spy. Are you quite sure that he is not?"

"Nope," Andrew admitted with a sigh. "He very well could be, and it wouldn't surprise me if he were. He has all sorts of connections, acquaintances, and sources but I've learned not to ask. He evades my questions whenever I do. But he is one of my best friends, and I've known him since I was thirteen. He's never been out of the country. Wouldn't a spy have to leave the country for extended periods of time?"

"He could be their handler," Clara replied pensively. "Does not a spy need some sort of associate or colleague at home to pass along information? If one man knew who all of England's spies were, you'd think he'd be a strong target for assassination. So it must be broken up between multiple people. And it is all hush-hush, of course, as espionage usually is."

Andrew regarded her for a moment before asking, "Are you a spy?"

Clara laughed out loud, and Andrew grinned at her. "No, Andrew, I am not a spy."

"Hmm, that sounded like spy talk there for a moment."

"I've just read my fair share of fiction," she replied. "I read a lot of everything, actually. And I have an overactive imagination." She held his gaze for a moment longer before looking away. He was looking at her in a funny way that did not necessarily make her uncomfortable, but it did cause a strange warmth to spread through her. There was a light in his eyes, aside from the candlelight, and a bounce in his mood. He was not playacting the part of the Duke of Brad-stone; he was Andrew, the Andrew she knew, jovial and ami-able. She wondered briefly why he did not act this way all the time.

Then the realization hit her. If he showed he had a pleas-ant side, the daughters and matchmaking mothers of society would hound him. People would flock to him, even more than they already did. She knew for the most part he had been spared the attentions of the title hungry wives-to-be, mainly because of his obvious disinterest in everyone and his general grumpiness. Clara realized he dared not let anyone know he was actually quite charming and agreeable. It was all just an act, a protective barrier between him and the world.

"What is it?" he asked. "You are smiling at me in the most peculiar way."

"I was just thinking," she replied.

"About?"

"You."

"Hmmm. What about me?"

"I think . . . I think I understand you a bit better than before," she admitted.

"How so?"

"I am not sure if I can explain."

"Try."

Clara paused to gather her thoughts. "I think your Stone Duke stature is more of a way to keep people from knowing the real you, because if they knew the real Andrew Macalis-ter, you would never get a moment's peace."

"And you think you know Andrew Macalister?" he asked.

"I did once," she admitted. "But that was a long time ago. I'm not sure if the Stone Duke hasn't trampled him down into submission. I get glimpses of the reckless young lord I used to know."

Andrew looked away. "Sometimes I wonder the same," he admitted to the darkness. "Having you here makes me hope that the Lord Andrew you knew has not been entirely suppressed. The Stone Duke is rather unpleasant, isn't he?"

Chuckling softly, Clara shook her head. "More than you could ever know. But I understand why he needs to be."

Andrew grinned with that slightly lopsided, boyish grin of his. She understood why he did not smile more often. He would have women falling at his feet, married and unmarried alike. He looked young, carefree, and virile. Much too handsome for his own good. His smile lit up his face, reaching all the way to his eyes.

"You should rest," he said and stood.

"You should too," she replied and nestled herself into the bed. He leaned forward, his face close to hers, close enough that she thought he was going to kiss her.

"Don't forget you are safe here, Clara," he said, his voice barely above a whisper.

"I know," she nodded. "And thank you, Andrew, for . . . well, for everything you've done for me."

"It has been my pleasure," he said and planted a soft kiss on her forehead. "If you need anything at all, do not hesitate to ask, Clara."

"There might be a day you will regret such a generous offer."

"Not possible," Andrew replied, snuffing out the candle before turning to leave the room.

"Sleep well, Andrew," Clara whispered after him in the dark.

"You too, Clara," he replied, and she heard the soft click of the door.

She leaned back in her pillows and sighed. Her sister's elopement did not make much sense before, but now that she had seen glimpses of her childhood friend, it made absolutely no sense at all. She could not understand why her sister had left to marry a footman. Christina had loved society, she loved fashion and gossip and balls and loved the idea of being a duchess. Everything Clara had seen of Andrew since the night of the birthday ball just made her even more determined to find out what happened to her sister. The Christina she knew would not have left this man for anything.

Gentle reader, the most astonishing news has reached this author's ears! A very reliable source has reported the Duke of B— proposed marriage to the scandalous Lady C—! One can only wonder what is going on at B— House. We will be certain to keep our readers apprised of any developments.

Chapter Six

It was three full days before Andrew saw Clara again for longer than a brief hello. He had his solicitors to meet with, Parliamentary proceedings to sit through, an important vote to take part in, and he had to put in an appearance at Brook's. So when his carriage rolled up to Bradstone House, Andrew was relieved to be home to enjoy what remained of the weekend.

"Thank you, Howards," Andrew said to his butler, handing over his hat and gloves. "How is everything?"

"Very good, your grace," Howards replied. "Not a thing out of the ordinary all day."

"Good. And where is everyone?"

"The marchioness is having tea in the lilac sitting room with Lady Norah and Lady Susanna before they go into supper."

Andrew nodded. "And Lady Clara?"

Howards's eyes softened just a little at the mention of her name. Andrew noticed she seemed to have that effect on people. "I believe Lady Clara is resting."

Andrew thanked the butler before heading up the stairs. He stopped to greet his sisters but did not stay to take tea with them. There was one person he wished to see, but first he wanted to change into a fresh set of clothing. Walton, his valet, was waiting for him in his dressing room, and it took only a few minutes for Andrew to feel refreshed and comfortable.

Andrew saw Martha the maid bringing up a large tray with domed silver dishes.

"Is that Lady Clara's supper?" Andrew inquired.

"Yes, your grace," Martha replied. "Doctor's orders for her to stay abed, so she is to sup there as well."

"Have Cookie send a tray up for me as well," Andrew said and opened the door. "I'll dine with Lady Clara tonight."

"Yes, your grace," Martha replied and set the tray down on a long side table.

Clara was sitting up in the bed, a book propped in front of her. She looked up at the sound of Andrew's voice and smiled.

"Good afternoon," she greeted him, setting her book down in her lap.

"Good afternoon to you," Andrew replied taking a seat in his tall wing-backed chair. Martha bustled about setting up Clara's food tray and before long a second tray was brought up and Martha settled discreetly by the open door.

"Thank you for taking supper with me, your grace," Clara said and took a bite of her roast.

"It is my pleasure," Andrew replied. He smiled at her, and they both tucked into their meals. They ate in silence until most of their meals had vanished from their plates. Andrew motioned for Clara's plate to be refilled.

"Really, I do not need any more food," Clara was saying as another serving was placed before her. "I ate a great deal at luncheon, I do not know if I can eat any more."

"Eat as much as you can," Andrew replied. "Did the physician come by today?"

Clara's brow furrowed. "Oh yes. The physician came by, and that man is a loon."

Andrews's brows rose. "How so?"

"He said I needed fattening up!"

Andrew let out a bark of laughter. "He said that?"

"He implied I was not getting enough to eat. My dining habits were beyond reproach," Clara replied stubbornly. "Since Jonathan usually could not bear the sight of me, I normally dined alone while he ate in his study or at his club or his mistress's townhouse. True, I was not allowed a second helping, but I was hardly starved."

They lapsed back into silence as she forced more food into her mouth. It was not necessarily an uncomfortable silence, just a heavy one.

"Please stop glaring at me while I eat," Clara said and set her fork down. "It really is unsettling to eat with you glowering at everything."

Andrew blinked a few times, not realizing he had been glaring. "I apologize. I assure you I did not mean to glare at you."

Andrew gave himself a mental shake. He was normally in such refined control of his features and emotions but seemed to forget himself around Clara. Her melting charm appeared to affect him as well. She was the exact opposite of him, he realized. Whereas he was dark and brooding, staring people down with his piercing blue eyes, she was happiness and sunshine, lighting up the existence of everyone around her. It was remarkable that even under the tyranny of her brother, her fire had not waned.

"The banns are to be called in Kent tomorrow," Andrew told her. "The messenger should be arriving in Cumberland next week sometime, so next Sunday they will be called."

"Lovely, thank you," Clara said, not meeting his gaze.

They lapsed back into silence. Andrew inclined his head towards her plate of half eaten food. "You do want to make sure you leave room for dessert. I thought I smelled an apple tart when I arrived, and Cookie's tarts are the absolute best."

Clara looked down at her plate. "That does sound divine. But I would hate for this food to go to waste."

"Nonsense," Andrew said, motioning with a wave of his hand for Clara's tray to be removed. "After everyone in the household, including the serving staff, is properly fed, all the excess is sent to the poor."

Clara's surprise was evident. "That is very kind of you."

"You may be surprised to learn that I am a kind person."

Nodding, she replied, "I suppose I never doubted that you were. I am mainly surprised at the differences between you and my brother. I had assumed all peers were as horrid as he. But you are not like him at all."

"I would certainly hope not," Andrew retorted. "I don't aspire to be great, but I do know right from wrong. I know my place in this world, and I know to appreciate it."

A warm smile crept across Clara's face again, and he was lost in the depths of her eyes. Brown warmth swam around him, dancing and teasing his senses, reminding him of simpler, happier times. Her bottom lip slipped a breath away from her top lip, and Andrew was overcome with an insatiable need to capture her lips with his. He wanted to know what she tasted like. He felt desire pooling in his blood, pulsing with a hunger for her, a longing he had not known this strongly in a long time, if ever.

A lovely flush rushed across her face, and he smirked, realizing she was not immune to him. It was reassuring, even if it just confused him more.

"Did you have a pleasant day?" she asked.

"It was normal," he replied. "Tedious and busy, as was the entirety of the week. I apologize for staying away. I wanted to allow you time to rest and . . . adjust."

"Adjust?"

"To the idea of becoming my wife."

"Oh," she replied, not meeting his eye for a long

moment. "Yes, I suppose that will take some adjusting." She paused and watched him. "You can make it up to me tomorrow."

"Really? And what would you have me do?"

"Good question," Clara said. "Let's see . . ." She paused to think, cocking her head to the side and pulling her bottom lip between her teeth.

"You are playing with fire, Lady Clara," he warned, not taking his eyes off hers. They widened in mock innocence, the audacity and daring of her behavior teasing and tempting him. She truly was unlike any other woman he had ever known.

"I do not know what you are talking about, your grace," Clara said with a little shrug of her shoulders. "You cannot possibly know what I was thinking."

"I'm not convinced I want to know what you were thinking," he confessed.

"Oh yes, you do. You want to know what went racing through my mind, what could possibly get me . . . excited."

Andrew swallowed. She was doing it again. Just her voice alone was almost his undoing.

Two can play at that game, Andrew thought.

"And tell me, Lady Clara," he drawled, dropping his voice to a seductively low octave. "What excites you?"

"There are many things that excite me, your grace," Clara said softly, her eyes slowly trailing up the length of him. "But you want to know what activity is most stimulating for me?"

He nodded.

"Do you want to know the most arousing thing we could possibly do in here together, alone?"

Andrew swallowed and nodded again, dumbly.

"Read."

He hadn't expected that. "I beg your pardon?"

"Books, your grace," Clara repeated, her seductive tone vanished. "I wish you to read to me tomorrow."

"You want me to read to you?" Andrew repeated, still

trying to clear his muddled brain. *Was that a euphemism for something?*

Clara narrowed her eyes at him. "What did you think I wanted you to do?" she asked. "Do you have a better idea of what you can do to make up days' worth of abandonment to this room? What other talents do you possess that could possibly entice me?"

Andrew's mouth had gone dry. She was a spitfire, this little blonde thing.

She laughed and leaned back into her pillows. "You are quite fun to tease, Andrew. And it is *so* easy."

"I have not a clue to what you are referring," Andrew replied, attempting to regain some semblance of composure.

Clara laughed again. "Yes, you do."

"Pray tell, what book shall I bring to our reading session tomorrow?" he inquired. "How about *Sense and Sensibility*?"

She narrowed her eyes at him. "How about Richardson's *Virtue Rewarded*?"

"Come now, Clara, it has to be Shakespeare's *The Taming of the Shrew*?"

She let out a tiny gasp before grabbing the pillow beside her and lobbing it at his head. Luckily he was quicker and ducked out of the way, but it did not stop him from laughing harder.

"You, your grace, are—are—" Clara sputtered, unable to find a proper insult.

"What am I, Lady Clara?" he asked, enjoying her ire.

"You, sir, are a scoundrel."

"Really, that is the best you could come up with?"

"I could say more, but such things are not fit to grace a lady's mouth," Clara said primly. "Now, I am tired, and I wish to rest. Good evening to you, your grace." She crossed her arms and turned her head away from him, her nose in the air.

Andrew laughed, watching as her features softened, and she tried not to laugh with him. Finally she threw her arms down in exasperation and huffed at him. He thought if she was standing she might have put her hands on her hips and stomped her foot.

"Oh, Andrew, will you cease? You can stay as long as you stop that racket escaping your mouth. I swear, how very unduke-like you can be."

"Why, thank you." He grinned at her. She grabbed another pillow and lobbed it at him, but this time he caught it and threw it back. She blocked it, and it fell to the ground beside the bed.

"Andrew Macalister!" she cried in outrage. "I have a head wound!"

Andrew's face fell in horror, his eyes flicking to the bandage still wound around her head.

"You are right, that was stupid of me," he admitted. "I apologize. Is your head feeling better? What did Dr. Lennox say?"

"That my head is healing," she admitted. "But he still wanted to watch for a fever or dizziness."

"I am happy to hear you are healing," Andrew replied. "You gave us all quite a fright." He frowned, remembering her collapsed at her brother's feet, the blood that had soaked through his coat and shirt.

"Well, remember that when you want to toss a pillow at my head," Clara chided. "The least you can do is rearrange my remaining pillows. They are all out of place and quite uneven now."

"Of course," he replied and leaned over her, fluffing and pulling her pillows back into place. "Better?" he asked.

He should have seen it coming; he should have seen the flicker in her eyes for what it was. But he did not see her lift one last feathery down pillow and whack him on the head with it.

He staggered sideways, reeling from the blow.

"I cannot believe you just did that!" Andrew exclaimed in mock irritation and true shock.

Smirking, Clara's eyes danced as she teasingly taunted,

"Believe it."

Andrew wanted nothing more than to capture her smirking lips with his and kiss her senseless.

"You, my dear, need to be very careful who you hit with pillows," Andrew said, his tone low and dangerous. He leaned towards her and her eyes blazed up at him, darting lower to his lips. He wanted to kiss her. He was going to kiss her. He was going to turn her bold words into moans, he was going to—

"Ahem."

Andrew silently thanked Martha for clearing her throat at just the right—or wrong—moment. He thought he also might throttle the maid for it.

Leaning away from Clara, the urge to kiss her still pulsed through him, but doing so would only complicate everything. She was injured and under his protection. Ravaging her in her sick bed probably was not the most gentlemanly thing to do.

He stood, removing his weight from the bed. She looked so innocent lying there surrounded by mounds of cloud-like pillows, her blonde hair pooling around her shoulders like a cherub angel.

"Are you going to stay for dessert, your grace?" Clara asked.

"I would like to," Andrew answered truthfully. "You have no idea how very tempting that sounds. But I really should be going. My valet will have a fit if I do not allow him two hours to dress me for this evening."

"Where are you off to tonight, if you don't mind me asking?"

"I don't mind. Tonight is the Sheffield Ball, though truthfully, none of us want to go. It is our brother Ben's birthday, and it always feels as though he is miles away when he isn't here on his birthday."

"Isn't he always miles away?"

"Yes, but once a year it is his day, and we don't know

where he is," Andrew explained. "It makes him feel that much farther away." It was true, he had been thinking about Bennett today more than usual. Truth be told, he missed his rambunctious younger brother with his big, barking laughter echoing off the halls. It had been too long since he'd been home.

"I understand how it feels to have a beloved sibling on the other end of the earth," Clara said, her tone trying to be reassuring. "My brother Patrick is at sea. I am sure wherever he is, Captain Lord Bennett is thinking about you all today as well."

"At least he does not have to put up with stodgy balls like the rest of us do," Andrew replied. "And that damned birthday ball always falls on my birthday."

"Your birthday was not so bad this year, was it?" she asked. "I mean, you danced the dinner dance with me, which should place it among your favorite birthdays, at least."

"It was a nice birthday this year," Andrew admitted. "Even though I do have to be another year older. Twenty-nine, practically an old man as Luke keeps reminding me. Have a pleasant evening, Clara. I'll stop by before I leave and bid you good night."

"I'd like that very much," she replied.

He leaned forward and kissed her forehead before turning and quitting the room.

Chapter Seven

It was two days later that Clara was alone with Andrew again. Each time he came to visit, she was encamped with one or more of his sisters, having tea or discussing books and ribbon colors. But true to his word, Andrew managed a few hours of uninterrupted time with her, though the doors were left wide open, and a maid was present the entire time, much to Clara's annoyance.

Andrew read to her after they had dined, and after Beverell brought in a traveling desk and his paperwork, he sat sifting through a stack of papers and correspondence. Clara had resolved to read quietly and simply bask in the comfort of his presence.

"Are you reading horticulture?" Andrew asked. Clara glanced at him over the edge of the book. It was open before her, but she was not exactly reading it.

"It is about the cultivation of roses," Clara explained. "To clarify: I like roses."

Andrew looked mildly appalled. "They are just flowers,"

he said, still trying to comprehend her choice of reading material.

"*Aux contraire*, your grace," she said. "There is so much more to the flower than you realize."

"Ah, but, *what's in a name? That which we call a rose by any other name would smell as sweet.*"

Clara rolled her eyes skywards at his teasing use of the famous quote. "I believe Shakespeare was very wrong."

"Enlighten me."

Clara set her book aside. "When you give roses to someone, you are personalizing your gift with a much deeper sentiment. Flowers are wonderful and beautiful, but there is meaning behind each one. A pink rose, for example, is for admiration and gratitude. Yellow is happiness and friendship. You give yellow roses to a companion when you admire and respect them as a friend. White is for purity and innocence and often reverence, which is why you send white roses when someone has died."

"What about those?" Andrew asked, indicating the vase of flowers sitting beside the bed. It was a bouquet sent the previous morning to Lady Norah who had them brought in to "brighten the room."

"Yellow with red tips symbolizes friendship falling into love, just as the yellow bleeds into the red, making the transition between the two states seamless and effortless."

"What about red ones?" he asked.

"A red rose is a symbol of a romantic love, of beauty and courage and passion. A bouquet with red and pink roses is for romance and passion, whereas red and yellow together is happiness and celebration."

Andrew looked at her in disbelief.

Shrugging, Clara continued. "As I said, I like roses. I like their beauty and simplicity and elegance. I like their variety. It is like speaking a secret language. I read somewhere that it came from Persia where women used flowers to communicate, as written language was forbidden. I was hooked at *forbidden*," she admitted with a mischievous glint in her eyes. "It was most amusing to watch as Christina was presented with bouquet after bouquet of roses that were screaming the wrong message."

"What did I send her?" Andrew asked.

Clara knew it was useless to pretend she did not remember. "You sent her a bouquet of pink and white roses every day."

"How dastardly of me," Andrew said, scrunching up his face in mock pain. "That meant what? I admire and am grateful for her purity and innocence?"

Clara laughed. "Basically. It was a very platonic sort of bouquet. Not something I would care to see from a suitor or fiancé."

Andrew gazed at her intently, his blue eyes twinkling as he thought through what she had said. "What color flowers should I have sent her?"

"Oh, I don't know," Clara said, brushing away her comment with a wave of her hand. "The ones you sent were satisfactory."

"What would you want a suitor or fiancé to send you?" he asked more directly.

Clara swallowed and looked down, afraid to read too much into his line of questioning. "Something a little more romantic. Red and white are for unity, whereas red and pink or pink and yellow would be appropriate as well." She hoped he wouldn't probe her further. It felt as though they were discussing something much more significant than the silliness of flower symbolism.

"It is interesting I had never heard of this secret language of roses before now," Andrew said looking back at his paperwork. "Does every lady know of this?"

"I think it is a bit of female common knowledge," Clara admitted. "At least the basics. Red is love, yellow is friendship, that sort of thing. All sorts of flowers and herbs are said to have spiritual and mythical meanings, but no one has published a book about it or anything. Though I would be the first to buy it."

Andrew nodded but did not look up at her. "Well, I can assure you it is not something completely known amongst the gentlemen in society. At least, it is not spoken of. How unseemly it would be to present the wrong message to a lady through the gift of a flower."

"Unless the gentleman is choosing the flowers himself, I can hardly think such a thing would happen," Clara replied. "I would think a gentleman would simply make the order for flowers to be delivered, and the flower shop would do the choosing."

Andrew's eyes found hers and a crooked grin spread across his face. "This is exactly what happened when I ordered flowers for your sister. It seems either my secretary or the florist knew the message I truly wanted to send."

"Which is why you should always specify exactly what you want when placing an order," Clara said.

Andrew chuckled and leaned back in his chair. "Very true."

She smiled, hoping their unusually heavy conversation was at an end. "What are your plans for this evening?"

"Another ball, I think," Andrew sighed and pulled a time piece from his jacket pocket. "I must be going. I need to stop by Brook's before, and I think I shall pay Halcourt a visit as well." He stood and rang the bell pull. It was only a few moments before Beverell was clearing away the desk and papers. Andrew bid her good night and left the room quickly.

The house was dark and silent when Andrew returned from the night's social engagements, tedious as they were. The servants had all retired for the evening or at least moved on to nighttime duties. They would be in their quarters and far away from the first floor bedrooms. Andrew knew

Martha would not be in Clara's room.

He stood outside the door, hesitant to enter. He knew it was a bad idea; being close to Clara was turning into an unhealthy infatuation, and that just would not do. Their marriage was out of a need for her safety. The balance and control he had cultivated over his life for the past twelve years was starting to crumble, and it was this woman's fault. Her teasing smiles and warm inviting eyes . . . she made him forget who he was, what he had become to survive.

Andrew had a plan. He would enter the room, bid her a polite good night, and then leave, nothing more. She might even be already asleep. There would be no teasing, no laughing or smiling or anything else that might make him want to touch her or kiss her or do something he shouldn't. Martha was not there this time to stop him; he had to be able to control himself.

Convincing himself of his self-discipline Andrew took a deep breath, expelling his uncertainty and insecurities as he exhaled. He knocked gently on the door and waited for an answer, but none came. He could not see a flickering of candlelight coming from under the door—perhaps she really had gone to sleep. Slowly, he turned the knob and slipped inside. The room was lit with moonlight from the window, its bright silvery glow casting long, dramatic shadows along the room. Silhouetted at the window stood Clara, leaning against the frame, dressed in a nightdress and silk wrapper, the moonlight glistening off the whiteness of the nightdress, illuminating her in a soft glow.

Turning her head, she pierced him with a small smile and gestured for him to come closer. There was no point in resisting. The air surrounding him was charged with something. The darkness paired with the brilliant light from the moon sent magic and energy dancing across his skin, every ounce of him anticipating touching her again.

Clara pointed out the window. "I can see Morton House from here."

Andrew looked to where she was pointing but only saw rooftops.

"Another street to the left and three houses down," she explained. "I used to count the chimneys between my bedroom and the park. There are twelve."

Andrew counted out twelve smoke stacks. "Are you certain?"

She nodded. "That is where my brother kept me as half a prisoner, half a toy for him to torture."

"Did he hit you often?" Andrew asked her.

"No, that was the first time," Clara admitted. "It shocked me when he did, I could barely react. He had been cruel before, but he never resorted to violence. Usually he avoided me, and when he was forced to be in the same room, he made sure we never touched."

"I'm sorry for what you had to endure, Clara," Andrew said gently.

"I would still be there if it were not for you," Clara said, turning her head to look up at him. She had removed the bandage from around her head, but her wound was not as terrible as he had feared. What had bled like a gunshot wound to her skull was nothing more than a three-inch cut just along her hairline. It was still dark and red, but once it healed, no one would notice.

"But I have been wondering, Andrew, why were you there?"

"To see you," he admitted. "I came to call and found the house in chaos. I heard smashing and shouting, and I ran up the stairs towards the noise. And then I saw you crumpled on the floor. I feared he'd killed you."

"And then you saved me," Clara whispered, her fingertips reaching up to tentatively graze along the edge of his jaw, her nails skimming the stubble that had grown throughout the day. "I thought you dashing before that. You cannot imagine what I think of you now."

"I don't mind."

Dropping her hand, Clara turned around to face him, her back to the window. "But really Andrew, I cannot thank you enough. You have no idea; your family is so loving and so wonderful. I've been without anyone else but Jonathan for three years. I'd have left if I could, but I have no funds of my own and nowhere to go. Thank you for . . . for your offer of protection. Though I do not agree with the decision, I do not want you to think me ungrateful."

"Clara," Andrew said, taking her chin in his hand and turning her face up towards him. "You were mine. You were mine to save."

Holding her gaze, he gently brushed his lips across hers, the softness of her skin only awakening his desire more. She was soft and warm, and her mouth was so very inviting. He knew he shouldn't be kissing her or taking such liberties with her, but she was impossible to resist. He was only a man long deprived of light, drowning in his life, starving for sunlight and Clara was a beacon. She was happiness and laughter and warmth, and he could think of nothing other than bathing in her light.

She pulled away from him and let out a nervous laugh.

"I should probably leave," Andrew sighed, resting his forehead on hers.

"Probably," she agreed.

"I apologize if I overstepped, Clara," Andrew said softly.

"Not at all," she replied, her voice barely above a whisper. "I am your fiancée. I would think that allows you some liberties. Besides, that was . . . nice. I had always wondered what it would be like to be kissed like that."

"That was your first kiss?" he asked.

Clara blushed and looked down. "Aside from the one neighborhood boy who stole a kiss on my twelfth birthday, but I would hardly consider that my first kiss."

Andrew was a little taken aback as the realization of her true innocence became clear.

"How old are you?" he asked.

"You should know to never ask a lady her age, your grace."

"I can do the sums if I need to," he replied.

"Three and twenty," she sighed.

"Twenty-three and never *properly* kissed," Andrew teased, wrapping his hand across the back of her neck, tilting her head towards his. "We will have to rectify that, you know."

"Right now?" she asked in a whisper.

"You have no reason to fear me," Andrew said, his voice low. "I could never hurt you."

Clara nodded as Andrew bent his head and kissed her again.

This time he was not going to be soft and reassuring, Clara realized, her knees nearly buckling at the sudden wave of desire that shot through her. His lips were urgent and passionate, teasing her lips apart, thrusting his tongue into her mouth, teaching as she learned to match his movements, trying to give as much as she was taking, hoping she was doing it right.

Christina had talked about kissing Andrew, but she failed to detail the heat of his lips, or the strength in his hands as he held her, the way her senses came alive, the dizzying wave that swept over her. Wanting to feel more of him, Clara pressed her breasts to his strong chest. His arms moved around her, one arm tight across her back and the other cradling the back of her head as his tongue danced with hers. Winding her hands through his hair, thick and soft, she pulled him closer.

His kisses turned harder and even more urgent, and she wondered how close he was to losing control, because she was not sure she could make herself stop. And they did have to stop, did they not?

Andrew pulled himself away from her a second later and took a step back, putting some distance between them. Clara was first aware of how cold she was without his warm arms around her, but she quickly realized she had to catch her breath. He was watching her, his eyes molten and dark with desire, and just seeing him look at her that way caused chills to run down her spine and pool in her toes.

Tentatively, Clara brushed her fingers along her bottom lip, feeling the wetness from his kiss. "You can stop looking at me like you think I might bolt or faint."

Laughing lightly, he shook his head. "I was not thinking any of those things."

Clara smirked. "Liar."

"I might have been worried you were going to run from me, but clearly my fears were for naught."

"I'm made of stronger stuffing than to run after being kissed by a man," she said, her breathing returning to normal, but her blood still hummed for his touch.

"That you are."

"And thank you," she continued, trying to remain light and aloof when she really wanted to run back into his arms and beg him to kiss her more and never stop. "It was most educational."

"Educational? It was not meant to be educational. It was meant to be arousing."

"It was that too," she admitted.

There was a glimmer of amusement in his eyes. "Good night, Clara."

"Good night," Clara said and Andrew quickly fled the room. The door clicked shut and it was a moment before Clara could move, much less exhale the breath she hadn't even realized she was holding.

She fell onto the bed, her mouth tingling.

"There is one way you can hurt me, Andrew," Clara said to the darkness. "You can break my heart, like you did five years ago."

The bright morning sunshine poured into the room as Martha pulled the curtains back from the window. Yellow rays hit Clara's face, and she pressed her eyes shut, trying to hold in the most wonderful dream.

"Good morning, my lady," Martha said as she moved about the room. "If you've no headaches, Dr. Lennox has agreed that you are no longer bedridden, so you are free to break your fast in the breakfast room."

"Wonderful," Clara mumbled, yawning as the maid left the room. She stretched and rubbed the sleep sand out of her eyes. Martha returned a moment later with a modest but beautiful arrangement of red, yellow, and pink roses, another from Norah's excess of admirers.

"It was kind of Lady Norah to have another of her arrangements sent up, it does add more color to the room." Clara glanced around the room, realizing it did in fact match the rose patterned wallpaper perfectly.

"Oh, no, my lady," Martha said, handing her the card. "These are for you."

"For me?" Clara asked in surprise and accepted the card. "Who could have possibly sent me flowers? I have not been out of this house in six days. The only gentleman I've seen is his grace, and . . ." Clara quickly looked down at the card in her hands and tore it out of the envelope.

Clara,

I have recently become aware of the hidden meaning of rose petals. I trust this bouquet will not be lost in translation.

Your Humble Florist,

Andrew

Clara smiled and looked at Martha, who was indiscreetly

smirking at her.

"*Who* indeed, my lady," Martha replied with a wink.

"Oh, stop," Clara laughed and swatted at her with her hand. "Bring them closer, please." Clara took a deep breath, inhaling the roses' sweet scent. Upon closer examination, she could see a single white rose and a single lavender rose intermixed with the pinks and yellows and reds. The sight warmed Clara's heart; she had not mentioned lavender roses nor the meaning behind single roses. He must have taken her advice and gone to the flower shop himself. She could only imagine Andrew, the Stone Duke, tromping into a florist shop on Piccadilly Street this morning demanding to choose his own blooms. She inhaled their scent again. Red and pink for romance and passion; pink and yellow for happiness and celebration. The single white rose said, "My feelings are pure," and the single purple said, "I am enchanted by you."

Clara smiled softly at her bouquet, afraid to hope.

"Splendid, you are awake!" Susanna exclaimed from the doorway, making Clara jump. "I saw those arrive, and Howards sent them straight upstairs. You must know how curious I was. They are beautiful, Clara, but whoever are they from?"

"They are from—well you see, I—" Clara sputtered but was interrupted by Susanna snatching the card from her fingers. Susanna read the card, glancing from the card to the bouquet then to Clara who could not help the flush that traveled up her neck and settled in her cheeks.

"Oh, Clara! How wonderfully romantic!" Susanna exclaimed and threw her arms around her.

"What's romantic?" Sarah asked as she came into the room, Norah only steps behind her, a fluffy grey cat positioned in her arms.

"This!" Susanna said, thrusting the card into her sister's hand. Sarah read through the card, a soft smile appearing on her lips before she looked longingly at the bouquet and then at Clara.

"That is a very sweet gesture," Sarah replied as she passed

the card to Norah. Apparently Clara would not be able to keep this to herself. She had a feeling not much was kept secret in this family.

"*Sweet?*" Susanna asked. "Oh Sarah, it is divinely romantic. Just think of the story it will make! He sweeps you off your feet at a ball and then saves you from your terrifying brother. While you recover, you fall in love over the simplest things, and he marries you, and you live happily ever after!"

"It sounds like those ridiculous romances you've been reading," Norah replied, sitting on the edge of the bed, her cat settling onto the thick coverlet.

"True love and romance do exist, Norah," Susanna quipped at her.

Clara felt the need to stop the Macalister sisters before they truly got the wrong idea.

"It was very nice of his grace to send these, but I am sure there is nothing to be gathered from it," Clara insisted.

"I don't know," Sarah said, pensively, tapping her finger against her lips. "Susanna may be on to something. The last person Andrew sent flowers was your sister, and those were some hothouse mix chosen at random. I'm not even sure they were roses."

"They were," Clara said absently as Norah handed the card back to her. "I remember the morning after our debut. Christina was so thrilled with all her arrangements that day she barely looked twice at any of them. There was no romance in any of them, no affection, and no honesty. They were all so false."

"That is how those types of arrangements are," Norah replied nodding. "Not that I'm boasting, but after my debut last season, I thought I would pick the gentleman with the arrangement that spoke to me most. But none of them spoke to me at all. They were just flowers; none had any meaning, and none of the presenters knew me."

With a nod Sarah added, "These flowers are special, Clara. Andrew rarely does anything like this. And he even signed the card personally. Normally Andrew sends his secretary and never pens his own name. But this . . . this is something special between you and Andrew. If a gentleman puts effort into something, it signifies something to him." Clara looked down at the cream card in her fingers, his long loopy scrawl strikingly black against the paper. She was afraid to place too much emphasis in the hidden meaning of some silly flowers. But were his sisters correct?

"Let us go down to breakfast," Susanna suggested. Clara nodded, threw back the blankets, and stepped behind the partition to dress with the help of Martha, choosing a morning dress of dusty blue muslin. Clara's trunks had arrived the day after she had, each one neatly packed with all her dresses and belongings from Morton House.

Sarah excused herself while Susanna and Norah moved the vase of roses around the room, determined to find the perfect place for them.

As they entered the breakfast room, a quick survey of the room told Clara they were the first to arrive, and she breathed a sigh of relief at the absence of the duke. She hadn't realized how nervous she was about seeing him again, though she had no idea why. It was just Andrew—the silly, teasing boy she had known years ago, even if he had grown into a delicious and handsome duke, to whom she was now engaged. It was pointless to be nervous.

Helping herself to eggs and toast arranged along the sideboard, Clara was careful to avoid the kippers, as they would surely make her sick, before settling down at the dining table across from Norah and Susanna. Sarah entered the breakfast room and smiled reassuringly at Clara as she began to fill her own plate.

Clara could never imagine her own brother smiling or laughing as Andrew had. Her brother would never tease or flirt. The more time she spent with Andrew, the more she was realizing he was still the same boy she had once known, though that side of him seemed often buried deep.

But then, why had Christina run away? Had she not seen this side of him? Why would she choose to run off with a footman instead of marrying Andrew? Could she have possibly loved the footman? The whole ordeal made no sense and was completely out of character for her society-obsessed sister. It was almost like something was missing, some chunk of information Clara was not privy to that was preventing her from understanding the whole picture.

Clara's thoughts were abruptly interrupted by very loud male voices echoing from the front hall.

"Oh dear," Sarah sighed, having taken a seat beside her.

"What is it?" Clara asked.

"By the sounds of it, the boys have returned from school," Sarah replied.

"I thought term was not out until June?" Clara asked, frowning as she tried to remember her own brother's school term patterns.

Sarah pierced her with a pointed look. "Exactly."

Two young men burst into the room, both red-faced and fuming. Their dark chestnut hair clearly defined them as Macalisters, and one was sporting a swollen black eye.

"Nickie!" Norah cried in alarm, jumping up and running toward them. "What happened to your eye? Were you fighting again?"

"My brother, Lord Nick," Sarah said quietly to Clara. "He and Norah are twins. And the other is our youngest brother, Lord Charlie. I'm not sure why they are home early from Eton."

"Nicodemus Hawthorne Robert Ewan Macalister!" Andrew's voice roared from the hall, and Nick winced at the use of his full and proper Christian name.

Andrew furiously burst into the room.

Norah turned defiantly towards her older brother, squaring her shoulders for the fight.

"Norah, get away from him," Andrew commanded.

"He's injured!" Norah exclaimed.

"Norah, I'm fine," Nick insisted.

"It is his own damned fault his eye is black, and I will not have you coddle him for his own stupidity!" Andrew yelled.

"Andrew, your language!" Sarah chided.

"It was not stupidity!" Nick cried, glaring at his brother. He was still shorter than Andrew, but only just, and his shoulders were squared for a fight, his fists balled at his sides.

"Then what would you call it?" Andrew demanded. "Having a laugh? It was stupid, reckless, and irresponsible. I should let you hang for this!"

"Andrew!" Sarah cried at him in dismay, rising to her feet. "Of all the things to say!"

"Nick!" Norah cried, rounding on her twin. "What did you do?"

"Tell them," Andrew commanded.

Nick swallowed and glanced at his younger brother before looking back at his sisters. "We, uh . . ."

"Barty thought it would be a great laugh if we pretended to be highwaymen," Charlie interjected.

"You did what?" Susanna cried in shock.

"And we might have held up a carriage," Nick finished.

"You could have been killed!" Sarah cried.

"We are all right," Nick replied. "And the bloke in the carriage is fine too. We did not have any bullets in our guns. We just scared him a little is all. But the prefect knew something was afoot and was waiting for us when we returned to the dormitory. He forced the answer out of us, and the headmaster sent us here straight away."

"He escorted you back to London," Andrew added. "He's suspended you for the rest of the term! I was barely able to calm the man down, the way he ranted and waved his arms about; you are lucky he did not expel you completely. I cannot believe your stupidity! What could you have been thinking? Were you even thinking at all?"

"We are fine!" Charlie repeated Nick's assurances.

"Yes, but is the man you tried to rob fine?" Andrew demanded.

Nick and Charlie exchanged a look between them.

"He was a bit shaken up, I reckon," Charlie admitted.

"But he was alive and swinging when we left," Nick added. "That is how I blackened my eye."

"Of all the irresponsible things!" Sarah shouted, rounding on her brothers, hands on her hips. It seemed for the moment Clara was forgotten as the Macalister siblings launched into an all-out shouting tirade, each yelling over the other.

"Be thankful he did not shoot you!" Susanna cried at them.

"Nick! How could you?" Norah yelled at the same time.

"You could have gotten your brother killed!" Andrew yelled at Nick.

"You've lost all the brains in your head!" Norah accused her twin.

"Are you both mad?" Sarah exclaimed.

"It was a mistake!" Nick cried. "I'm sorry! *I forgot!*"

The room went eerily silent, and all Macalister eyes bore into Nick and Charlie.

"How convenient for you to forget such a thing," Andrew said, his voice dangerously calm. "The rest of us are, unfortunately, not so lucky. I am certain Sarah, Susanna, or Norah will never forget that night. I will not. Luke and Bennett will not. It must be a privilege to be you and not remember."

"It was not that we forgot it happened at all," Charlie quickly explained, "we just did not make the connection. You are right, we were not thinking."

"That much is obvious," Andrew snapped. "You should have a great deal of time to *think* at Bradstone Park. You shall have no one to *think* with the entire time except for each other. I also imagine it would be best for you and your thoughts to stay indoors in the evening; stay off of the horses and out of the lake."

"You are sending us away?" Nick asked horrified. "We just got home!"

"I feel you had best leave now while your trunks are still packed," Andrew added. "You will also have plenty of time to study for your exams, as I will have to persuade Eton to accept them. I expect perfect results."

"You cannot do this!" Charlie cried. "You cannot banish us to the country!"

Andrew narrowed his eyes at his youngest brother. "I can, and I will. If you thought this little stunt was going to be overlooked, you were sorely mistaken. I can handle almost any sort of frivolity, any sort of carousing or acts of stupidity. But this is unforgivable."

"Andrew, please," Nick begged. "We've only just returned to London."

"And you shall be leaving today," Andrew replied. "Sorry to spoil your plans, but you made the mistake. Now you must live with the consequences." Andrew turned to leave but stopped and turned to his brothers again. "And if I hear that even one toe is out of line, you might want to consider a life outside this family."

The sound of silver clanging on porcelain caught Andrew's attention, and his eyes landed on Clara's, his gaze furious. Clara realized she had dropped her fork onto her plate. He held her gaze for a long moment before storming out of the room, slamming the door behind him.

"Well," Sarah said, obviously attempting to break the tension. She glanced at Clara and saw the fear in her eyes and forced a smile, attempting to offer her reassurance. "He might have gone a bit overboard, but his reasons are genuine."

"Of course," Clara said, nodding absently.

Had she been wrong about him? Had Andrew Macalister—the laughing, free, and reckless boy she had once loved as a child been completely stamped out by the Stone Duke?

That could not be right, she had seen him laugh and flirt, and he'd sent her roses, for goodness' sake. But who was this shouting at his brothers in the breakfast room? How could they be the same man?

Was he just a cold-hearted, high-handed, uncharitable man with a title? If he was, how could she possibly expect to find a happy marriage with him? It was better that she planned to leave him. She wouldn't allow herself to have any feelings towards the exact thing she wanted to get away from, pink roses and a sweet card be damned.

Gentle reader, a report was made that the Duke of B— was seen stomping about at Gormant's Hothouse Flowers early this morning. As it was nearly dawn, the claim cannot be substantiated, but if the Stone Duke was choosing flowers, one must then believe they were for his bride-to-be. Since the formal announcement came days ago, all of London is on alert for the sign of the couple's eventual downfall.

Chapter Eight

*A*ndrew tore from the house, his every limb shaking, hot rage coursing through his veins. He wove his way towards the mews, eager to put as much distance between himself and the breakfast room as possible. This was not how he wanted his morning to go. Clara was supposed to come into the breakfast room, preferably alone, and sweetly thank him for the flowers. He was then going to ask her if she rode, and then he was going to invite her for a ride around Hyde Park.

"Well done," Andrew muttered to himself. He sought out his horse, a beautiful Hanoverian warm-blooded animal. Titan, as Andrew had christened him, nuzzled his head into Andrew's palm, his chestnut coat fine and soft from the excellent care of his groom.

"Seems you've made a right mess of things," Luke said from behind him.

Andrew nodded, not looking back at his brother. "You heard, did you?"

Luke snorted. "I think everyone in Mayfair heard."

Turning to regard his brother, Andrew asked, "Are you aware of Nick and Charlie's transgressions as well?"

Facing Andrew, Luke braced himself against the doorway post, one brow raised in a perfected look of detached amusement.

"It is unforgivable," Andrew stated. "I will not tolerate such behavior out of either of them. How could they have forgotten?"

"Andrew, they were just boys out for a thrill. Sowing their oats and all."

"But if those oats had cost them their lives? Or that bloke they were pretending to rob?"

Luke held his brother's gaze. "I understand the emotional weight you have behind this, but I don't think their lack in judgment means they don't mourn for Father and Sam. In our own ways, we have all mourned their loss differently."

Andrew nodded, knowing his brother was right. He felt the seriousness of the conversation fade away, felt the anger seep from his bones. It was stupid and reckless, but at least everyone was safe. He did not want to endure another tragedy.

Looking between his horse and Titan, Luke asked, "Do you think Titan can out run Ulysses?"

Andrew looked across the barn to the tall bay at the end of the row, and then back at his brother, raising a dark eyebrow in question.

"Or did you forget how to ride?" Luke taunted.

Giving into Luke's bait, Andrew turned to the stable boy standing at the far side of the row of stalls. "Saddle him up."

The saddle boy's eyes widened in surprise, but he quickly hurried to do as instructed. Andrew was not sure what made him do it. His anger at his brothers? Clara's influence in his life? Something made him choose the reckless route this time. It might have been a bit careless, but he needed to be somewhere, anywhere else. Not where his brothers' guilty faces were finishing breakfast, not where his sisters would look at him with pained expressions, and not where Clara would frown at him, horror and revulsion reverberating through her deep brown eyes.

He would never get the look in her eyes out of his mind. It made him sick to know that she had seen him lose his temper. What she must think of him now . . .

Sighing to himself, he mounted and led Titan out onto the street, pausing momentarily for Luke to catch up. Andrew had always felt at home on a horse. He had been born to be in the saddle. Titan had been a gift from his father a few years before his death, and Andrew had intended to take the black horse into the cavalry with him.

But that was a different life, before the night that changed his life—all of their lives.

"Ready when you are," Luke said as they reached a long stretch of road at Hyde Park.

"You honestly think you can best me?" Andrew asked, walking Titan in a circle. "You think that your bay can outrun Titan?"

Luke bent down and patted his horse on the neck. "I think Ulysses can handle it."

Andrew grinned confidently. "I'll even give you a head start."

"Why thank you, your graceness!" Luke exclaimed and dug his heels into his horse's side. With a jump, Ulysses took off down the path, and Andrew counted to three before urging his horse after him.

There really was no benefit in giving Luke a head start, and Andrew quickly surpassed him. He was not known as the best rider in the family for nothing. Andrew even held back for the last few hundred yards to give Luke the idea that he might have a chance of winning before taking off at breakneck speed to finish strong.

Luke was laughing as he caught up to him at the end

of Rotten Row. "I don't know how you do it. That Austrian horse isn't even bred for speed."

"It must be the rider then," Andrew replied audaciously.

They walked their horses back towards the house, Luke stopping to chat with a few other gentlemen and young ladies before catching up with his brother. Andrew, of course, did not converse with anyone.

"Do you wish to return?" Luke asked. "Or are you going to avoid the house longer?"

"It was your idea to have a race."

"But you succumbed to my bait quite easily," Luke said. "You were desperate for a reason to leave. And I don't think that anyone with the last name of Macalister was the reason for it."

"I needed time to let my temper cool down," Andrew admitted.

"You are really going to marry the girl?" Luke asked. "After what her brother has done, after what her sister did to you five years ago?"

"It would be unfair of me to punish Lady Clara for the sins of her siblings," Andrew replied. "And would you trust her safety to anyone else? You know what Morton can accomplish with just his words."

"She was truly bleeding on the floor?" his brother asked.

"And Morton stood over her in glee," Andrew recalled. "For nothing else, Lady Clara deserves better than what her brother and sister have provided for her. Abandoned in the wake of her own sister's scandal, only to have her brother treat with her with such disdain. It is a marvel she's maintained a pleasant demeanor. The same treatment would turn anyone else bitter."

"Lady Clara is really getting to you, isn't she?" Luke asked as they rode through the front gates of Bradstone House.

"I am certain I don't know what you are talking about," Andrew replied coolly, tugging off his riding gloves. Except he did know exactly what his brother was talking about, and it annoyed him that Luke had assessed his mood so accurately. Lady Clara had somehow dug her way into his senses. Dancing with her had been happiness; talking with her and discussing silly flowers had been pure contentment. And he had sent her flowers that morning. Not only sent, but personally selected the flowers from the vendor on Piccadilly.

What *had* he been thinking?

But after the way she had looked at him earlier, he was certain that any potential interest she had had in him was long gone.

As much as Clara wanted to deny her growing affections towards the duke, she was so utterly confused. How could his personality swing so fluidly back and forth between pleasant and cold? How was she to know which one was true, which man he was now, the cold Stone Duke or the charming Andrew?

He had berated his brothers, in front of her, with the same expression that she had seen on her own brother's face so many times. True, Andrew hadn't known she was in the room, and she hoped he would have behaved more gentlemanly had he known she was there. But he had been too blind with fury to take an inventory of the room before exploding with rage. And just knowing he had that level of anger and rage inside him made her a tad uneasy.

She had replayed the scene over and over in her head all day long, running over the words and the level of insult he had taken from his brothers' actions. There had been something else, something almost painful. Underneath his tirade, he had seemed to be genuinely concerned for their safety, and that was something that Jonathan never felt for her.

Clara did not see Andrew for the remainder of the day, which she was grateful for. He had not been there to escort his sisters to the theatre, so Sarah declared they would go without him. Clara had chosen to stay in, not feeling ready to face the world again, even with the Macalister family as her champions.

Deciding she needed a book to lull her to sleep, Clara threw her legs over the side of the bed and crossed the room to the dressing table. She pulled on her thin silk dressing robe, hastily tied the sash, and quietly left the room.

Something boring to sooth my busy mind, she thought. Something to make her think of anything but *him*.

Without a candle to light the dark hallway, she moved slowly, careful of where she was treading. She made it down the stairs without tripping and silently padded her way through the front hall. She had counted the doors to the library on her tour of Bradstone House earlier in the day and easily found the library door now. It was slightly ajar, but as she peered in, the room appeared to be vacant. The moonlight cast eerie shadows along the carpeted floor, but it allowed enough light for her to read the titles from the spines of the books.

"Hmmm, what could we read to put us to sleep?" she murmured to herself, skimming her fingers over the spines. They were organized alphabetically by author, and reading through them, each one seemed less interesting than the next.

"Not geology . . . philosophy will just give me a head-ache . . . Ah, astronomy." Pulling the thick tome from its place on the shelf, she flipped through a few pages. Her eyes swept over the first few lines, and she understood it well enough to be completely bored by it.

"Planning on star gazing, Lady Clara?" a deep voice asked. She jumped, the book slipping from her grasp to the floor, the thud it made on impact echoing throughout the entire house. Whipping around, she saw Andrew standing in the doorway, his face illuminated by a streak of moonlight.

"I was just looking for something to help me sleep," she

replied.

"Hmmm," he said, taking a sip of whatever was in his glass. It was a dark liquid, so she assumed it was wine.

"Good night, your grace," she said awkwardly, half skipping to the door in escape.

"I wanted to apologize to you," he said, taking a step into the room, securely blocking the doorway.

"Now?" she asked. "Here?"

"I was going to do it tomorrow," Andrew explained, setting his glass down onto the table beside the door. "But now seems as good a time as any."

"You have nothing to apologize for, your grace."

"I am sorry you were present to witness the scene earlier today. What goes on between brothers should be dealt with in private, not the breakfast room."

"You need not make apologies to me, your grace," Clara said. "It is your house."

"Yes," he said, his eyes glancing about the room expressionlessly. "It is my house."

"And that gives you permission to act as you see fit."

"But it was very impolite and very ungentlemanly of me to do so in your presence. My brothers were . . . out of hand."

"For parading as highwaymen?" she asked. "Please excuse my impertinence, your grace, I can understand the issue of their judgment, but you seemed much more angered than you should have been."

"I could not care less about their stupid stunts," he replied. "I mean, I care about my brothers, but, as they say, boys will be boys."

"Then what—"

"Did you know that I was not supposed to be the duke?"

"Yes," she replied. "Jonathan told me of your brother and father dying when he came home from Eton without you. But he never mentioned how they died."

"My father and brother were gunned down by highwaymen," Andrew replied, and Clara's heart dropped at the sadness in his eyes.

"Oh." And Clara understood. The pain in his eyes . . . the care and concern for his brothers. How had she not known about this before? How could she not know about such a tragedy in his life? Good lord, what else did she not know?

"So you see, my reaction was more than warranted."

"I see that now, your grace," Clara agreed.

"Why are you still addressing me that way?" he asked.

Her mouth had gone dry as she fought for a response, something clever and witty, to find a foothold of control, for with him she felt none. His gaze was slowly trailing down the length of her body. Her silk robe did not leave much to the imagination as it hung on her curves in a very tantalizing way. She had the urge to wrap her arms around her midsection in an attempt to shield herself from him, but something made her still. Something about him was powerful and predatory and *male*.

His eyes met hers and did not waiver as he moved closer. He was clad in black pantaloons, a waistcoat and shirt, but no cravat, leaving the top of his shirt open in a V. She could see part of his collarbone and a small amount of his chest. She felt very tempted to touch him, just to see if his skin was as soft as she imagined.

She took a hesitant step back, not necessarily afraid, but not sure she wanted him near. Her rational thoughts seemed to scatter when he was too close. A few more steps and her back would be against the bookcase.

Standing directly in front of her, Andrew still had not dropped his eyes from hers. Slowly he brought his right hand to cup the side of her face, rubbing the pad of his thumb over her cheek, a trail of fire left in its wake.

"Thank you for the flowers," she said, her voice barely above a whisper.

"You are very welcome," he replied.

"They are beautiful."

"Much like you are. Do you ride, Clara?"

"Horses," she replied, smirking.

One side of his mouth turned up into a smile. "Would you like to go for a ride with me tomorrow?" he asked. "Hyde Park has some breathtaking views from horseback."

"I did not bring my horse with me to town."

His smile melted into a devilish smirk. "I would be pleased to mount you, my dear."

"Oh," she said, tilting her chin up in challenge. "Then I would enjoy that very much."

His bright smile and his bright eyes were causing her knees to weaken, her heart to crescendo in her chest.

"Are you going to kiss me again?" she asked, too aware of the bookcase pressed up against her back now, leaving no room for her to run. After the events of the breakfast room, she would think she would have been terrified of this man, but she could find no fear in her body. Shimmers of something else, but no fear.

"Do you want me to kiss you?" His question was simple enough, but words escaped her.

"I . . ." she began, intending to tell him to leave her alone, but her eyes and thoughts betrayed her, and he knew it. One look at his perfect lips, and she was lost. Slowly those lips descended upon hers, and she was lost in the magic and the beauty and the fantastic sensations running throughout her body. Slowly and possessively, he teased her lips apart and let himself in, tasting her. He tasted like wine and sweetness and everything she should not be doing.

Clara purred as the hard length of his body was pressed against hers, his warmth and strength cradling her. His lips wove long and slow kisses across her mouth, his tongue playing a torturous game with her own. She moaned with pleasure against him, arching her back, pressing her breasts against his chest. His hand came up to cup her breast through the thin silk of her night rail. She could feel everything through it, and he could too. With his thumb he rubbed the bead of her nipple, hardening it into a peak, as a similar sensation rose deep in her core. It was wrong, she shouldn't kiss him. How could she know he was not the same as her brother? Arrogant, mean, and controlling.

But he was gentle as he kissed her, his tongue stroking hers in a slow steady torture, his hands gentle as he cupped her breast, kneading her through the silk.

He had completely justified his motives earlier when he had yelled at his brothers, she thought. It was because of the deaths he had experienced that had caused him to react thusly. But the image of his hateful face bellowing at his younger brothers suddenly popped into her head, and Clara pushed him away, breathless.

He did not resist, but he did not move away completely either. He stayed mere inches from her; she could still taste the sweetness of his breath, the heat from his pulse. For a long moment he stared at her, his dark blue eyes almost black with desire, boring into her with such an intensity, Clara was not sure what any of it meant.

"I am not that man, Clara," Andrew stated hoarsely, and she nodded.

"I know."

His hand came to cup her cheek, gentle and careful like she was a frightened foul.

"You . . . you make me want to be me, and I am grateful for that." He kissed her again, lightly and sweetly before pulling away, stepping away from her.

She nodded but did not move away from him. Placing her hands on each side of his face, Clara leaned up on her toes and kissed him again, just as gingerly as he had kissed her.

"Good night, Andrew," she whispered before disappearing out the door, the astronomy tome long forgotten on the floor.

Chapter Nine

ndrew woke the next morning with a pounding head. A troupe of dancing elephants could not have caused more pain had they been parading on his temples.

Walton arrived muttering about something, and Andrew groaned as his valet pulled the heavy drapes back. The bright morning sun hit him like a brick.

"Having a bit of a lie in, are we, your grace?" Walton asked impertinently, moving about the room as he prepared Andrew a bath.

Rubbing his eyes, Andrew inquired, "What time is it?"

"Nearly ten, your grace," Walton said, holding out Andrew's dark blue dressing robe. Feeling as though his head might burst with any sudden movement, Andrew slowly moved off the bed, and his valet helped him into his robe. Ten o'clock? Luckily he did not have any meetings that day and was not needed in Parliament.

"Are the girls already up for breakfast?"

"Yes, and they have already finished," Walton said, and Andrew stumbled across the room to where a spread of coffee and muffins had been laid out. Walton handed him his cup of coffee before turning back to supervise the filling of the hip bath. The last of the footmen were coming in with the warm water and Andrew was grateful for its temperature. It looked very soothing.

"I have been asked to relay a message, your grace," the valet said, pulling clothing out of Andrew's wardrobe. "Lady Clara would like you to know that if your offer of riding still stands, she would very much like to go."

"I asked her to go riding with me?" Andrew asked, looking around at his valet.

"She seems to think you have."

When had he asked her to ride?

The library, he remembered, though the details were lost in a drunken fog.

"Is that wise?" Andrew asked. Being near her did not seem to be wise. "I mean, with her head injury?"

"I am not a physician, so I really could not say. What shall I tell her?"

"Oh, tell her that would be all right, I suppose, if her head is not bothering her," Andrew replied, frowning. "No, wait, tell her I'm sorry for . . . that I had hoped I did not . . . did she say anything else, Walton?"

"No."

"She did not mention anything about last night?"

"Should she have, your grace?"

"No, no, of course not."

"Are you all right, your grace?"

"Yes, I'm fine," Andrew replied, racking his mind to remember what he said to her, wanting to hit Walton for ending each sentence with such a surly "your grace." For the life of him he could not remember what had transpired in the library. It was all an alcohol-induced blur.

"Would you like me to tell her that you have already

gone out?"

"No!" Andrew replied a bit too eager. "Tell her yes, no, I mean tell her no, I have not, I mean . . ." Andrew shut his eyes, pushing away the pain along his skull. "Please inform Lady Clara I would be honored to take a ride with her and to meet me in the front hall at eleven."

"Very good, your grace."

What have I done? he asked himself. He had kissed her, that much he remembered. But what else had he said?

The previous evening, he had arrived home later than planned, completely forgetting he was appointed as his sisters' escort for the evening theater. After taking dinner in his study, he had consumed two entire bottles of wine while looking over his notes from Parliament, not fully aware he had had so much to drink. On his way to bed, he had heard someone muttering to themselves in the library and had walked in to find Clara there and barely clothed in what should really not be considered proper night clothes.

He did remember that. He remembered the way her backside had been deliciously molded by her thin night chemise, her golden-blonde hair hanging loose over her shoulders hiding her lovely, pert breasts.

Everything after that was lost in a drunken haze, though he had a vague sense that he had touched her, and not in the most gentlemanly way.

Settling himself into his now-lukewarm bath water, he sighed. He hardly drank in excess, and when he did it was always a challenge to remember what had transpired while under the influence. Now he had to pay the price and face Clara without the clear knowledge of what had occurred between them.

Promptly at eleven o'clock, he stood in the front hall wondering what had possessed him to ask her to ride with him in the first place, especially after his embarrassing display of behavior yesterday morning. But when he saw her walking down the stairs, smartly dressed in a dark brown riding habit which perfectly complimented her soft complexion and eye color, he did not mind in the least that his drunken self had taken control the night before. She smiled softly as she drew near, the faintest glimmer of fondness dancing through her eyes. Whatever he had said the night before must have prompted her forgiveness of his deplorable behavior the previous morning.

"You look well rested, Lady Clara," he said. "I take it you slept well?"

Clara quickly glanced at him, and seemed confused by his words. "Actually, I did not, your grace. But facing the prospect of being mounted can do wonders for one's mood, wouldn't you agree?" Her eyes twinkled with her teasing words.

"Indeed," he replied curtly and led her out of the house, perplexed by her choice of words. They sounded vaguely familiar. He had inquired earlier if Lady Clara had brought a horse with her to town and had been informed that she had not, so he requested a suitable mare of even temperament be selected and brought to the front of the house for her. The cream buckskin stood patiently beside Titan, an entire head shorter than him, looking very unimpressive and very uninterested in their outing.

Clara stopped walking and looked at the horse in disbelief.

"Is there a problem?" Andrew asked.

"This is the horse I am to ride?" Clara asked doubtfully.

"This is Hillie," Andrew replied, petting the horse's muzzle. "Is she not suitable?"

"She's beautiful," Clara said. "But I grew up in the country, and I don't mean to be rude, but . . ."

"Do you wish for something livelier?"

"If possible, your grace," she replied. "For she will be as bored as I am if I ride her."

"What sort of horse do you have at home?"

"A thoroughbred," she replied proudly. "He's black, and

his name is Magnificent, Maggie for short."

"You have a male horse named Maggie?" Andrew asked, and Clara nodded. He chuckled as he handed Hillie's reins back to the groom and instructed him to saddle a specific thoroughbred. Taking Titan's reins from the groom, he led Clara towards the mews at the back of the house. A rich chocolate-colored horse was being led out of his stall towards the hitching post to be saddled.

"This is Homer," Andrew said, pleased at the delighted look on Clara's face.

"Hello, Homer," Clara said gently, running her gloved hands along the tall horse's muzzle and neck as the grooms worked quickly to saddle the horse.

Homer was only a hand shorter than Titan, but he was very gentle with Clara as she climbed atop him, her legs elegantly nestled to one side, long cane gripped in one hand. Andrew mounted Titan and the two of them set off towards Hyde Park. They walked through the park along the same path he and Luke had taken the morning prior.

"We really mustn't waste such a beautiful day, your grace. I have always wanted to race along Rotten Row!" Clara laughed, throwing him a smile full of challenge.

Before he could respond, she tapped the cane into the horse's flank and Homer leapt into action, racing towards the Serpentine. Andrew wondered briefly if it would be ungentlemanly of him to surpass her, he paused long enough to count to three, before urging his horse after her. After a few moments, though, he realized she was a good distance away and he was not gaining on her. Urging Titan on again, Andrew willed the horse to go faster, realizing that this time he was not going to win.

Clara dared not look behind her, knowing what she would see. She was giddy with excitement, knowing she

had out-ridden him. She knew that was not an easy feat—
Andrew was a natural born rider. She smiled to herself,
knowing he would not share in her glee.

At the end of the long stretch of Rotten Row, she
brought Homer around, slowing him down as she turned,
leaning down to pat the horse on his neck. It was still early
enough in the day that there were not many people in the
park, mostly nurses and governesses with their young charges
happily throwing bits of bread into the water, laughing at the
geese and ducks that came to feast.

Hearing the thumps of hooves approaching, she turned
in her saddle to watch Andrew arrive firmly in second place.

"You've beaten me," Andrew stated in anguish, pulling
his horse to a stop beside her. Clara could not help but laugh
out loud. He narrowed his eyes at her. "I say, are you laughing
at me?"

Clara laughed again and nodded. "Oh, Andrew, I learned
how to ride in the years since we were children running
about Morton Park."

"You took off so fast it quite caught me off guard,"
Andrew replied. "We will have to have an official rematch to
determine who the real winner is."

"Oh, no, I won this one fair and square," Clara laughed.
"But by all means, let us have a rematch. I will best you again,
your grace."

"No one has outridden me in a long time," he said,
propping his hand on his hip and looking her up and down.
"You, my dear, may have triumphed this time, but it will
never happen again."

"You should not underestimate me, your grace," Clara
replied, challenge flashing through her brown eyes. Riding
was the one and only area Clara was ever overly competitive,
and this man was the main reason. "It would do you well to
remember that."

"Oh, believe me, I will," Andrew replied, steering his
horse around the bend of the Serpentine. Clara turned her

horse to walk steadily beside him. It was already a warm day, and she could feel little beads of perspiration collecting at the base of her neck. Clara was happy to just be outside, to enjoy this brief reprieve before she must figure out what to do with herself. She was merely a temporary guest in his home, though unbeknownst to her host.

"I would have never have guessed you were such an accomplished rider," Andrew commented, unaware of the thoughts rampaging through Clara's mind.

Clara laughed. "I did not used to be. I remember when you were friends with my brother, the two of you would ride all day, all over the property at Morton Park. Jonathan would never let me come with you and for good reason. I was appalling on horseback. One summer, when I was ten, you argued with him and told him to give me a chance, which he eventually did."

"You lost control of your horse," Andrew said, smiling at the memory. "We had to chase after you. I managed to grab the horse's reins and slow him down."

"Which caused me to fall off my horse," Clara finished. "Into a pond."

Andrew chuckled. "You climbed atop my horse and told me I was your hero. You even kissed my cheek and declared you would marry me someday."

"Goodness, don't remind me," Clara groaned. "I was an embarrassing ten-year-old girl."

"At least you were not wounded when your horse dumped you into the pond," Andrew added.

Clara nodded. "My pride was bruised. So the next year when you and Jonathan were at Eton, I rode and rode for hours every day to get better so I could show you I was not such a silly girl. Then the next summer Jonathan came home from Eton, angry and without you. And you never returned to Morton Park."

"That was the summer I inherited," he replied, his face clouding with emotion.

"What happened between you and Jonathan?" she asked. "I asked him, of course, but each time I inquired he became angrier. All he ever said was you were not the friend he thought you were."

Andrew shifted his weight in the saddle.

"I do not know what he would mean by that," Andrew replied, frowning. "When I became the duke, your brother decided he no longer wished to be my friend."

"It is as simple as that?" Clara asked.

"Yes," Andrew replied, looking at her, though she did not believe he was telling the complete truth. "We'd had an argument just before I learned of my inheriting, though over what, I cannot remember." His eyes unfocused for a moment as if recalling something. Whatever it was, he did not share. "I was called away to the headmaster's office. When I returned to my dormitory, he was nowhere to be found. I was packed up and sent home within the hour. I did not see him again until I returned to school three months later. And our friendship simply . . . ended. There was never an official falling out or a 'farewell and good luck.' We simply stopped speaking. Eventually, I realized he despised me, though I doubt I will ever know the reason for it."

"He hates me too, you know," Clara replied. "And like you, I have no idea why." She glanced at Andrew before asking, "What would you have done had you not become the duke?"

Andrew stared straight ahead, not answering. After a long moment, it seemed to Clara she had overstepped her bounds, wherever they were, and she opened her mouth to apologize.

"I had planned to join the army after Oxford," he answered slowly. "I wanted to ride in the cavalry. But fate had other ideas."

"You inherited," Clara stated, and Andrew nodded.

"As the heir, Sam was never allowed to join us on our escapades. He was not allowed the same level of freedom that we, as spares, enjoyed. Growing up at Bradstone Park in Kent was like a dream come true for the reckless, headstrong youth that I was. There are endless green rolling hills covered in orchards that slide up to the cliff and shoreline. We would ride for hours, myself, Ben, and Luke; Sarah often weaseled her way into coming with us, though she never enjoyed riding as we did. We would rise early in the mornings, escaping before our governess could wake us for breakfast. Cookie would make up a basket of breads and cheeses and a jug of fresh milk. We would take off on horseback into the depths of the estate. A footman would find us at lunchtime, bringing another basket of food, returning to the house mum about our location. And we would simply ride our horses; jumping fences and puddles, swimming in the lake, enjoying our freedom. No governess to keep us in line, no tutors to push Latin and mathematics. Mother knew we would come back; she never forced us home before we were ready.

"Once, Sam snuck out of his lessons, and Father was furious. I always felt sorry for my older brother. He was only five years my senior, and I felt guilty that we were allowed the luxury of amusements that he was not. His life was secluded; he only saw his tutors. Father did not send him to Eton or Oxford. He only saw us—his siblings—at dinner. He took breakfast and luncheon with his tutors or alone. When he died and I inherited the title, my initial reaction was that my life was over. I was no longer allowed to have fun; I was no longer allowed to live. So I rebelled. I drank and gambled and—" he paused and a faint blush ran up his face, glancing at Clara sheepishly. "Well," he continued and cleared his throat. "I made sure I did not stop living my life as I chose to.

"About a year after my inheriting, four or five months after my mother's death, I stumbled home in the middle of the night, nearly eighteen years old and drunk as can be. On my way up to my new room, I heard this strange noise. I followed it through the halls, drunk and stumbling until I came to the nursery. It was crying; I had heard my younger siblings crying. Luke and Susanna were there with Ben and Sarah, comforting Norah, Nick, Charlie, and Mara as they cried out for their mamma. I realized then that my fun really was over. I had responsibilities; I had a duty to uphold. Everyone was counting on me to make everything right and to be good and to step into Sam and Father's shoes."

Clara chewed her lip, reeling from his confession.

"It was not seamless," Andrew continued. "But I figured it out eventually. And now, this is what you have." He glanced again to her, meeting her eager gaze. "You asked me at the birthday ball if I ever did anything dangerous, and the answer, Clara, is no. I never do anything dangerous or reckless or remotely entertaining. I would never do anything to jeopardize my position, my title, or the safety and wellbeing of my family. I sit in Parliament; I escort my females in society. I tend to my tenants' needs and the requirements of my estates. I provide for my family, I make sure my investments and crops are prospering. For twelve years I have done my duty. I have been deprived of joy, of life. Until I met you."

Clara looked up at him, startled, his mouth curving into a lopsided smile.

"You, Clara, are the first thing I have done for myself in twelve years."

Her brows furrowed, she asked, "What about Christina? You almost married my sister."

"That was for the title," Andrew replied with a shrug. "I was not in love with her; I barely knew her."

"You are not in love with me," Clara reminded him. "You barely know me."

Andrew frowned. "Your father thrust her on me after one dance at a ball. I essentially made my purchase and expected delivery on my wedding day. This engagement between you and I is different."

"And now you've decided to amplify the excitement in your life?" Clara asked, becoming irritated. "And somehow

I am your excitement? How does being engaged to a social pariah constitute as different?"

"Clara, I—" Andrew began, but he was cut off by the arrival of his groom. Looking around, Clara realized they already returned to Bradstone House, the horses finding their own way home because Clara certainly hadn't been paying attention to where they were going.

Clara avoided looking at the duke as they reentered the house, feeling uncertain and unsure. She did not want to know what he had meant, she did not want to hear his dismissive tones or subtle set downs, just like everyone else in the *ton*.

"There you are!" Susanna's voice rang through the front hall, and Clara jumped. Susanna came rushing down the stairs, her face worried and flushed. "Where have you been?"

"We went for a ride through Hyde Park, Andr—your brother and I," Clara replied, stumbling over the duke's name. Susanna glanced quickly between the two before deciding it was not worth pursuing.

"We are going out, and we must get you changed out of that riding habit and into something suitable for Bond Street," Susanna said, slipping her arm through Clara's and pulling her up the stairs.

"You are going shopping?" Andrew asked, frowning.

Susanna nodded. "Of course. You want the *ton* to accept Clara as your fiancée, she needs to leave this house in the company of someone other than her fiancé. Shopping with me will indicate I have given my support to the union, which, of course, I have."

"She has a point, Clara," Andrew agreed. "It might be beneficial to be seen together to help convince the *ton* of the reality of this engagement."

"Whatever you think is best," Clara replied, following Susanna absently up the stairs.

Shopping seemed to be the Macalister girls' answer to everything. Feet hurt? Buy another pair of shoes. Feeling ill?

A nice brisk walk down Pall Mall will do one's constitution good.

"A little bit of shopping will improve your mood," Susanna replied, patting her hand as they set off down Bond Street. "And some fresh air will not hurt either. Trust me. Shopping is always the answer."

Norah and Sarah accompanied them to Bond Street, and they seemed to have a genuine love for shopping, possibly closer to an obsession. Their enthusiasm seemed odd to Clara, who had never overly cared for shopping, but their exuberance began to rub off on her. They did not look for anything in particular; they simply wandered through the stores looking at everything, purchasing items Clara knew they did not need.

Clara followed Susanna through the shops on Bond Street, chatting about ribbons and flowers and wedding plans, surprised when she found herself relaxing. She'd never enjoyed shopping with her sister, but here she felt a little more comfortable in her skin and in her position. And Susanna's exuberance was intoxicating.

Two hours and several purchases later, Susanna and Norah's parcels and packages were handed up into the carriage as the quartet set off for ices at Gunter's.

"There is something quite relaxing about spending a day wandering looking at lovely things," Susanna admitted, linking her arm with Clara's. "We have been given the great gift of privilege, and not everyone is so lucky. If buying a few extra ribbons or bolts of fabric helps these merchants put food on their tables, then I am happy to oblige. I'd rather spend money in a way that would help someone than sit and stare at it. Donating is good and all, but these people are the ones who will benefit from our generosity. Direct action always reaps the most rewards."

"And you like pretty things," Clara added, though she was touched by Susanna's perspective of their shopping exploits. Susanna had the right of it, though Clara had never thought of it in those terms. There was something to be said for saving one's income, but if that income was plentiful, there were ways it could be used to help someone else.

"Well, yes, there is that," Susanna admitted, beaming at Clara. "But what lady does not?"

Clara laughed, and they walked arm-in-arm down the street to spend more of their privileged funds at various establishments.

Upon returning to Bradstone House, Clara was grateful for a few moments alone with her tumultuous thoughts. Her heart twisted at the thought of not going through with the engagement, of leaving Andrew as her sister had. Over the past week since she'd taken up residence in Bradstone House, Clara had nearly forgotten she had no intention of marrying Andrew, too caught up in silly conversations and vases of beautiful roses. He was only marrying her out of some misplaced need to keep her safe, something she still could not quite comprehend.

She lay on her bed, bright golden rays of the afternoon sun filling the room with light and warmth, quite the opposite of her mood. Confusion and irritation coursed through her as she thought about Andrew and her sister and the mess that had become her life.

For as long as Clara cared to remember, she had always had a *tendre* for Andrew Macalister. When she was a child she had fancied herself in love with him. When he became the Duke of Bradstone and his friendship with her brother came to an abrupt end, she was certain she would see him again. She studied hard, wanting to keep up with him intellectually, learning Latin and maths, even some bits of science, all to make sure she would have something smart to say to him. She also strived to become a graceful and sophisticated lady, so when he saw her again he would be sure to take notice. Throughout her teen years, her childhood crush transformed into a challenge. She knew it was impractical to morph herself into exactly what Andrew could be interested in, so she strived to be someone worthy of his caliber of gentlemen.

Then, one week after her eighteenth birthday, after eight years of lessons and studying and learning to shoot and ride and doing everything she could think of to impress him, he appeared at her debutante ball and danced with her twin sister.

To say she was crushed would be an understatement. He took her heart with him as he led Christina onto the dance floor. She managed to hide her hurt over the following weeks, through his engagement to her sister, through the scandal of Christina leaving him at the altar, and when her father made her tuck tail and run back to Cumberland, she was secretly grateful to be away.

Here she was, five years later, engaged to the one man she could never shake from her heart. He laughed and teased and kissed her, but he was also cold and domineering.

She was beginning to understand both were different sides of the same coin.

One thing was for certain—if she did not belong in society, and she was not convinced she did, then she needed to remove herself from the situation. But the only way to be certain would be to try and fit in, especially with the Macalister family, because she would never know for sure if she did not try. If she was not careful, she would find herself in deeper than she had been as a child. If the odd, tingly feeling that accompanied any thought of Andrew meant she was in danger of her childhood crush resurfacing, then this time it would be with grown up and mature expectations and desires. She had been hurt by Andrew once before, when he chose Christina over her, so Clara knew she could survive it a second time. Her engagement to him was not real, not in any way that mattered to her. She could weather the scandal of her own abdication, and she would walk away from him in the end, if that is what it took to maintain her dignity. The mere impasse she had bought herself would conclude, and she would not hold him to a promise he made out of a misplaced sense of duty. She would not become his wife out of pity. If that outcome should come to pass, she needed to be ready and able to walk away.

Gentle reader, it seems the Duke of B— has taken to showing off his fiancée in public. The pair were spotted in a rare moment of riding through Hyde Park. Lady C— has not been seen for nearly a week and was later the same afternoon spotted with Lady R—, Lady S—, and Lady N— shopping along Bond Street. The quartet purchased ribbons and a pair of satin slippers. Does this increase in ventures indicate the Duke of B— is ready to let his pet out into the world? We all wait with anticipation to see where they next appear.

Chapter Ten

*I*t was five mornings later when Andrew saw Clara again, in a much different scene than the breakfast room fiasco the prior week. Everyone had already tucked into their meals, coffee and tea and chocolate steaming before them, when Andrew entered the breakfast room.

Sarah, Susanna, and Norah were chattering to each other with Clara in the middle, looking much more animated than he had seen her before. The bruising on her face had faded, though he suspected she had covered some of it with a powder. She looked almost back to normal.

"What do you have planned for the day, ladies?" Andrew asked as he filled his breakfast plate.

"I thought some sightseeing was in order," Sarah replied. "Clara hasn't been to London in years, and I would like to see some of the sights as well."

"We were thinking the museum, the gardens, the tower, and definitely the animals," Susanna continued. "What do you think, Clara?"

"Sounds lovely," Clara replied smiling. "It will be nice to venture out of this house."

"You were out of the house last week," Andrew said and took his seat.

"Really, Andrew? Surely she is allowed out more than once in a week?" Susanna asked before Clara could respond.

"Exactly," Clara said, smiling and tilting her chin at him. "Besides, I should experience more of London than your arrogant and haughty stares."

Andrew wanted to roll his eyes at her, but he was finding her spunk endearing.

"What do you say, your grace? Will you join us?" Clara asked.

"Absolutely," he answered. "How about after luncheon? We can do ices at Gunter's."

"Might I inquire what is the reason for your obsession with Gunter's?" Clara asked, looking around at the occupants of the table.

"Family secret," Andrew replied.

"Andrew loves ice cream," Susanna answered, ignoring his response. "I mean, absolutely *adores* ice cream. He is willing to pay extraordinary sums each year to have Gunter's personally cater his events. Gunter is, of course, just enamored to have the patronage of the Duke of Bradstone and deems it pertinent to give Andrew whatever he wants. He makes excess strawberry ices just to make sure it is always available when Andrew stops in."

"And he stops in normally once a day," Norah added.

"Really?" Clara said, turning towards Andrew. "It is curious, your grace, how you keep in such fine physical shape if you indulge in sweet confections so frequently?"

"The usual," Andrew replied, inwardly groaning at his sisters' attempt to irritate him, and now it seems they pulled Clara into their game. "Fencing, riding, boxing. Normal gentlemanly pursuits."

"Boxing?" Clara asked, her eyes flickering out of focus for

an instant, a hazy memory resurfacing. "Like prize fighting?"

"Not quite that plebeian," Andrew replied, glancing at one of his sisters, but Clara did not look to see which one. "I frequent Gentleman Jackson's when I feel the desire to beat something to a pulp."

Norah stood up abruptly, glaring at him. "Excuse me," she said stiffly. "I have lost my appetite." She stomped from the room, practically slamming the door shut behind her.

"Andrew, can we not make it through one breakfast as a family without someone throwing a fit?" Sarah asked.

Andrew set his fork down, regarding his older sister. "I will not apologize if Norah took offense to my words."

"Why would Norah take offense to prize fighting?" Clara asked.

"You remember Norah's twin from the other day, Nick, with the blackened eye?" Susanna asked and Clara nodded. "Well, our dearest ducal brother has deemed it ungentlemanly for Nick to partake in prize fighting, which is a bit of a strange passion of Nick's.'

"It is ungentlemanly for any gentleman to partake in prize fighting," Andrew quipped. "Think of the scandal it would cause, were people to find out the boy fights for money."

"But he's good," Susanna responded. "And no one knows it is him, he uses a pseudonym, like a stage actor."

"You are not helping his case," Sarah said.

"He needs to find a more respectable pursuit," Andrew continued. "Some sort of goal that does not involve beating another man with his fists. Why will he not consider joining the army?"

Susanna scoffed. "Yes, let's send him off to be fodder for Boney's bullets. We already have one brother involved, do we really need another?"

"I did not say I was going to enlist him against his will, Susanna," Andrew grumbled. "I'm not an ogre. I just think he should focus more on his studies and less on fighting."

"He just wants you to take notice of him," Sarah interjected. "He only wants to make you proud."

"The point is moot," Andrew said, ending the conversation. He took a bite of his toast and changed the subject. "So, the museum, the gardens, the tower, and the animals. Sounds like a full day. I would be happy to meet you, if that will please you, Clara," Andrew said to her.

"If you can manage with your important schedule," she replied cheekily.

"I have a session starting in half an hour," Andrew said, glancing at the time piece on the far wall, realizing he'd better be off soon or he'd be late. "But it should be over after one o'clock. I would be happy to meet you at Gunter's or wherever else you deem fit."

"Gunter's sounds wonderful, your grace," Clara replied and took a sip from her cup.

"We will have some calls to make this afternoon," Sarah added. "And the Garden Club Ball is this evening, don't forget, Andrew."

"Yes, of course," he replied.

The social season was in full swing and each night it seemed there was at least something requiring their attendance.

"Luke is so difficult to pin down, it falls upon you to escort through the week," Sarah reminded him. "We will attend the theater Wednesday evening."

"Will we not go to Almack's?" Susanna objected.

Pursing her lips, Sarah stared at her younger sister pointedly before the realization hit and Susanna quickly took a sip of her tea. Both girls looked from each other to Clara, who was seemingly oblivious to the exchange or the meaning behind it.

"Yes, the Garden Party and the theater," Andrew replied trying to cover over Susanna's gaffe. "I will make note of it. Also, Mara will be arriving in a week and has requested everyone to be gone from the house so she may have peace all day in order to prepare for the musicale on the following Friday."

"Goodness, however will we occupy ourselves all day?" Susanna asked.

"I'm sure you will find something," Andrew replied and dabbed his mouth with his napkin.

"It seems we have a busy schedule ahead of us," Clara commented. "And please don't allow my presence to prevent you from attending Almack's. I do not mind staying home for an evening."

There was a brief pause while Susanna and Sarah considered it before an almost convincing chorus of, "No, of course not!" "Don't be silly!" and "We can miss Almack's this once." But Andrew knew it wouldn't be this once, and he knew that Clara realized this as well.

"Splendid." Andrew pushed back from the table and stood up. "If you ladies will excuse me, I am off. Important assembly vote today, don't you know?"

"Andrew, ladies do not discuss politics, as you well know," Sarah chided him.

"Ah yes," he replied. "Whatever would I do without Sister Sarah? I might forget to tie my cravat or wash behind my ears." He winked at Clara before exiting the room.

Clara watched his retreating back as he left the breakfast room, curious of his mood.

"Sometimes he can be so very infuriating," Sarah muttered.

"He was teasing you, Sarah," Susanna explained. "You know he only says such things to get a rise out of you."

"Yes, well, he's been unusually teasing lately," Sarah said.

"Hmm," Susanna murmured. "I wonder why." She shot a side glance at Clara and winked. Clara pursed her lips. Andrew's perceived change in character had nothing to do with her, she was certain.

They finished their breakfast and quickly retrieved their gloves and bonnets before being ushered out the door, the burley footman, Beverell, in their wake.

"Do keep up, Beverell," Susanna said kindly.

"Yes, my lady," Beverell replied. Clara glanced from Susanna to Beverell, noting the way the Macalister family always seemed to be pleasant and kind to their servants. Andrew knew each person's first name, as did his sisters, and they were polite and courteous to their employees. They smiled and conversed not on a level of friendship, but on a level of mutual respect, and in return, the servants of Bradstone House adored the Macalister family. She saw how each time Susanna rang for tea there were extra biscuits waiting on the tray, how the footmen hurried to bring in warm water for Norah's bath, working quickly as not to lose the heat. It was no wonder the Macalister staff was willing to bend over backwards for their family. The Macalister family treated their servants like fellow human beings and not like lesser creatures.

"Garnet," Susanna called up to the coachman. He tipped his hat to her. "We wish to see the museum, the gardens, the tower, and the animals. Could you direct us the quickest way?"

"Of course, my lady," Garnet replied. Beverell helped each lady into the carriage before shutting the door with a soft click. Norah had not made an appearance in the front foyer.

Susanna shrugged when Clara asked her about Norah. "I don't particularly want to be in Norah's company if she is going to be in such a mood."

"Susanna," Sarah chided. "That is awfully rude of you. As a lady you must rise above the immaturity of your younger sister."

"Do you wish to endure her pouting and glaring, Sarah?" Susanna asked.

"Well, no," Sarah admitted as the carriage rolled into motion. "But you need not say such things aloud."

It was an unusually warm, late spring day in mid-May, and Clara was grateful for Susanna's choice in taking the open carriage. The streets were packed with carriages and carts all blocked by an overturned cart of vegetables that had spilled its load into the street. Garnet deftly and swiftly maneuvered them through the side streets until they pulled up to the front of the British Museum. What would normally have been at least an hour drive through the traffic had taken them less than twenty minutes.

Clara watched as Susanna thanked the coachman for his proficiency before linking arms with her and leading the way into the museum, Sarah and Beverell in her wake.

Perhaps, Clara thought, *there is something to that proverb about catching more flies with honey, after all.*

Andrew was eager to leave the Palace of Westminster's stifling rooms. The day had turned hot and humid, and he would rather spend the afternoon with Lady Clara and her tempting, teasing smiles instead of surrounded by hundreds of his sweaty, smelly peers.

Musing about Clara was how he got through his days in Parliament lately. Her dark eyes dancing with mischief as she chewed on the inside of her cheek, her hair falling golden and silky down around her shoulders as he pulled the pins from her hair. The feel of her pert breasts pressed against him, her nipples tightening under his attentions.

He hailed a hackney and gave the direction to Gunter's, promising a tip if the driver could get there quickly. It had taken him longer to get out of session than he had originally anticipated, and he was eager to get to Clara.

The hackney came to an abrupt stop a few minutes later, and Andrew poked his head out to see vegetables covering

Piccadilly.

"No way around it, guv'nor," the hackney driver called down to him. "Been like this all morning."

"I'll walk from here," Andrew said and handed himself out of the hired carriage. He flicked the driver a few coins before setting off down the road, careful to avoid the smashed vegetables along the street. He hurried down Piccadilly, passing his club and turning right once he got to Berkeley Square. It only took him a few more minutes from there for Gunter's Tea Shop to come into view. He was relieved to see his own carriage sitting a few carriages down from the confectioner's front doors.

He spotted Clara beside Sarah outside the shop, very pretty in her pale yellow day dress, a coordinating ribbon laced through the brim of her bonnet. As she spied him across the street, she gave a little wave as a bright smile spread across her face, and he could not stop the smile that formed on his face in return.

"Hello, your grace," Lady Clara said to him as he came across the street.

"Good afternoon, Lady Clara," he said.

"Goodness, Andrew, could you have been tardier?" Susanna chided him, coming out of the shop.

"Actually, I could have," Andrew replied and offered Clara his arm. "There was an overturned cart just down Piccadilly."

"They still have not cleared that away?" Sarah asked, frowning. "It was there when we passed by hours ago."

Andrew removed his top hat as they stepped inside the confectioner's shop.

"A pleasure as always to see you, your grace," Mr. Gunter said as he stepped out from the back room. "A strawberry coming right up."

Andrew nodded his thanks.

"And for Lady Susanna?" Gunter asked.

"I have been eyeing this peach for a few days now,"

Susanna said, pointing at a light brown confection. "I think I will try that one please."

Sarah declined a serving of ice cream and Gunter looked lastly to Clara.

"Have you lemon?" Andrew asked, realizing that was what she was searching for. Gunter's face fell and he looked down nervously.

"I apologize, your grace," the man said mournfully. "Lemon is not on today's list. I assure you it will be available the next time we see you."

"It is not a problem," Clara said, smiling sweetly at the man. He softened a little under her gaze. "I would like to sample the strawberry, since that is all his grace seems to order."

"Of course," Gunter said and busied himself with their order. He presented their cups of frozen cream and apologized again for not having the flavor Clara preferred. Andrew dropped a few coins into the man's palm, knowing Gunter would have lemon ice cream the next time they came by.

"Really, your grace, you need not frighten the poor man," Clara said as they settled into the seats arranged outside on the patio walk. "It really is not an inconvenience. I am capable of eating another flavor if my favorite is not available."

"Yes, but one of the privileges of being a Macalister is always having your preferences available to you," Andrew replied, taking a bite of his ice cream.

"I have it!" Clara exclaimed, her eyes lit with amusement. "I know why you enjoy Gunter's so often! The cool temperature of the treat must keep you from overheating!"

"I beg your pardon?"

"Well, you are always dressed in black, your grace," Clara explained, a smile dancing on her lips. "It's as if you are in mourning. Surely such a dark color would cause you to overheat throughout the day. The ices help keep you cool."

Andrew's brows rose at her teasing tone, but he did not answer. Clara smiled brightly at her jab.

"How was the museum?" he asked, ignoring the snickers emanating from where his sisters sat. Just as he had intended, Clara launched into a long explanation about what she saw and how interesting the entire outing was. Having never been to the museum, she prattled on about the collection of Greek vases, Roman and Egyptian antiquities, gems and natural specimens from the travels of Captain James Cook.

Andrew, for his part, listened intently, interested in her thoughts on the things she had seen, and also the sound of her animated voice that he found calming. It relaxed him after his stressful morning in Parliament.

"What time do you need to be back for the afternoon session?" Sarah asked him.

"I think today I will skip the afternoon session," Andrew replied. "Morning was almost a waste of time, and we are much further from that vote than I had originally thought. No one will miss me." He caught a look between Susanna and Sarah and knew his uncharacteristic actions were being noted. However, today he felt like throwing caution to the wind, taking the reckless way out, in the tamest sense of the word.

Clara had not noticed anything amiss with his change of afternoon plans. "What do you have planned for the afternoon?" he asked her.

"We have some calls to make," Susanna answered for Clara. "You are coming, Clara, no arguments. We also need to make an appearance in Hyde Park for the afternoon crush. We will want time to rest before we begin to dress for the Garden Club Ball this evening. You are welcome to accompany us on our calls, Andrew."

"An excellent idea," Andrew replied, fully aware he had just agreed to chaperone their social calls. An entire afternoon of weak tea and dry biscuits accompanying the required polite social gossip, who ran away with who, who cut who, that sort of thing. He had just signed up for an afternoon of misery, but it also meant an afternoon spent with Clara, and that alone was reason to endure the mind-numbing repetitiveness of the conversations to come.

Andrew tried his best to play the part of the attentive guest, but occasionally he felt his mind start to wander, usually to the indecent things he wished to do to Clara. The taste of her mouth, her soft skin, supple curves beneath his hands. The breathless way she moaned as he trailed kisses down her throat, his hands aching to wander further down to her center, her heat.

The clanking of porcelain drew his attention, and he glanced around the room, assessing what he had missed. The ladies were rising, dipping into polite curtsies. Belatedly, he realized it was time to leave and he should also rise, but as he stood to his feet, he realized another part of his anatomy had opted to stand as well. Turning quickly away from the ladies, who were thankfully ignoring him, he strode the perimeter of the room, pretending to examine a painting on the far side of the room. Checking to make certain no one was watching, he did his best to readjust himself, vowing to keep his thoughts—and parts—under better control.

"Lovely oil painting you have," Andrew said to their hostess as he passed.

He opted out of the carriage ride around Hyde Park for a brief nap in his unnaturally cool room. The afternoon of social calls had exhausted him, and he fell asleep on his bed fully clothed, which was how Walton found him hours later.

Andrew awoke with a start as his valet let out a shriek of terror at the sight of him sprawled on the bed.

"I am so sorry, your grace," Walton apologized, catching his breath, hand across his heart. "I had not expected to see you there. I thought you dead."

"Not yet, Walton," Andrew replied groggily. "Have the girls returned?"

"Hours ago, your grace," his valet said and began pulling out pieces of his evening attire. "They have already begun to dress for the evening."

"I assume it is time for me to dress as well?" Andrew asked, though he knew the answer.

"Yes, your grace," his valet said.

Andrew looked at his reflection in the mirror. Hair disheveled, face pink from sleep. Clothing wrinkled. Hell, he even still had his boots on. He glanced at the formal black on black evening attire Walton had pulled from his wardrobe. Black was ever so boring.

Walton went to work quickly, and soon Andrew was dressed in his formal evening attire, his valet fluttering about him, making last minute adjustments.

A loud pounding on the door startled them both and Andrew strode forward and yanked the bedroom door open.

"Morton's returned, Andrew," Bexley said, standing on the other side of the door. "I've just run halfway across Mayfair, but it was him. We need to get to Halcourt's as soon as possible."

Grabbing his top hat from Walton's hands, Andrew followed Bexley hurriedly down the stairs.

"I apologize, your grace, I did not know Lord Bexley was here," Howards said as the two men descended the last stairs.

Bexley shrugged. "I came in through the kitchens. More efficient."

"Is Luke here?" Andrew asked the butler.

"I have not seen Lord Luke since Saturday last, your grace," the butler replied.

Andrew swore and looked at Bexley. "He's in London still," Andrew told him. "Check the Mall—he has probably taken rooms."

Bexley nodded. "I'll find him."

"Ready my horse," Andrew said to the butler who bowed and quickly left to do his master's bidding. Andrew yanked his gloves on, looking at Bexley. "Find Luke. Tell him this is of grave importance: he must escort the ladies to the Garden Club Ball, they are not to be out of his sight. Send word to Connolly and Redley to meet them there. They are attending anyway."

Following Andrew out of the house, Bexley tugged on his own hat.

"I don't trust Morton," Andrew added as Titan was brought around the house and Andrew quickly mounted. "I don't want him near his sister. I cannot have her in danger, Bexley."

"We will keep her safe," Bexley promised, mounting his own horse. Andrew nodded, and the two friends took off down Park Lane, parting at Upper Grosvenor Square where they both vanished into the night.

Chapter Eleven

rriving at Aster House, Halcourt's Mayfair residence, minutes later, Andrew was quickly shown in to Halcourt's study. The room was draped in scarlet and mahogany and smelled of cigars, but it was the abundance of books and papers scattered around the room in neat piles that was most curious. Untidiness did not fit with Halcourt's meticulous personality.

"Ignore the mess," Halcourt said, struggling into his evening jacket, a bundle of papers clutched in his hand. "I'm reorganizing."

"I've sent Luke to escort the ladies to the ball, so I have a few minutes," Andrew said to his friend, setting his hat and gloves on a table. "Are those for me?" Andrew pointed at the papers in his friend's hand.

"No, another matter," Halcourt replied.

"Bexley saw Morton," Andrew informed him, lowering himself into a brown leather arm chair.

Halcourt nodded, pouring him a finger of brandy from

the decanter on his desk and offering Andrew the drink. "Your engagement announcement in the papers is likely the culprit for his return," Halcourt said.

"What have you learned?" Andrew asked, accepting the drink and taking a long sip, prepared for whatever his friend needed to tell him.

"Morton is flat broke," Halcourt began. "He has blown through the entirety of the Morton funds and is in deep with a dicey set of fellows who work out of the docks. Your new fiancée was meant to be payment for part of his debt."

Andrew ran his hand through his hair and silently cursed.

Halcourt continued. "The morning he threw her out of Morton House he had arranged her to be picked up from the street. He would spin some story about how she ran out in an overly-dramatic fit and was scooped up by some no-good criminal, and he was helpless to save her. There would be a search, of course, but she would never be found."

"That is appalling," Andrew replied, his voice calm, but his mood was anything but. "How could he sell his sister?"

"You forget that Morton hates his sister."

"Yes, but to do something that horrible?" Andrew shook his head, unable to comprehend that level of hatred. "There is more to this, I am certain."

"Oh, there is," Halcourt answered. "My guess is that he's trying to get his hands on the Patterson gold."

"Patterson gold?"

"Miss Solana Patterson was a very wealthy heiress, the daughter of some sugar cane farmer. Her father brought her up to town, debuted her with great success and married her off to the highest bidder. However, Old Patterson was no idiot; he knew his daughter's suitors were only after his money. She was not to receive a dime until his death, and then the money would be held in a trust to be passed along to the daughters of his daughter's daughters, and so on. Over a hundred years and some smart investing by the Patterson women, the funds have more than quadrupled the original amount. Clara's mother, Lady Meredith Masson, was the last Patterson heir, and her daughters are the sole beneficiaries of the trust. Only her daughters can access the funds, once they are five and twenty. If they die without issue, it goes to the sons. Jonathan Masson is such a son."

"But there is another Masson. Patrick, I believe."

"He's away in the war. He will not bother Morton."

"So you think that Jonathan Masson wants to get his hands on the Patterson fortune?"

"I think he had Lady Christina kidnapped or threatened, and it was convenient she died in childbirth at that back country parsonage," Halcourt replied. "When he realized it was only Lady Clara standing between him and the money, he knew what a convenience it would be if Lady Clara was kidnapped from his doorstep."

"I cannot believe this," Andrew said and stood up, pacing the length of the room, weaving around piles of books stacked throughout the room.

"People kill for a lot less, your grace," Halcourt said to him.

"Is there any proof?"

"Possibly. We think we have found Lady Christina's footman husband. He has a grand house just south of the Scottish border. He has been making a great deal of noise lately and claims to have been paid off by some great lord and said if the lord does not pay up the rest he is owed, then he will start being more specific with his information. He's ready to start naming names."

"Does Morton know of this?" Andrew asked.

"It is possible. The individual I've tasked with finding him will have him here within a fortnight. Once the footman sees your face his expression will tell if he's the one or not. And I'm sure that he can be persuaded to tell the entire story truthfully."

"Morton wants Clara dead."

"I think he would not mind if it happened," Halcourt replied. "He is too cowardly to actually get his hands dirty, but I think that is his end goal. He wants that money. And he is desperate."

"Then it is a good thing I intend to marry her," Andrew stated, his mind springing into motion. Morton, he could deal with later. One look at the clock told him he was going to be late to the ball.

"Best be going," Halcourt said, noting Andrew's glance at the time piece.

Andrew stood and picked up his hat. "Keep me informed of any more developments."

Halcourt nodded in agreement, and Andrew set off for the ball.

As promised, the members of Jonathan's staff who found themselves needing employment presented themselves at Evans, Smith and Watson Employment Agency and were promptly placed in positions around the country. Molly was one of those fortunate to escape Jonathan's employment, and Clara was relieved and grateful to have her former maid returned to her. Molly had been her lady's maid at Morton House, but since Christina's elopement Molly had been assigned other duties in addition to being Clara's maid. With Molly here, Clara felt a little closer to her normal self.

Although her trunks had arrived from Morton House weeks earlier, Clara still accepted the use of a gorgeous sage-green gown from Lady Norah. The color was a luxury she'd never been afforded. This once, she wanted to try and see what it would feel like to be a part of this family, of this life. She wanted her attire to be appropriate for the Garden Club Ball, especially if she was attempting to convince the *ton* her engagement was not a lark.

Clara thought she did look rather nice in the sage-green

gown. Her reflection was a bit of a shock to her. She was used to simple dresses meant for walking and day wear; even the evening dresses she had worn before were never this elegant. The pink gown she had worn at the Macalister Birthday Ball had been the nicest gown of the lot. The dresses and gowns her Great-Aunt Bridgette had paid for were lovelier than her country attire, but this dress was more exquisite than Clara had ever worn before. It was a soft satin with a wispy sprinkling of minute pearls carefully interwoven into the delicate embroidery along the bodice and bottom hem. Her golden hair had been curled and teased into a myriad of plaits woven into pinned curls. There were even a few curling over her hairline, dropping fashionably along her forehead, and more importantly, concealing her healing wound. She adorned herself with pearls borrowed from Sarah, and as she looked at her reflection one last time, Clara realized that she looked like a lady—a sophisticated, intelligent, desirable London society lady. She felt confidence surge through her veins.

Wrapped in her own cream shawl, Clara descended the stairs, her eyes darting around the front hall in search of Andrew. She was excited to see him, excited to be out with the Macalister family. But the tall, dark-haired man standing in the foyer was not Andrew.

"Luke!" Norah exclaimed as she rushed down the stairs. "We thought you'd left already!"

Lord Luke glanced up the staircase and his mouth split into a wide grin.

"I had planned on it, but his graceness begged me to escort you lovely ladies to the Garden Club Ball."

"Clara, this is our brother, Lord Luke Macalister," Sarah said, introducing the roguish brother. Clara had met him once before, years ago when Andrew was courting her sister.

"Be careful, Clara," Susanna teased. "It is rumored that his eyes alone can charm a young lady senseless."

Lord Luke offered her his other arm. "And we all know

how reliable rumors can be, don't we, Lady Clara?" he teased with a wink.

Clara accepted his arm. "Quite right, my lord. I have asked your sisters to simply call me Clara and would appreciate if you would do so as well."

"Sounds reasonable of you," Luke replied. "Since you are to be my new sister, you may call me 'my lord,' or simply 'Lord' for short." He threw her a teasing grin.

Clara wanted to roll her eyes. "Andrew is otherwise indisposed for the evening?" she asked as they stepped outside to the waiting carriage.

Luke handed Norah and Susanna into the carriage after Clara before offering a hand to Sarah, positioning himself beside his widowed sister. It was a tight fit with three to a bench but the three ladies were slim enough to make it work. Thankfully, it was a short drive.

"His grace begs your forgiveness for the change of plans, but relays the message that all is well, and he will meet you there."

"I certainly hope it was important," Norah huffed, gazing out the window.

"Oh, you know Andrew," Luke commented and managed a shrug in the tight carriage. "One hair out of place is reason for an uproar. I assure you it is nothing to worry about. Something about a missing duck returning to London, and Andrew needing to get him back in his row." He spoke the words to the group at large, but he was looking directly at Clara, and she heard what he was not saying: her brother had returned to London.

Clara tried to not let the rocking of the carriage bounce her into Norah, but every jolt made Clara want to leap out of her skin. It was nerve-wracking to know Jonathan had returned to London. Her brother would be angry, for sure, but what would he do? She was engaged to Andrew, banns had been called twice in Kent and once in Cumberland. There had been an announcement in the newspaper for goodness' sake. She was out of his reach, just as Andrew had intended.

But would it be enough?

It was all so stressful, and Clara could feel the beginnings of a headache making her even more anxious. She had to keep her mind occupied so she would not think or worry about Jonathan and what he may or may not be doing. Andrew said he would protect her. But how could he protect her when he had sent his giddy younger brother in his place?

With Andrew absent the night seemed less enchanting. The duke's jovial brother did not offer the same level comfort and security as his brother. Luke was tall and handsome, but something about him stuck Clara as odd. Perhaps it was his eyes, she thought, watching the siblings' idle banter during their ride in the carriage. Luke's eyes were an unusual shade of lavender blue, striking and laughing at the same time, though guarded. There was something more to Lord Luke, a depth he seemed keen to hide.

Clara soon discovered Luke was not the only bodyguard Andrew had directed. Arriving at their destination moments later, the ladies were handed out one by one, each passed to a tall male figure before being quickly ushered inside.

"Good evening, Lady Clara," a tawny-haired man said as she descended from the carriage. "I am Lord Emmett Connolly, the Viscount Barrington. His grace has sent me to make sure you have an enjoyable evening. It would be my pleasure if you would allow me to escort you inside."

"Yes, of course, my lord," Clara replied, a bit taken aback by the fact Andrew had sent someone other than his brother to escort her. "Are you a friend of his grace, Lord Barrington?"

"One of his oldest and dearest," the man replied as they stepped inside.

"Who else has his grace sent to protect me from the evils of the world?" Clara asked in partial jest.

"Lord Bexley and Lord Kensburg are also here at the

request of his grace."

"Gracious, what does Andrew think will happen in the middle of a ball?" she asked, glancing around at the occupants of the front hall where they all stood queued to be announced to the ball.

"You would be surprised how much goes unnoticed during a ball," Connolly replied. "Morton could pop in and out and no one would notice."

"Is he going to?" Clara worried.

"It is not likely," Connolly admitted. "You are not to worry about it—Andrew's orders."

"And does everyone usually obey what Andrew commands?"

Connolly laughed. "Usually. Most people stay out of his way, he has a certain dark air about him, you know. But there are a select few who knew him before he was the duke. Our loyalty is based on friendship and respect, not rank."

"Who are these people you are referring to?"

"Our little troupe of friends," Connolly explained. "Myself and Bexley, Halcourt, and Trevor, though we have not seen Trevor since he was sent off to fight in the war. And Redley, of course."

"Why 'of course'?" Clara asked. She noticed whenever someone mentioned this Redley person they always followed it with "of course."

"His grace and Viscount Kensburg are cousins," Connolly explained. "Andrew's mother and Redley's father were siblings. Redley arrived at Eton just after Andrew inherited the dukedom and has never left Andrew's side. We tried to get rid of him; he was Andrew's younger cousin after all, though only by several months. But once we got to Oxford we realized we actually liked Redley. He is a peculiar sort, but a top-notch gentleman. It is difficult to explain why he is a bit odd, but once you meet him you will understand."

"What about his grace's spy friend?" Clara asked. "Which one is he?"

Connolly let out a bark of laughter. A few people near-est to them turned at the sound, glanced at Connolly, then at Clara for a fraction longer before pointedly looking away. "Spy friend? I'm assuming you are referring to Halcourt. That is rich, Lady Clara. Goodness, I am beginning to understand what he sees in you."

"Was it so difficult to see before?" she asked, not sure if she had just been insulted or not.

"Well, yes and no, if I'm being honest," Connolly admit-ted and turned his striking green eyes down at her. "You are quite beautiful, though don't tell Andrew I said so, for he might get cross with me. He is quite protective of you, you know."

"I hadn't noticed," she replied dryly.

"But you are Morton's sister," Connolly continued. "They are akin to mortal enemies. You are also Christina Masson's sister, the girl who jilted him at the altar. I admit it was a shock to find out you were the girl he was going batty over. No offense, of course."

"None taken," Clara replied. Moments later they were announced to the ballroom, Clara included in the group of Macalisters and Andrew's friends. Clara did her best to ignore the inquiring looks as she entered the ballroom. Some leered in disgust and yet others were just overly curious.

The Garden Club Ball was as grand as every other ball she had ever attended, but there seemed to be an abundance of flowers everywhere. Vases overflowing with arrangements were crowded on every flat surface. Roses hung in spheres from the ceiling, greenery woven into garland hung along with walls. Trees were tucked into the alcoves. The middle of the room was sectioned off with a rectangle of knee high garden hedge, a tree in each corner. The guests had also taken on an unspoken garden theme with their evening attire as well. Ladies were dressed in pastels, pinks, lavenders, greens and yellows, little flower buds decorating their elegantly coiffed and curled hair.

Clara stood with Susanna, Connolly, and Luke and a red-haired gentleman who was introduced to her as Lord Bexley, another of Andrew's friends tapped to play bodyguard.

A tall, blond gentleman arrived at their group, and she was introduced to the Viscount Kensburg. He smiled politely at her but did not speak, which Clara found odd. After observing him for a few minutes, she realized his quick grey-blue eyes were taking inventory of the room. The Macalister cousin exchanged a wordless observation with Luke before they both slipped away from the group.

Having disappeared to her own group of friends within moments of arriving, Norah stood on the opposite side of the ballroom holding court with the fashionable crowd, Lady Laura included. Clara met two of Susanna's friends, Miss Gemma Scott and Lady Monica Summers, both smiling sweetly at her, no doubt privy to their scheme. Their presence indicated their support of her, and Clara was grateful.

A few gentlemen stepped up to request a spot on Susanna's dance card, each one shooting curious glances at Clara before disappearing into the crowd. Luke had commandeered Clara's card, writing in name after name along each black line. It seemed her bodyguards were also responsible for dancing with her.

The Garden Club Ball was proving to be a successful crush as more people packed into the room, but still there was no sign of Andrew. Clara knew better than to be worried, but his absence made her anxious. He had a calming effect on her, and while she knew she would survive without it, she desperately wanted his support.

"Have you heard about Miss Griffin?" a gossiping voice said behind Clara. "Her father inherited, and now she's *Lady* Eleanor."

"What a social-climbing little gnat," a second voice replied. "She's almost as bad as Lady Clara. It's amazing how she weaseled her way into polite company." Clara stiffened, determined not to let the words bother her. If there was anything polite about this company, Clara had failed to see it.

"Oh, do tell," the second lady said with a laugh.

"She is apparently *engaged* to the Duke of Bradstone," the first lady said. "He must be having some sort of laugh about this. I daresay he only intends to jilt her as her sister jilted him. He is just keeping her as some sort of pet."

"Pet?" the second woman asked. "That sounds . . . titillating!"

"You would think so, Maurine," the first lady said. "It is sad she does not realize he's just having a laugh at her expense. This is certainly some grand old scheme to amuse the duke."

"I don't ever recall Bradstone having a sense of humor."

"Mark my words, he has no intention to marry her," the first woman replied. "You know he and the Earl of Morton hate each other. It must just grate on Bradstone to have to endure her presence in his house. If I were him I'd toss that old rug out the door. Once I'm done treading its threads, of course!"

"Oh, you are so delightfully wicked!" the second lady laughed.

Clara turned her head to deliver the two gossipmongers the coldest, haughtiest stare she could muster, trying her best to imitate Andrew's best glares. The two ladies stared back and Clara raised one blonde eyebrow in challenge before looking forward again, nose tilted slightly up.

She danced the first set with Connolly, who was pleasant enough, but he did not eliminate her uneasiness. Luke returned to her side for the second set and was all grins and laughter in an attempt to ease her concern, but Clara did not miss how his eyes darted around the ballroom, watchful and intelligent, much like his cousin's. She decided there was something else to Lord Luke, and Lord Kensburg as well, something she could not quite put her finger on.

"You dance like an angel fallen from the Heavens," Luke

proclaimed dramatically as he led her away from the dance floor.

Clara frowned. "I dance like Satan?"

Luke's eyes darted to hers, his mouth forming into a grin as he saw she was smirking at him. "Oh, well done, Clara. If Andrew does not keep you in the end, then I will."

Couples were already taking their places for the third set, a set of waltzes, which were to begin next. Clara scanned the crowd, her eyes searching for the tall, handsome duke she desperately wished she could call her own, in more than just name.

Catching a glimpse of a lanky, dark-haired man, her breath caught in her throat, but as he turned she saw it was not her brother. She felt her palms start to perspire, her brother's hateful face swam before her eyes, and she swallowed down the rush of panic.

Jonathan is not here, she told herself. In London, yes, but not here in this ballroom.

Sensing her discomfort, Luke bent his head to hers. "I say, are you well?"

Clara nodded, glancing around the room again, fighting down the panic and fear rushing over her. Like the night of the Macalister Birthday Ball, the crowd swam before her eyes and parted just the right way, just as Andrew walked into the room. The sight of him sent a surge of relief down her spine.

"Quick, Luke, waltz me to that side of the room," Clara said tapping her hand quickly against his arm. Luke glanced beyond her, realizing the reason for her request and complied, sweeping her into his arms just moments after the dance had begun. It took only two rotations for them to move to the other side of the dance floor and Luke stepped out just as Andrew stepped in, and no one was the wiser. The two brothers even managed to not knock over a garden shrub.

Holding Clara in his arms, Andrew felt a jolt of excitement. His overwhelming concern for her safety, his worries over her brother and his despicable motives, all of it paled to having his hands about her waist, seeing the brightness in her warm brown eyes.

She smiled up at him, incapable of masking her enthusiasm. "Hello."

"Hello," he said returning her exuberant smile, unable to hide his own delight. "I hope you've had an enjoyable evening?"

"Oh yes," she replied. "I was not left alone for even a moment. Your brother and Lord Barrington were as attentive as a pack of wolves circling their prey."

"I may have overreacted a little," Andrew admitted with a shrug. "But until I knew the exact nature of the situation, I wanted to make sure nothing could happen to you."

"And the situation?" she asked. "Has it been adequately taken care of?"

"No," Andrew replied. "But we have done all we can."

"I take it you still don't know where Jonathan is?"

Reluctantly, Andrew shook his head. "I'm sorry, Clara. We know he has returned to London, but he is being smart about his whereabouts. He seems to realize we have found him out and isn't taking any chances."

"Found him out?" Clara asked, her brows pinching in confusion.

"He has been behind some rather despicable plots," Andrew replied. "I don't want to say any more just now, Clara, but we will talk later. Just know you are safe."

Clara scoffed as the waltz ended, stepping away from Andrew and his comforting arms to curtsy. He bowed but did not break their eye contact.

"You seem to doubt my ability to keep you safe," Andrew said as the second waltz began.

"I don't understand any of this," Clara replied. "You entrusted me to your brother who cannot take anything seriously, Lord Barrington who seems even less capable, and Lord Bexley who is a ridiculous mixture of the two. And let's not even mention your cousin!"

"Don't underestimate them, Clara," Andrew replied. "These men would give their lives for me, and, by proxy, you."

"That is what I don't understand," Clara continued. "I appreciate your hospitality and your kindness, your grace, but you don't owe me anything further than that."

"As your fiancé, I do owe you just that," he stated.

"And is that all?" she asked. "Is there to be no more between us than simply your desire to protect me from Jonathan?"

Andrew opened his mouth to speak, though he had no idea what he intended to say. His thoughts and emotions were a jumble of confusion when it came to Lady Clara. He wanted her in his life—he did not want to be without her. But she had only reentered his life scarcely two weeks earlier. How could he be certain of his feelings, of himself, in just under a fortnight?

He clamped his mouth shut and felt himself mentally pulling away from her. He saw how her expression changed as she watched his walls go up, the warmth draining from his face. She nodded and looked down.

"I did not think so," she said softly. "I am appreciative of your efforts, and I am grateful for your concern."

"I am your humble servant, Lady Clara," Andrew heard himself say and he hated himself for the distance in his voice. He did not even understand his attachment to Lady Clara. Maybe his friends were right; maybe he was in love with her. But you cannot fall in love with someone in two weeks, can you? Besides, would it be so horrible to be in love with the woman who was to be your wife?

As he twirled her around at the end of the waltz, Andrew caught the sight of Luke and Redley's heads bent together, Redley's intelligent eyes darting around as Luke spoke to him. Luke had spent one year as a Royal Marine but decided officer and military life was not for him and sold his commission after only thirteen months. Sometimes it seemed there was more to his jovial younger brother than met the eye, but he never had the heart to ask him of it. Luke would tell him in his own time. But now, it seemed, his brother's unnatural observation and detection skills were proving to be handy. Andrew went through the proper motions of bowing to Clara as she curtsied, all the time watching Luke and Redley's reactions as Bexley came hurrying towards the dance floor, as well as someone can hurry in a crowded ballroom. Bexley said something, pointed towards the other end of the room and Andrew turned to see the back of Connolly hurrying through the balcony doors in pursuit of someone unseen.

"We need to go," Andrew said, gripping Clara's hand and pulling her off the dance floor, hoping no one would notice their hasty exit.

"What has happened?" Andrew quietly demanded as they came to where Luke stood with Redley and Norah.

"We need to get Clara out of here," Luke replied as Bexley came up with Susanna, having just pulled her from her dance partner. Andrew looked at Clara's lovely face and saw the color drain from her as she understood Luke's comment correctly.

"Bexley, you remain here with Sarah, Susanna, and Norah," Andrew instructed, glancing at his red headed friend. Bexley nodded. "Redley, fetch the carriage, please."

"I'm coming with Clara," Susanna said to her brother as their cousin hurried away. "It would be inappropriate for Clara to leave with three gentlemen. If I come it makes the exit much more reputable. Isn't that what we are going for?"

Andrew did not want to endanger or involve Susanna, but her reasoning was sound. He nodded to her in agreement before turning back to Bexley. "I'll send the carriage back for you as soon as we are safely home."

Silently and as politely and properly as they could manage, their group of four moved through the ballroom towards the front doors and outside where Redley stood, the door to the awaiting carriage open. Andrew handed Susanna and Clara into the carriage, glancing at Redley who nodded. Andrew was grateful for his brother and cousin's watchful eyes and quick thinking. He was not sure what Jonathan Masson would do, but he was not about to jeopardize Clara or the safety and wellbeing of his sisters, to wait and find out. Susanna and Clara were safely inside the carriage, and Andrew set his foot on the step to hoist himself inside.

Three quick shots rang out like blasting cannons in the front entry of Caraway House. Andrew turned and saw a man raise his pistol and fire a fourth shot, aimed directly at him.

Chapter Twelve

lara ducked as the fourth shot rang out, splintering the wood of the carriage wall, sending shards and splinters into the carriage. She was barely aware of the slumped form struggling to get inside the carriage as it pulled away from Caraway House.

"Andrew!" Clara cried and she and Susanna yanked on his jacket, hauling him into the carriage. He sat back against the seat opposite them and stared at the girls in shock.

"Are you injured?" Clara asked. Susanna was visibly shaking, and tears were starting to run down her cheeks. Clara set her hands over Susanna's and gave her a reassuring squeeze.

"I am unharmed," Andrew answered, his eyes not leaving Clara's face. "Are you—"

"We are not hurt," Clara said, glancing at Susanna's tear streaked face and then back at Andrew, giving him a confident nod. Clara felt shaken, to say the least, but Susanna looked likely to be overcome with panic.

The highway robbery, Clara remembered, and her newfound-friend's reactions made sense.

"What happened?" Clara asked as clearly as she could, impressing herself with the evenness of her voice.

Andrew ran his hand through his hair, a mannerism she had come to cherish. It indicated her Andrew was present and not the Stone Duke. "I heard the first three shots and turned to see where they had come from. There was a man standing directly behind me with his pistol pointed at me. It was Luke, or Redley maybe, who tackled the bloke just as he fired his fourth shot. It went wide and hit the carriage. The sound must have startled the horses because they took off and my foot was still entwined in the footstep. I leapt into the carriage as it jumped into motion. For a second, I thought I was going to go under. It was quick thinking for you to pull me in."

They sat in silence for the quick trip back to Bradstone House.

Luke was there to help them out of the carriage as they arrived, having ridden ahead on horseback. Andrew descended before Clara and lifted her out of the carriage. She did not protest; the warmth of his hands eased the anxiety and dread she had been experiencing all evening long.

"I promised we'd talk, Clara," Andrew whispered to her as they stepped into the house. "But I need to check in with Luke and see what he knows." He steered her into the blue drawing room. "Wait for me in here, please?"

Clara nodded and agreed, sitting hesitantly on a high-backed chair, her back straight in agitation as she fought back tears and exhaustion.

Andrew spoke with Luke in hushed whispers just outside the open drawing room door. Susanna came in, bussing her cheek with a tight smile before escaping to her room. Redley entered the foyer moments later and handed a parchment to Andrew before disappearing to the depths of the house. Clara could not make out anything that had been said, though she was certain it all had to do with her and the danger she was creating for them all by remaining under their roof.

Andrew reentered the room, took her hand, and pulled her along with him towards the back of the house and into his study. Turning towards her, pulling her to him, he wrapped his arms tightly around her. Clara relaxed in the warmth of his embrace, eager for his warmth and comfort.

"I am so relieved you were not injured," Andrew said, his face pressed tightly into her hair.

"I feared for you too," Clara admitted. "Especially when you were slumped in the carriage fighting to get inside."

"It would seem you saved me this time," Andrew said and set her away from him. Stepping to the sideboard, he poured himself a drink, downing the contents before pouring two more and offering her one. Normally she wouldn't have accepted, but it had been an exceptionally trying evening. "I am thankful for Redley's quick thinking. Luke said it was my cousin who knocked the shooter out of the way, or else Bennett may be the duke now."

Clara took a sip of her drink and it burned her mouth. "That is not funny."

"No," Andrew said, looking into his cup, as if all the answers he sought might be mixed in with the liquor. "It is really not funny at all."

"Who was the shooter?" Clara asked.

"I know it was not your brother," Andrew replied. "I did not recognize him. Redley is handling things with Halcourt, and they've taken him into their custody."

Clara nodded, but she could not contain herself any longer. "You said you had information on my brother. Am I to believe that Jonathan's evil plots and this shooter are connected?"

Andrew took another swig of his drink and did not meet her eye. He set his glass onto the mantle and ran his hand though his hair. "This has all become a much bigger mess than before," he said absently, not looking at her.

"Please tell me what is happening," Clara asked him, her voice soft.

"Tell me about the night your sister ran away."

That caught her off guard. "What does that have to do with anything?"

"I think it is the beginning of everything," Andrew replied. "Please, just tell me."

Clara huffed, not sure where he was going with this line of inquiry but willing to comply. "Christina said good night to me. She hugged me tight and told me she loved me. It seemed innocent at the time, maybe a little extreme. We were sisters, twins, but we were never overly close. Father made sure of that. Christina and I were physically identical, but somehow Christina was the chosen one in Father's eyes; he thought there was something special about her. At first we thought it was silly, we used to joke about it. As we got older, Christina had more dresses, and she had her hair styled in the current fashion. I was an afterthought. We were identical, same blonde hair, exact same color eyes, complexion, height, everything, but somehow next to her, I started to look painfully plain."

With a deep sigh, she sank into the chair below her. "It bothered me a little," she continued, not looking at Andrew. "Really, I thought it silly. I never loved shopping or gossiping as much as she did. She thrived in society; she was born to be a glamorous society host, I was merely along for the ride. That is why she and Father accepted your suit so quickly. You were exactly what they wanted, young and rich, and you had an incredibly prominent title. She gushed over your wealth and your looks and how lucky she was. I loved Christina, but I will be the first to denounce her for being shallow and vain." Clara paused again, watching the flames in the grate, flicking and dancing into the darkness. "The night before your wedding, she came into my room and hugged me tight. She said she was only acting to keep me safe and happy. I asked her if she was happy, and she smiled and said she would be very happy very soon."

Clara took another sip of her drink and looked up to Andrew, watching her intently. "The next morning I went in to wake her. She had slept awfully late, especially for her wedding day. But Christina was not in bed, she was not in her rooms. We searched the house; she was nowhere to be found. Father sent me ahead to the church to make sure no one noticed she was missing. I told everyone who asked that she was on her way, that it was only wedding nerves. An hour past when the ceremony was to begin, Father arrived with the letter I gave you. First he asked me to *be* her, to put on her dress and do my hair up, he told me I could marry you and be Christina, and no one would ever know. There would be no scandal; there would be no crying off. But I refused, and he was so heartbroken over her departure that he did not argue with me. So I walked up the aisle and handed you the letter she left for you."

"You did not read it?" Andrew asked.

Clara shook her head. "Father did, and he told me later what it said."

"I barely had a chance to talk to you," Andrew said. "Afterwards, I mean. I read through her words about how she could not be trapped with me, that I was cold and uncaring and I would never know how to love. She said she found her true companion in her father's footman and she was eloping with him. I read through the letter twice; the second time was so I could think about what I wanted to do." He claimed the chair opposite her, his face tight with unshed emotion. "In truth that only hindsight can reveal, I was relieved. I did not want to go after her, but I did because I had to keep up appearances. I had to maintain a respectable image, make sure nothing tarnished the Bradstone name." He scoffed and drained the rest of his glass. "I drove all the way to Gretna Green, hearing only whispers of them as I went. They had a six hour start on me and were long gone by the time I got there. I took my time coming home, thinking about what a narrow escape I had just had. However, she was right about one thing. I was cold, and I was uncaring. And that only intensified once she left."

He stood abruptly from the chair, setting his glass on the table and crossed to the fire, facing the flames in the hearth, bracing an arm against the mantle, a curl of dark hair falling across his brooding brow.

"Andrew, she was wrong," Clara said as she rose out of the chair, closing the distance between them to stand beside him. "She never tried to get to know you. All she wanted from you was your fortune, your title, and the position in society it would give her."

"She was right, though," Andrew replied and turned his head to look at her, his face pained. "You know I never even kissed her? She was my fiancée, and I never kissed anything except for her hand."

"Really?" Clara asked, her brows rising in surprise. "She told me you had kissed her, numerous times."

Andrew laughed. "I barely touched her. Thinking back on it, I'm not sure if it was the rules of propriety that held me back or if I just did not want to."

"I think maybe you did not want to," Clara answered. "I mean, you've kissed me."

He smiled at her. "And you let me. Why?"

Clara shrugged. "I don't know. I thought it might be exciting."

"Exciting?" Andrew asked, his voice low. He cupped his hands around her face and leaned in to kiss her again. "Is it still exciting?"

"Very much so," she replied. She knew she shouldn't let him kiss her. It was difficult sometimes to not listen to the rumors, the whispers of other people speculating. They revealed her deepest fears. Why now, after all these years was he showing her attention? Was he keeping her just to have a laugh? She was afraid to hope his kisses meant more. She could not bear the gentle look in his eyes—what if it was not genuine?

She took a step back from his enchanting embrace. "Andrew, please tell me what is going on."

He kissed her again, softly and yet urgently, his lips strong against hers before setting her away from him.

"We think that Jonathan might want you dead," he finally answered.

"That is not exactly new information," Clara replied. "He is not my biggest admirer."

"No, Clara, I mean he wants you dead so he will inherit your mother's money."

"What?" Clara said, her brows pulling together in confusion and took a step back. "That is madness. Jonathan is a horrible brute, but it is difficult to believe he would result to murder."

"He nearly killed you not two weeks ago," Andrew reminded her. "And he is broke, and therefore desperate. He has completely spent the entire Morton fortune. He's had three years of failed crops and several bad investments, not to mention his lavish lifestyle and gambling debts. He is in deep to a set of dodgy moneylenders. When he kicked you out, the day I arrived and brought you here, he had planned for someone to kidnap you off the street. We think he bribed the footman your sister ran away with. They threatened your life if she did not go with them. And Christina went away with them against her will to protect you."

"Oh my goodness," Clara gasped, tears rising to her eyes. "Christina ran away to protect me?"

Andrew nodded. "Halcourt believes he has found the footman. He's been living well off Morton's payments throughout the years, but since Morton's funds have run out completely, the payments stopped and the footman has been spinning his tales. Word of that somehow reached Halcourt, I don't even want to know how, and he sent someone to fetch the footman. And he has the man who shot at us in custody; he should be able to shed some more light. We think he was hired by your brother."

"I cannot believe this," Clara said. "You think Jonathan wanted to have me kidnapped? And then what, killed?"

"Raped and killed probably," Andrew replied, wincing at her shocked expression. "Or sold to a brothel. I'm sorry to be blunt, darling, but I'm trying to be honest and not leave anything out. I'm sure he did not care what they did to you as long as you died in the end. And that we know for sure, we have the men who were sent to kidnap you. They were awfully upset you were gone when they arrived and were more than willing to divulge everything they knew about Morton."

"That vile pig!" she exclaimed, shaking in anger and hurt that her brother would do something so horrid. She paced the length of the room and back again. Something her brother said rang through her mind, his random statement making sense now.

"He did something to Christina," she said. "He said something the day after the birthday ball, that morning when he was shouting awful things at me."

"What did he say?"

"That he'd gotten rid of one sister, and I would be useful payment for something," Clara replied. "I did not understand what that could mean at the time but now . . . My God, my brother tried to kill me!"

"Clara, they are not coming for you," Andrew said soothingly. "Morton will not be able to hurt you again."

"But what about your family, Andrew?" Clara asked, turning towards him. "I cannot willingly put them at risk."

"You are not putting anyone at risk by marrying me," he replied. "I would not have you anywhere else. You are safe here; my sisters are safe here. This is not your fault, Clara."

"But what about Christina?" she asked. "He did something to her! I don't even know how she died!"

Andrews's brows furrowed, an internal debate evident across his face as he hesitated to tell her.

"You know?" Clara whispered. "Please, Andrew, tell me what happened to my sister."

With a tight sigh, Andrew relented. "Christina arrived at a parsonage in West Sussex, filthy, sick, alone, and very pregnant. She died that night giving birth, and the baby died as well."

Clara leaned into Andrew, his arms coming around her, her emotions coming to a head as her heart broke for her sister. Poor Christina, having to endure all of this alone, knowing what people thought of her when she had only been trying to protect her sister. Christina had hugged Clara and told her she loved her and that she would be happy. She was giving Clara the ability to live and be safe. But Clara was not safe, not really. If Jonathan wanted her money she would never be safe, no matter what Andrew said or who he stationed at the door.

Clara was not aware of time as she sat and absorbed the warmth of Andrews embrace, but the idea that she had money worth killing for stuck out in the myriad of confusion. This lone idea was preposterous, but it found a foothold, and her mind swirled around that one datum.

"Why does Jonathan think my inheritance will save him?" Clara asked, her resolve strengthening around such an absurd idea. "There isn't enough to live on."

"Clara, how much do you think there is?" Andrew asked, his confusion evident in his tone.

"I don't know," she replied and looked up to meet his gaze. "I never thought to inquire because I don't have access to it yet. I asked Father once and he said there were only pennies, that Mother had spent it all. Jonathan had told me that nothing split between two sisters was still nothing. I never gave it much thought."

"The money that your mother spent was on investments which highly paid off, Clara," Andrew told her. "There is over forty thousand pounds."

Clara stepped back, blinking in amazement. "What? Are

you certain?"

Andrew nodded. "You are a very wealthy young lady."

"But it is not mine, not yet anyway," Clara said. "I will not have access to it for another two years."

"Or until you marry," Andrew reminded her.

Clara glanced at him, worrying again over her decision to marry him. The closer and closer they got to her self-imposed deadline, the more likely it seemed she might have to go through with it. Jonathan was no less contained than he was a fortnight ago when this entire nightmare began. It did not look like that was to change any time soon.

But, she had money to live on, on her own. She simply needed to survive her brother until her twenty-fifth birthday. But it was something.

Clara looked up to Andrew's face, and her heart tightened at the thought of leaving him. She actually wanted to marry Andrew. She wanted to love him and be his wife, but she would not do so if he could not feel the same about her.

"Thank you for this information, Andrew," Clara said, stepping away, completely dislodging herself from his limbs. "It is horrible to think that Jonathan literally wants me dead for my money, but I feel better knowing. I only wish we hadn't been shot at. It upset your sister terribly."

"Susanna will survive," he replied. He crossed the study to the decanter of the amber liquor sitting on the side mantle and poured another hefty portion of it into the glass before tossing it back, draining the contents.

Clara could sense she was being dismissed, though she was not sure why it bothered her.

"Good night, Andrew," she said quietly before turning.

"Clara, I—" he began but clamped his mouth shut.

"Yes?" she asked, spinning around, her eyes searching his, watching as his bright blue eyes melted into smoldering warmth and then hardened back into ice. The distance between them when his icy façade was in place was alarming. How could he be so amazing and yet so terrifying? She understood why people in society avoided him. The Stone Duke was menacing and frightening. She was fairly certain she did not care for the Stone Duke at all.

"I hope you sleep well," he said.

"Thank you. I hope you sleep well too," she replied. She turned to leave again, and this time he did not stop her.

Gentle reader, what began as a prime opportunity to examine the relationship between our favorite society couple, turned into a night of disappointment. Though arriving with the M— family, Lady C— danced many sets with varying gentlemen before disappearing for the night. One can only wonder what was so important to exit a lovely jubilant ball with such lively entertainment and company. Perhaps we will never know.

Chapter Thirteen

A ndrew spent the following day in Parliament, arguing over farmer reforms. As a glorified farmer himself, he had a particular interest in the outcome of the bill, but it seemed all his peers wanted to do for now was argue. By the time he arrived home, his sisters had left for the evening, and he wanted to think about anything but politics.

"Is it proper for me to be annoyed with you?" Clara asked as he wandered into the library in search of a book to settle his mind. He turned to survey her, a startled expression flashing across his face.

"That is a two-part answer, my dear," he said, turning back towards the bookshelf. He had come in here with a purpose, now just to remember what it was. Clara's presence had completely befuddled him. He glanced back at her and noted her confused frown. The sight of her, in what looked like a night gown, curled up on the sofa was all too enticing.

"How is that a two-parted answer?" she asked.

"Well, for one, it begs the question of why it would not be proper for you to be annoyed with me," he responded and ran his hand along the spines of the book, trying to get the sight of her out of his mind, the way the soft shadows from the dimming fire were dancing shamelessly upon her creamy complexion.

Ah yes, the book Sarah and Susanna had suggested to him, what was it called? *Pride and Prejudice*, he remembered. Sarah had raved about the unknown author's other work, *Sense and Sensibility*, and Andrew was willing to read nearly anything. He scanned the shelves for the thin volume, but did not see it sitting in its place beside its sister.

"And secondly," he continued, wondering if one of the meddlesome females in his house had it tucked away somewhere, possibly on their third or fourth read before he had a chance to read it once. "It makes one wonder what I could have possibly done to annoy you. I say, have you seen—" He stopped his question as he saw the book in her hands and realized she had the blasted novel. Clara glanced down at the book she was reading and frowned again.

"Never mind," he said abruptly. "What is it I have done to annoy you?"

Clara smirked at the book, but appeared to keep that bit to herself, which he was fleetingly grateful for.

"You left Lord Kensburg here to watch me," she accused. "Just as last night, you deployed your lackeys to protect me. It is a little excessive, Andrew."

"Last night and today were necessary," Andrew replied. "Or have you forgotten you were shot at?"

"Yes, but I doubt anyone could have gotten into Bradstone House," she replied. "Have not you told me how safe I am here?"

"Yes, and you were exceptionally safe today with Redley on post," Andrew replied. "Redley has a keen mind and is more than capable of watching over you."

"I thought you said the shooter was in custody?"

"Yes, but who knows what else your brother has up his sleeve," Andrew acknowledged. "We cannot find him so we don't know what other dredges from the underworld he has conjured to wreak havoc on our lives. Redley was merely a precaution."

Clara studied him for a long moment, turning over his words. "I thought you would have joined your sisters on their outing," she said. "You need not stay in on my account."

Andrew sighed. "A night off once in a while can be a good thing. I am not required to attend every event I am invited to."

Clara snickered. "No, but you do."

Andrew shook his head turned away. "I do what is expected of me."

Clara straightened and set the book down. "You, my dearest duke, have made it your life's purpose to be exactly what society expects you should be, and that is your problem. It is as if you looked up 'duke' in the dictionary and beside it found a list of attributes, and you set out to master them all. What you have failed to realize, Andrew, is that you can be whoever you want to be, and you will still be the Duke of Bradstone. Nothing can take that away from you now. You can fail or succeed, and it will still be yours."

Andrew shook his head. "You don't understand."

"I think I understand all too well, and it scares you," Clara said, folding her arms across her chest. "But enlighten me."

"I was not supposed to be the duke," he said, urging her to understand, his voice strained with years of frustration over that one fact. "I ran free and wild while Sam was drilled for this position. And suddenly he was not there and I was supposed to step into his shoes." He sighed, pulling his hand through his hair, his eyes burning with long buried outrage. "Everyone expected me to *be* Sam, to be my father, to be perfect and ducal and take up the reins and not look back. So no, I had no idea what I was doing. And yes, I have strived to make sure I do it correctly, what I think society deems as correct. I have endeavored to make sure no harm or trace of anything negative befalls my family. I have tried to do right by my ancestors and my ancient title and prove that even though I was not born to be the duke, I could still do a passable job."

"Do you not see that in doing so you have sacrificed yourself?" Clara asked, rising and moving to stand beside him. "No one expected you to be Sam or your father. Everyone expected you to be you. You can be both, Andrew. You are Andrew Macalister and you are the Duke of Bradstone. You don't have to sacrifice one for the other. When was the last time you did something you enjoyed? Something fun that made you laugh? Do you even enjoy your life?"

Andrew turned to look at her, realizing she was not aware of the impact she had on his existence. He pulled her closer to him, setting his hands on either side of her face, running his thumbs across the soft plains of her cheeks. She was warm and soft, and her brown eyes turned to molten chocolate as he leaned down and kissed her firmly on the lips, hoping she could understand some of the intensity he was feeling, even if he could not properly voice it.

"You, Clara," he whispered. "You are what I enjoy. You make me laugh and smile in ways I have not done for years. With you in my life, by my side, I have learned to live again."

She was his and, whether she knew it or not, he was never letting her go.

Clara could sense the transformation in him, the intensity of his kisses, the urgent way he moved his hands along her sides, roaming across her back. The strength of her own passion nearly took her breath away, her knees swaying beneath her, and she groped for him, eager to be closer, to feel more.

Gently but with an unmistakably erotic force, Andrew's tongue rolled with hers, loving and stroking in a metaphorical mating game. She met him thrust for thrust, matching her actions to his, willing and eager to accept what he had to teach. He wound a hand into the soft tresses of her hair, massaging her scalp, wrapping his other arm around her and pulling her close into him. Her body fit into his as if she had been created specifically for him. The proof of his arousal pressed hard against her belly as she wound her hands into his hair, pulling him to her, closer, wanting more.

Andrew's mouth moved to her neck, along her jaw, nipping at the delicate patch of skin just below her ear. Her throat hummed with a breathless moan, every nerve in her body jumping alive, eager and willing to feel. Tingles shot down her arms, her torso, pooling into a spot between her legs, tightening and pulling. What wanton things she was feeling . . . but she did not care. Perhaps it was time she lived up to the rumors everyone whispered behind her back.

"Clara, you need to leave," Andrew whispered against her neck, his voice hoarse with desire. She shook her head. Pulling his lips away from her skin, he stared into her eyes, his blue eyes flittering back and forth between her brown, searching for the truth, the permission she was giving him.

"I'm not leaving, Andrew," she said defiantly, leaning up on her toes to press a wet kiss at the pulse beneath his jaw. His eyes closed and his jaw dropped open as he sucked in a breath. She wanted him—*this*—more than anything. She wanted a piece of him, one tiny piece of the man he kept so hidden from the world, one thing to take with her when she left, to remind her of true happiness.

With a feral sounding growl, he claimed her mouth again, pulling her down to her knees with him, and then her back was on the ground, a scratchy rug beneath her. Kneeling, Andrew pulled off his jacket and waistcoat, and yanked at his neatly tied cravat. He moved to the buttons holding up her silk nightgown and undid them with ease. Tugging the gown off her shoulders, he ran his hands over her bare breasts, his eyes dark with desire. She shuddered with pleasure, gooseflesh peppering across her skin, from the coolness of the air or from the intensity of his gaze, she did not know. She did not care.

"You are so beautiful," Andrew whispered, trailing a single finger down between her breasts, swirling under one and up around her nipple before doing the same to the other. His touch burned, or froze, or left a trail of sparkling magic, she could not know for certain, but it was glorious. It pulled at the tightening between her legs, pleasure shooting down from her nipple as he trailed his finger across, pinching between his thumb and forefinger, rolling back and forth. He bent and took her nipple into his mouth, his tongue hot and wet as he swirled it around the tight peak, smiling at her sharp intake of breath at each pass.

"You want something," he whispered in her ear and Clara nodded, whimpering into his chest. "Tell me what you want."

"I cannot explain," she answered into his shirt, fighting to find the words.

"Try," he coaxed.

"I want . . . *you*," she whispered. She did not understand it, but she wanted to satisfy the fire stirring within her. "Here." She tugged on his hand, moving him down across her stomach, down between her legs. "I need you to touch me here, where it hurts and aches to be touched. I don't even know what I mean by that, or if it is something that is done, but—"

"Oh, it is definitely something that is done," Andrew growled in a harsh whisper, leaning down to capture her lips, cupping the soft mound between her legs and stroking one finger along her wet slit.

It was as though Clara was so close to something unbelievably magical, but with each teasing stroke, she was not quite there. Each pass Andrew made, his finger slick with her moisture, each time he thumbed across the little nub at the apex, she felt a tightening sensation, something deep inside her longed to be stroked.

"*Please.*" The word was enough, and he slipped his fingers into her most private folds, and she gasped at the sensation. Clara arched her back and bucked her hips into his hand in a most wanton fashion, but she did not care. She could not care anymore. She just wanted him and all he had to offer.

She moaned into his mouth as his fingers worked miracles deep inside her. His lips moved down her neck, to her breast, and all she could do was feel and enjoy and take pleasure in what he was giving her. Something was building, something she never felt before, but she felt it coming on like a beam of sunshine on a cloudy day. Suddenly, she was drowning in light as each ray burned through her, wiping away the chill in her bones, and all that was left was warmth.

"Oh God," Clara gasped, panting, racing to catch her breath. She looked up into Andrew's handsome face, smiling rakishly down at her, and she could not help but smile. In that one moment, she no longer felt embarrassed or out of place. She felt brazen and bold, and she felt perfect. He leaned down and planted a soft kiss on her lips before lifting himself off of her, moving to sit on the edge of the sofa.

"Where . . ." she began, but stopped, trying to find the words in her pudding of a brain. "Where are you going?"

Andrew closed his eyes, an almost pained expression moving across his face.

"Why did you stop?" she asked, her brow pulling together. "I mean, there is more? Surely that cannot be all men and women do together?"

Andrew shook his head, his eyes still closed, as if the sight of her might change his mind. "Not tonight, I'm afraid."

Tears pricked her eyes as she swallowed his words of rejection. Swallowing the hurt that was bursting to the surface, Clara tugged her nightgown up over her shoulders and stumbled to her feet.

Clara looked to Andrew, hoping to see something of the man she had just shared an incredible experience, but his features were dark and unreadable. Did he regret this? Had she pushed too far, asked too much? Oh, what had she done?

Clara stood straighter, her anger mixed with despair as she found the strength to leave the room, determined not to cry here in front of him. She had done nothing wrong. She'd wanted something, and she'd taken it. Men did it all the time.

Chapter Fourteen

---

week later, Clara awoke to a warm and sunny morning; the wet and gloom and humidity that had hung over London for the past week seemed to have burned away, leaving a brilliant blue sky and sunshine. A rare occurrence, but something to be cherished.

"His grace mentioned we all need to be gone from the house today," Clara said absently, sipping on her morning tea, trying not to overthink or over-worry about all the things that needed to be dealt with in her life. Her growing attachment to Andrew; her unease about her brother's unknown whereabouts; the knot in her stomach every time she considered leaving Andrew as her sister had. "The primrose day dress for today, please, Molly. And the straw bonnet, I think, the one with the yellow ribbon. That one should hide this ugly scar."

Clara leaned forward towards the mirror, Molly pausing her brush strokes as Clara examined the crusted over wound from her head injury weeks ago. The pain and tenderness had subsided, as long as she did not push directly onto the wound, but the cut had hardened into a dark red scab. Once it healed completely it would be nearly undetectable in her hairline.

Molly finished twisting Clara's golden hair into an intricately woven knot at the base of her head, and Clara dressed in the lovely yellow dress, wondering what she was to do with herself all day long. She found Sarah sitting with an exasperated Norah in the front sitting room. Picking up an errant embroidery wheel, Clara glanced up at Susanna as she came bustling into the room, her gloves tucked inside the bonnet she held in her hands.

"This is completely ridiculous," Norah said, tossing aside her book in exasperation. "It is insulting for Mara to ask us all to be gone from the house. I cannot believe Andrew is going along with this."

"Can you not?" Susanna asked her sister doubtfully. "Andrew does whatever Mara demands."

He does whatever any of you demand, Clara mused.

"What have you planned?" Clara asked out loud, hoping she was included in someone's plans. Penniless and alone on the streets of London for the day did not sound appealing, though desperate for someone to allow her to tag long seemed almost worse. Maybe she would call upon her aunt and uncle, or even Great-Aunt Bridgette.

"I was thinking we could shop for a few hours before stopping for some luncheon," Susanna replied. Shopping. Clara was not surprised. "There are calls to make after one o'clock, then of course the promenade through the park."

"I am attending a reading with Lady Laura and her mother," Norah said. "If they arrive before Mara, I am leaving without welcoming her."

"That is very rude of you," Sarah chided. "Politeness is next to goodness."

Clara did not think the quote was accurate but did not correct the marchioness.

"It is her own fault for being late," Norah said with a shrug.

Sure enough, ten minutes later, Lady Laura and her mother, the Countess of Swanley, arrived to collect Norah.

Clara stood politely with the Macalister sisters as the countess and her daughter were announced to the sitting room. Norah beamed brightly at her friend before conducting introductions around the room, not looking Clara in the eyes as she said her name.

"Pleasure, my lady," Clara said, dipping into a curtsy.

"You are engaged to his grace and have already taken up residence?" the countess asked, her nose turned up. Her daughter, Lady Laura, sneered at Clara.

"Yes, my lady," Clara replied. "My brother was called out of town unexpectedly."

"It is so difficult to plan a London wedding when not in town," Susanna added, smiling sweetly at the countess. "We simply insisted she be our guest until she is to be our sister."

"How wonderful for you to have an extended visit and acquaint yourself with polite society," the countess said. "If I understand correctly, you've been out of the country for the past couple years?"

"Not so far as out of England, my lady," Clara replied. "Simply Cumberland. Though sometimes that seems like an entirely different country." Clara smiled sweetly at her.

Lady Swanley smiled pleasantly, though a malicious glint flickered in her eyes. She looked to her daughter and Lady Norah and announced, "Let us be off, girls. I would like to avoid the summer heat, and it is getting warmer out there as we dawdle in here." She spun around without looking again at Clara and practically ran into Andrew as he came around the corner.

Clara hadn't seen Andrew in a week. Despite what Sarah had intended, he had not appeared to escort them each night, and Luke had been retained for the position. Andrew's absence hadn't gone unnoticed by the *ton*, much to the delight of the gossipmongers. His distance was only fodder for their theories of Andrew's lack of commitment to Clara.

Over the past week Clara had tried to harden her heart and prepare herself for the worst. Either he rejected her, or she did it to him; it was bound to happen. But seeing him here, dressed for the day, handsome as ever in a dark grey coat and black breeches, Clara's breath nearly caught in her throat.

"Oh, your grace, I do beg your pardon!" Lady Swanley apologized in a breathless voice. Lady Swanley dipped into a deep curtsy, Lady Laura following suit.

"Of course," Andrew replied, glancing about the room. His gaze latched onto Clara's, and he held it for a long beat. Clara nearly forgot to breathe.

"We were just enjoying a quick visit with your sisters and, erm, fiancée," Lady Swanley explained, smiling graciously at the duke. "Duke, you remember my daughter, Lady Laura?"

Andrew tore his gaze from Clara's and nodded to the young lady but did not add further conversation. Lady Laura opened her mouth to say something, but barely a squeak came out before clamping it shut.

"Lady Norah wished to accompany us as we went for a reading at Hammer and Sons Book Sellers," the countess explained.

Andrew looked at Norah and nodded. "Very good." He looked past Norah, his eyes landing on Clara again for a brief moment before moving to Sarah. "Mara has not arrived?"

Sarah shook her head. "Not yet."

"We are most eager to attend the musicale tomorrow evening," Lady Swanley interjected quickly, trying to keep his attention. "My dear Laura is quite accomplished on the pianoforte you know, though I am certain no one can compare to the beauty Lady Mara creates. We are looking forward to hearing her play."

With a curt nod, he said, "Enjoy your outing, madam,"

before turning to quit the room.

No one moved for a long moment, Susanna shaking in barely suppressed laughter. A heartbeat later Howards arrived at the sitting room door.

"Might I show you to the door, madam?" the butler asked.

The countess nodded curtly, hurrying after the butler, calling for Laura—and by extension, Norah—to follow. Norah exchanged a look with Susanna before hurrying after her friend.

Clara, Sarah, and Susanna remained standing for a few seconds longer until they heard the front door close. Susanna slumped down into the chair in a very unladylike fashion, doubling over in a fit of giggles.

"Well," Sarah said, reclaiming her seat as well, "that was interesting."

The *clop clop clop* of horses' hooves on the stone walk outside alerted them to the arrival of another carriage. Clara stepped over to the window and saw the Bradstone crest emblazed on the carriage door, a small feminine form moving up the front steps. A few seconds later the front door was opened and a sweet, girlish voice echoed in from the front hall, a child-like ring to it, and Clara remembered Lady Mara was only thirteen.

Lady Mara was before them within moments, beaming at her sisters. Lady Mara was very beautiful, dressed in a traveling dress of satin pink. She had glistening dark brown curls that bounced as she moved her head. She looked rather like a porcelain doll all done up, a child playing in her mother's gowns. Her face was round and exuberant as she took in each of their faces.

"Mara-Bug," Andrew said affectionately from behind her, and she turned to run into his arms. Clara could see the admiration in Mara's eyes as she hugged him, her arms wrapping around his neck as he bent to lift her into his arms, lifting her off the ground, his arms tight around her slim form.

"Oh, I truly missed you all," she said, beaming, and he set her back on the ground. She went to Sarah's arms next, hugging her just as tightly as she had Andrew. Susanna stood and hugged her youngest sister as well before Luke bowled into the room and scooped her into his arms and spun her around.

"Where is Norah?" Mara asked looking around.

Sarah and Susana exchanged a glance. "She sends her apologies for not being here when you arrived," Sarah answered.

"She claimed you were late," Susanna added. "And that she could not be expected to wait around all day for you to arrive like you were the queen."

Mara shrugged. "Just wait until I am a queen, and then she will pay for this transgression."

Clara wondered if she were serious.

"Really, Mara," Andrew chided affectionately, glancing at Clara. "This is Lady Clara Masson," Andrew said gesturing to Clara. "She is to be my wife."

"It is a pleasure to meet you, Lady Clara," Mara said, dipping into a curtsy, and Clara did the same.

"And you, Lady Mara," Clara replied.

"Please, just call me Mara," the young lady said. "It seems you are on familiar terms with the rest of my family, so I insist we be friendly as well."

"Then I am simply Clara, if you please," Clara said. This little creature was a mystery, Clara thought, watching as she chatted with her siblings. She was every inch a Macalister. She had Norah's luster to her dark hair, Susanna's sweet round face, Andrew's proud demeanor and Luke's humor and lavender eyes. Clara was not quite sure what to make of Lady Mara Macalister. She had been expecting her to be giddier, more child-like, and less . . . *mature*. The creature before her was serene and serious, though she had a bright smile upon her face that reached all the way to her eyes. But despite the maturity of her clothing and demeanor, she was, undoubtedly, a young girl on the brink of womanhood.

"I am so pleased to be home, even if for a short stay," Mara said, her expression not changing as she revealed her demands. Her tone, while full of youthful sweetness, was firm and commanding. "But I must insist you all leave the house. I am in dire need of practicing if I am not to make a spectacle of myself tomorrow evening, and if any of you are here I will be distracted and tempted to talk to you. Especially you, Clara, as I know nothing about you."

"Of course," Clara agreed, though to what, she was not sure. Mara was a disciplinarian and the most elegant of society hostesses rolled into one, yet she was a child.

Clara chuckled to herself as they left the music room, Mara gracefully and gently ordering the remainder of her siblings about.

"May I inquire what has amused you?" Andrew asked, glancing towards her.

Clara shook her head. "I am afraid for you."

"How so?" he asked.

"When Lady Mara makes her grand entrance into society, you had best be prepared to fend off the hordes of gentlemen who will descend upon your house, seeking her favor," Clara explained, glancing back at his youngest sister.

Andrew frowned in displeasure. "I try not to think of it."

Clara laughed at his sullen expression, and he looked down at her, his face softening a little. "You really are a grump, your grace."

Susanna came into the front foyer, handing her bonnet and gloves to her maid for assistance. Clara let go of Andrew's arm to do the same, Molly expertly tying the ribbons under her chin.

"What have you planned for the day?" Andrew asked Susanna.

"Shopping on Pall Mall," Susanna replied. "I am in need of ivory lace gloves."

"Have an enjoyable time in session this afternoon," Clara

said, taking her gloves from her maid.

"Actually, I am not going to the afternoon session of Parliament," Andrew said, his gaze on Clara as Molly did up the buttons of her gloves. "I am afraid you will miss lace glove shopping today. I am taking you hostage."

Clara's brow rose, almost afraid to be excited about spending the day with Andrew. They had not spent any real time alone together during the day since she had outridden him in Hyde Park.

Offering Clara his arm, Andrew said, "I felt the day warranted a little luxury and a little rebellion." There was a glint to Andrew's eyes she could not quite place, almost mischievous, which was strange as Andrew was never mischievous, but Clara could not shake the feeling that he was up to something. She nodded to Molly who quickly followed them out the door.

Susanna glanced with curiosity, and Clara answered with a shrug, neither having an explanation for Andrew's mood nor really wanting to give one.

"Will we be safe?" Clara asked Andrew cautiously as he handed her into the waiting carriage.

"Quite safe," he replied, following her in and settling on the opposite seat. "However, we still do not know where your brother is. Morton is proving cleverer than I would like to give him credit for. It seems the shooter has no information regarding Morton or who hired him. It seems it was all done through multiple people in gaming hells."

"That is unfortunate," Clara said as they rolled away from the front of Bradstone House. She glanced out the window at the massive structure that had come to feel like home. She wondered how long it would stay that way.

He looked glumly out the window, and Clara fought the urge to box his ears. The man was aggravating with his changing moods. One minute he was all smiles and charm and the next he was brooding. The inconsistency in his moods was difficult to keep up with.

Frustrated, she asked, "Are you going to be like this our entire outing?"

"Like what?" he asked, not looking at her.

"Brooding and disagreeable and unpleasant. Because if you are I'd much rather spend the rest of the day shopping with Susanna and Sarah."

With a sigh, he turned back at her. "I do not mean to be disagreeable, Clara."

"Yes, but you are."

"I will try my best to better my mood for you," he replied dully and looked out the window again.

"See, there you go again, brooding and unpleasant," Clara sighed. "This outing was your idea; you could at least try to enjoy it."

He did not look at her again, and she resolved herself to leaning back in the comfortable, well-sprung carriage and waiting until this madness was over. She just had to wait out his mood and hope he snapped out of it before their outing was concluded.

They sat in silence for another ten minutes or so as the carriage rolled through London to their mystery destination, before coming to a stop. Andrew had the carriage door open and was gone before she could look to see where they were. She stepped out from the carriage with Andrew's assistance, gasping when she saw where he had brought her.

"Andrew," she said breathlessly, breathing in the deep floral aroma wafting in the air. She had heard of Vauxhall Gardens before, but had never had a chance to see them for herself. The gardens had been on Susanna's list of sightseeing locations, but they never made it.

"I thought you might like to tour the gardens," Andrew said gently.

The damn irritating man! She wanted to gather him into her arms and kiss him senseless!

"Thank you," she said, her eagerness nearly busting from her as he led her to the entrance, dropping a few coins in the collector bin for their entrance fee. She nabbed a map and program as they walked by the entrance booth and scanned the basic layout.

"I am told they have a spectacular collection of roses," he said, his shoulders relaxing, energy returning to his eyes.

Clara nodded eagerly. "They are said to be the very best."

The gardens were magnificent. Row upon row of greenery and shrubbery stretched out as far as she could see in every direction save for the one from which she had just come. Statuary and mason work accented the many *alleés* throughout the carefully manicured lanes.

"Vauxhall Gardens really comes to life at dusk," Andrew explained. "They have fireworks and music and performers. But during the day it sits in its simplicity to be viewed at one's leisure."

"It is wonderful," Clara said, her smile soft across her lips. She was truly touched by his gesture. "At night you wouldn't be able to appreciate the beauty in its manicured rows and floral accents. It is perfect just as it is during the light of day, it does not need gunpowder and music to give it more magic."

She walked along the paths, smelling each blooming flower, basking in the minimalism applied to such a large space. Rows of trees matched with bushes and shrubs and flowering plants, it was cultivated and civilized, but it was still wild in its own way.

"See, look," Clara said to Andrew as she pointed to flowering bush. "See how all the others are white and this one decided to be red? It is as if it is rebelling against nature, against all the attempts to control it. But it is nature in itself—it cannot be controlled, not completely. It will act as it pleases and dare someone to cut it down."

"Someone will probably come cut it down," Andrew answered. "Some gardener who thinks he knows how things should be will come and snip it out. It might have been better for that red flower to be white than for it to be plucked and discarded."

Clara looked up at Andrew curiously. With each moment she spent with him, she understood him more and more, the reasons for the change in him, from the carefree Andrew Macalister she knew as a child to the Stone Duke before her.

"But then it wouldn't be who it truly is," she answered softly. "A red flower cannot be white, no matter how hard it tries. It was born red, it should stay red. There is nothing wrong with it being red. It can be red and still be as beautiful."

They walked on, finally coming into the rose garden. It was separated from the rest of the walks but still a part of the larger cultivated elegance. Here, the roses were not planted in rows but allowed to grow more wild and untamed, much as wild roses.

Clara bent to smell a bright white flower, full of petals. She inhaled its sweet scent and offered the flower to Andrew who dutifully bent and smelled the flower, as he had done for every other flower that day. They had not spoken much, just walked in silent companionship down the rows of trees and shrubs. Clara did not mind the lack of conversation. It was not uncomfortable; she was content to just be beside him.

Andrew leaned away from the flower and nodded just as he had with the others. She wanted to ask him what had prompted him to bring her here, to want to spend a few hours with her, why he was such a conundrum after the warmth of beauty in their intimacies last week followed by his cold shoulder. Sometimes she felt so close to him, like a covert companion in their own clandestine world. When he smiled, he was sharing something special with her and only her, as if she was in on his private joke, his personal secret. When he kissed her, she felt cherished, beloved, and desired, like he would never get enough of her. And then there were times he was miles away, his eyes concealed and face masked over by the Stone Duke. He turned cold and autocratic and entirely frustrating. His attentions to her were confusing, and she refused to hope what he could possibly feel for her. Her own emotions were frightening on their own, to think he might feel the same things, and to have that proved false, Clara did not want to consider it.

He turned them down a partly secluded avenue. The trees formed a canopy overhead blocking out the brilliant summer sun. The thickness of the trees also restricted their view of the remainder of the gardens. They were, as Clara realized suddenly, quite alone. Even Molly, who had been following at a discreet distance the entire afternoon, stood with her back to them at the entrance to the avenue.

Her gaze fluttered to his, and she realized he'd been watching her, heat dancing through his eyes.

"We've seen all that Vauxhall has to offer," Clara said, cross at herself for becoming aroused by his heated stare. "Have you an idea of what to do with the rest of our time?"

Gently and without words, he tugged the ends of the ribbons tied prettily under her jaw, slipping the bonnet from her head. Placing his hands on either side of her face, the pads of his thumbs rubbing across her cheekbones, he leaned into her, whispering, "Something I've been longing to do all day."

Clara closed her eyes as his soft lips descended upon hers and reveled in the feeling of his kiss. It was a soft and sweet kiss, not lacking in passion, just intensity. His mouth moved over hers, tempting and teasing her lips apart and she complied because she wanted to kiss him again, wanted to feel the magic of his touch swirl through her. She felt loved when he touched her, craved it when he was away. She was not convinced she could walk away from this man, clear and free. A part of her heart would always belong to him, as it always had.

Eventually he pulled away, leaving her thoroughly aroused, smiling softly down to her, his touch gentle as he brushed his thumb over her bottom lip. His face was open and bright, and Clara refused to believe what she saw in his eyes, not daring to trust her own assumptions on things that had not been said aloud. She knew how she felt, and she was far past falling in love with this man, though she truly had no choice, no ounce of resistance towards him. She'd loved him since she could remember, and now it sat in a hard, painful knot at the base of her heart, terrified he would not love her in return. She could not expect him to, could barely even allow herself to hope.

He fit her bonnet back on her head, tying the ribbon. Smiling at her, he linked his arms with hers again, and they continued down the secluded avenue, Molly strolling along discreetly behind them.

Gentle reader, this author can only conclude the Duke of B—'s behavior towards Lady C— is not what a marriage is founded on, but rather a testing of the marriage waters. From a reliable source, it is known that the Duke of B— intends to choose a proper society wife to be his duchess, by the end of this season! His arrangement with Lady C— is only to boost his image to the marriage minded ladies keen on becoming a duchess, as Lady C—'s past indiscretions in Italy made her unsuitable for such a role. Who will be the one to snare this prime catch after all?

Chapter Fifteen

little bit later that evening, as Andrew stood just outside the doorway to his theater box, he began to notice something different about the evening compared to those past.

People were paying attention to him.

Normally he was able to fade into the background at such events. People expected him to be there and noted when he was not, but his icy demeanor kept people at bay. No one sought him out, no one stopped to speak with him.

That was, until tonight.

Andrew was not eager to go to the theater, as his sisters and Clara were. He wanted to stay home with Clara, secluded in some corner of the house where no one would find him, and her smiles would be for him only.

Instead, he was at Covent Garden, enduring another torturous performance and intermission promenade. Very few people were actually concerned or even remotely interested in the actual theatrical performance they saw tonight.

Andrew did not even know what it was called. Most people wanted to be seen and see who would be seeing them. It was an endless charade of splendor and pageantry, and sometimes he wished he could be rid of it all. Especially since the ladies of the *ton* were braving his foul glares for the first time in a very long time.

Miss Petunia Barfield stood before him, flanked by her sisters, Marianne, Rosemary, and Annabelle. They each smiled sweetly at him, batting their eyelashes, flashing flirtatious grins, completely ignoring Bexley, who stood beside him. Susanna had been joined by Lady Monica and had gone off to stroll through the hall during intermission; Sarah had left with Clara to see to the ladies refreshing rooms. Norah had disappeared off with her friends as well.

"Yes, of course," Andrew said absently to whatever Miss Barfield had said, hoping that the Barfield sisters would take his bored voice as a hint to leave him alone. He was not really paying attention to what they were saying anyway. He knew he shouldn't scowl, but it was very impolite to continue to talk to someone when it was clear they were not interested. Their inane chatter only increased his irritation.

"And of course Lady Norah said we must come and say hello," Miss Barfield was saying, dropping his sister's name as if she hoped to impress him with her connections. Miss Rosemary, Miss Marianne, and Miss Annabelle agreed, their dark red curls bouncing as they nodded enthusiastically.

"Speaking of sisters, have you seen which way mine went, Bexley?" Andrew asked, turning toward his friend.

"Which one, your grace?" Miss Barfield asked looking at the masses surrounding them.

"I believe I saw Lady Radcliff in that direction," Miss Rosemary said, pointing towards the opposite direction of the refreshing room.

"Lady Susanna was that direction, I believe," Miss Marianne added, pointing in the opposite direction.

"Shall I fetch her for you?" Miss Annabelle asked.

Losing his patience, Andrew turned his scowl onto the eldest, and poor Petunia seemed to wither on the spot.

"Of course, your grace," she said and took an unconscious step back. "I did not intend to chatter as long as I did. It is a great fault of mine, Mother always says. Please enjoy the remainder of your evening."

He simply nodded and they quickly left, practically scurrying away. Individually, the Barfield sisters were tolerable at best; as a group, they were overwhelming. He turned away from the crowd to avoid another matchmaking mother and glared at Bexley.

"This is not my fault, Andrew, no matter how much you may wish to blame me," Bexley laughed.

"You and your tricks and games, you are certain you know nothing about this?"

"About the reaffirmed interest the ladies of the *ton* suddenly have in you?" Bexley laughed again. "Believe me, I *wish* I knew something about this!"

"This is exasperating," Andrew muttered. He needed a drink, something stronger than the lemonade and watered down wine Covenant Garden was willing to offer.

"It is quite comical," Bexley replied. "Lady Clara's absence has made it all the more obvious."

Two more minutes and he was going in after her, Andrew decided, scowling in the direction of the refreshing rooms.

He was thankfully spared the embarrassment of storming into the ladies refreshing rooms by the appearance of Clara a mere thirty seconds later. She smiled at him, an odd but attractive glint to her brown eyes. They seemed to sparkle more than usual.

"Is something amiss?" he asked, thinking his cravat pin was out of place.

"I will tell you later," she said, her lips twitching up in amusement. "It is too enjoyable to share it with you just yet."

"What—" but he was cut off by the arrival of two young

and fashionably dressed young ladies and a crusty old earl.

"Bradstone, have you met my daughter?" the old Earl of Mackingdale asked, indicating the blushing blonde beside him. "Lady Ava, this is the young duke I was telling you about. Quite a strong arm in Parliament. Going to do this country some good in the years to come."

"How splendid," Lady Ava purred.

"And this is my niece, Lady Josephine," Mackingdale said, indicating the second lady, a pretty girl with more of a reddish tint to her blonde than her cousin bore. Andrew recognized the two ladies, but he could not pin down where he had seen them recently.

"A pleasure, your grace," Lady Josephine said and curtsied. Andrew bowed and introduced Clara and Bexley, who were both doing their best not to burst out in laughter at Andrew's expense. Really, the amount of interest and attention he was receiving this evening was ridiculous. Andrew, for his part, tried not to growl.

What sort of manic ghoul had possessed the ladies of the *ton* this evening? He glanced around the hallway, taking in the interested stares from many of the female population in attendance. More than five women openly stared back, one winked, and he looked quickly away. First the Barfield sisters, and now this?

"Ah, I think I see an acquaintance of mine," Lord Mackingdale said, coughing into his handkerchief. "Excuse me."

"Your grace, we had such a wonderful evening at your birthday ball last month," Lady Ava said, smiling up at him, a saucy glint to her eyes. He nodded in response and realized that was where he had seen them recently. These two were the gossiping chits he had eavesdropped on during the birthday ball.

"It was so delightful to have a private dishing of Gunter's ices that evening," Lady Josephine added, her tone holding a double meaning. "One can only imagine what other treats you have to offer." Andrew was thankful he did not let on to his shock, though the same could not be said for Bexley.

"It was a wonderful evening, was it not?" Clara asked, stepping into the conversation to cover for the coughing fit that Bexley was trying to recover from.

Lady Ava turned her gaze onto Clara and narrowed a fraction. "It was. I must admit I was most surprised to see you there. I did not think it was something Lord Morton would allow you to frequent."

"He was most gracious to allow me to attend with my aunt and uncle," Clara fibbed. "It was a wonderful time, wouldn't you say, your grace?" Clara turned her sparking eyes onto him.

"Most certainly," he replied. Clara held his gaze for a moment longer before looking back at Lady Ava.

"His grace was even generous enough to dance the dinner waltz with me," Clara continued, to the annoyed expressions on the ladies' faces. Lady Ava looked at her cousin and smiled, a malicious look in her eye.

"Wherever did you get such a beautiful gown, Lady Clara?" Lady Josephine inquired, glancing down at Clara's gown, a soft golden satin with intricately embroidered vines across the bodice and hemline.

"Thank you, Lady Josephine," Clara replied. "I simply fell in love with the fabric when my aunt, the Dowager Countess of Desborough, suggested it to me."

"Your aunt is the Dowager Countess of Desborough?" Lady Josephine asked, gulping in surprise. The Dowager Countess of Desborough was a finicky old lady who was not to be trifled with, and was a good friend of Andrew's grandmother. A young lady could be ruined with just a bad word from the countess. Andrew suppressed a laugh as the two ladies fluttered with this new information. He was a little surprised to be reminded that the Dowager Countess was Clara's great aunt. She had mentioned her great aunt before; he had just forgotten exactly who that said aunt was.

Clara nodded. "Great aunt, if we are being technical. She

was quite generous to see to a season for me. Who knew I would end up engaged to a duke?"

"Yes, who indeed," Lady Ava replied, apparently regaining some of her composure. "I thought maybe you acquired such a garment in your travels on the continent? I say, how is Italy?"

"Goodness, I've never been that far away from home," Clara replied with a laugh. "Everyone has been asking about my journeys outside of England, but I've never left the country. Where has everyone been getting such ridiculous information? I've been in the Lake District for the past five years."

"Visiting your sister?" Lady Josephine asked.

"Sadly, no," Clara replied without missing a beat. "My sister passed a number of years ago. I was quite saddened by her death. We were twins, after all."

"Yes, but you must have had some communication with her after she, erm, disappeared," Lady Ava said, glancing not so discreetly at Andrew. "She was, as you said, your twin."

"I am afraid to disappoint you again, but I have no idea where my sister ran off to when she disappeared," Clara replied, and Andrew could hear the slight hurt in her tone. He stared at the two young ladies, hoping his displeasure was quite obvious. He wanted them to leave. Now.

"If my sister left in such a scandalous fashion, I don't know what I would do with myself," Lady Josephine said with a laugh in her voice. "It would certainly be quite a while before I showed my face in proper company again."

"Well, it has been five years," Clara acknowledged. "I daresay that would qualify as quite a while."

There was a soft knock, and Andrew looked to the doorway to see a young lord looking very uncomfortable. *Salvation at last*, Andrew thought, recognizing Lady Ava's older brother. He smiled apologetically.

"Your grace, Lord Bexley," the young lord said, nodding to each of them.

"Ah, Lord Hemsworth," Andrew said, hoping the relief

he felt was not apparent in his voice.

"I am terribly sorry to interrupt, your grace, but Father is asking for my sister and cousin to return for the second half of the program," the young viscount replied.

Lady Ava glared murderously at her brother, while Lady Josephine looked thankful for Hemsworth's arrival.

"Of course, if Father wishes it," Lady Ava said, smiling at the gentlemen. "It was so wonderful to have a chance to speak with you, your grace. I certainly hope we see more of each other in the future." She winked at him.

Andrew nodded, mainly because he was at a loss for what to say. Lady Ava sauntered out of the box, swaying her hips just a tad too much with Lady Josephine quickly in her wake.

"I apologize, your grace," Lord Hemsworth said, blushing. "Sometimes a sister can be quite a handful."

"Quite right," Andrew replied. It seemed all he could manage to say this evening. The viscount nodded again before hurrying after his sister.

Clara glanced at Andrew, one curved brow raised in either question or humor, he was not sure which.

"That was interesting," Bexley said chuckling. "I say, Andrew, what has come over the ladies of the *ton* as of late? Such a shame all your brooding and glares and haughty stares are for naught." Clara snickered and reclaimed her seat along the front row.

"Oh, shut it," Andrew grumbled and Bexley clapped him on his back.

"I think this is partly my fault," Clara replied.

Andrew turned to regard her. "In what capacity?" he asked.

"As I heard it in the refreshing room," Clara began, "the marriageable ladies have taken your behavior towards me as a sign you are amiable to a marriage prospect."

"How does that even make sense?" he asked. "I am going to marry you. Shouldn't that indicate I am removed from the marriage mart?"

"You would think so," Clara agreed and continued. "But since I am deemed so far beneath you, despite the fact that I am the daughter and sister of an earl, but apparently my supposed misdeeds on the Continent have cancelled out that fact. Everyone seems to think our engagement a grand scheme you have concocted as revenge against my family. There are bets on how soon you break off the engagement." She turned to regard him, her mouth twitching in laughter. "The most popular wager is you will jilt me at the altar as my sister did to you."

Bexley burst out laughing, and Andrew glared at his friend.

Clara laughed lightly, as if the whole thing had been created solely for her enjoyment. "Lady Ava has been declared to have the best chance to win your affections after you are done with me."

Andrew scowled as Clara and Bexley laughed at his expense. "Oh, will you two cease?"

"Come now, your grace," Clara said, turning her laughing eyes up at him. "There is only one solution."

Andrew held his breath, hoping she was going to say what he wanted her to say. That he should just marry her, that there was no other respectable option.

"You should marry Lady Ava," Clara concluded, giggling. "She apparently has set her cap for you, your grace. If I bet against myself, I will split the winnings with you."

Andrew scowled at the empty space in front of him.

"That will certainly not happen," he grumbled, trying not to be annoyed or cross, but finding it very difficult to be anything but.

"And why is that?" Clara asked.

Andrew turned his blue eyes onto her, eyes he knew were betraying what he was truly thinking. "Because, Lady Clara," he replied, his voice low and thick with emotion. "With you beside me, I barely noticed she was here."

Clara's expression faltered for a moment, but she recovered and shrugged, laughing off his comment. The music started, signaling the beginning of the second act and Susanna returned with Sarah and Norah at her heels.

Clara glanced at Andrew as they both turned back towards the stage. "But, I don't think you actually want me for your wife," she said to him in a low tone that no one else would hear.

"Why would you think that?" he asked.

Her brow rose over her eye and she leveled an incredulous look at him. "Your actions sometimes say otherwise."

"Clara," he said, leaning towards her. "If I hadn't wanted to marry you, I would never have asked."

Clara watched the remainder of the opera, not understanding the words of the female lead's song, but understanding the want and the sadness behind it. The melody filled her with sorrow and longing, but she was adamant about not letting Andrew see it.

The chatter she'd overheard was not surprising. No one seemed to believe he would actually lower himself to marry her. Her rank and pedigree seemed to not matter. Clara knew she was worthy for him as a person, but as a society wife? No one would take her seriously as the Duchess of Bradstone. Would she spend her days having her husband jumping in to fight her battles? Would everyone whisper about her for the rest of her life, wondering how the duke could have made such a colossal mistake? She would never be accepted, not after what her brother had spread about her. She wanted things to be different, she wanted to be a proper *ton* miss who Andrew could take as a wife and make his duchess, and she could smite all those who dared say anything negative about her. But it was a fairytale, and she was too old to believe in happy endings. Her parents hadn't gotten one. Her sister certainly hadn't gotten hers. It was time she grew up and faced the world with her head held high. Two more years ,and she could take her funds, all of them, and leave without a backwards glance.

Perhaps she could find work as a paid companion to some elderly lady. Or work as a governess. Though, finding such work without references to support her credibility would be difficult, especially in light of the scandal that would occur when she broke the engagement with Andrew.

Maybe she should just stow away to Italy and tour the continent under an assumed name, and then when someone asked her how the weather in Italy was at a particular time of the year, she could boldly answer them with a response gained from firsthand experience.

Once back in Bradstone House, she dressed for bed, but sleep eluded her. Again she braved the dark hallways in search of something to read, something to put her spinning mind to sleep.

The front foyer was pitch dark as she tiptoed across, her bare feet soundless on the grand marble floor. She turned down the dark hallway, pausing outside the library door. Three doors down, the door to Andrew's study, was ajar, light pooling in the darkened hallway, a thin strip of amber shooting up into the darkness. She heard voices and at once turned to leave, it was quite improper to eavesdrop, but the sound of her name made her pause.

"Clara's social suicide, Andrew," Bexley's voice said and Clara's breath caught in her throat. "Sure she is a true gem and a joy to be with, but you have to know what this will do to you."

"I know," Andrew said. "She's not the most popular person."

"Morton certainly made her damaged goods," Bexley said. "You survived him once; can you image what he would do to the both of you?"

"Bex, everything I have is wrapped up in this dukedom,"

Andrew replied. "You know I would never do anything to jeopardize that."

"I know," Bexley replied. Clara could not bear to hear any more. Braving the darkness and the fact she might be heard tearing up the stairs, she ran away from the library door, away from Andrew and his laughing friend who could seem so nice in one instant, but it was truly refreshing to know what he really thought. What they both truly thought of her.

She tumbled onto her bed, wrapping the soft down comforter around her and up over her head, wanting to block everything out. Was there no one who was not gossiping about her? She wanted to un-hear their words, she wanted to go back in time and prevent herself from ever attending the Macalister Birthday Ball.

That was not entirely true, Clara realized, even as tears ran down her face. If she had never gone to the ball, she would never have danced with Andrew, and the magical evening would have never happened. She wouldn't know her brother wanted her dead for her money and had probably had her sister abducted for the same reason. She knew more and had experienced more in her short time here than she had in her five years stuffed up in her brother's property. She could not go back to that, not now or ever.

But to hear Andrew say such things about her, it completely tore her heart apart. It had been stupid, foolish, and childish to think he could feel the same things towards her, that their time together as children had meant something to him.

Who was she fooling? Their time together as children? It was perhaps two summers over which she formed an embarrassing attachment, thinking him her one true love. As a teenager he had tolerated her because she was his friend's sister, but as an adult had made it perfectly clear how he felt about her. He'd almost married her sister!

Clara squeezed her eyes tighter, blocking out the night and wishing his words did not sting like needles to her heart.

She'd tried to remain impassive, tried to keep him out of her heart, and she'd been a fool to allow even the faintest glimmer of hope take root.

Her tears carried her into a restless sleep, where coherent dreams eluded her, only echoes of her fears and Andrew's hurtful words trailing through a dark abstract mist she was tumbling down.

Clara awoke with a start, her breath catching as she came fully to consciousness. Blinking away her dream, she rolled over to see the thin sliver of moon shining in her window. The moon was not interested in the plebian comings and goings of the citizens of the city, any more so than Andrew was interested in her. He was here as a comfort, as a friend, and would leave her all too soon, just as this moon would slowly move through its phases. He would laugh and smile at her first, and then take his beautiful face and fade into darkness.

Part of her wanted to believe he was falling in love with her. He was gentle and kind to her, but after hearing his words tonight, she could not trust what was said to her face. How could she trust his affection for her when he said the opposite when she was not around? She would stay here where she was safe, but the moment the danger was over, the moment her brother was no longer a threat to her or anyone she cared about, she would leave. She could not marry Andrew knowing he would end up resenting her in the end. She would manage without Andrew and his teasing, boyish smiles or the way he could make her feel like the most beautiful, most important person in the room with one look. She would learn to live without him, again, and in time he would fade from her memory.

Clara closed her eyes to the sight and willed the pain to go away, though she was certain it never would.

Andrew glared into the fire. He wanted to hurl the half

empty decanter of brandy into the flames, just to watch the fire flare up and then die away. He wanted to make Lady Ava pay for her arrogance. Attempting to insult Clara all the while trying to win him for herself? It was laughable.

"It was rather humorous to watch you deflect the attentions of Lady Ava," Bexley said to him. Andrew glanced at his friend, knowing that all jokes aside, Bexley was only here for support. Andrew was in a very dangerous mood tonight, and Bexley seemed to sense that. He was not sure if Bexley wanted to make sure Andrew did not pummel some unsuspecting victim or take off to Mackingdale's London residence and string Lady Ava up by her expensive stockings.

"It is tiresome," Andrew stated, taking a sip of his drink. He knew he would do no such thing to Lady Ava. He would not want to give her the slightest bit of attention, even negative, or she would be singing their engagement to whoever would listen.

"Oh, come now," Bexley said. "Laugh a little, Andrew. It was quite humorous from where I sat."

"Did you see how they treated Clara?" Andrew asked.

"I saw," Bexley replied. "I could also tell how well she handled them."

Andrew ran his hand through his hair, pride rippling through him at the thought of Clara's set-down to the incorrigible ladies. "Not once did she cower," he said. "Not once did she let on to how she was actually feeling. She was brilliant."

"And you could tell?" Bexley asked. "How she really was truly feeling?"

"She was mortified," Andrew explained. "And she was hurt, but she set those girls down without missing a beat. Her continued strength, despite her almost ruined reputation, amazes me. I think she could manage it."

"Manage what?"

"Being my wife."

"Clara's social suicide, Andrew," Bexley said. "Sure, she is a true gem and a joy to be with, but you have to know what this will do to you."

"I know," Andrew said. "She's not the most popular person."

"Morton certainly made her damaged goods," Bexley said, shaking his head. "You survived him once; can you image what he would do to the both of you?"

Andrew sighed, knowing his friend had a point. "Bex, everything I have is wrapped up in this dukedom. You know I would never do anything to jeopardize that."

"I know," Bexley replied.

"But—" Andrew began, but a sound in the hall caught his attention. Bexley looked at the almost closed door. They listened for another moment before deciding it was nothing.

"But I need Clara in my life," he continued. "I need her to thrive. I was not living before, I was going through the motions. I was merely surviving. Clara somehow breathed life back into me. I feel like anything is possible. I cannot let that go."

"I have noticed a change in you over the past couple of weeks," Bexley admitted. "The gents and I all have, actually. We just worry about you, Andrew. We know what you have been through, and while you will not ever lose our support, society is a fickle creature. Lose their favor and it is hard to gain it back. Society rules our world, as disheartening as the thought is, it is true. Parliament, the Crown, the blasted Patronesses of Almack's, everything is connected. Don't jeopardize all that you could accomplish by falling in society's eyes."

"I have considered this," Andrew replied. "Maybe not all the way through, maybe I am blinded by my need for her. I cannot expect you to understand, but someday you will."

"Are you in love with her?"

Andrew laughed. "I don't know," he replied. "Sometimes it is so much more than that. I feel an undying urge to be near her, and hear her laugh, to know what she thinks about something. But I'm overly worried about her, about protecting her. I cannot get her out of my mind, and the only thing I can think of is to marry her. I cannot lose her, that is for sure."

"Sounds like you are in love with her," Bexley replied.

"Maybe I am," Andrew replied with a shrug. "It does not matter. She will be my wife, and everything will be fine." Andrew sighed and took another sip of his drink. "Thank you for listening, Bex."

"Not a problem, old chap," Bexley replied. "Whatever you choose, we will support you, regardless of whether or not we understand. Just remember to return the favor when I come crying to you, heartsick and love-struck for some inappropriate chit."

"Lord help us when that day arrives," Andrew teased.

Bexley tossed back the remaining contents of his glass and shook his head. "I fear for the world when I decide to find a wife."

"Be careful," Andrew advised. "I've heard that a wife will find you whether you are looking for one or not."

Bexley laughed. "Then it is I who should be afraid!" He stood and looked back at Andrew. "Is it safe for me to leave? You aren't going to go traipsing into Old Mack's house and demand satisfaction on Lady Clara's behalf?"

With a laugh, Andrew shook his head. "No, I am quite sane. Go and enjoy your evening. I will not be good company tonight."

Bexley nodded and left, patting Andrew's shoulder in a comfortable, brother-in-arms sort of way as he passed.

It was late; Andrew could see the clock ticking away towards the early hours of the morning. He had no desire to move, even if the thought of his bed was inviting. He wanted to make certain Clara was asleep, that there would be no light coming from beneath her door as he passed, though he was not certain he would be able to stay away if he knew she was awake.

Andrew watched the amber liquid swirl around in his snifter, the light from the crackling fire illuminating the color of the alcohol, casting faint shadows across the empty study. Slowly he took a sip, letting the spiciness of the brandy wash over his mouth and burn his throat on the way down. The sensation was a welcome distraction from his brooding thoughts, but did not erase them.

Andrew shivered despite the warmth of the room. Above all, he wanted Clara safe. Morton was last seen at a known gambling hell, but as far as they could determine, he was not staying anywhere in the vicinity. He was proving very competent at covering his tracks. Morton had caused enough problems in their lives, both his and Clara's, and he just wanted to be rid of the man. Andrew did not appreciate feeling helpless against Morton.

Andrew shivered again, thinking about the way Clara made him feel. Damnation, he was in love with her. He had never been in love before, so he was not expecting to immediately recognize the signs, but a silly grin spread across his face as the full impact of the realization hit him. He was in love with Clara. He was mad with worry for her safety, and he desired her immensely, his self-control had nearly failed him once. The way she handled herself and those twits they had encountered at the theater made him radiate with pride. He was in awe of her strength and courage and amused with her feisty wit, especially when it was directed at someone other than himself. And her smile made him melt like a green schoolboy. The way Clara's eyes had laughed tonight at the opera had challenged his self-control. She had looked like a drop of sunshine in her golden dress, and that was truly what she had come to be to him—happiness and light, warming his mundane existence, reminding him what it felt like to be alive.

Andrew ran his hand through his hair, hauling himself up from his chair and clopped up the stairs. He paused in the corridor outside Clara's room, looking at the oak door he knew Clara was behind.

Pushing the door open, its well-oiled hinges were silent as he crept into the room. It was irrational, but he just needed to see her. Moonlight filled her room, her sleeping form a small shadow in the center of the bed. The coverlet was pulled up to her ears and she was burrowed underneath, like she was trying to hide away from the world. Lightly, he traced his fingers along the top of her hair, grazing the edge of her scar before he removed his hand and took a step away, closing the drapes and darkening the room before he left her to sleep in peace.

Chapter Sixteen

The following day, Clara managed to keep a strong and resolved expression plastered on her face. It was a warm, bright day and she was determined to enjoy it. She maintained her composure while in public, only letting her face fall and her sadness creep into her eyes when she was alone in her room. Molly's gaze was worried as she assisted Clara in dressing for that evening's festivities and Clara was thankful for her maid's momentary lapse into silence.

Upon entering the foyer, Clara was informed that Andrew would be arriving at the musicale after them, and Mara was already there. Clara worried for a moment about Andrew's whereabouts. The last time Andrew had not appeared to escort them it was because her brother had returned to London and they had subsequently been shot at. Lord Bexley, it seemed, had been sent in his place.

Clara smiled politely at the earl, still remembering the sting of his words the night before.

"Not to worry, Lady Clara," Bexley said, offering his arm.

"Andrew was called away on an urgent personal matter, nothing to do with your brother at all."

Clara nodded but did not comment. It really was not her business where his grace had gone.

She sat silently between Norah and Susanna in the carriage, Sarah beside Lord Bexley opposite them. Clara appreciated Bexley's loyalty, but he really needn't be here if he did not even like her.

Clara followed along behind the Macalister family demurely as they entered Radbourn Mansion a few streets away from Bradstone House. It was an impressive structure on Berkeley Square, almost as grand as Bradstone House. The entrance hall was just as grand, with marble floors stretching along the length of the house, the elaborate wooden staircase leading up to the music room, and the guest and family bedrooms another floor above.

"Dearest Sarah," their hostess, the Countess of Longfield cooed, and the familiarity between the two struck Clara as odd. They embraced, and the Earl of Longfield bussed Sarah on the cheek.

"Aunt Michele," Sarah said and realization struck Clara in the head like she had been hit with a ball of snow. The Bradstone and Radbourn families were related. The story Connolly had told her the other night about Andrew and his cousin—Redley was the oldest son of the Earl and Countess of Longfield. Norah embraced her aunt next, and then Luke appeared at her elbow, seemingly out of thin air, and Clara glanced at him, startled to see him there.

"Luke, my boy, you are more handsome every time we lay eyes upon you," Lady Longfield said, kissing his cheek. "Which is entirely too rare," she added with a stern but affectionate look. He smiled his rakish smile at her, and she smiled back because it was quite impossible to not succumb to Luke's charm. He was much like his brother that way, when Andrew deemed it worthy to show he actually possessed a charming personality.

The countess turned her eyes onto Clara and to the lady's credit, she did not look too shocked to see her there. Her gaze flicked to someone behind Clara, and Clara expected Bexley to step forward, but it was not the earl's deep voice who answered the countess's silent query.

"Aunt Michele," Andrew said, and Clara turned abruptly to see him standing behind her. He glanced down at her, his eyes twinkling in the soft candlelight, and he offered her his arm.

"Andrew," Lady Longfield said, and he leaned down to plant a kiss on his aunt's cheek.

"May I have the pleasure of introducing you to Lady Clara Masson, my fiancée," Andrew introduced her to his aunt. Clara dipped into a proper curtsy, her head bowing. Lady Longfield eyed her up and down, her eyes searching and judging. Clara desperately hoped she would not find her wanting.

Lady Longfield's face broke into a sweet smile, betraying the girl who was behind the middle-aged woman's façade. "Lady Clara, it is wonderful to meet you," the countess said.

"It is a pleasure to meet more of his grace's family," Clara replied.

"He cannot hide from us all the time," Lady Longfield replied, winking at her. "He likes to think he is coarse and brooding, but the poor boy has a family and tends to forget we exist."

"I do not forget you exist, Aunt," Andrew said in a gruff tone. "Hence my presence."

Lady Longfield's gaze was affectionate, almost sad, but they quickly moved past to the earl, who bowed over Clara's hand and stoutly shook Andrew's with a stiff, "Bradstone."

"Andrew, dear," an aged voice said and Clara turned to see an elderly but elegant woman beam up at Andrew, her blue eyes bright, eyes that looked painfully familiar.

"Grandmother, how are you?" Andrew asked gently as he bent to place a kiss on her weathered cheek.

"I'm alive, if you ever dared to see for yourself," she replied sharply. "Now, who is this?"

"Grandmother, this is my fiancée, Lady Clara Masson," Andrew said, smiling at Clara. "Lady Clara, this is my grandmother, the Marchioness of Radbourn. Grandmother, Lady Clara's great aunt is the Dowager Countess of Desborough."

"You are Bridgette's niece?" the marchioness asked, her eyes lighting up. "Why, I had tea with her last week, and she did nothing but sing the praises of her only relation who had a brain between her ears. I did not realize you and she were one in the same. How wonderful that it is you who has finally caught dear Andrew's eye. Better you than your snobbish hussy of a sister."

"Yes, well," Andrew said, much as Sarah did when she could not think of anything else to say. "We will be taking our seats now. Is Grandfather inside?"

Lady Radbourn nodded. "In the back corner, of course, though he cannot be guaranteed to actually hear the performances or stay awake."

Andrew led Clara away, smirking at her shocked expression.

"Grandmother has taken to her role of cantankerous old marchioness with full gusto," Andrew commented. "She claims that with her few years left, she does not have time to beat around the bush and chooses to say what she thinks."

Clara swallowed, recovering her wits. The Marchioness of Radbourn had quite succeeded in shocking her. "Of course," she replied. "Though I had not realized so many of your family would be in attendance this evening."

"The Ralston family is my mother's family," Andrew explained as they strolled down the hallway and into the well-lit and very large music room. Chairs were set up in rows, with a slightly elevated stage area where the performers were set to perform. "Mother and her brother and sister were very close, and after they each married and began to have children, they decided that their children would perform for an audience each season."

Clara took a program from the footman by the door and glanced around the room. The room was beautifully decorated in blues, whites, and golds with beautiful damask wallpaper adorning the walls. Clara glanced twice at the elderly gentlemen in the corner sitting in a wheeled armchair. He had a peculiar looking ear trumpet in his lap and appeared to be asleep.

"Grandfather," Andrew said, nodding towards him. "He uses that contraption to hear, though it really does not work. Let's not wake him." He turned her away from his elderly relative.

"You performed at these events?" Clara asked, knowing he must have but wanting to make him say it.

"Yes," he replied and shrugged. "Family traditions are hard to break."

"What do you play?" Clara asked.

"The piano," Andrew replied. "There were not many dukes who can play the pianoforte as well as they could shoot a target dead on." He winked at her.

"He plays beautifully," Sarah added, coming up to them.

"What about yourself, Lady Radcliff?" Clara asked. "Do you play?"

"I play the harp," Sarah replied. "As does Luke."

"Lord Luke plays the harp?" Clara repeated, surprised.

Andrew nodded. "Yes, and he will not be happy that you just divulged that family secret, Sarah."

"Oh pish posh," Sarah replied with a wave of her hand. "He can play the violin as well."

"Bennett took piano lessons but was never any good. Susanna and Norah chose the violin as well," Andrew explained.

"And Nick and Charlie?" Clara asked. Luke joined them, jumping into the conversation.

"Nick took lessons in the French horn, of all things, though I don't remember him being very proficient," Luke answered.

Clara frowned as she read through the program. "Lady Mara's name is the only name listed here."

"Well, after Mara proved to be a bit of a prodigy some years ago, the other cousins refused to play with her," Andrew explained.

"It is less of a Ralston Family Musicale now," Sarah added.

"It is basically a Lady Mara Macalister concert," Luke said.

"But you still call it the Ralston Family Musicale?" Clara asked.

Andrew shrugged. "Family traditions are hard to break," he repeated.

Susanna joined their group just then, looking directly at Clara.

"Lady Clara, would you like to take a quick turn about the room?" Susanna asked.

"Certainly," Clara replied and stepped away from their troupe, linking arms with Susanna. She could feel Andrew's gaze on her as they looped the room once, smiling politely at the acquaintances of Susanna's as they passed.

"A turn about the room, Susanna?" Clara asked once they had completed one rotation and on their way to the second.

"I just needed some movement," Susanna explained. "And also the refreshing room. That receiving line was much too long."

They left the music room and went down the corridor to where a refreshing room had been set up. They stepped inside the room, a long mirror along one side with plush comfortable chairs along the opposite side. Susanna winked at Clara before stepping behind one of the privacy curtains and Clara did the same.

Tittering feminine laughter came into the room, just on the other side of the curtain. Clara glanced at the drapery to confirm it was completely closed.

"Really, who does she think she is?" a feminine voice asked.

Her friend laughed. "Oh, I know! It is so humorous. Throwing herself at Bradstone, as if he would even look twice at her. How she convinced him to offer her marriage is beyond me." Clara tensed as she realized the subject of this gossip.

"She's pretty," the first girl said. "Oooh, maybe she's blackmailing him?"

"Lady Susanna has claimed her as a friend, though we all know that is a lie if ever one was told. I don't think they've ever spoken two words before this month."

"I just cannot imagine why Bradstone's family is going along with this farce," the first girl wondered.

"Makes you wonder what on earth is going on at Bradstone House," the second girl agreed. "And to think Lady Radcliff is allowing such behavior. Surely she could have talked some sense into the duke."

"You don't think he's trying the goods before purchasing the cow, do you?"

The second girl laughed. "Goodness, you just called her a cow! That is rich! But really, why would he want to sully himself with a lady such as her, though she can barely be considered a lady. She's quite disgraceful and quite scandalous, don't you know?"

"Perhaps that is what Bradstone sees in her," the first girl suggested. "I heard she's been mistress to an Arabian prince all these years."

"It was an Italian viscount," the second corrected. "I also heard she killed her sister so she could take her place and have the duke, but the late Morton wouldn't allow it. So she killed him too."

"Explains why the new Morton hates her so," the first girl said. "I cannot image he would allow such behavior if he were in town. Oooh, maybe she killed him too!"

Their tinkling laughter cut through Clara as the girls retreated to the corridor and tears prickled the edges of her eyes. She was not fooling anyone. People were still choosing to believe Jonathan's lies over their own eyes.

Clara stepped out from behind the privacy curtain to an empty antechamber. She was not sure if she wanted to laugh or cry.

"Clara," Susanna said softly, and Clara turned to see her step out from behind the second screen. Clara managed to plaster a smile on her face, hoping she could appear unaffected, at least until she was in her room at Bradstone House and she could cry herself to sleep.

"It is all right, Susanna," Clara said and dug into her reticule for a handkerchief.

"No, Clara, it is not all right," Susanna said, placing a gloved hand on her arm. "I have half a mind to storm out there and put those two harpies in their place."

Clara dabbed her forehead and discreetly at the corners of her eyes. "Let's not make a scene," she pleaded. The room had turned warm and muggy, and Clara felt like she was melting. At least the pink of her cheeks looked like a healthy flush instead of dire embarrassment. "I barely even heard what they said, and I am not going to let two malicious ladies put me out for the remainder of the evening. Please, let us return. I want to hear your sister play."

Susanna did not argue, simply nodding, the angry glint not leaving her blue eyes. Clara had seen that look on Andrew before, and it was startling how much they looked alike when they were glaring. She walked alongside Susanna, wary of the way her friend's shoulders were shaking.

Clara stopped before they reentered the music room. "Fine, Susanna, let's have it."

"I don't know what you mean, Clara," Susanna said in a harsh whisper, stopping a few steps away.

"I can tell those ladies upset you," Clara said. "I wish you wouldn't allow them to, as I am not allowing them to bother me."

"You are very wrong, Clara," Susanna said, turning towards her. "I have gotten to know you well over the past month and have come to adore you as a sister. I am sick and tired of the horrible things said about you. I want to string your brother up by his ears and make him admit that he made it all up. I cannot imagine how you have survived thus far."

"It has been trying," Clara admitted.

"Anyone else would have tucked and run by now," Susanna continued. "Thank goodness my brother was sensible for once and offered for you."

"Susanna, we are friends, are we not?" Clara asked.

"Of course," Susanna replied, taken back.

"No, I mean actual, true friends. Not just because your brother says we need to be friends or because I am to be your sister. We are actual friends?"

Susanna's face softened. "Yes, Clara. I quite like you better than Norah most days."

"That is not exactly saying much," Clara muttered.

Susanna laughed. "And this is why we are friends. Now what is this about?"

Clara bit the inside of her cheek, hesitating to ask something so dastardly. "If my engagement to your brother ends, can I ask you for help?"

Susanna frowned, her brows pulling together. "I do not understand."

Clara sighed. "I have not intended to marry your brother from the beginning of our engagement."

"I am still not certain what you are talking about."

"When I awoke after being hurt by my brother, I was a bit vulnerable," she admitted. "I had nowhere to go, no funds to my name, and my brother wanted me dead. When Andrew offered to ease all that, I accepted, but only to buy myself some time. I never intended for it to go this far."

"But, Clara, you seem to actually like my brother," Susanna replied. "And he likes you."

"If I thought for a moment that Andrew could actually love me, I would marry him without hesitation," Clara replied with a sigh. "But his temperament towards me has been so hot and cold, I do not even know what to think anymore. One moment he is charming, and the next he is cold and distant. Compound that with what everyone claims about this engagement—"

"You must know Andrew does not think of you the way those girls insinuated," Susanna asserted. "If you are unwilling to believe it from him, then believe it from me. Never since he inherited the dukedom have I seen Andrew be more himself, more the Andrew we all used to know, than he has this past month with you."

Shaking her head again, Clara looked down at the glistening marble floor. She wanted to believe. She wanted Andrew to love her, to want her, to choose her as she was. But it was too much; it was too farfetched. Andrew had already overlooked her once; she did not want to feel that rejection gain. He was a duke and she . . . she was not fit to be a duchess.

"I want you to be happy, Clara," Susanna continued. "And I want Andrew to be happy. I think you both are the key to each other's happiness. Besides, once you are a duchess no one would dare speak an ill word of you. You can cut everyone if you chose to. In fact, we should find out who those insipid girls were and make sure they are never on any guest lists. And they can wonder about that for the rest of their lives."

With a laugh, Clara linked her arm through her friend's. "I say, Lady Susanna, you have a hidden vicious side that I think I quite like. So much different than prim and proper."

Susanna shrugged. "Prim and proper will get you places, but it gets old and boring after a while. Vicious and malevolent are far more enjoyable from time to time."

"Remind me to never get on your bad side," Clara replied, clucking her tongue. "You would make a formidable enemy."

"Marry my brother, and you shall never have to worry about it," Susanna countered, grinning.

Clara's amusement faded. "If only it were that simple."

Susanna watched her for a long moment before replying, "If it should come to pass that you and Andrew do not suit, and your engagement is broken, I will aid you in any way you require. You are my friend, Clara, and that is whether or not you are married to my brother."

Clara managed a smile. "Thank you, Susanna. You have no idea what your friendship means to me."

Clara followed Susanna to their seats, sitting between Andrew and Sarah, all the while straining to maintain a glimmer of decorum and a polite expression on her face. She regarded the other attendees, a bit curious as to the identities of the ladies who had spoken such mean things about her, but she was not as determined as Susanna was, who was twisting around in her seat, staring at each person as they walked by, straining to recognize the voices they had heard. Sarah swatted Susanna with her fan, and Susanna glared at her sister before facing forward with her hands properly clasped together in her lap.

The musicale finally began, Mara taking her seat at the pianoforte, every inch a lady. Her proper posture, her soft smile, and the overall regal air about her. She was like a strange lady-child, the paradox amusing to Clara. Barely a teenaged young lady but dressed as a duchess. She was very accomplished on the pianoforte and simply magic to behold. Her hands flew across the keys, graceful yet powerful in the music she was creating. The sounds of Mozart and Vivaldi washed over Clara, the notes cascaded throughout the room. Mara moved with the music, her head dipping in intensity, a small smile crossing her youthful face in lighter parts of the music.

Part of the way through the program, Clara glanced to her left at Andrew. He was toying with the signet ring on his right hand, twisting it around and around as if anxious about something. This was startling; what did he have to be anxious about? She hoped it had nothing to do with her brother but feared it might.

Turning back to the performance, Clara tried to relax and let the music calm her, enjoying the warm length of Andrew up against her left side. They were not touching, but she could still feel the warmth radiating from his body. She remembered him without his shirt, the way he had been a week earlier, and remembered the heat and feel of his body pressed up against hers, the way his fingers had stroked her from inside as he led her to release.

She squeezed her eyes shut in an attempt to control her thoughts as a rush of heat swept through her, and she dared a glance at Andrew. He was smirking down at her, as if he knew exactly where her thoughts had wondered. Her eyes widened in challenge, and he looked towards the performances and then back at her, indicating she should be paying attention. She made the same motion with her eyes, and he smiled, lifting his right shoulder in a slight shrug. They both turned back to the recital.

At its conclusion, she rose with the other fifty or so people in attendance and applauded Mara's performance. She had thoroughly enjoyed the concert. Lady Mara had been quite impressive.

"Lady Clara, my grandmother has a lovely garden full of roses. Would you care to take a tour before we go in for dinner?" Andrew asked, as they walked up the aisle of chairs.

It would seem outwardly rude to refuse, so Clara nodded her acquiescence, placing her gloved hand on his arm, and went with him out the far doors. She tried to ignore the stares that followed them—some supportive, some rude, but speculative stares all the same. She knew they were making a scene as he practically paraded her out of the room, and she tried desperately not to care.

The cool night breeze hit her face, a welcome reprieve from the heat of the music room. Besides, she had resolved to take what he had to offer for the remainder of her time with him, and if he wanted to walk through the gardens unchaperoned, then who was she to refuse?

Chapter Seventeen

ndrew was doing his best not to burst with nervousness and excitement. He was anxious, thankful he was wearing gloves, afraid she would feel his palms perspiring.

He ignored the shocked look on Sarah's face, the bemused look on Susanna's, and the confused, alarmed and distressed looks on the various ladies they passed on their way out of the music room. He wanted to laugh at all of them. To think they doubted his commitment to Clara.

"Have you enjoyed your evening?" he asked, chiding himself for his cool tone.

"Yes," Clara replied absently as she strolled beside him. "Your sister is a prodigy."

"She wants to play with the new Royal Philharmonic Society," Andrew said. "Though I doubt they'd allow a lady."

"Or a child," Clara added.

Andrew glanced at Clara in worry. Something about her demeanor seemed off.

"Are you well?" he asked, and she turned her gaze to meet his.

"Perfectly," she replied, though the dimming light in her eyes said something else.

"Are you worried about your brother?" he asked. "Because, allow me to reassure you—"

"Yes, I know," Clara interjected. "I am well protected under your house and soon with your name. Your soldiers in Andrew's Grand Army will make certain no harm comes to me."

"Your sarcasm indicates you do not agree."

"I don't agree with any of this," Clara replied with a shrug. "I cannot understand what possessed you to take such a giant risk in proposing to me. I can only conclude you did so in a moment of worry and now wish to rescind your offer. But, you are too polite to do such a thing."

"I assure you, I do not wish anything of the sort," he said, halting their progress into the gardens.

"I wouldn't hold it against you if you did," Clara said gently.

"Clara, I have no desire to break my promise to you," he replied. "In fact, I brought you out here to renew my commitment to this engagement and to you." He pulled a jeweler's box from his jacket pocket, pulling the ring from inside.

It was a strong gold band with a diamond half the size of Clara's nail, flanked by two equally impressive sapphires.

"This is the reason I was late this evening, and I apologize," Andrew said to her, slipping the ring onto her finger. "I received a missive this evening that it was ready, and I rushed to pick it up. I know it is not traditional to give a ring before a marriage, but I wanted you to have something from me," he explained. "There are the Bradstone jewels you will have access to, and numerous family pieces that have been passed down. But I wanted this one thing to be between you and I, Andrew and Clara, not the duke and duchess."

Clara stared at the ring, held in its rightful place as he

held her hand in his. It sparkled in the dimming moonlight, stark against the white of her glove.

"Hopefully this will prove my desire to marry you."

"You don't even want to marry me, Andrew. Not really."

"Why would you think that?"

"Because you proposed to me under threat of my life," Clara said with a laugh. "And I was not exactly given a choice."

"If you had the choice now, would you change your mind?"

Clara paused for a long moment before answering.

"If I thought there was a chance, a possibility you could love me—that this marriage would not turn into a thicket of pity and resentment—I would never leave your side," she admitted. "But I do not know what to believe anymore. One moment you are charming, the next there is a frozen tundra of distance between us. You tell me one thing, but your actions tell me something different. I will not be your pet, or the source of some revenge trick. What my sister did to you was unforgivable, but I will not be some pawn in your vengeance." She took a few steps away from him and Andrew was thankful for the distance, lest he be tempted to pull her into his arms.

"Is that really what you think?" Andrew asked, his brows pulling together. "That this is some sort of game? That I am getting some sort of entertainment from this, at your expense?"

"Are you not?" she asked him.

"Whatever gave you that impression?" Andrew demanded.

"Idle chatter in the refreshing rooms," she said with a dismissive wave of her hand.

"I do not care what other people think of you," Andrew replied, taking hold of her hands. She still did not meet his eyes. "What they think does not matter. I am choosing you, regardless what the *haute ton* thinks of my decision."

"You had a choice once and you chose my sister," Clara reminded him. "Am I to be her replacement? A second choice—an afterthought?"

"Clara, I am terribly sorry for any hurt I caused you all those years ago," he replied. "But you have to understand, I did not have a say in the matter."

"I was there, Andrew!" Clara exclaimed. "For years I had watched you parade about with Jonathan, never giving me a second thought. Then, the night of my debut, you walked right up to Christina, bowed, and asked her to dance. You barely glanced at me. I spent my entire life in her shadow, in Jonathan's shadow, and the one person who had barely managed to notice me looked right past me when it mattered most. No one forced your hand, no one coerced you into proposing. Like everyone else, you chose her over me."

"Is that what you think happened?" he asked delicately. "Darling, I am afraid you are terribly wrong. I did see you, since the first day I met you. You were always following after Jonathan and me. Christina would stay in the house, but you chased after us. You were the bright parts in my summers at Morton Park. After I inherited, every time something got me down I would think of you and your light and your freckles, and it would cheer me up. The night of your debut ball, I went to see you. After all those years, I had not forgotten about you."

"Then why did you dance with my sister?"

Andrew sighed. "I thought she was you."

Clara blinked at him dumbly.

"You two looked so similar," he continued, "and I hadn't seen you in seven years. She smiled so brightly at me. I thought she was you, smiling at me in friendly recognition, a reflection of the feeling I had buried but not forgotten. I only realized my mistake at the end of the dance when she mentioned you by name, I looked back at you and realized my mistake. I figured I would dance with you next, but your father had already set his cap for me and Christina, and I would never get that chance to dance or speak with you.

"Each time I called I was brow beat into escorting Christina to the park or to Gunter's or a ball. Then your father practically guilted me into proposing to her, claiming I had paid her too much attention to cut off my suit. He said it would harm her reputation. The papers were practically announcing our engagement. I felt trapped. I did not want to be the villain and bring about the scandal of stopping my suit. But I did not want her for a wife. I resigned myself that if she and I were married at least you would still be in my life, and I wouldn't lose you completely. Then she left me at the altar, your father whisked you away, and I thought my chance at happiness was lost.

"So there you have it," Andrew finished and ran his hand through his hair. "In the most important moment of my life I could not tell you and Christina apart. I chose wrong. But I never overlooked you, Clara, I always saw you."

Clara shook her head. "I know you to be a kind and generous man, the *ton's* greatest hero, swooping in to save the day. But what if you cannot save me?"

"Clara," Andrew said, desperate for her to understand. He cupped her face in his hands, wiping away her tears with his thumbs. "It is you who has saved me. I love you, darling. That cannot be denied."

"Andrew, I don't know what to say," Clara said, shaking her head.

He stepped closer, eliminating any space between them. Slowly he raised his hands to her face, placing feather-light kisses on her lips.

"Say you'll marry me," Andrew pleaded, cradling her head in his hands, he kissed her softly on the lips.

Clara shook her head again, pulling out of his arms. "I need a moment to think."

"We've been engaged for weeks, Clara," he reminded her. "What else have you to think about?"

"Andrew, I never intended to actually marry you!" she

exclaimed. "Not when you were just offering to keep me safe. That is no way to start a marriage, a relationship we'd both have to live with until one of us died!"

Frowning, Andrew asked, "Then what did you intend to do?"

"I intended to break it off," Clara said, her voice small. "Once Jonathan was no longer a threat, I intended . . . to leave."

Andrew felt his stomach drop to his toes. The past weeks when he'd been tumbling head over heels in love with her, she'd been . . . planning to leave him?

He could feel his features changing, hardening into granite, pushing every ounce of pain and hurt down deep within him to where he could not feel it at all.

"Andrew, please," Clara began reaching for him but he cut her off, stepping out of her reach.

"This is for you," Andrew said, handing her the soft jeweler's box. "As my wife, you will need a wedding band."

"Andrew, you cannot possibly still want to marry me after what I've just said to you."

"My wants and desires are immaterial in this matter," he replied. "I have made you a promise, and I intend to keep it. Whether or not you decide you will be there is up to you. I've dealt with one Masson daughter leaving me at the altar. Another might go without notice."

He bowed to her stiffly and made his exit from the gardens.

How lovely of her to tell him now of her true intentions. At least this time he could prepare for the scandal. What he could not prepare for was the hole left in his heart. It was only fair, he assumed. He'd broken her heart the first time, it was her turn to do the same to him.

Clara stared after him, her mouth agape as she watched

him walk away. It took her a few seconds to recover but quickly she caught up to him, not wanting to remain outside in the gardens alone. Her brother did want her dead, after all.

The moment she stepped back into the music room, she knew her mistake. The ring on her finger shone bright like a lighthouse beacon at the edge of a rocky cliff. A sure sign of his commitment to her. Who gave a lady a ring before the wedding? A man desperately in love, that is who. And it was blatantly obvious.

Andrew did not look at her as she walked beside him towards where his family stood. Clara swallowed the lump in her throat, holding her head high. She was determined to make it through the rest of the evening, despite the awful turn it had taken.

The first person she saw was Susanna, whose eyes lit up like fireworks on Guy Fawkes Day. Unable to hold her glee in any longer, Susanna rushed the last few feet to wrap her arms around Clara in a very unladylike way. Clara chuckled and patted her soon-to-be sister-in-law's back before Susanna pulled away, her face in a brilliant grin.

"Did I not tell you, Clara?" Susanna asked excitedly, Clara managed a faint smile at her exuberance. She was not sure what they looked like to everyone else, but they could not look the epitome of a couple happily in love.

"I do not believe this!" a feminine voice rang out, echoing off the halls and the entirety of the Macalister family, plus Clara, Bexley, and everyone else in the room turned to see what could have caused such a noise.

Striding out of the crowd came Lady Laura, fuming with anger.

"Oh lord," Clara heard Norah mutter behind her.

"Your grace, you cannot possibly be serious!" the young lady screeched at him. "What could you possibly be thinking?"

"Lady Laura, please calm down," Norah said stepping around Clara and taking her friend's hand. Lady Laura shook her off, rounding on Norah.

"You let this happen!" Lady Laura accused, glaring daggers at Norah. "We told you to fuss the hussy out, to get rid of her. And you are encouraging the match?" Clara could see the change in Norah's posture, her back straightened, chin slightly raised. Clara had come to recognize it as the Macalister fighting stance, like a snake about to strike.

"Laura, please, be reasonable," Norah replied in a calm, albeit dangerous tone, much more proper than the screeching Lady Laura.

Lady Laura apparently did not appreciate Norah's condescending tone, and Clara had her first glimpse of what a wronged young lady was capable of. Laura glared murderously at Norah, raising her hand to strike her. The entire room seemed to gasp as one.

Faster than Clara could have thought possible, Andrew moved and caught Lady Laura's slim arm, halting the assault on his sister. Lady Laura looked up at Andrew in shock.

"If you dare lay a hand on my sister, I will forget you are a lady," Andrew threatened in a low tone. Lady Laura's murderous stare returned, and she yanked her hand way.

"How could you choose this *trollop* over the much more qualified ladies of the *ton*?" Lady Laura demanded, pointing an elegantly gloved finger at Clara.

"My reasons are not any concern of yours," Andrew replied, his voice a little louder. "But hear this: Lady Clara is who I choose to marry, and if you or anyone else has a negative word against her or my decision, they will answer directly to me."

Lady Laura seemed to regain some sanity, realizing she had just prodded a lion with a hot poker. She shrank back from his grace's livid glare and nodded demurely. Her father was behind her a second later, tugging on her arm to leave.

"Father, please release me," she snapped, pulling her arm away and turning around in a huff. "We are not leaving."

"I think it would be best," the earl said, looking around

uneasily. The crowd around them had turned into a violent mob looking for their chance to pounce into action.

"I have a right to be here," Lady Laura said as she brushed the blond curls back from her face.

"You should listen to your father," Andrew said, nodding to the earl.

"No, thank you," Lady Laura replied. "I was invited."

"I am uninviting you," came the Marchioness of Radbourn's elderly voice and she stepped from the crowd. "You have no manners at all. Swanley, take your daughter out of my house at once." Lady Laura's shocked face was worth having been screeched at, Clara realized, as the lady was forcibly removed by her father.

Norah mouthed an apology as she took a few steps back to stand beside Sarah. Clara watched as the Marchioness of Radbourn turned back to Andrew, not a shred of disgust on her elderly elegant face.

"Well," the elderly marchioness said, glancing between Andrew and Clara. Stepping forward, the marchioness took Clara's left hand into her own, examining her new ring. It felt as though the entire room held their collective breath, waiting for the marchioness' approval.

"This is very beautiful," the marchioness said softly to Clara. "I don't recognize this, is it new?"

"Yes, my lady," Clara replied. "His grace said he purchased it just today."

"This is special, young lady," the marchioness said softly, looking into her eyes, her voice low enough so only the two of them could hear. "Now listen well, girl. I've known Andrew his entire life, and he is a rare sort of gentleman. He has the ability to love very deeply, you just have to remind him he is still allowed to do so, even though he is a duke." She smiled softly at her. "You remind me of my Mary. You have backbone and you have heart. Hold onto him tightly and he will not disappoint." She stepped away from Clara but did not drop her hand, pulling Clara the few steps to meet Andrew in the middle of the room and linked their hands together. Even through their gloves, Andrew's hand felt like ice beneath hers.

"I am very happy to have you as a member of this family, Lady Clara," the marchioness said a little louder, leaning in to kiss Clara's cheek. She released their hands and turned towards her guests.

"Shall we eat?" she asked. The congregation of guests turned as one herd, conversation and laughter filling the silence almost immediately.

Andrew still held her hand, pulling it into the crook of his arm.

"Shall we dine?" he asked, his voice hard.

"Please," Clara pleaded, fighting the tears prickling at the corners of her eyes.

Please, just look at me. Please let me apologize.

He did not turn his hardened gaze to her, and her apology died in her throat.

Goodness, what a mess she had made of things.

Lady C— has landed the Duke of B—! What this author had believed from many sources to be simply a lark for the duke, has instead been declared by himself before his family, an act he would only make if he intended to actually wed the lady. A great many ladies may swoon over this, but do not despair. It is only a matter of time before whatever alluring spell the scandalous lady has created comes to an end, and the duke's common sense returns.

In other news, the darling Lady M— performed beautifully at a musicale. The night was only marred by the disgraceful outburst of one Lady L— and this author was hesitant to conceal the identity of such a rude person. Utterly disgraceful performance by a jealous ninny who nearly struck Lady N— for interfering! One can only hope Lady L— has learned her lesson and will behave more properly in the future. Especially if she hopes to one day win over the heart of the Duke of B—.

Chapter Eighteen

*C*lara sat slumped on the settee the next morning, flicking through the morning gossip paper, her eyes not truly seeing the words as they swam before her eyes.

Despite the formal announcement nearly three weeks earlier, it seems their engagement was now gossip rag official. Perfect.

Andrew Macalister loved her. Of all the wishes she'd ever hoped to come true, this one was now her reality. He loved her, and he wanted to marry her. Not out of a sense of duty, but because he wanted to be with her.

And she'd bungled the whole thing.

She set her cup of tea onto the small table and leaned back in the sofa, pinching the bridge between her eyes.

"Something wrong, my lady?" Molly asked as she moved about the room, pulling together the pieces for Clara to dress for the day.

Everything, Clara wanted to tell her maid, but she managed a thin smile.

"Finally I grace these pages because of something I've actually done," she replied.

"It is a splendid match, if you don't mind my saying so," Molly replied.

"I don't mind," Clara answered, reading through the short commentary. It detailed the events of the Ralston Musicale, though focusing more on the outburst of Lady Laura than the musical accomplishments of Lady Mara.

A soft knock came from the door, and Clara nodded, permitting Molly to answer it.

"It is Lady Norah, my lady," Molly said, and Clara nodded her permission to enter. Norah came in, dressed smartly in a pastel blue morning dress, her grey fluff ball of a cat tucked in her arms.

"Good morning, Norah," Clara said, setting the paper aside.

"Good morning," Norah answered. She sat down hesitantly on the chair across from Clara and looked about the room, as if it were the most fascinating thing possible.

Clara frowned. "Was there something I could help you with?"

Norah stroked her hand across the back of her cat, who was content and purring very loudly. "I have a favor to ask of you."

"Go on."

Norah sighed. "I do not despise you."

"I did not think you did," Clara replied.

"I have not been very welcoming to you since you became engaged to my brother," Norah continued. "And for that I apologize. I fear I believed the gossip about you—not the part about you being some Italian count's mistress, but the parts about what my brother truly thought of you. I should have believed my own eyes when I saw how he was falling for you. And you for him."

Clara cringed, but Norah continued, not noticing Clara's

discomfort.

"Lady Laura was out of line last night," Norah said. "But despite her vile outburst, she is still my friend and, though you might not understand, I need her friendship right now. I do not want our continued association to derail any potential friendship you and I might develop."

"You said you needed a favor?" Clara asked, hoping to hurry along whatever Norah was here to say.

"It seems you have my brother's ear, and since you are to be his wife, I had hoped you would speak to him about something for me."

"I cannot imagine my opinion could change Andrew's opinion on anything," Clara stated. "What is it you wish me to speak to him about?"

"My brother, Nick," Norah explained. "Our birthdays was last week, and we were supposed to spend it together. But, because he was banished from London, we spent the first birthday in our lives apart from each other. Despite his idiotic tendencies, he is my twin, and he has a good heart. I miss him terribly, but when I mentioned to Andrew that he should be allowed to return, my request was met with disapproval."

Norah leaned closer to Clara, putting a hand on her arm. "Please, would you speak to Andrew and ask if Nick may be allowed to return?" Norah's turquoise eyes welled with tears as she made her request. "This has been a very trying year, and it would be nice to have my brother with me these next few weeks."

"Could you not join him at Bradstone Park?" Clara suggested, but Norah shook her head.

"I need to remain here," Norah replied, somewhat forcefully. "I would hate to miss any engagements during the season."

"I suppose I could remind Andrew that it was very upsetting for you two to miss your birthday. I know how saddening it is to be away from family, and I can remind Andrew of this, and of your attachment to your twin. However, I cannot promise he will be amenable to my suggestion," Clara replied.

"He will listen to you, I am certain of it," Norah said, standing. "Thank you, Clara."

Norah was gone for barely a moment before there was another knock on the door.

"It is Lady Mara, my lady," Molly said after a moment.

"Yes, of course," Clara said. Mara came into the room alone, and Clara wondered at the whereabouts of her governess. Though as a Macalister, she wouldn't put it past Lady Mara to slip the eagle eyes of her governess.

"Good morning, Clara," Mara said with a slight curtsy.

"Good morning, Mara," Clara replied somewhat cautiously. "Please, will you not join me?"

"Yes, thank you," Mara said and sat primly on the edge of the chair across from Clara, though she declined a cup of tea.

"Have you enjoyed your stay in London?" Clara asked Andrew's youngest sister, and the young girl nodded.

"I do enjoy London, though Andrew prefers to keep me tucked away in the country," Mara replied. "I wonder if he realizes that if I do not spend an acceptable amount of time in town before my debut, I will be no better prepared than the unsuspecting daughters of the country squires, brought up to London to make a match. I fear that the sophisticated rakes of London might make easy prey of me."

Clara was not sure if Mara was being serious. However, Clara did recognize the vaguely veiled threat hidden in her statement.

"Have you discussed this with your brother?" Clara asked.

"Of course," Mara replied, as if the suggestion was ridiculous. "Andrew, the dear, thinks I am being silly."

"Is there any way I can be of assistance?" Clara asked, realizing this must be Mara's end game.

Mara tilted her head curiously. "How wonderful of you to offer. You know, I think you are a good match for my brother. For one, you are not a dolt."

"Thank you," Clara said, wondering if she should be offended or threatened, something other than completely bewildered.

Rising, Mara paced to the window. "I am happy for my brother to have found such a splendid match in you," she began, only throwing Clara's confusion to another level. "Andrew is very dear to me. He is my eldest brother, and I say that in truth because I really do not remember Sam. Andrew is a bit of a hero to me, and I do worship him quite shamelessly. However, he is also ridiculously protective of me."

"I understand how his protective nature can outweigh his more rational thought," Clara agreed.

"Most definitely," Mara said, turning away from the window. "However, as the youngest of this clan, it often comes with the privilege of being suffocated. I am lonely in Kent with only my governess and tutors for company. I miss being around my siblings, but now that they are older and have more worldly things to attend to, I fear I am being left behind."

Clara definitely understood that feeling. Christina had run off and left her behind to deal with the scandal. Patrick had left her to deal with Jonathan on her own. She knew the feeling of abandonment all too well.

"Are you suggesting I intervene on your behalf?" Clara asked.

Mara shrugged, a mischievous glint in her blue eyes that Clara had definitely seen in the other Macalister siblings. "I only ask that, as his wife, and my eventual sponsor, you help my brother make informed decisions in regard to the handling of my tutors, activities, and residence."

"Did you assume I would not do so without your request?" Clara asked.

Mara shrugged again. "I could not be certain. But after seeing him with you, even this short amount of time I have been here, I see a change in him, and I can only conclude you are the reason. I know he will listen to you, or at least take your opinion into consideration. Since in a few short years you will be my sponsor, it seems we should be on the same side."

Clara hadn't realized there were opposing sides to be on, but she was beginning to understand. Mara wanted a champion, someone to stand up for her and her desires. As the youngest of nine living Macalisters, she had been foisted off to the country in the charge of adults whose purpose was to teach and train and shape her into a glamorous society lady. Clara felt her heart softening towards the prim girl, so bent on pleasing her brother. She knew that feeling as well, the desire to please to gain approval, acceptance, even love. What was surprising was that this lovely Lady Mara felt that way.

Clara looked at the girl again, this time seeing a true thirteen-year-old, sheltered out of sight by her gruff guardian, taught by cold tutors and grilled by a stern governess. A young girl, on the edge of womanhood, who knew she deserved better.

Clara nodded and rose. "It is unfortunate you are not with us in town more often, Mara. I hope we will see more of you in the future."

Mara beamed. "I hope so too, Clara." She took a few steps towards her, and before Clara realized what she intended, Mara wrapped her slender arms around her, hugging her tightly. Clara hesitantly returned the embrace, not sure what had come over the prim and proper Lady Mara. Clara felt her heart swelling at the gesture and patted the young girl's back, leaning down to kiss her softly on the head.

Regaining her composure, Mara pulled away and nodded. "Very good. Shall I see you for luncheon?"

Clara wanted to laugh out loud, but kept herself in check. "Yes. I believe I heard something about a picnic."

Mara's adolescent eyes lit up, though there was no change in her expression. "That sounds lovely. It was very nice to have a chance to speak with you, Clara. Please enjoy the rest of your morning." And with a quick curtsy, the female and miniaturized version of Clara's fiancé left the room, closing the door with a soft click.

Clara sat down on the couch again and took a sip of her now-cold tea, wondering what she had gotten herself into. It seemed she was the new champion of the Macalister siblings, and she dared not wonder what all that entailed.

The weekend passed without incident, and Clara did not see Andrew at all. True, he was present at breakfast and dinner and escorted the ladies to the various social engagements, but he was cold and unfeeling. He was the Stone Duke. Clara longed for her Andrew Macalister, but the man she loved had shut her out behind a wall of stone and ice.

It was Sunday tea time when things took a turn for the worse.

Settled on the various couches and settees in the lilac drawing room, Susanna, Sarah, and Norah all looked to her, expecting something, and after a moment Clara realized what they were waiting for.

"I'm not the duchess yet," Clara said to the expectant looks of the women who had become like sisters to her, and would soon legally be so. "You pour, Sarah, it wouldn't be proper for me to do so."

"We're not opting for propriety, Clara," Sarah said, turning the handle of the teapot towards her. "We're opting for practice. Forgive me, but I've never seen you pour tea. I think we should make sure you know how."

Norah shot her an amused look and Clara sighed, resigned to oblige. Clara took the teapot lightly in her hand even though it was quite heavy, holding the lid in place with the other, gracefully pouring four cups of tea, careful to allow as little as possible to dribble between pours. Her hands and fingers worked lithely and efficiently as she added the correct servings of milk and sugar in each cup: black for Norah, three sugars for Susanna, and just a splash of milk for Sarah before fixing her own.

"Very well done," Sarah said, accepting her cup.

"Despite what the *ton* thinks about me, I was raised a lady," Clara said as she offered Norah and Susanna their respective cups. "I had the typical upbringing expected of a young lady of quality. I was even instructed to pour tea."

"I have not forgotten, Clara," Sarah said. "I simply wanted to make sure it was not something we needed to cover. Being a duchess is a difficult duty."

"And you would know *everything* about being a duchess, wouldn't you, Marchioness?" Susanna asked, goading her sister.

"My title is irrelevant, I simply want to—" but Sarah was cut off by the clattering of china as Norah dropped her cup, tea spattering all over them as she hunched over, gasping for breath before she fell to the floor. Sarah gasped in horror as Clara knelt down beside her to-be sister as Norah fought to breathe.

Andrew glanced up as he pulled off his gloves and hat, handing them to the waiting footman. It was Susanna's voice that had caught his attention, calling frantically for help as she ran down the stairs.

"What has happened?" he asked. Susanna looked terrified.

"It is Norah," she cried, her voice full of worry. "She needs a doctor. She cannot breathe."

Andrew immediately ordered for Dr. Lennox, following Susanna up the stairs to the lilac drawing room.

"We were having tea," Susanna explained. "Norah fell on the floor gasping for air."

Andrew took the stairs two at a time, reaching the drawing room before his sister. Clara sat on the floor beside Norah, her hand under Norah's neck, tilting her chin up as Norah gasped for air.

"What happened?" Andrew bellowed.

"We don't know," Clara answered, her eyes frightened. "I've tried to keep her breathing, but I do not know what is wrong."

Her handkerchief tucked tightly in her hand, Sarah sat down on the settee, her hand trembling as she took her teacup in her hand. Andrew took a quick assessment of the room, his eyes narrowing in on the tea setting, interrupted by tragedy. Clara, Norah, Sarah, and Susanna had been served tea, but by who? Molly, Clara's maid, stood sullenly in the corner, pressing into the wall, her face awash with grief.

"Sarah, don't," he commanded as the pieces fell together in his head. "You said you were having tea? Have any the rest of you had any from this pot?" Clara, Susanna, and Sarah shook their heads. "Don't drink the tea."

Sarah glanced down at her cup in disgust and set it away. Molly moved to remove the tea tray, her hands shaking as she moved the pieces back to the platter. Molly had been a maid in Morton's household, and Andrew had been grateful when Molly applied for the position of Clara's lady's maid. He thought having a familiar face might make Clara feel more comfortable.

Narrowing his eyes, Andrew watched as the maid's gaze darted nervously around the room. Her appearance in his house now seemed too convenient.

"Stop," he commanded, and Molly froze, but did not look up at him.

"Andrew, what—" Clara asked, but he ignored her.

"You, Molly, is it?" Andrew asked and she nodded. "Did you prepare this tea?"

"I brought it up from the kitchens, your grace," Molly said feebly.

"Yes, but who brewed it?" Andrew asked. He picked up the teapot and yanked the lid off. Hot amber liquid swirled around, the dregs of tea leaves twirling in circles with the motion of the liquid, but there were three whole leaves that stood out.

"What the devil did you put in here?" he asked, slamming the lid back on. Sarah took the pot from him and looked inside.

"There are three whole leaves in here," Sarah said faintly. "Tea leaves aren't whole."

"Molly, what did you do?" Clara asked, her voice sounding heartbroken, and Andrew strained not to look at her, not wanting to see the hurt cross her face, knowing she had been betrayed yet again by someone close to her. He did not want to care.

"I—I—I—" Molly stammered but was saved from answering by the arrival of the physician.

"My sister has been poisoned," Andrew replied. Dr. Lennox nodded, kneeling beside Norah, feeling around her throat and abdomen.

"Let's get her to a bed," Dr. Lennox said. "And fetch some water and a clean cloth." Andrew bent to Norah's side, easing his gasping sister into his arms, quickly carrying her two doors down to a guest bedroom. He lay her gently on the bed, stepping away to give Dr. Lennox space to work. The doctor felt for her pulse before bending his ear to her chest and listening directly to her heart, then her lungs.

"Poisoned, you say?" Dr. Lennox said, Norah's limp and weak form seemingly small on the large canopy bed. "With what?"

Andrew rounded on the maid, who was standing uncomfortably by the door, restrained by Beverell.

"Tell us what you put into the tea," Andrew commanded, his voice low and authoritative.

"I don't know, your grace," Molly replied shaking her head. "I did not do anything to it."

"You did," Clara said, yanking her maid's chin towards her like an irate mother would to do a child. "You came from my brother's household. No one from his grace's staff would hurt a member of this family."

"I'm sorry," Molly whispered, her voice shaking.

Andrew swore and walked the length of the room to the window.

"It was hemlock," Molly said, her voice cracking in a sob. "Or some variation—I'm not certain. It was meant for you, my lady." Molly had not taken her eyes off Clara.

"Is there any of this tea left?" Dr. Lennox asked and another maid stepped forward with the evidential teapot. Lifting the lid, he glanced inside, nodding to himself.

"Without knowing exactly what variation, there is little I can do. Hemlock poisoning can be deadly, but it does not react well to heat. The boiling water might have burned off most of the toxin."

"Have you more?" Clara demanded from her maid.

Molly shook her head. "I was just given those three leaves. Lady Radcliff always pours, and you are always the first to drink, so I thought nothing of it when I put the leaves in the tea this afternoon. But Lady Norah drank first."

"That does not excuse your actions," Clara snapped at her. "You are henceforth released from your position. However, you are not to leave the premises. You will answer for what you have done."

Andrew nodded to Beverell, who pulled her out of the room.

"Is there anything you can do for Norah?" Clara asked the physician.

"Activated charcoal should help absorb some of the toxin," Dr. Lennox said as he opened his bag on the table. The miscellaneous jars of tonics and herbs he carried clanked as he sifted through them to find the correct one. He pulled a small glass canister filled with sand-like black crystals and snapped the bag shut. Andrew watched as he mixed a spoonful of the powder with a spoonful of water, nodding to Clara as she moved to the other side of Norah to aid in its dispersal. Tilting Norah's head, her mouth opened and Dr. Lennox poured the mixture down Norah's throat. Norah choked and sputtered but swallowed most of the poultice down.

"Keep her restful," Dr. Lennox said to Andrew as they stepped out of the room. "And keep her body temperature up, don't let her get cold. Bed warmers and downs if you must, or a hot bath and a roaring fire. Only time will tell, but the next twelve hours are critical. I have something else to give her, but I'd need to speak to your cook."

"What is it?" Andrew asked, his brows pinching together.

Dr. Lennox looked a bit embarrassed, but he answered Andrew truthfully. "My mother was an herbal healer in the village where I grew up and she did well enough to send me to Cambridge to study medicine. My brother accidentally ingested hemlock as a child and she gave him a horrible smelling drink of coffee grinds, mustard powder, and castor oil. It made no sense to me, but he survived and lives to this day. There may not have been much stock in Mother's herbal remedies, but it will not hurt to try."

"By all means, try everything," Andrew said.

"Absolutely, your grace," Dr. Lennox said, hurrying down the stairs, asking the butler the direction of the kitchen.

Worry over Norah's health was overpowering his anger at her poisoning, but the rage still simmered in his blood. Someone had tried to poison Clara, and Norah had paid the price.

Clara came out of the room, standing a few feet away, her arms crossed around her midsection, like she was trying to hold herself together.

"She will survive, Andrew," Clara said, though she seemed as though she was trying to convince herself. "From what the doctor said it was the small dosage combined with the heat from the tea that probably saved her. Three hemlock leaves could take down a grown man if ingested fresh. Norah barely had a sip."

Andrew knew she was right, but he was still wracked with worry for his sister. What if his sister died? If he lost another sibling . . .

Andrew shook his head, trying to clear his thoughts so

he could figure out what to do next.

"Where is she?" he asked. "Your maid?"

"Beverell left with her," Clara replied. Andrew turned, hurrying through the hall and down the stairs, seeking Howards who was standing beside the front door.

"Where has Beverell taken the maid?" Andrew asked.

"Your study, your grace," Howards replied. Andrew did not spare a glance for Clara or offer her an arm as they both practically ran unceremoniously down the long hallway towards the study.

Chapter Nineteen

The maid's tearful confession was proving to be more of a hindrance than informational.

"Molly, please try and calm down," Clara was saying to her, though Clara looked fed up with her maid's dramatics. "What you know is no good if we cannot properly understand you."

"I'm sorry, milady," Molly sobbed, gulping in great gasps of breath. "I am so v-very sorry about everything that has happened. It was not my f-fault, or my idea. I was just a p-p-pawn in their stupid *games!*" Molly sobbed over the word "games" and her speech was lost again to her tears.

This is ridiculous, Andrew thought. The maid was wasting time.

"If you do not tell us what we want to know, I will have you hanged," Andrew snapped at her. "You attempted to murder a member of one of England's most prominent families. Answer my questions, or I will have you strung up like the common criminal you are."

This only made her wail louder, and Clara glared at him for his tactlessness. He shrugged and moved away from the sobbing woman and poured himself a drink and then another for Clara. Stepping back to them, he offered Clara the alcohol, which she took after a moment's hesitation. She took a long sip, swallowing quickly before thrusting the crystal into the maid's hands.

"Drink this," Clara ordered. "You need to calm down, Molly. I will not be able to stop his grace if he decides to have you arrested. However, if you help us he will be much more lenient. We just want to know what is happening and why."

Molly downed the contents of the cup, dabbing at her watering eyes with the corner of Clara's delicate handkerchief.

"Now, who is behind this?" Andrew asked, standing before her, feet apart and shoulders squared, his arms folded across his chest in irritation.

Molly passed the glass back to Clara. "My brother," she said and looked at Clara, "and your brother, the earl."

"Who is your brother?" Clara asked.

"Joseph Baker," Molly replied. "He used to be your father's footman."

The name rang a bell. "The footman Lady Christina ran away with, perchance?" Andrew asked.

Molly nodded. "She did not run away, they forced her to leave with him. They threatened your life, Lady Clara."

Clara nodded; they knew this already. "Do you know my brother's motivations?"

Molly shrugged. "I swear I do not know. When he came back, he told me he wanted me to apply to be your lady's maid and to insinuate myself in his grace's household. He said he needed me close to you. He only gave me those leaves a few days ago, though I had to persuade him to tell me what it was. He was not going to tell me, but I told him I had to know what it was so I knew how to properly administer it."

"But why?" Clara asked, her voice falling. "Why would you want to hurt me?"

Molly started to cry again. "I'm sorry, milady, but he threatened my brother's life. Joey's been living up near Scotland in a big mansion, and the earl told me he'd cut off his head if I did not do as he asked. I was afraid for my brother's life, you see. I had to help him."

Clara shook her head, her face falling in exhaustion. Yet another victim of Jonathan Masson's smooth-talking tongue. Someone else's life the earl had destroyed.

"Is there anything else?" Andrew asked. "Any other assassination attempts we should know about?"

Molly shook her head. "No, I know nothing more of the earl's plans. I am just grateful he does not know about sweet Mary."

"Who?" Clara asked.

"Mary," she repeated, her tone a tad patronizing. "The baby your sister died bringing into this world. Only she did not die."

"The baby or Christina?" Clara asked.

"Both," Molly explained. "When news came of your sister's death, I made my own subtle inquires. I went to the parsonage where she died, though they did not see me. I saw Lady Christina and her baby, and I knew she had faked her death, and I could only imagine why. So I kept my peace, knowing that everyone was better off thinking Lady Christina had died in childbirth."

"My sister is alive?" Clara asked, her eyes wide, brimming with tears.

"Last time I saw her," Molly replied.

Reeling, Andrew poured himself another drink and another for Clara, though she declined. All this time, Christina was alive? He was shocked, though Clara must have been enraged. After all Clara had to endure at the disappearance of her sister, her time away from London, away from him. Andrew watched his new fiancée, hoping for some insight into her thoughts, but her face was blank and devoid of emotion.

"Where is this parsonage?" Andrew asked, and Molly gave him the name and location. He waved in Beverell, and the footman came forward to take Molly to another room. "And send for Halcourt, please," Andrew instructed the footman as the maid was removed from the room. Andrew did not sit beside Clara on the settee, watching her for signs of distress, searching her face for some sign of her thoughts.

She looked to be breathing normally, though anyone else might have melted into hysterics. Andrew could only imagine how he would react had he learned Sam was alive after all this time—would he be angry? Pleased? Relieved? He wanted to say something, anything, to ease the distress of the past five minutes—of the past twelve hours—but for once he was at a loss for what to say.

Clara was not as stunned as she ought to be. Of everything that had happened over the past three weeks, this was not so farfetched. Jonathan wanted to kill her for money she did not know she had, and he was instrumental in Christina's disappearance, who had not died as previously thought, which meant Clara's year of mourning was for naught. Though if she hadn't stayed away from London until now, she wouldn't have met Andrew again as she had, and she would not be basically taking her sister's place as his fiancée. Just thinking of the circle of events was causing her head to spin.

"Where on earth did you find a footman such as Beverell?" Clara asked absently as Andrew shifted his weight back and forth the between each foot. He did not seem to know what to do with himself.

"My brother, Bennett," he replied. "He has a habit of sending us people as gifts."

"People as gifts?" Clara asked, slightly appalled.

"Not how it sounds," Andrew answered. "In his travels he occasionally comes across people who are in a bad situation. He removes them from their circumstances and sends them here, where he knows I will offer him employment."

"How many has he sent you?"

"Over the years?" Andrew thought for a moment. "Eight. He assured me that each one had come willingly, and we've never had any problems with those we have taken his advice and employed."

It certainly helped explain the staff's complete devotion to the Macalister family. The long-lost Bennett was just another Macalister do-gooder.

"Where is Beverell from?" Clara asked, not sure if she had ever heard him speak more than three words.

"Brussels, I think," Andrew replied.

"Is Beverell his first name or surname?"

"I never thought to ask," Andrew replied. "You are rambling, Clara. Please, tell me how you are feeling."

Clara sighed, not even sure she understood the wash of emotions this new development sent crashing through her. "I am surprised, I think that would be the best way to describe how I am feeling. But I am not overset by the news. To think we were all here assuming the worst of Christina and she was enduring hardships no person should have to withstand. She must have known what Jonathan was capable of to feel the need to fabricate her own death."

"Sometimes I envy your empathy, Clara," Andrew said, softly. "You should be livid or hurt by your sister's deception, but instead you worry about what she has had to suffer. Your ability to think of others first is one of the most wonderful things about you."

Clara tilted her head up towards him. He stood, towering over her, and she wanted nothing more than for him to wrap his arms around her, to press a soft reassuring kiss to her lips. But that was not how things were to be between them.

"Do not think I will put my sister before my own happiness," Clara told him. "If she truly is alive, she is not taking you away from me."

"You will, of course, stay here while I travel to this parsonage and verify your maid's claims."

"I will not," Clara replied, and he sighed as though he knew she was going to argue. "I have to see what happened, Andrew. This could have been me. Father could have chosen me instead of Christina; *you* could have chosen me instead of Christina. I could be the one missing, presumed dead, hiding in a parsonage to protect myself and my child. That could be *my* child. Christina was my sister, Andrew, and I lost her. I've lost everyone. My parents, my twin sister—gone; my younger brother went off to war, and my older brother has tried to have me killed. Don't you see? All I have is you, and you can give this to me. Let me come with you. I have to see this through."

"Clara, we cannot just up and leave London on some wild goose chase," he argued. "Who is to say if what the maid says is even true? It could be a lie spun by your brother."

"Molly said she saw Christina with her own eyes," Clara countered.

"And Molly just tried to poison you, and Norah was harmed in the process," he reminded her, glaring. "Are you so quick to trust Molly? Or your brother?"

Clara took a deep calming breath, trying to find the words to explain to him what she had felt for years.

"Everything that I was ever told about Christina's disappearance seemed off," Clara said. "This seems right."

"Or do you just want so desperately for your sister to be alive?"

"I want to know I am not stepping into her life!" Clara exclaimed.

Andrew glared. "I explained to you the differences between you and your sister, but you are quick to deny any truth to those claims."

"I do not doubt your sincerity," Clara began.

"Then what?" he demanded. "You intended to treat me the same as your sister, why should you want anything different?"

Clara turned away from his angry face, realizing how deeply she had hurt him. But she had no words to fix this, how could she?

"You intended to use my name as protection against your brother, hoping to be free of us both in the end," he stated. "And now we are both stuck."

"I've been stuck since the very beginning!" Clara cried, rounding on him. "Since my brother decided he would rather have a fortune than a sister. Since you decided for me the best course of my life. Have I no say in any of this? Have I no right to an opinion about my life? I woke up in your house with you announcing our engagement to everyone you met, each of my hesitations and concerns met with arrogance and now, *now* you are angry with me because I never wanted any of it?"

"If you never wanted it then why did you agree to it in the first place?" he asked.

"Because I've been in love with you since I was a child!" she exclaimed. "Because I did not think you'd ever love me in return!"

"Why would you think I could never love you?" Andrew asked. "Christ, Clara, you love me, and I love you, and still you deny any of this is true?"

"It does not make sense," she insisted. "Who is to say a year from now you will not realize what a mistake you've made? When your duchess is shunned from polite company or you have Jonathan Masson for a brother-in-law?"

"It is called *trust*, Clara," he chided. "It is part of loving someone; you trust they will be there for always."

"Well forgive me if trust does not come easily to me," she snapped. "I have not had the greatest experience with people following through on their promises."

"Yes, and you planned to demonstrate that to the fullest extent of the truth."

"Planned to, yes," Clara replied. "But I never said I would go through with it!"

"Well, now we will never know, will we?"

"I am sorry if I hurt you," Clara said. "That was not my intention."

"Yet, you knew it was a possibility from the start," he snapped. "Again, a Masson lives up to their vile nature."

"That is not fair," Clara said, recoiling from his dark glare.

Andrew laughed. "You know what is not fair? My brother and father dying and throwing me into this blasted dukedom. A fiancée who runs off with your footman. And another fiancée who intended to do the same thing!"

"God, you are so bloody stubborn!" Clara cried. "If you would just stop being so arrogant and heavy-handed, you might—"

Andrew's lips crashed against hers and Clara's words were lost, forgotten completely. His lips were urgent and demanding, and Clara realized this was not a kiss of a gentle lover. This was punishing. This was fueled by pent up frustration and tension and hurt.

Well, two could play that game, Clara decided. She wanted him, wanted this.

She pushed at him, propelling them backwards, until his knees hit a large leather chair and he sat, pulling her with him. Her shawl wrap fell to the floor as she kneeled over him, her knees resting on the cushion of the chair. Clara pressed her breasts to his chest, kissing him in long searing strokes, like he had done to her.

"Clara, we cannot," Andrew said against her mouth.

"You don't have a good reason why we shouldn't so this," she whispered, nipping at his jaw, the stubble scratchy against her swollen lips. "You want to, and I want to. Besides, you started this."

"God, Clara," he moaned, trailing his hands down her back to her bottom, squeezing the soft flesh and muscle. "Stop testing my control," he pleaded and pulled away a fraction. She opened her eyes to see his blue ones, dark with arousal, staring deeply back into hers.

Clara bit at the lobe of his ear, whispering, "Then let go."

With a suddenness she was not expecting, Andrew picked her up and practically thumped her onto the nearby sofa, pressing his knee down between her thighs, his mouth hungry and frantic. It nearly undid her, the sheer power and ferocity of his desire breaking free from the herculean control he held so tightly.

She tugged his shirt ends up out from his trousers, pulling the fabric over his head. She nearly gasped in shock, gazing at him in wonder and amazement.

His dark hair, normally so nearly coiffed, was tousled, curling around his ears and across his brow. Silhouetted by the dimming flames, his skin seemed to glow golden in the dying light. A light dusting of dark curls scattered across his chest, a dark line forming from his navel down, down into his trousers.

Her gaze followed that line, before her eyes darted up to meet his, a smirk across his lips.

"Enjoying your view?" he asked.

Clara sat up and kissed him firmly on the lips, opening her mouth to his, the urgency returning, their breaths coming in quick succession. She ran her hands through his dark curls, his hair soft and thick against her fingertips, and he moaned into her mouth with pleasure. Clara loved that such a simple thing could illicit such an arousing response, and that she was the one he was responding to.

His hands roamed over her breasts, thumbing her nipple through her day dress, trailing kisses down the swell of her breasts. With long nimble fingers, he managed the buttons along the back of her dress, the garment falling limp around her shoulders. Shrugging her arms out of the frock, the fabric fell loosely around Clara's hips. Soon the laces were pulled from her stays and the stiff whalebone garment was discarded on the floor.

Hungrily he captured her nipple in his mouth, suckling through the thin chemise. His hand moved slowly up the length of her leg, leaving a trail of tingling fire from her ankle to the soft flesh of her thighs. His fingers found the small nub of nerves at the apex of her thighs, a burning flooding though her limbs with each caress. Slipping one finger inside, then another, he moved inside her with abandon, his restraint long gone. Clara moaned his name, lost on the breath of his kiss as he moved his fingers inside her, twirling the nub as the waves built inside her again. She arched into him, giving him better clearance to create such wicked feelings inside her. Deep at her core she could feel the building, the burning, and the impending release, but he removed his fingers as her inner muscles ached to clench around him.

"Not yet, Clara," he said kissing down her neck, shivers racing across her feverish skin. She remembered from before, the passion and pressure that had released and sent her into a spiraling place of pleasure. She wanted him to feel that this time.

Reaching for the falls in his trousers, she pulled the laces from their loops, reaching down beneath the folds to grasp him in her hand, and release him from his imprisonment.

The long hard length of Andrew sprung free, proud and strong, thumping against her soft stomach.

"Can I touch you?" Clara asked, her voice hesitant.

Taking her hand in his, he guided her to his length, his hand grasping around hers as she took him, pulling her hand up and down, showing her how to stroke him.

Capturing her mouth again, Andrew groaned into her kiss. Clara moved her hand up and down again, relishing that the movement could cause him such pleasure. He was soft beneath her fingers yet hard as granite.

His hands went between her legs again, one finger, then two, stretching her, readying her for his intrusion. Clara had seen the size of him, and while he was not enormous, she was still a small woman.

"I don't want to hurt you," he muttered, his tip pressing against her entrance, both soft and hard.

You will not, she thought as he pressed into her, but she was wrong. What started with a tightening, a stretching to accommodate his size, turned into a searing pain, and she gasped. He withdrew a small amount and pressed in again, and this time the pain was less. Again he withdrew and pressed in, and again, a little further each time, until he was completely sheathed in her, and Clara was certain there was no greater feeling in the world.

Each thrust into her went deeper and deeper into her soul, each plunge a whisper of a promise that she longed to hear but refused to acknowledge. If ever she had felt more loved, more cherished that she did there on the sofa with him, she could not remember a time. Even as his kisses turned frantic, and his thrusts went deeper, it pulled at her heart, and her own passions, and she met him thrust for thrust.

This is what Clara wanted from him. This release of his own inhibitions, his own control he stacked against himself. The part of himself he held too close, so afraid the world might see and judge, and find lacking. But God, was he glorious. He was handsome and tender, and in this instant, he belonged to her, and her alone.

Clara could see in Andrew's expression the ecstasy he was experiencing, and he pummeled into her hard, finally stilling for a long moment as he buried his seed deep within her. Her own release did not peak as it had before, but Clara did not mind. The feeling of him inside her was fulfillment enough.

Neither one moved for a long moment, five minutes?

Hours, maybe? Clara did not know. Slowly, she came became aware of their surroundings, the waning light of the day, the weight of Andrew against her, his face buried in her neck, his hardness twitching inside her. With reluctance, Andrew pushed himself off her, withdrawing and sitting against the other end of the settee, where they had just made love, because that was the only thing Clara could think to call such a shattering experience.

"Now you'll have to marry me," Andrew said darkly.

Clara scoffed. "The joke is on you, your grace. I'd planned on marrying you for some time now."

"You said you—"

"I said I had intended at the beginning of our engagement to never see it through," Clara replied, pulling her stays around her. "My thoughts on the matter changed, Andrew."

"Clara . . ." he began, but his voice trailed off.

"Tighten these as best you can, please. I am without a lady's maid, and I'd rather not scandalize the entire household when I escape to my room."

He obliged, tugging her laces tight, but not nearly as well as Molly had. Tugging her dress over her head, Clara managed to straighten the gown as best she could, fumbling with the few buttons she could reach.

"The final banns were called in Cumberland today," Andrew reminded her as he found his own clothing. He'd slipped his arms through his waistcoat, but chose to hold his jacket in his arms.

Clara nodded. "I suspected they would be. That is it then? We are to be married in what, ten days?" The date had been set weeks earlier, but now that it was ten days away it seemed more . . . permanent.

"It seems that will be the way of it," he replied.

"Lovely," Clara managed, ignoring the tight ball of emotion nearly choking her. "I shall check on Norah. Good day, your grace." She managed a light curtsy before wrapping the shawl around her shoulders and barely buttoned day dress, before leaving him in the study. She did not flee or cower, but walked with a confidence she was certain she was faking, but there was no way she would let him know how her heart was torn in two.

Chapter Twenty

The following day Clara stood for a new wardrobe fitting, finally agreeing that while the clothing her great aunt had provided was lovely, as the Duchess of Bradstone she would need more clothing and more elegant gowns, in addition to a wedding gown. When Madame Deveraux arrived with her army of seamstresses and assistants, Clara harnessed her inner duchess and insisted that the fittings be done in Lady Norah's chambers.

"She has the best lighting in the house," Clara explained to the dressmaker.

"Yes, of course! *Absolument!*" Madame Deveraux exclaimed with a snap of her fingers. Susanna, who Clara had begged for help, lead the way up the stairs, the band of assistants carrying the numerous pattern books, fabric samples, and designs up the stairs after her.

Clara caught Andrew eyeing her suspiciously, and she shrugged.

"Norah likes fashion," Clara explained. "If she were well

enough to come downstairs and enjoy this then she would, but since she's not, we will go to her."

"Mountain to Mohammad?" Andrew asked.

"Precisely," Clara replied, smiling sweetly before hurrying after the dressmaker. Norah was thrilled to participate and Clara let her have almost free reign with the designs and colors, looking to Susanna and Sarah to rein her in.

By luncheon, Lord Nick Macalister arrived at Bradstone House like a hailstorm descended upon an unsuspecting patch of rose buds: fierce and blustering. Most of Nick's yelling was a bit unintelligible, and though his flailing arms and finger pointing were rather theatrical and comical, Nick was lucky he did not flail or point at Clara because she was fairly certain Andrew would not have tolerated his brother insulting his bride-to-be, despite the turmoil of their relationship.

"Are you insinuating that I do not have adequate protection for my own sister?" Andrew asked in a very calm and yet very intimidating tone.

"I am telling you in no uncertain terms that I think you do not," Nick replied, his blue-green eyes flaring with anger.

Andrew stood up. "Hear this, Nicodemus: It was my decision to bring you to town to see your sister and no one else's. I can send you away just as quickly. I suggest you think that over as you attend to her sick bed. Tread carefully because my memory is not so short to have forgotten the reason you were asked to leave this house in the first place."

Steaming and red-faced, Nick turned on his heel and stormed off, slamming the breakfast room door.

Andrew slowly returned to his seat, taking a sip of his tea and glancing at Clara's bemused expression.

"What?" he asked. "At least I did not yell this time."

"You still ordered him about and issued ultimatums," Clara replied. "He's your brother, not a servant or one of your lackeys in Andrew's Grand Army. Treat him with a little respect."

Susanna and Sara stared at her wide-eyed.

"He does not need respect," Andrew replied, ignoring his sisters' expressions. "He's nineteen, and he's a hot-head. He needs to grow up."

The rest of the day proceeded normally enough, some social calls with Sarah and Susanna, joining the *beau monde* for the ride around Hyde Park. The silly social customs that she had been denied had started to feel almost normal. And it was amusing to watch everyone treat her with a confused respect, as if they did not want to but felt compelled to be polite.

The peace she had found during the day was interrupted that evening with the arrival of Joseph the footman.

Dinner had just been served *en famille*, a lovely spread of beef, ham, and duck—no fish to be seen.

Clara paused, her fork halfway to her mouth, as Howards hurried into the dining room with a note for Andrew. Watching the fury race across Andrew's face as his eyes danced across the paper was confirmation that something had happened.

"Excuse me, ladies," Andrew said, rising from his seat and sending Clara a dark look. She did not bother to say anything to Sarah or Susanna and she jumped up and raced after him.

"Andrew, what is it?" Clara asked as she came into the foyer.

Andrew was pulling on his gloves but did not look at her. "The footman has been returned to London. I am off to Halcourt's to see what he has found out."

"I am coming with you," Clara said.

"Absolutely not," he replied. "This is not suitable for a lady."

Clara leveled an incredulous look, crossing her arms. "I am not some weak-minded debutante who faints at the first sight of trouble. Take me with you."

"I am certain you will not faint, but I do not want you anywhere near that man," Andrew said, crossing the distance between them and placing his hands on her shoulders. "I want to keep you safe and try to shield you from as much of life's ugliness as I can. And that man, Clara, the one who kidnapped and possibly raped your sister, is ugly."

Clara tilted her chin up in defiance, realizing he was trying to shock her. It was not working. "I am going with you. I am the only one who knows what that footman even looks like. You might interrogate the wrong man and not even realize it."

If Andrew had been prone to growling like an angered lion, she imagined he might have done so. His expression would have matched such a sound. "Go and fetch your cloak."

Controlling the jubilant smile that wanted to burst from her, Clara hurried to her room and was back down the stairs within moments, breathlessly pulling her pelisse around her shoulders. Andrew stood waiting, looking very sharp in his top hat and evening cloak, and looked up irritably as she came down the stairs.

"Quickly, please, Clara."

"Yes, yes, I'm coming," she said. "Your sisters will make excuses for us then?"

"For the theatre this evening?" Andrew asked, and they hurried out the door. "We should still be able to make it in time."

Clara fought a discontented groan, and her face must have shown her displeasure because Andrew laughed as he handed her into the carriage.

"As the Duchess of Bradstone, you must—" Andrew began, but Clara cut him off with a dismissive wave of her hand.

"Yes, I understand about duty and appearances and all that," Clara said. "I just thought this might take longer."

"Not likely. Maybe we should stay in tonight," Andrew suggested pensively. "I would hate to force you into society after the ordeal of this evening."

"If you think we should attend the theatre, then we will attend," Clara stated. "It is the proper thing to do after all."

Leaning forward, Andrew snatched her hand off her lap, pulling the silk of her glove with his own gloved finger. "Maybe I don't want to be proper," he said huskily. "Maybe I want to spend the evening with my improper fiancée doing improper things to her."

Clara snatched her hand away and he chuckled. Throughout the day his icy walls had been thawing a bit towards her.

"How can you even think of such things while we are headed to interrogate the man who abducted my sister?" Clara asked.

Andrew shrugged. "I always think such things, especially about you and most certainly when you are cooped up in a coach with me. To think of all the things that we could do in a coach traveling around the city. Most improper."

Clara shook her head incredulously. She glanced out the window and realized they were heading to a part of the city she had never been.

"Where are we?" she asked him.

"Halcourt has a residence he uses for these sort of things," Andrew explained. "It is not in the most fashionable part of town."

"He has a residence he uses for interrogations?" she asked. "Are you certain he's not a spy?"

"I've known Halcourt for years, we were lads together at Eton," Andrew explained. "He is his father's heir, and his father spends a great amount of his time out of the country. Halcourt's two younger brothers are Bow Street Runners and somehow the entire Aster family seem well-connected to every aspect of London: the slums, the *haute ton*, the docks, politics, the church. Halcourt has a connection or an ear to the floor in every part of town, and most of the country. That is how he heard about Joseph the footman to begin with. But a spy?" Andrew shrugged off the question. "If he is, he hasn't bothered to include me in the secret, and for that I do not mind. He wields a great deal of power in his sect of life, and his brothers are respected Bow Street Runners. With Halcourt it is best to look the other way and just be satisfied with the results."

"I suppose if he was some sort of spy or contact or aid, it would be a need to know sort of thing," she concluded.

"And I don't exactly need to know," Andrew replied, nodding.

"He will not be angry with you for bringing me along?"

Andrew was silent as he thought for a moment before answering. "Halcourt is a very old-fashioned sort of gentlemen. He prefers things done in a certain way, pays respect to those it is due, and he likes the boundaries that separate men and women. But angry? No, he will not be angry. He respects me enough to trust my judgment. Plus, you are my fiancée, and he will feel that affords me some level of control over you."

Clara's brows pulled together as she tried to figure out why these two men were possibly friends.

"*I* don't think that affords me control over you," Andrew said quickly, holding his hands up in defense. "I'm just saying that Halcourt does."

"It seems you two are very different," Clara said. "I would assume you would not completely view me as your property once we are married?"

Andrew smiled at the challenge in her voice. "I have learned over the course of our acquaintance that it would be very unintelligent to view you as my property. Despite my recent behavior, I do believe you have a choice in how your life should unfold. Thus far you've dealt with unpleasant treatment at the hands of the people who should have loved you most. None of your life has been in your control. I apologize for adding to that burden when I insisted we wed. Truth be told, I was a little frantic with desire to protect you. I still am, but I want you to know you have a choice. If you show up to the church, it will be your decision. You do not owe me anything."

"Thank you, Andrew," Clara said.

A moment later the carriage rolled to a stop. The door popped open and Andrew descended before turning to help Clara. She looked up at the modest red-bricked town home, wondering if Halcourt's neighbors knew what went on at this residence. Andrew and Clara did not dawdle in the front, Andrew taking her hand and pulling her along behind him and into the house.

Clara saw Redley first as they entered the house and then Luke, which was surprising, as she had not seen him in days. They both nodded at her, and she smiled tersely back, not exactly knowing what to expect.

"Ah, your grace," a tall dark-haired man said as they handed their cloaks and gloves to a footman.

"Halcourt," Andrew said, inclining his head. Clara looked finally upon the face of her fiancé's spy friend and realized he could not be a spy. She was certain one important ability for a spy was to blend in. Viscount Halcourt certainly did not blend in. He was too severe in appearance to be considered classically handsome; his nose was too thin, and his eyes were too dark. He was not unattractive, yet if she had met him under different circumstances she might be afraid of him. She was not certain she was not afraid of him now.

Halcourt turned his intelligent eyes onto her and frowned, glancing at Andrew for an explanation. It did not occur to her until later that he knew who she was without an introduction.

"She is the only one who knows what the footman looks like," Andrew answered his friend's silent query. "It is important we have the correct man, not just another of Morton's schemes."

Halcourt nodded, though Clara was not certain he agreed with Andrew's borrowed reasoning. Halcourt led the way down a dark hallway, Andrew and Clara directly following with Redley and Luke behind them. Andrew nodded to his brother and cousin as they passed, but did not express any surprise in their attendance.

"They arrived just an hour ago," Halcourt explained as they wound their way through the house. "I sent for you just after. As you can imagine he did not come quietly, nor is he cooperative. He may appear a bit roughed up." He glanced back at Clara with uncertainty.

"She can handle it," Andrew said, squeezing her hand in support.

Halcourt nodded and turned the last corner, knocking on the door before opening it.

Clara was surprised at the ordinariness of the room and its furnishings. It looked to be a library, with tall shelves lining each wall of the room stocked full of books and artifacts, with a balcony alcove directly above her. A few chairs were scattered around the room, dark wood and dark fabrics. It was a very masculine room. It struck her that the room had no windows and the door they had come through was the only entrance and exit. A solitary man sat in the middle of the room, ropes around his wrists and ankles and wrapped around his torso, securing him to the chair. Another man stood leaning against the bookshelf, boot crossed at the ankle. He looked nearly as unkempt as the man tied to the chair but less injured.

Halcourt closed the door, leaving Luke and Redley in the hall, and Andrew led her to stand directly in front of the incarcerated man. His left eye was purple and practically swollen shut, but upon seeing Clara, his right eye grew large with recognition. His cheek was bruised, and there was a scabbed-over cut on his jaw. He looked as though he had put up a decent fight when he encountered the man sent to escort him to London.

"My, you do look just like her," Joseph the footman said, blinking his good eye at her. "I remember you, obviously, I just forgot how identical you two were."

Andrew and Halcourt looked at Clara for confirmation and she nodded. "That is him."

"Right," Andrew said and pulled her out the door, and she managed to yank her hand from his tight grasp.

"I'm staying, Andrew," she said in a low tone, her eyes dancing with challenge. He accepted her challenge and planted her in a chair in the hall. Luke and Redley stood nearby.

"You are not going to be in there, Clara," he said, crossing his arms. "I agreed to bring you with me, but I never agreed to allow you to be in the room while we talk to him. You are staying put."

She opened her mouth to object, but he cut her off.

"I'm not budging on this, Clara," Andrew said, giving her a dark stern look, and she realized he was not going to allow her inside that room, no matter how much she begged.

Clara reluctantly nodded in acceptance. With a hard look to Luke, who was standing near her chair, Andrew stepped back into the room, Redley following before shutting the door.

Aside from Luke, she was quite alone in the hallway. Clara hoped this would go quickly; something about this house made her skin crawl. She could hear nothing but muffled voices from the interrogation room, and she leaned forward to hear better.

Luke cleared his throat, and a thought occurred to her. She smiled at him and stood up.

"Could you direct me to a refreshing room?" she asked.

Luke's raised his brow. "I'm sure your fiancée would be happier if you just stayed put."

"I'll be quick, I promise," she said sweetly. "Honestly, it is very urgent. A chamber pot then?"

Luke looked pained, but sighed and pointed up the

stairs. "First door on the right, the bedroom has a chamber pot. Be quick. Andrew will have my hide if you are not back when he returns."

"Splendid," she said, smiling and swept past him and up the stairs. Hoping there might be a door or a sliding panel that would lead her to what she was actually looking for, Clara walked along the hall, thankful that her evening slippers were silent against the wooden floorboards. She did not want Luke to know what she was up to. She tried the first door on the left, but it was locked, as was the second. The third knob turned and opened, and she smiled at the small empty room, an almost identical doorway on the opposite side of the room. She slipped inside silently, finding exactly what she was looking for.

Chapter Twenty-One

*A*ndrew was not happy Clara was in the residence, even if he had managed to keep her in the hall. Halcourt, he could tell, was not happy about it either. Whatever they needed to do to get information out of this man, he did not want Clara to be even remotely aware of what Halcourt intended.

"Bradstone, this my associate, Ian Carlisle, Lord Westcott," Halcourt said, nodding to the unkempt man leaning against the bookcase. Andrew nodded to him, but barely spared him a glance. His attention was focused on the man tied to the chair in the middle of the room.

"Do you know why you've been brought here?" Halcourt asked the man.

The footman shrugged. "I've an idea."

"Please state your name for the record," Halcourt said.

The man scoffed. "What record? This isn't exactly legal proceedings."

"On the contrary," Halcourt said, pacing in front of him.

"This is entirely legal. This house is leased to the name of a Bow Street Runner, and there are three law enforcement agents present in this house. After we have concluded this interrogation, you will be sent off to Newgate to await trail." Halcourt paused in front of the man. "Or perhaps not. The value of the information you give us can aid greatly in your future. Do you understand?"

The footman gulped and nodded.

"Your name, please," Halcourt asked.

"Joseph Baker."

"And prior to residing in Northumberland, where were you living?"

"I was a footman in the Earl of Morton's household," Joseph answered.

"Please describe the events of the evening of Friday, June twenty-fourth through Sunday, June twenty-sixth, the year 1808," Halcourt inquired.

Joseph the footman looked confused and Andrew clarified, his tone sharp. "When you eloped with Lady Christina Masson."

"Ah yes," Joseph said. "She was quite in love with me, you know. Ran away with me to Gretna Green."

Andrew's jaw tightened, and his fists clenched painfully at his side.

"The accuracy of your information is also vitally important," Halcourt said absently, trailing his hand over the spines of books along the wall. "I will know if you lie."

Joseph looked uneasily at the pair of them. "Who are you?"

"Who I am does not signify," Halcourt replied and continued on his circle around the chair. "However," Halcourt pointed his finger at Andrew, "his identity is rather important. That is the man whose fiancée you abducted five years ago."

Joseph's good eye widened a fraction, and Andrew felt oddly satisfied. He was accustomed to the attention his name earned him and often used it for his own gain, usually in Parliament, but this was the first time he had enjoyed the fear that raced across the man's features when he realized who he was dealing with.

"So, I suggest you start with purest truth," Halcourt said softly and deadly, his voice dancing just above a whisper. "Because it is this man whom you so wronged who will decide your fate."

Joseph cringed and looked down, his chest wrapped tightly to the chair with extensive ropes. Andrew began to grow impatient. He wanted to take Clara home and away from this. He knew only bits of Halcourt's business with the Crown and knew that not even his Runner brothers would be able convict him if something were to get out of hand. He appreciated the connections Halcourt had to the underbelly of society, but it disgusted him at the same time. He remembered why he never asked Halcourt for specifics, and Halcourt seemed uninclined to enlighten him.

Andrew was, however, surprised when Halcourt pulled a hot poker from the fire and poised it above the man's thigh ready to strike it down.

"Whose idea was it for you to run off with Lady Christina?" Halcourt asked, his voice much louder and more threatening than it had been a moment ago. Joseph shook his head. Halcourt shoved the hot poker into the man's leg, the golden hot tip searing through the man's trousers and into his flesh. Joseph roared in pain.

Behind him Andrew heard a soft gasp, and he turned to see blonde hair disappearing from the alcove above. He should have known she'd find around his orders and demands.

"Whose was it?" Halcourt asked again pulling the poker from the man's leg.

Joseph shook his head again. "I cannot," he gasped. "You may throw me in Newgate, but he'll find me. No one can touch him! He will see to the end of me!"

Halcourt jabbed the poker into the other thigh and Andrew felt his stomach turning over at the smell of burning flesh filling the air. The footman's screams echoed in his ears, and he wanted to close his eyes. He had seen his share of brawls and fights, but torture he was not accustomed to.

"Morton," Joseph gasped. "Morton told me to do it, threatened my sister's life, beat her to a pulp. She's all I got you see, I had to protect her. I knew . . . I knew what he would do to her if I refused. So I did it, I took the earl's money and ran off with his sister. He threatened Christina too so she would come quietly. But I did not intend for her to die. She ran off and died in that parsonage and that was not my doing. You have to believe me! He will kill me, I swear to it. My life is over once I leave this house."

"And the man that shot at his grace and Lady Clara?" Halcourt asked.

Joseph shook his head and Joseph raised the poker again.

"It was all Morton!" he gasped just as Halcourt moved to stab him again. "He told me to stay put, that I was not needed in London. He chastised me for playing such a failing part in the whole scheme. He said if he wanted something done right he would never again turn to a mere servant for services."

"How did he contact you?" Andrew asked. "Where did you send your replies?"

Joseph apparently realized what he was asking and was shaking his head again. "He sent a note," he explained. "But I never sent a reply. He just assumed his note would be orders enough. But I'm done taking orders from that prick. That is why I started shouting my mouth about, I wanted him to feel out of control, bullied around a bit. But if he knew I was here telling you all this," he let out a low whistle, and Andrew had to agree. Jonathan Masson had not taken lightly to Andrew leaving his company of merry lords and speaking out against him. He understood the footman's fear of the earl.

"If there is anything else, you know where we are,"

Andrew said to Halcourt. Andrew did not want this man killed on his account, even if he had abducted Clara's sister. The man should be punished, but he was another victim of Morton's hate. The cycle had to stop somewhere. "Let him see his sister. Arrange passage for them both to the colonies. I want them out of this country and as far away from Clara as possible." He took another step towards the ex-footman, his glare hard. "I do not want to see either of you again. I am sparing your life because it is not my place to expedite your death. But I will not hesitate next time."

Joseph nodded. "Yes, your grace."

With a final glance to Halcourt, Andrew turned and quit the room.

Clara's mind was spinning with what she had seen. There was no denying it, Molly's story had been true up until now. It was likely her sister was alive somewhere.

Clara's head bumped on the pane of the carriage window, lost in her thoughts. Over the past month her entire life had shifted, moved off its axis, and with this information about Christina came another wave of uncertainty. What would Christina say when she found Clara was engaged to her former fiancé? What would Clara say to her sister who had fooled everyone into thinking she was dead? She was elated to hear that her sister was alive all this time, but what new complications would her twin's reappearance bring into her life?

Clara looked to Andrew, her cheeks glistening wet in the dim lighting of the carriage. "If I asked you to do something, would you agree to it?"

"Most likely," he answered.

Clara felt her chest seize in pain. She regarded him for a long moment, the hopelessness and loneliness washing over her. Fear that she'd destroyed any chance they might have at a happy life together rippled through her as she took in the concern that was plain on his handsome face. She regarded him for a long moment, before crawling across the carriage and situating herself in his lap, her arms wrapping around his neck. He did not hesitate and wrapped his arms tightly across her back, holding her to him, his lips grazing along her hair, across the physical scar her brother had left her with. The invisible ones were much worse. Clara's chest shook as it rose and fell, each wave of sobs washing over her. Andrew tightened his grip on her, and Clara was soaked in the comfort she so desperately desired.

It might have been the two fingers of brandy she drank before she went to bed, but Clara slept rather peacefully throughout the night. She was drained physically and emotionally, but the next day she woke to birds chirping outside her window and the sun sending warm rays across her cheek. At breakfast, she told Susanna about Joseph Baker and the suspicions about her sister being alive, mostly because she needed someone else to know what was going on. Clara watched her newfound friend sipping her tea, her cheeks ashen and almost wished she could have had the same reaction. Clara did not consider herself a whimpering miss, but she should have been frightened or upset by what she saw the night before, by what she had been through the past few weeks. She wondered how Andrew was feeling, if watching his friend jab a burning poker into another man's leg had bothered him as much as she thought it should bother her. What a pair they made.

"I have a solution to your problem," Susanna announced an hour later. Clara had taken up reading in the lilac drawing room but she had barely made it through two pages in as many hours.

"Do tell," Clara replied, setting the book aside. "If it will improve anything, I am eager for a suggestion."

"You and Andrew need to travel to Petersfield to determine if your sister and her child live, am I correct?" Susanna asked and Clara nodded. "So," Susanna continued, "let us all go."

"I beg your pardon?"

"We have a home there," Susanna explained, sitting demurely on a chair opposite Clara. "Well, in that general direction. Let us adjourn to the country for a few days for an impromptu house party."

Clara frowned. "I thought Bradstone Park was in Kent?"

"It is," Susanna answered. "But I'm speaking of Foley Cottage. It is near Petersfield."

"How would an impromptu house party solve anything?" Clara asked.

"If the family leaves London together, no one would think twice about you coming with us," Susanna explained. "It is brilliant actually. No one would even know you were not with us the entire time. Sarah and I can have a quick rest in the country while you two go figure out this business with your sister."

"Goodness, Susanna, you might be on to something," Clara admitted, tapping her finger against her lips. "But the wedding is next week. Can we be back in time?"

"Foley Cottage is about a day's carriage ride," Susanna replied with a shrug. "If we leave first thing in the morning we will have ample time. The rest of us may get some rest; you and Andrew, I suspect, will not." Susanna's brow arched up above her eye and she gave Clara a quizzing glance.

Clara ignored her, not wanting to decipher the subtext of Susanna's questioning brows.

"Let's do it then," Clara decided and rose from her chair. "Come, let's inform Sarah of our plans, and she will help us make everything ready."

Susanna blinked at her from a moment, before asking, "Do you wish to run this by Andrew first?"

Clara shook her head. "If he chooses not to come, that is his decision," Clara replied, walking through the room. "This concerns my sister, and I am determined to find out what has happened all these years. He will not deny my going, not when you are all travelling with me. Besides, he is not yet my husband. I still have a few more days to determine my own fate."

Andrew was not expecting to return to Bradstone House and find it in a state of chaos. Apparently his sisters were packing for a holiday.

Andrew frowned, watching the maids carry bundles of clothing down the halls, footmen lugging trunks up the stairwells.

With a glance to the gentleman beside him, Andrew led the way through the halls, in search of one of the females in his life who might shed some light on their change in plans.

He found Susanna and Clara in Clara's bedchamber, discussing the amount of gowns required for a quick sojourn out of London. Clara was a sight to behold, smiling and laughing about some nonsense she and Susanna had bought on Bond Street days earlier. Andrew suppressed a sigh, watching Clara giggle at an anecdote regarding his poor footman being completely encumbered with a mound of towering parcels from their excursions. Apparently the last hat box slung on his arm was too much for the girls to take, and both girls doubled over in a fit of giggles. It was wonderful to see Clara smile and laugh, and he was grateful to his sisters for helping Clara to cope with her ordeal over the past two weeks. He knew what good friends could do to a person's disposition, especially in the trying times life had a way of putting in one's path. He was happy she found that in his sisters, particularly, it seemed, in Susanna.

"Sorry to interrupt," Andrew began, clearing his throat.

"Andrew!" Susanna said brightly. "It is about time you returned. We had planned to leave without you!"

"Yes, and where are we going?" he asked, crossing his

arms, watching the maids moving gowns and day dresses from the wardrobe.

"To Foley Cottage, of course," Susanna said dismissively.

"Susanna has this harebrained idea that is actually quite ingenious," Clara explained. "We are to all go Foley Cottage for a house party, when really it is to mask you and I going in search of Christina. Susanna says the parsonage where she was last seen is near Foley Cottage?"

Andrew glanced at Susanna, his gaze hard. Susanna blinked at him in challenge. "I said it was sort of close." Turning towards Clara, Susanna said, "I will leave you now and tend to my own packing. Good luck." Susanna winked at Clara before quitting the room.

"This parsonage is at least a two-hour carriage ride from Foley Cottage," Andrew informed Clara. It seemed Susanna was aware of this.

The bright light in Clara's eyes dimmed for a moment before she smiled sweetly at him. "Well, that is closer than it is to London. We will be back in time for the wedding next week."

Andrew glanced at the gentleman waiting behind him in the hallway and the dark-haired man shrugged.

"Sounds like a marvelous plan," Andrew replied to Clara. "In fact, we can add one more to our numbers." Stepping into the room, Clara gasped as the gentleman followed Andrew through the doorway.

"Oh, my goodness," she said, her hands flying to cover her mouth. "Patrick!"

The young man smiled at her, a warm teasing smile that only a younger brother could give to his older sister. Clara went tumbling into his arms, and Patrick laughed, wrapping his arms around her.

"Clare-bear, you are all grown up!" he teased and kissed the top of her head.

"Oh, posh, Patrick, I was grown up when you left," Clara said, looking up into his eyes. She smiled brightly at him, reaching up to ruffle his hair. "You, on the other hand, have grown so tall! And your hair, you really need to trim it. Oh, Patrick, whatever are you doing here?"

Patrick laughed as she squeezed her arms around him again and glanced over her shoulder to Andrew. Andrew nodded and took a few more steps into the room.

"I went to the Home Office to inquire where he was, nearly a fortnight ago," Andrew explained, taking up the tale. "I did not intend to have him shipped in from the far reaches of the sea, though I thought maybe if he was near he could be sent for. Imagine my shock when he appeared at Brook's this afternoon."

"My captain received a letter from his grace," Patrick continued. "He granted me shore leave for the duration of your engagement. Said it was a wedding present."

Clara glanced to Andrew. "You will never guess who his commander is," he said, his eyes flashing with humor.

"Your brother," Clara said immediately, her lips broadening into a bright smile. "Of course he is."

"A very strange set of coincidences, don't you think?" Patrick asked. "I just happened to be under Captain Lord Bennett Macalister's command."

"Indeed," Clara agreed and looked back at Andrew, her eyes twinkling. "This truly is the best gift you could have ever given me," Clara said, reaching for Andrew's hand. "Whatever shall I do to equal such a gesture?"

"I do not require anything," Andrew said. "Just show up to the church and stay away from my footmen."

Clara and Patrick laughed, and Clara squeezed Andrew's hand again. He excused himself, leaving brother and sister alone in the drawing room to reconnect after three years apart.

Clara could not believe her eyes; her long lost Patrick

was sitting beside her. He looked well, his dark hair curling at the base of his neck and his brown eyes bright and clear. Looking at the two of them one could not tell they were brother and sister. Patrick looked more like Jonathan, more aristocratic in his features. The eyes were the only way the two brothers were different. All the Masson siblings had brown eyes, but Patrick and Clara were blessed with the twinkling gold flecks in the brown that Jonathan and Christina lacked.

"You filled out," Clara observed, glancing at his informal attire. He was not wearing his military uniform, choosing instead a dark brown coat with a cream waist jacket and cream breeches.

"Three years on a ship will have that affect," Patrick laughed. "Captain Macalister had me scrubbing floors and climbing ropes to the top of the mast the first days aboard his ship. I learned to be quick though. I'm very useful if the ropes tangle themselves."

"Goodness, to think of you at the top of a ship's mast . . ." Clara said, her eyes sparkling with pride. "I am so very happy to see you, even if you did not come home to the best circumstances."

Patrick shrugged. "But look at you, dear sister, about to be a duchess!" he said and clicked his tongue. "Who would have thought?"

Clara smacked him on the arm and he feigned injury. "Are you implying I am not fit to be a duchess?"

"Quite the contrary, actually," Patrick replied. "I am very happy for you, and you seem very well-suited to his grace."

"Yes, well, after what Jonathan has been saying about me it is a very advantageous match," Clara agreed. "Though Andrew is quite wonderful, once you get to know him."

Patrick scoffed. "Yes, I am sure. Just like a shark is nice after you pet him once. And what do you mean about Jonathan? What has he done now?"

"He absolutely hates me, Paddy," Clara said. "You have to

know what he has said about me."

Patrick shook his head. "Away at sea for the past three years, Clara. We don't exactly have access to the gossip pages."

Clara sighed and regaled her brother with the tales their elder brother had put out into the world. "The *ton* somehow thinks I was involved with Christina's elopement, that I actually killed Christina or that I am Christina masquerading around as the other twin. I have been on the continent as the mistress of some wealthy foreign aristocrat, specifically at times an Italian viscount. I went away into the country to give birth to a bastard child. I have also become a fortune hunting leech and an upstart looking to extend my reach. Oh, and Jonathan has been trying to have me killed to gain access to Mother's Patterson money."

Patrick looked at her, wide-eyed in shock. "No one can believe any of that?"

"Oh, it would seem that everyone does," Clara replied. "Except the part about Jonathan trying to kill me for mother's gold. No one knows about that."

"The Patterson funds?" Patrick asked. "Is it even worth killing for?"

Clara nodded, her curls bobbing alongside her face. "Oh, yes, there is over forty thousand pounds." Patrick let out a low whistle, and Clara nodded again. "Mother invested well."

"Apparently so," he said. "Now I know who to go to for a loan. Though I would suspect you will be marrying into much, much more."

Clara glanced around the elegant and finely-decorated room. "Yes, though I never dared ask Andrew how much exactly."

"Wise of you," he answered, nodding. "Best not to look like a fortune-hunting leech trying to extend your reach."

Clara laughed and squeezed her brother's hands. "Oh, how I have missed you, Patrick. You will join us on this impromptu house party? There is an alternative reason for going, and it does involve you." Clara swallowed and forced the words past her lips. "Christina might be alive."

The words felt so foreign coming from her lips, but the tightening in her chest was no longer so. Patrick's eyes flew open in shock, and Clara chuckled.

"You have a better reaction to this than I did."

"How is that possible?" Patrick asked with a sigh as he leaned back against the cushions.

Clara launched into the story about everything that had come to light over the past four weeks, her brother watching her carefully. She told him about Jonathan's abuse that lead her to waking up in Bradstone House and her engagement to Andrew. How the family was shot at and Norah poisoned, all because her brother wanted her dead, to take possession of a fortune she hadn't even known existed. How Molly, her maid, had seen Christina with her own eyes, and now Clara needed answers. She needed to close that part of her life before she could hope to move forward.

"We are to set out to Petersfield where she was last seen alive," Clara said. "You must come with me, Paddy. She was your sister too."

"Yes, of course, I will come," Patrick agreed, giving her hands a squeeze. "My darling sister, how much you've had to endure in my absence. I am so sorry this has happened to you."

Clara shrugged. "I've managed. You have no idea how unbearable it has been with just Jonathan to live with."

"I think I can remember," Patrick replied. "He was the reason I left. Though it is hard to imagine he would say such things about you."

"Andrew does not think he openly said them, just hints and veiled comments," Clara explained. "Servants talk and soon things spiraled until I was a barely accepted member of society. The past few months have been grand, let me tell you."

"So I am to walk you down the aisle and give you away?"

Patrick asked.

"If you please," Clara replied.

Patrick kissed the backs of her hands. "It would be my honor, Clare-bear. At least then I can fulfill some brotherly duty to you and make certain he goes through with it."

"I think he's more worried about me not going through with it," Clara admitted. "I've made a mess of our relationship, and it has barely begun. Additionally, our family does not have the best history with weddings when it comes to the duke."

"With our shared history it is a wonder Bradstone would even look at a Masson again," Patrick said. "Not that you are not lovely enough to attract a duke, just that *you* should land *this* particular duke is a feat on its own."

"Yes, I am well aware," Clara sighed.

"I am sorry you have had to endure Jonathan without me, but I can feel confident leaving again knowing you have the duke as your protector. You will be quite safe from our brother's evil doings."

Clara wished her younger brother was correct, but she could not help but recall how someone, presumably hired by Jonathan, had shot at them leaving a ball. Or how he had infiltrated a conspirator into the household and Norah had been poisoned. Clara felt safe at Bradstone House, but she would feel much safer if Jonathan was under control.

Clara managed a brave smile, happy to have her brother here. "Come, I want you to meet Andrew's sisters. And he has a brother with whom you probably went to Eton, Lord Nick Macalister."

"Oh, yes, I remember Lord Nick," Patrick said and rubbed his jaw as if the memory of an old injury had resurfaced. "He and I brawled a few times on the front lawn. Usually over nothing, if I recall. If he is in residence then I imagine it will be an interesting evening. Perhaps he can show me around town afterwards."

Clara scowled at her brother. "Please, let's not encourage

him, Paddy. He is a good boy, and you are too—you both need to just grow up a little."

Patrick smirked as they paused before the bedroom door. "I will leave the growing up and respectability to you, my dear duchess sister."

Clara rolled her eyes and pulled open the door, eager to have her old family entwined with her new one.

Gentle reader, a reliable source said the Duke of B— and family were to enjoy a last minute holiday at home before the wedding next week. One can only hope the Duke of B— comes to his senses while on holiday at Foley Cottage in Kent.

Chapter Twenty-Two

Early the following morning, they were off. Three carriages departed from Bradstone House with two riders. Clara sat in the first carriage with Patrick, both eager to make up for the years they had been separated. Susanna and Sarah were in the second carriage, with the third carrying the various maids, valets, trunks and other luggage. It never failed to amaze Andrew how much six people needed to pack for four days away from town.

Norah opted to stay behind with her brother Nick so he could tend to her.

"It is for the best, really," Susanna had told Clara. "Norah's constitution isn't the strongest under the best of circumstances, and with her recovery still early, she really shouldn't be moved. Besides," Susanna had added with a wink, "Norah is a horrible traveler. Even just trips around the city in the carriage make her sick. She is the worst to travel with."

Andrew had chuckled at Norah's expense, which was

probably mean-spirited of him, but Norah had been in a rare sort of disagreeable mood lately, and he only hoped she would snap out of it soon. Clara had managed to befriend Sarah and Susanna, and while Norah was polite, she had not warmed up to Clara as the others had.

After a few hours they paused to switch horses. Andrew opted to switch with Patrick, who was eager to stretch his legs after so many months at sea.

"You are to ride in Clara's carriage?" Sarah asked as they stood outside the Crown and Pig Coaching Inn while the horses were changed. Sarah eyed Andrew suspiciously, her gaze darting between the engaged couple.

"Is that a problem, Sarah?" Andrew challenged. "Am I not allowed a few moments alone with my fiancée?"

Sarah's lips pursed into a flat line. "A few moments is one thing, but we are still a few hours from our destination. That length of time is not entirely proper."

"Oh come now, Sister Sarah," Susanna chided, linking her arm through her older sister's. "Give the bridegroom and his bride a chance to be alone. What do you think they will get up to in a carriage?"

Sarah eyed both Clara and Andrew before giving a curt nod. "Keep the curtains opened at least."

"Goodness, Sarah, they're practically married," Susanna said. "If this were London, and they were carousing about town, that would be one thing. But there is no one here, and we are with family."

"Such things from you are worrisome, Susanna," Sarah replied.

"I'm not about to go along in a carriage with a gentleman who is not my husband," Susanna said innocently. "But this is Andrew and Clara. I daresay they've earned a little leniency."

Sarah sighed and nodded her permission, though Andrew was not really waiting for her blessing.

"Lovely," Susanna said, tugging on her sister's arm. "Now, let us get out of this heat and into the shade before I am covered in freckles."

Clara chuckled under her breath before glancing at Andrew beneath her long lashes.

"Your sisters are enchanting," she told him.

"My sisters are a handful," Andrew replied. "They interject their thoughts and opinions into every aspect of my life."

"But they care," Clara reminded him.

"Patrick cares about you," he told her, offering his arm.

"Yes, I know he does," Clara replied, linking her hand through his arm. "But he is not here permanently. At the end of his leave he will sail off into the sunset, and I will be left here again, alone."

"You know you are no longer alone, Clara," he said, and she glanced up at him quickly.

"Yes, I know," Clara replied. "You and your family have been wonderfully welcoming." He handed her into the carriage before settling himself along the opposite bench.

They traveled together for a while in silence. Glancing to her, he made an effort to pull her into conversation.

"You will like Foley Cottage, I think," he said. "For one, the kitchen is divine. Whatever pleases you, the kitchen will prepare."

"The food at Bradstone House has been marvelous, Andrew," she replied. "I wonder, does the kitchen at Foley Cottage offer a variety of desserts?"

He caught the hint of a double entendre, and he could feel his heartbeat quickening, his temperature rising. Despite his irritation towards her, he could not help but remain utterly enchanted. He'd forced himself to stay away from her since the debacle at the musicale, and that only resulted in the explosive tryst in the library two days earlier. He ached to hold her, to feel her soft skin and supple curves beneath his hands.

"They have the most delectable desserts available any time of the day," he replied, pushing the memory from his thoughts.

"What if I choose to indulge every hour of every day for a whole year?" Clara asked coyly.

"Then the kitchen staff would be quite exhausted from the constant work to keep you satisfied."

She smiled demurely and looked out the window. "It is not the kitchen's staff I'm worried about, but another staff entirely."

Andrew let out a bark of laughter, and she winked saucily at him. "Oh Clara, where have you been all my life?"

"Right under your nose, you goose," she replied.

He tilted his head to regard her, taking in how truthful her statement was. She had truly been there all along.

"Don't think me the most horrid person in the world for saying this . . . ," he began, but he stopped, unable to find the right words.

"But my sister's abduction might have been the best thing for both of us," she finished for him.

He looked embarrassed, but she laughed her tinkling laugh.

"Don't look so ashamed, Andrew," she chided. "I happen to agree. I miss my sister terribly, and I have begun to appreciate the sacrifice she made for me. But I came to a realization last night after spending some time with Patrick."

"A good realization?"

She nodded. "When you and Halcourt were talking to Joseph Baker, who is, for all intents and purposes, my brother-in-law, I had the strangest feeling that he had come to care for Christina. He seemed devastated that she had run off and supposedly died in that parsonage. He admitted to the abduction but was horrified at the thought of killing her. I wonder if they had come to some sort of understanding. They both acted out of love for their siblings, they were bound together by the threat of Jonathan. And it was a few years after her abduction that Christina ran away. I wonder if she only did so because of what she was afraid Jonathan would do if he found out she was with child. A Patterson heir would impede his plans, and Joseph looked grief-stricken that Christina and their child had died."

Clara's compassion for a man who had caused her so much pain surprised him. "This was your revelation?"

Clara shrugged. "I want to believe that Christina was not miserable the entire time, that she was able to form some sort of connection, even mutual respect, with her husband. They were forced into the situation together; I can only hope they were able to make the best of it. Joseph did not seem capable of handling that hot poker in his thigh or the thought of going to prison. I cannot imagine him actually causing bodily harm to Christina."

Andrew had not considered this, though truthfully, he had not given much thought to Christina's circumstances after she left him standing at the altar. But now that he did consider it, he realized he hoped the same thing.

"I suppose I am incapable of seeing only the bad in everyone I meet," Clara concluded. "I could say the same for you too."

"I do not see the worst in everyone, but I can recognize the evil some people possess."

"You do not think Joseph Baker possesses such an evil," she stated.

"Why do you think that?"

"Because you secured his passage abroad, for both him and Molly. That was a very generous thing to do, though it was not surprising. Sometimes it seems as though you want to save everyone in the world."

Andrew looked out the window, a little unnerved by how well his fiancée had pegged him down. He had never been accused of having a hero complex, but he made sure he did some good with the position he had so tragically inherited. It was the least he could do to honor Father and Sam.

"No, I could not have him ordered to his death," Andrew admitted. "Removing them from the country seemed a decent alternative. We never have to see them again and they have the opportunity to start anew. They too were victims of your brother's hate."

Clara's gaze was intense, and her brown eyes sparkled with some unshed emotion as she looked down at her gloved hands. She pulled her lip to the side and chewed the inside of her cheek, her brow furrowing before asking, "I am curious about something, but I am afraid you will not be honest with me."

"When have I ever not been honest with you?" he asked.

Her face relaxed slightly. "All right. I want to know what happened between you and my brother. You said you had been a firsthand recipient of his vile nature but you have never elaborated."

Of all the things he thought she would inquire, that was furthest from what he expected. He sighed, deciding he should probably share the story with her.

"Morton and I were boon companions at school," Andrew began. "I was Morton's lackey, as were Trevor and Connolly. We were Morton's little troupe, his little band of miscreants. We did his dirty work. He always said his 'illustrious title' made him better than us, since we were all second sons or lower and as such we had to do his bidding. And we did. We did his bullying, his taunting. Once we even beat someone up for him." Andrew sighed, running his hand through his hair.

"When Mother sent a note requesting Luke, Ben, and I return home for that weekend, I refused to go. She wanted to have a grand family affair for Mara's first birthday. I knew it would irritate Mother, but at the time I thought the whole idea was silly. I did not want to go to my baby sister's birthday party. I was ten days away from being seventeen; I was head strong and a bit rebellious. Luke and Ben went ahead and I stayed behind at Eton. The carriages brought my brothers to London where they joined the rest of the family before continuing on to Kent and Bradstone Park. On the last stretch of road before reaching Bradstone Park, the coaches were attacked, and my father and brother were killed."

"How awful," Clara said.

Andrew nodded. "I was the only one not present, and only because I did not want anyone telling me what to do."

"Had you been there, the outcome might've still been the same," Clara said reassuringly, giving his arm a light reassuring squeeze. "Or you could have been killed too. You could not have prevented it from happening."

"I know," Andrew said, nodding. "The day I was told of my father and brother's death was the last day I was friends with your brother—I've told you this. But there was something that happened . . ." Andrew trailed off, frowning over the memory. It was not that he was bothered by what had happened, though he should have been. It was more he did not understand it. "We'd been arguing about something, and Morton was rather put out with me. Our argument turned into a brawl and somewhere in the middle of it . . . Morton kissed me."

Clara's brows shot up in shock. "I beg your pardon?"

"That was about my reaction," Andrew replied. "But I was a lad brawling with my best mate, and to have him do that in the middle of it all, well, I believe I reacted rather badly. I hit him again, and we were broken up moments later by Halcourt, who was a prefect. Halcourt had always been a rule follower. It seemed he had been sent by the headmaster to fetch me and I left straight away, worried I'd be expelled for fighting. It was then I learned of my father and brother's deaths. Afterwards, I ignored what Morton had done, pretended that it hadn't happened, I suppose. We did not have any contact that summer. I missed my examinations, but Eton sent tutors to administer them to me at home. When I returned that fall as a duke, everything changed. I did not want the attention I received, suddenly it did not matter I had been a terrorizer on the school yard, everyone it wanted to be my friend. Connolly and Trevor stuck by me and later

Bexley and Halcourt, who were a year behind us, got added
to our little group. Redley arrived one day from somewhere—he never really explained where—and we welcomed
his companionship and his fists.

"Morton . . . pretended I did not matter. That our friendship had never meant anything, and he certainly never mentioned what he had done. At first he ridiculed me for not
being there to save my father and brother. He told everyone how it was my fault they were dead. And when no one
seemed to listen to him, he started to make things up. He
told everyone I had confessed to orchestrating their murder."

"No one could have possibly believed him," Clara said,
horrified.

"At first no one did," he replied. "But slowly, he poisoned
a lot of the boys against me. Some claimed to have heard me
rant about how I hated my family and how I wanted them all
dead, especially Father and Sam, so I could be the duke. The
professors did not know who to believe and as a precaution,
Bow Street opened an official investigation."

Clara gasped. "That is appalling!"

Warmth spread through Andrew as he watched her
dark eyes full of disgust, grateful the disgust was not aimed
towards him. He felt a weight lift off his shoulders, realizing
he'd worried she might believe Morton as well.

"I'm glad you feel that way," Andrew said softly. He
could not hide the years of pain from his eyes; he could no
longer mask his expression with her. He had tried so hard for
so many years to be exactly what he was supposed to be. He
was not born to be the duke, but he had made every effort to
fulfill his duties correctly, to do it right. He needed to prove
he deserved it, that he hadn't slipped in and stolen it from
its rightful owners. For years he had strove to force those
hateful, horrible things Morton had said about him out of
society's mind with his actions, and he felt he had been successful, though the tinges of the rumors enhanced his Stone
Duke facade.

"Andrew, I would never believe such a thing about you," Clara said gently. "How could you think that of me?"

"There is something about Morton that people respond to. It is amazing, and I was once fully susceptible to it. Whatever he says somehow people take as the gospel truth. They actually opened an investigation. The Bow Street Runners came up to the school and went through my room and interviewed my classmates. They went to Bradstone Park."

"What did they find?" Clara asked when he paused.

"Nothing," Andrew said, the corner of his mouth pulling up into a half-smile. The memory of his mother, red-faced and in her blacks, standing at the front door to Bradstone Park blocking the Bow Street Runners entrance to the house. "Mother wouldn't let them inside. Said that anyone who believed the vile things said about me were less than human, and she would not allow an investigation into something that was clearly a horrible set of tragic events. The highway men had killed Father and Sam, and I was not involved."

"And they believed her?"

"She was the Duchess of Bradstone," he replied with a shrug. "No one doubted her, and no one dared question her." He glanced at her carefully. "I am relieved that you do not believe Morton's version of things."

"I would never," she replied. "I am surprised that anyone else would as well."

"Truly?" Andrew asked, skeptically. "People have believed what he has said against you."

"I am certain that Jonathan hates me. I've given up trying to understand him or his motives. Besides, his words did not do you as much social damage as they did me."

"I had some cleanup work to do in order to repair my reputation," Andrew admitted. "Even after Mother put an end to the investigation, Morton still ran his mouth. When I made my bows to the King and took my place within the *ton* I had my work cut out for me, but eventually everyone stopped talking about my supposed patricide. I did everything I could to be exactly as one would expect a duke for twelve years."

"Hence the Stone Duke," Clara surmised.

"Partially," he replied. "I took a page out of Mother's book: if I was stern and unrelenting, people would do as I said. But I also thought it was who society expected me to be. My father was a stern man, though he loved his children, he was distant. We never doubted his love for us, but he was not a warm person. I thought that was what a duke was supposed to be. My hardened personality earned the moniker. I never much cared for it, though I understood the need for it. As for Morton . . . I never breathed a word of what had happened, until here and now with you. I suspect he panicked, thinking I would spill to everyone so he set out to discredit me."

"Then he likely did the same to me," Clara admitted. "Just after Patrick had left for sea, three years ago, I saw . . . Well, first I had noticed the name of someone he had been corresponding with, and it was a gentleman's name." She laughed lightly. "It's so strange how bits of old memories stick with you. One little thing will latch on to a more important memory, then that tidbit is forever connected, even if it has no other relation. Frederick Meyers. 15 Grosvenor Square. I only remember the name because, as children, Christina and I used to play with a Sally Meyers, and I wondered if there was a relation. And my birthday is on the fifteenth of April."

Clara sighed and looked out the window. "Naturally I inquired after the letter. Jonathan was very displeased and told me to stay out of things that did not concern me. My brother has never been overly warm to me, but in the past ten years or so his resentment has grown stronger and his demeanor colder. I learned to not ask questions where he was concerned."

Clara turned her gaze towards his, her eyes hooded and guarded. "The truth is, there have been few people in my life that I could truly rely on. Most of the things promised to me have turned out to be lies or ended in betrayal. I put on a good face, but sometimes I feel as though I am barely holding my life together—barely holding my emotions in check from spilling all over everything. Sometimes it feels I am strung together by the tightest frayed string, and one more snip will send me tumbling into destruction. A person can only handle so much betrayal in life before they turn hard and cold. Perhaps that is what happened to my brother. But I've been given little reason to trust anyone."

"As you say, trust does not come easily," he said. "Though I have a family that loves me past the point of suffocation, my time in society has not been easy. Having to convince everyone I did not have my brother and father murdered while navigating who was genuine and who was merely near me because I was a duke was not easy. I was fortunate to have a select group who I could place my trust in. It surprised everyone when I offered for you, when I chose to trust you. And to have you not reciprocate that trust . . . well it was very confusing."

"Truly, I did not intend to hurt you," Clara said softly. "I hope I can show you that I am someone you can trust."

"And I hope you will learn to trust my affections for you," Andrew replied.

Clara did not respond, she just nodded and looked out the window again.

Her hesitation, though rational, still irritated him. Finally he had opened his heart to someone, and to have her reject him was stunningly painful. And he had to prove himself to her? He did not doubt her love for him, how could she not trust his feelings?

Begrudgingly, Andrew realized she had a point, her past relationships had not proved the best foundation of trust. Andrew understood that—even related—though he had moved through his past hurt. Now he simply had to wait for her to move through her own distrust.

As the sun began to wane in the afternoon sky, the front

drive of Foley Cottage came into view.

"Foley Cottage," Clara asked, not looking at him. "Is it truly a cottage?"

"Well, no," Andrew admitted. "But it is more modest than Bradstone Park."

"That sounds rather wonderful," Clara said, watching as her new home came into view.

Much smaller than Bradstone Park, Foley Cottage was three stories tall, stone with ivy crawling up the sides, the windows framed with white edgings. The carriage pulled into a circle in the front of the house, a streaming fountain in the middle of the loop.

Clara was introduced to the housekeeper and butler, Mr. and Mrs. Singer, as the members of their house party traipsed inside and disappeared to their bedchambers, weary from a long day of traveling.

Foley Cottage truly was a modest country home. It sported six bedrooms, two family suites, a dining room, one sitting room, a music room, an extensive library with a study alcove, a long gallery, and a massive and modernized kitchen featuring what Andrew informed Clara was the newest Rumford model of stovetop oven. He escorted Clara through the house as he explained the improvements and modifications he had made to the structure, the décor, and the furniture.

He hoped his eagerness to share this place with her was not as evident as he felt, this solitary world where even his siblings rarely infiltrated. He explained how he had all the portraits removed and replaced with landscapes because he did not want his ancestors staring down at him every moment of every day. The previous year he had commissioned the rebuilding of the church that lies to the west, adding a family pew containing a firebox and a walled garden with a fish pond.

"It feels like a home, Andrew," Clara said, placing her hand on his chest and kissing him softly on the cheek. "It is perfect."

Brushing an errant curl back from her face, he said softly, "I am glad you approve."

They gazed at each other for a long moment before Clara's eyes slid away and the moment was broken.

"I think I would like to speak with Mrs. Singer before dinner," Clara said, stepping away.

"Of course," Andrew replied. "Feel free to make whatever changes you feel necessary and to your liking. It is to be your home as well." He hoped.

"Thank you," she replied. "I will see you for dinner?"

"Yes," he nodded and bowed, somewhat formally, and he wanted to smack himself on the head for his cold behavior. With an odd glint to her eyes, she dipped into a curtsy before leaving him alone in the long galley.

Chapter Twenty-Three

The following morning, Clara crept into Andrew's room, silent in the early morning darkness. The grounds were lit with an eerie glow as the first rays of light began to hit the countryside. Sitting on the edge of his grand four poster bed, Clara brushed the dark lock of curls from his brow, leaning down to kiss his cheek.

"Andrew," she said, giving his shoulder a light shake. "Wake up."

He mumbled something in his sleep as his arm snaked out and wrapped around Clara's waist, pulling her down onto the bed beside him. His face turned to nestle in her hair and he breathed deeply.

"Andrew, you are awake, do not deny it," Clara said with a laugh.

"I do not deny anything," he murmured. "Especially whatever seductive nymph has entered my bed."

"Andrew, get up," she said, pushing on his arm. He tightened his hold and pulled her closer.

"I am up," he muttered.

"Goodness, Andrew, I cannot breathe!" Clara laughed. "Will you wake up and dress?"

"Whatever for?" he asked, blinking at her slowly. His face was so wonderfully handsome, red from sleep with stubble growth along his jaw and cheeks. Clara traced a finger from his brow down his nose. Andrew's eyes drooped in contentment.

"If you get up and get dressed, I promise to make it worth the effort," she told him.

Andrew sighed but released her. "I will hold you to that," he said as she rolled off the bed.

"Walton will be in momentarily," Clara said, righting her skirts. "He was gracious enough to allow me a moment to wake you myself."

"You are friendly with my valet?" Andrew asked, sitting up, the sheet and duvet falling down his broad chest. Clara did her best not to stare, ignoring the level of impropriety they had just ventured into.

Turning towards the door, Clara replied, "I am to be your wife, Andrew. Of course I know your valet. Now, dress and meet me in the front hall."

"Clara, the sun isn't even up yet," he complained, his hair tousled from sleep. Clara was very tempted to return to his side, run her hands through his soft curls, and refuse to leave the room, or the bed, all day.

"So it is," she said with a glance to the window. "Best hurry then. We wouldn't want to miss the sunrise. Oh, and dress for riding."

"Why are we riding before the sunrise?" Andrew asked. "We aren't set to leave for Petersfield until well after breakfast."

Clara's brown eyes glinted with mischief. "We can go to the parsonage tomorrow," she replied. "Today, I am taking you hostage."

"Well, if that is the case," Andrew replied, flipping the

blankets from his lap. Clara turned and fled the room before she was reminded what lay beneath those blankets.

Twenty minutes later Andrew appeared in the front foyer, dressed smartly in brown trousers tucked into black boots, a cream waistcoat and a jacket of—

"I say, your grace, but you are wearing blue," Clara realized in amazement marveling at the sapphire blue of his coat, highlighting the blue of his eyes.

He glanced down at his coat. "Is that all right?" he asked.

Clara wanted to laugh but she simply smiled. "It looks rather nice on you, in fact."

He nodded towards the basket in her hands. "What have you there?"

"Fresh milk, a fresh loaf of bread, and some cheese," Clara replied, watching as a wide grin split across his face. It was the same basket his cook used to prepare for him as a lad.

They set off on horseback for the sunrise Mrs. Singer had told her about, one that rose gently from the direction of the house, but dipped down on the other side, stretching out across the valley below. The summer morning brought a low foggy mist that shifted across the grounds like a gentle caress. The air was damp as the morning dew settled onto the landscape, cool and crisp as they made their way briskly towards their destination.

Clara pulled a thick quilt from her saddle bag and spread it out on the grass.

"The basket please," Clara said, settling in the middle of the quilt. Andrew handed over the basket of milk, bread, and cheese before sitting stiffly beside her.

Clara leaned against his shoulder as they sat on the hill, watching the sun rise over the horizon, an early morning breeze pulling a few strands of hair free from her coiffure. She was going to give it one day, she decided. One day to be in love and to have Andrew love her; one day to prove to him, and hopefully herself, this was real and could be trusted.

"What else have you planned for the day?" Andrew asked.

"Well, I thought we could redo our race from Rotten Row," Clara replied. "Though I will best you again. I suspect there is a bit of exploring we could do on horseback." She leaned away to regard him. "Have you a pond or lake we could swim in?"

Andrew laughed. "No, unfortunately, there is no bit of water suitable for swimming. But we can race again, if you would be prepared to admit defeat."

"You should be the one ready to eat your words, your grace," Clara chided, rising to her feet. "I am on an unfamiliar mount on unfamiliar land. You have a distinct advantage over me."

"I am willing to give you a head start," he replied, rising. He helped her fold the blanket and return it to her saddle bag.

"Oh, no," Clara said. "I am not riding with extra weight. We can leave the blanket and basket here and return for them later."

"Leave them here?"

Clara glanced around. "Is there any one around to pinch it? Or shall we leave a note saying, *By order of the Duke of Bradstone, do not touch my basket!*"

The lopsided grin appeared across his face, the one she had come to cherish.

"Fine, we leave the extra weight here," he agreed. "But then I am not racing in his hat." He swept the beaver skinned top hat from his head.

"It was a bit ridiculous you wore it to begin with," Clara admitted. "But my bonnet will stay as well. And my spencer jacket," she added, slipping her fingers beneath the buttons and releasing them from their loops. Her blouse beneath was a soft cream and much more comfortable to ride in.

"Can't have you be the only one carousing about the countryside half nude," Andrew said, pulling off his own jacket, but he needed Clara's assistance to be rid of the tight-fitting garment. She happily complied, but not without giggling at his expense.

Both without jackets or hats, Clara and Andrew mounted their respective horses and moved down the hill towards a more even patch of ground. The valley below was lush and green, speckled with white and blue flower buds lasting through the end of springtime. Andrew pointed out the eastern property line, the long stretch of woods at the very far end of the valley.

"What is that?" Clara asked, shielding her eyes from the sun as it rose higher in the sky, bringing bright rays of light. She was pointing towards the southern end of the valley, where upon a small rise in the elevation sat a ruin of sorts.

"That is a turret ruin," Andrew explained. "I have no idea what it was before that, and no one in the area knew anything about it. It has simply been there as long as anyone can remember. It was used as a hunting hide from time to time."

"It looks part of a medieval castle that once sat upon that hill," Clara said.

"Except there is no record of there ever being a castle there," Andrew replied. "Nor a fort or lookout tower or anything of the sort. It is simply a single turret in the middle of the countryside."

"We shall have to investigate," Clara said with a nod.

Andrew laughed. "Are you trying to weasel a way out of this rematch?"

Clara's brow rose. "Nothing of the sort. Merely finding an activity to occupy us while you lick your wounded pride."

"Would you like the five second lead count?" he asked.

"I would not," she replied. "I will not have you give any reason for my success other than my superior riding skills."

"Then you cannot be put out when I trounce you thoroughly," he replied.

"Deal," she said. They set out the race perimeters and moved their horses to a starting point.

"When that crow lands on that tree, we go," Andrew said and Clara nodded in agreement, not taking her eyes from the crow as it flew towards the lone tree in the middle of the valley, the end point for their race. The second the bird landed, they both leapt into motion.

Clara beat him, again, though it truly was no contest. She laughed at the incredulous look of astonishment as he came up firmly behind her. For a moment, she thought she'd pushed too far, that the Stone Duke was about to make an appearance, but he laughed with her, proclaiming her the better rider.

They rode across the countryside, jumping over low fences and bits of thicket, laughing as Clara's horse nearly dumped her into a stream. They quizzed each other about their favorite sweets, seasons, colors, and Shakespearean sonnets. They discussed the two wars England was fighting, the farming reform Andrew was working through Parliament, and the idea of investing in the steam engine. Clara learned that despite growing up on an apple orchard, Andrew still adored apple tarts. Andrew learned Clara preferred dogs to cats.

Returning to where they'd watched the sunrise, they found the basket refilled, as Clara knew it would be. They dined on strawberries from the hothouse, wine from his private stores, and bits of cold ham fresh from the farm down the road.

"Tell me about your mother," Clara said. "If I am to be the Duchess of Bradstone I should know what I have to live up to."

"She would have liked you, I think," Andrew said, taking a bite of a strawberry. "She had a strength and an impishness that was quite unbecoming of a duchess, but she turned it into a power. She was a force to be reckoned with, but she was still lovely and kind."

"She sounds like an amazing woman," Clara said softly. "I wish I could have known her. What was her name?"

"Mary," he answered. "She died about six months after Father and Sam, in childbirth. It seems she was with child when they died." Andrew smiled at the chuckle that escaped from Clara.

"Seriously?" Clara asked, choking down a burst of laughter. "I mean, it is horrible that she died at all, but birthing another Macalister? Were there not enough of you?" Clara covered her mouth. "Goodness, forgive me. That was quite rude."

Laughing, Andrew shrugged. "I am not offended. I'd often thought the same thing." He paused and took a sip of his wine. "There is a peculiar thing with all of our birth dates, you know. We were all born in May, and Mother lost all the children not to be born in May. Mara almost died when she was born, and the doctor said she was born too close to April."

"That is silly," Clara replied. "What month a child is born has nothing to do with its survival rate. How many did she lose?"

"Ten."

"Ten!" Clara exclaimed incredulously.

He smiled again and nodded. "Mother spent most of her time pregnant."

"I'll say," she said softly.

"Perhaps there is something to it. Nevertheless, only the May babies survived. Which is another reason Mother started the tradition of the Macalister Birthday Ball. She wanted to celebrate the children she had in this world and remember the ones she had lost."

"When was your father born?"

"May," Andrew answered. "He has five siblings too, all born in May."

"So what if we have a child who is not to be born in May?" Clara asked.

Andrew stared at her, and Clara felt a blush rush up her neck, coloring her cheeks. Their children. She hoped it would happen, in fact, he needed it to happen. Andrew would need a son eventually, and hopefully more than one. He was the spare, and while she hoped his spare would never be needed, they knew from firsthand experience there was no controlling the matter.

"I don't believe in it, Clara," Andrew said with a shrug. "I'm just saying it is a weird set of coincidences. If we have a child that is not born in May then it will be loved just as if it were born in May. But please let's not have ten. Ten is a bit much."

"I agree," Clara said, popping a bit of ham into her mouth. "Four or five, but not ten. I don't want to spend my entire life pregnant."

"What about your mother?" he asked. "You never mention her."

"There isn't much worth mentioning, I am afraid," Clara said with a sigh. "She was silly and vain; it's no wonder where Christina got it from. Mother taught us all sorts of useful things, like how to bat our eyelashes to make a man do our bidding." Clara turned her gaze to him, looking up at him from beneath her lashes, batting them slowly at first, then quickly, then slowly again.

"Yes, I can see how that would be useful," Andrew said, looking way, his voice tight.

Clara laughed. "She always told us to put our bosoms first when we entered a room. And that our reticule should always match our shoes. And to never wear plumes if they were not necessary. Useful things like that."

"She does sound delightful."

"I suppose she felt she was helping us, in her own way," Clara replied. "She and my father did not get on very well after Patrick was born, and she never really recovered from his birth. She would have fits of supreme sadness followed by giddy happiness. It was difficult to know which mood she would be in on any particular day. Then one day she fell ill during a winter chill, and never really recovered. She died before we made our debut."

Clara stood and brushed the crumbs and grass from her skirts.

"Enough talk of our mothers," she proclaimed, offering him her hand. He accepted, but rose without putting any weight on her. "I want to see that turret ruin. And I think I'd like to walk, as we've been in the saddle nearly all day."

"Then we shall walk," he said, offering his arm, and they set off across the meadow.

They strolled down the hill and across the valley as though they were walking along Bond Street, shopping for wares. Andrew entertained her with anecdotes from his elaborate childhood. With ten siblings, the levels of mischief they had accomplished impressed even Clara, who had only snuck out of her brother's house to attend a ball.

As they neared the end of the valley, a crack of thunder rang through the sky, startling both Andrew and Clara.

Turning, Andrew realized as they walked towards blue skies scattered with harmless clouds, behind them had blown in a dark threatening storm.

"We're too far to make it to the horses," he said.

Clara agreed. "We will have to make a run for this turret then. Has it a roof?"

"If memory serves correct, I believe it does," he answered. "We run?"

"Yes," she said.

They made it to the bottom of the hill before the skies opened above them and within moments they were soaked through. The dampened grass made climbing the hill difficult and more than once they both slipped down, pulling the other along for the ride, giggling in the rain. Finally they reached the top of the rise.

Laughing, they tumbled through the splintered wooden

door and into the round room of the turret.

"Well that did not go as I planned," Clara laughed, shaking her bonnet, water pooling around her boots on the stone floor.

"Oh, you did not intend for us to get drenched in a storm?" Andrew teased, winking. "I rather thought you were capable of controlling the weather."

"No, darling, that was supposed to be in your part of the vows."

"Remind me to make note of that," Andrew replied, bending down near the hearth.

The room was circular with a set of stairs along the wall spiraling up to the top of the turret where it opened onto nothing. There was no door leading to the roof, though it thankfully did have a roof. It was a most peculiar building, but for now, Andrew was thankful it was here.

The room contained a table with a long bench and a hearth built into the rock of the wall. The chimney went up the exterior of the turret, and Andrew hoped it was clear, or any fire they would light would surely fill the room with smoke if some bird or varmint had decided to make the chimney its home.

There was a scattering of hay and wood, though the fireplace had not been used in some time. At the very least the wood was dry, though he did not have anything to light it with.

"I don't see a flint rock or anything to strike a flame with," Andrew said absently, running his hands along the top of the stone fireplace. "I could use my ring, perhaps." He twisted his signet ring around his finger, wondering if that would produce enough spark to light the bit of hay in the hearth.

"Andrew, we don't need a fire," Clara said.

"Clara, we do if we do not intend to freeze," he replied, turning around to regard her with an amused gaze, but the laughter drained from his face as he took her in.

Her dark gaze was almost predatory, and he saw reflected in the depths of her eyes the same thing that raged through him all day. Lust, pure unadulterated lust.

"We don't need a fire to keep up warm," Clara amended, taking a step closer to him.

Tilting up on her toes, she pressed a feather light kiss to his neck, under his jaw, nipping at the sensitive skin along his ear.

Without overthinking it, Andrew met her lips with his, kissing her deeply, tasting her, taking as much as she was giving, and she was apt to comply. She was a quick learner ,and their previous jaunts into indiscretion had proven her a successful study.

Winding his fingers in her hair, he pulled the pins free, her pale golden tresses falling free like waves of light around her face, its texture smooth and soft. Andrew pulled his lips from hers, leaning back just a fraction to see her beautiful face and inviting eyes. His hands cradled her face and he ran his thumbs over her cheeks and the pads of her full lips. Her gaze was clouded with desire, as lust and wonderment reverberated through him, knowing he could elicit such a response from her. She was his. Somehow the moon and stars had aligned and forever he would have her. No more dark unending moods that threatened to overtake him; no more refraining from joy and laughter. Her light and beauty was his alone.

With a possessive and rather feral growl, he recaptured her lips with his, claiming her need as his own. His arms wrapped around her, and he found the bench behind him, stumbling as he pulled her down with him. Her own passions were unsurprising, and he welcomed her onto his lap as she climbed atop him, her legs spreading to straddle him, her skirts soaking wet from the rain bunching around her hips. He was rock hard beneath her, straining against the fall of his trousers.

Her hands deftly undid his cravat and pulled the fabric

from his neck before moving her fingers to the buttons of his waistcoat, slipping each circle from its loop, her hands roaming over his chest as each layer was removed. It was not easy, as both his garments were soaked through and unwilling to cooperate, stiff and sticking to his skin, and it took both their skill and laughter, to tug his arms loose.

"Your blouse is next to go," he whispered against her mouth.

"I've about as many layers as you do," she admitted, pressing her breasts to his chest as he fumbled with the loops and buttons at the neck of her blouse, loosening them enough for the garment to slip from her shoulders. His fingers pulled the laces from her stays, Clara's hot mouth moving along his jaw, her hips grinding against his.

Running his hands down her back, her blouse fell around her as he pushed the fabric from her shoulders and arms, her breasts bared to him. Her nipples had hardened into little peaks in the cold, or in arousal, and Andrew bent to take one in his mouth. Nipping and sucking, he swirled his tongue around the little bud, Clara's soft moans and gasps echoing off the stone walls of the turret.

His mouth found her other breast, and he bit down on it gently, enjoying the way Clara's breath caught in her throat before turning into a soft moan of pleasure. He suckled, his tongue loving the peak, again and again, kneading her other breast, plump and heavy in his hand. Arching her back, her breast pressed further into his mouth, the other filling his hand as he fondled, his thumb flicking across her taut nipple.

She was glorious, this little fiancée of his. Her curiosity and passion had him begging to be inside her, but they shouldn't do this here, now. Clara deserved something more dignified than a rough tumble in a ramshackle old castle turret.

"Clara, we need to stop," Andrew said in a harsh whisper.

"No," Clara practically growled.

Andrew tried to stop her hands to dislodge her, but she was much stronger than he realized.

"Why must we stop?" Clara asked, pulling back to look into his eyes. Her brown eyes were dark with desire, her pink lips swollen from their kisses. "Why must we *always* stop?"

"I don't *want* to stop, Clara," he answered, closing his eyes and resting his forehead against hers. "But I am trying to be a gentleman. You deserve much better than a toss on a stone floor. You deserve a bed and a fire and champagne and flowers and more comforts than this turret can offer."

Clara kissed him roughly, and he lost himself for a moment.

"I don't care what I deserve, Andrew," she said, nipping his lip as he had done to her. "I care about what I want, and what I want is you. We have our entire lives to enjoy soft beds and fireplaces but this is how I want you now."

The little argument Andrew had remaining vanished, and he gave in, claiming her mouth as hungrily as she was his. Clara rocked her hips over his hard erection, pressing into her soft warm center he wanted to bury himself in. If she wouldn't believe the declaration of his love, perhaps she would believe him in this way.

"I need to touch you, Andrew," she whispered in the wake of a moan. Her hands tugged on his shirt ends, freeing the fabric from where it was tucked into his trousers and pulled it over his head.

Greedily, her eyes roamed over him, her hands trailing down his chest and torso, the muscles in his chest tightening instinctively as her fingers passed over, leaving trails of spark and sensation as they went. Clara bent her head and licked his nipple before glancing up at him. Andrew nodded, and she did it again. Sparks of energy shot down to his erection, pulsing with need for her, to be buried deep in her depths.

"Darling," he said hoarsely, pulling her head up capturing her mouth with hungry urgency. She wound her hands around his neck, pressing her breasts to his chest, skin on skin, and it felt glorious. His hand found her under her mass of skirts, skidding a finger along her opening before slipping his finger inside. She was wet and waiting for him.

She broke off their kiss and buried her face into his neck, a soft moan escaping from her chest as he stroked her deep inside, faster and faster until he could feel her clenching around him in anticipation before she gasped and cried out his name. He quickly tried to undo the folds of his trousers, not even realizing he was trembling until her hand came over his and took the task over.

He looked up into her bright brown eyes alight with passion and pleasure.

She kissed him soundly on the mouth, her hands unlacing the folds, taking him in her hand as he sprung free between them. She guided him to her warm opening, teasing the tip inside just enough to feel her moisture, and he groaned with pleasure. As she removed her hand, Clara slid herself onto him, slowly taking him into her, rocking her hips as she went. He watched the pleasure wash across her face, her mouth open as a moan passed across her lips, her head tilted back in abandon. Just watching her take her pleasure almost made him come.

In one quick movement, he lifted her into his arms, twisting to lay her down on the table behind them, thrusting into her as her heels came up to rest on the flat of the table.

Christ, Andrew thought but could not manage a verbal accolade, the angle of her hips pulling him deeper inside her. Aided by the height of the table, he thrust into her again and again and again, slowly at first but soon her breathless moans urged him on, her hips rocking with the him and with her own will.

Andrew was lost. Her glorious release of inhibitions empowered him, and he was no longer in possession of his own actions. He held her hips, delving deeper into her with each rhythmic thrust. With each invasion came a little breathless moan from Clara as she lost herself in their lovemaking. He watched her find her release, her muscles clenching around him, pulsing with ecstasy. He came a moment later, the sight of her pleasure sending him over the edge, his last few thrusts sending his seed deep inside.

Andrew slumped against her, her arms wound around his neck, holding him close to her heart. He could feel her heart thumping against her ribcage, matched beat for beat by his own.

Pulling himself from her and tucking himself back into his trousers, he lifted her from the table, her limbs limp in the aftermath of her release, and settled on the floor, leaning against the wall. Clara's eyes fluttered open, still stormy with their passion and found his, a sleepy smile spreading across her face. Andrew leaned forward to press a soft kiss onto her forehead. She smiled softly and closed her eyes again, curling up beside him.

Andrew leaned back against the wall and took a deep breath, hoping to clear his head, but he was still stimulated and pulsing from their lovemaking. Their first time had not been an anomaly, as he had feared. His desire for her had not waned, even the slightest. Never had he experienced anything quite like what he did with Clara. Perhaps it was the love and care he felt for this woman, but there was something about her that made him pause and forget himself. Glancing at Clara's face awash with peace, it made him warm, but not aroused. He never thought he would care this much for another person, never thought he could love someone as he did her.

"What was this Clara?" he asked, hesitantly, worried his query would break the spell cast over the turret ruins. "What was today?"

Clara sighed softly. "A reminder, I think," she replied, her voice barely above a whisper. "Of what it felt like to be loved. A chance to trust it is all real."

"It is real for me," he whispered. Andrew wrapped an arm around her and rested his head atop hers, breathing in her lovely rosewater scent.

If today did not convince her that his feelings were true, he did not know what more he could do.

Chapter Twenty-Four

🌹

The following morning Andrew stood with Clara and Patrick just outside the parsonage adjacent to the parish church in Petersfield, a two-hour drive west from Foley Cottage. The dwelling was not in the best repair and looked as though it needed a new roof, at the very least.

Andrew rapped his knuckles on the weathered wooden door and took a step back, smiling encouragingly at Clara. She took a deep steadying breath, attempting to wrangle control of her nerves.

A plump older woman opened the door, wiping her hands on her apron and blinked up at them. She looked from Clara to Andrew, then past him to where his carriage stood at the end of the drive.

"May I help you?" she asked, holding her hand to shield her face from the sun.

"Yes, madam, I wonder if perchance you could be of assistance?" Clara asked sweetly. "We are in search of someone, and were told they might have lived here in the recent past."

The woman looked back and forth between the two gentleman and Clara before opening the door wider. "Please come in, and we can see if we can find who you are in search of."

"Thank you," Clara said and stepped inside, followed by Patrick. Andrew nodded to the woman before ducking inside after Clara. They were led to a drawing room that looked as though it also doubled as a music room. It was a small room, and the large pianoforte made it a tight fit but Clara and Patrick took a seat on a worn, rose-print embroidered sofa. Andrew chose to remain standing.

"Who would you be looking for?" the woman asked.

"Our sister, Lady Christina Masson," Clara replied.

The woman's eyes widened, and she nodded, her eyes misting. "Yes, of course, I should have known. You look just like her. Let me fetch the missus."

Clara turned to look at Andrew, her blond eyebrow rising above her eye.

"At least we know we're in the correct place," Patrick said.

"Indeed," Andrew replied and set his arm against the mantle. It wobbled a bit and Andrew removed his arm, worried the whole thing might fall.

A few moments later a gentle looking woman came bustling in, hair loosely tied back in a bun, and more grey hair than there was brown. She was an older woman, but her face was kind and tired. She smiled warmly at them.

"Hello," she said politely and Clara rose from her chair. "I am Mrs. Roberta Willis, the reverend's wife."

"Hello, Mrs. Willis," Clara said and dipped into a slight curtsy. "I am Lady Clara Masson. My brother Lieutenant Patrick Masson. My fiancé, the Duke of Bradstone."

Mrs. Willis, to her credit, did not miss a beat. She curtsied, wincing as though it hurt her joints to do so. "It is a pleasure, your grace. Welcome to Petersfield. My housekeeper tells me you are looking for someone?"

Clara nodded. "Yes, our sister in fact. We were informed she may have resided here?"

The housekeeper came in with a tray of tea, setting it down nervously down on the table, the porcelain clinking.

"Will you take tea?" Mrs. Willis asked.

"That would be lovely," Clara said. Andrew and Patrick declined.

Preparing their tea allowed for Mrs. Willis to gather her thoughts, Andrew realized, watching her hand shake as she poured the heavy pot of tea in an attempt at civility, not looking up at either one until she had finished. After handing Clara her cup, the reverend's wife sat back in her chair and Andrew reassessed his assumptions. The woman looked exhausted, he realized. And she was much older than he had originally guessed, putting her age closer to his grandmother than his aunts'. Her dress was tidy, simple brown for day wear, but it hung heavily on her thin frame.

"I knew your sister, my lady," the reverend's wife said softly and looked down sadly into her tea cup.

"We truly mean her no harm, madam," Clara said. "We only wanted to inquire about her wellbeing."

"I'm afraid that is not possible," Mrs. Willis said. "She has passed on."

Clara set her cup down. "Yes, we were informed. But recently we have learned she did not die when we were told she had."

"Yes, but since then she has, in fact, died."

Clara's brow furrowed, and Andrew could sense her frustration.

"Perhaps if you told us what happened, we might better understand," Patrick suggested.

The older woman nodded, taking another sip of her tea, the cup clattering on the saucer as she replaced it before setting it on the table.

"When we first met Christina, she told us her name was

Tilly," Mrs. Willis began. "That was just over three years ago. As good Christians, we could not in good heart leave her on the street. From what I understand she was trying to get to Portsmouth and from there I have no idea what she planned. We could tell Tilly was a young girl in trouble, so we brought her here and bathed her and it was that night she birthed her daughter. Tilly barely gave us any information about herself and we let her keep her peace, knowing she was running from someone. It was not our place to force her to tell us. She stayed with us for a few months, she and her sweet baby girl, but Tilly never fully recovered from childbirth, physically or mentally. She was sad and broken and there was nothing we could do for her. We prayed, hoping she would find salvation, find purpose and meaning for her life." Mrs. Willis paused and dabbed at her eyes with a handkerchief, sighing as she continued. "Tilly had a difficult time with the rain in the spring and fell ill one day and never recovered from the fever."

"When did she pass?" Andrew asked, handing her his handkerchief as hers was running out of dry corners.

"A year ago, this past March," Mrs. Willis replied. "Seeing you is like seeing her here once again."

"And what of her daughter?" Clara asked. "Do you know where we could find her?"

Mrs. Willis nodded. "She went into town with the reverend. They should return any moment."

Clara sat up straighter. "She's here?"

"Of course she's here," Mrs. Willis said. "We could not bear to send the child away after her mother passed, and we've come to love her as our own. It is just . . ." Mrs. Willis paused again, wringing her hands in Andrew's handkerchief.

"Just what, Mrs. Willis?" Andrew prompted.

The reverend's wife dabbed at her eyes again. "You see, the reverend and I are getting on in years. Sometimes it is difficult to keep up with a three-year-old. She has a tremendous amount of energy." Even as she chastised the young girl her eyes were filled with warmth and adoration. "And this . . . this is not the place for a young girl. We have not the funds to pay for an education, and she's a bright little thing. One of the women in town offered to teach her with her own children, but we worry that will not be enough for the young girl."

Voices rang in through the front window and within moments the reverend was in the drawing room, handing over packages to the housekeeper. Mrs. Willis rose to her feet and introduced them, quickly explaining the reason for their visit.

"We don't often get visitors from outside the parish," the reverend said. "When I saw your carriage, I thought maybe the King had come to call."

"Almost dear, but not quite," Mrs. Willis said. "Now, Reverend, where is Mary?"

The reverend twisted around, looking for the little girl who was hiding behind his legs.

"Come out dear, these fine people have come to see you," Mrs. Willis said.

A petite blonde girl peeked her head around the reverend's legs, and Clara gasped. The little girl's eyes were quick and intelligent and very brown, and she possessed the same rosebud mouth as Clara. Her hair was the same shade of blonde, pulled back from her face in a plait down her back. She glanced back and forth between Andrew, Patrick, and finally Clara, stepping around the reverend and sticking her chin up defiantly. She stared him straight in the eyes, and Andrew could not help but shake his head. She was a miniature spitfire.

"Mary, please meet the Duke of Bradstone," Mrs. Willis said. Chin still in the air, Mary dipped into a quick curtsy. "And this is a Lady Clara and a Mr. Masson. They are relations of yours."

"Hello," the little girl's voice rang out, defiant but clear and sweet. "Have you come to offew me a job?"

"Hello, dear," Patrick said, stooping to the girl's three-year-old height. "My name is Patrick, but I suspect you could call me Uncle Paddy."

"Wobbie says when wich wewations come to see you they've come to offew you a job," Mary explained, her "r's" sounding like "w's." Andrew was enchanted.

"Robbie is the baker's son," Reverend Willis provided. "He has some interesting thoughts on the world."

"No, we've not come to offer you a job," Andrew replied, the idea laughable.

"Why have you come then?" Mary asked.

"We came to see you," Patrick replied.

Clara knelt beside her brother, eye to eye with the young girl. "Hello, my darling," Clara cooed at her. "Your mother was my sister. My name is Clara."

Mary's mouth popped open in surprise. "Like me?" she asked. "My mamma named me Mary-Clare."

"Yes, almost the same," Clara replied, and Andrew could hear the emotion in her voice. Turning, Clara glanced at Andrew, and he gave her a curt nod in agreement, knowing what she was asking. She rose and addressed the reverend and his wife.

"We are grateful to know that my sister's daughter lives," Clara said. "We would like to offer her a home."

"Now just a minute here, missy," the reverend said shaking a finger at Clara, and his wife pulled his arm down.

"Mary, dear, please head to the kitchen and see if Ms. Doggins needs any help with preparing tonight's dinner," Mrs. Willis said, giving the little girl a stern look. Mary nodded and scurried quickly out the room. "Please," Mrs. Willis continued once the door was closed again. "We do not mean any disrespect, but you must understand we've come to love Mary as our own. We are getting older, and some days it feels like she keeps us young. But it would be a relief to us in our ending days to know she is well taken care of."

"She would never want for a thing," Andrew assured her.

"She will be raised as the daughter of a duke, with all the privileges that entails. A proper education, to say the least. You can rest assured she will be loved for always."

"When poor Tilly came to us, we had no idea what that dirty young girl would do to our lives," the reverend said and slumped into the nearest chair. He too looked exhausted. "She was a troubled girl, but I do not regret our decision to help her. She made us promise never to tell the truth. We helped her fool the lord who came looking for her, and we lied for her, knowing we were helping her in the end."

"Was this other lord perchance the Earl of Morton?" Patrick asked.

Reverend Willis nodded. "How did you know?"

"He is our brother," Clara replied.

"Tilly eventually told us her name, and we sent him a letter as she requested and he came down here, pompous and full of air," Reverend Willis said. "We told him Tilly had died in childbirth and her baby with her, but he refused to believe us. Tilly warned us we would have to give proof and sure enough he made us dig up the grave. In it he found the body of a young mother and her baby, obviously not Tilly and Mary, but the bodies of a mother who had died in the area just before Tilly came to us. The earl believed the ruse, which was a miracle because I thought for certain God himself was going to smite us down for our deception. Tilly was so troubled and fearful of someone finding her that we could not refuse her requests. In the end, I stand by my part in this. I would have never allowed that man to take her."

"She and Mary have brought us such joy," Mrs. Willis said, dabbing at her eyes again with Andrew's handkerchief. "It broke our hearts when Tilly passed on. We knew there was a reason Tilly did not want anyone to know about her or Mary, so we kept our peace and maintained her secret. We . . . we were never blessed with children of our own, so it has been such a gift to have Mary here with us."

"We could not in good conscience let her go with just

anyone," the Revered said, glancing at his wife. "And lately it has been on our mind, wondering what will happen to the girl once we pass on. We've prayed on it profusely, and then you two turn up on our doorstep like a gift from the Heavens."

"We are happy to give the girl a home," Clara said gently, handing her handkerchief to the reverend. He accepted and blew his nose loudly before dabbing at his eyes with what Andrew hoped was a clean, dry corner.

"It would be such a relief to know she is cared for," Mrs. Willis added sadly. "It just breaks my heart to give her away, because she is so much more to us than that."

"Why don't you join us at Foley Cottage?" Andrew suggested, realizing that this would be an important transition for the girl and for the parents who had fostered her since her mother's death. "Come be our guests at our home, and you can see where she will live. Spend a few days with Mary there so she can see she is not being sent off to live with distant relatives who will not treat her well. We are only a two-hour ride from here. You can see for yourselves that she will be cherished as you two have cherished her. After, you are welcome to visit as often as you wish as I am sure Mary would like to see you from time to time."

"Your grace, that is awfully kind of you, but completely unnecessary," Mrs. Willis said, a little wistfully.

"I insist," Andrew replied. "It will help put your mind at ease. There is no one else in residence at this time, so you are welcome to stay as long as you like. The future duchess and I unfortunately must return to town on the morrow, but we would feel more comfortable knowing Mary was safe and sound at Foley Cottage." The reverend exchanged a look with his wife and he could see acceptance of his proposal pass between them.

It did not take long for the reverend and his wife to pack for a short stay at Foley Cottage. Andrew went into Petersfield proper and hired a post-chaise for the reverend and his wife as all five of them would not fit into his carriage for two hours.

Andrew watched as Patrick assisted with loading the two traveling trunks onto the post-chaise and Clara came out of the house, handing a small case to the footman before coming to stand beside him. She slipped her gloved hand into his and gave him a light squeeze.

"Thank you," she said softly. "You did not have to do this."

"Of course I did," Andrew replied. "She is obviously your sister's daughter. It is only right she is with her family. But we cannot forget about Morton. He made them unearth a grave, Clara. He blackmailed your maid into poisoning you, threatened a footman to abduct a lady. Don't think he would stop at killing an innocent child."

"Then we will have to protect her," Clara said, turning towards him. "Jonathan will have to walk through fire and hell to get to her."

Andrew saw the determination in her eyes and he nodded. "I just wish we did not have to bring her into this."

"I agree. But we don't have a choice. She's safer at Bradstone House surrounded by servants and Macalisters than she will be here."

"No," Andrew said with a shake of his head. "I will not have her in town, not where Jonathan can catch wind of her existence."

"Then where do you suggest we hide her?" Clara asked, folding her arms across her chest.

"We leave her at Foley Cottage until it is safe to bring her to London," Andrew replied quickly.

Clara nodded, determined. "And what do we tell the *ton*?"

"Once your brother is dealt with, once we have assured her safety, we tell the truth," Andrew answered. "We wanted to find out what happened to Christina all those years ago and we tracked her to the parsonage and found her daughter here. She was born perfectly legally in wedlock. Aside from her parent's elopement there is no scandal to her name."

"With the exception that her father was a footman," Clara added.

"Yes, but she is also half Masson, and she will be raised as the daughter of the Duke of Bradstone."

"You know everyone will take this as evidence of one of those stupid rumors, that I've been in the country to give birth," Clara said.

"Perhaps," Andrew replied. "But like every other rumor we have weathered, we will beat this one down as well. Besides, if need be we will have the reverend reveal the story of how Christina came to them. They must have a grave marker for her somewhere, a real grave marker."

Clara nodded. "I'd like to see it before we leave," she said softly. "I'd like to finally say goodbye to my sister."

Andrew smiled down at his wife. "Of course," he replied.

Mary and Mrs. Willis arrived a moment later. Mary looked hesitant, but she kept a proud look upon her face. Andrew felt the twinges of pride developing deep within him. This tiny little girl had endured so much, having her mother taken from her, expecting to be some wealthy relation's paid companion. He wanted to give her everything she never thought she'd have.

Andrew stood beside the carriage with Mary as Clara and Patrick went with the reverend's wife down the little hill in the direction of the parish cemetery.

"Does this howse have a name?" a little voice asked him and he looked down upon her sweet face.

He stooped down and picked her up, carrying her around the front of the horse.

"Certainly he has a name," Andrew replied, holding Mary in one arm. He looked up at the horse. "Who do we have today? Oh yes, this one is Bentley, and this one is Beauford." The matching bays twitched their ears.

"Those awe not good names for a howse," Mary decided,

hesitantly rubbing her fingertips along the horse's nose. Bentley nuzzled closer to the soft touch and Mary giggled.

"Then what should a horse be named?" he asked.

She thought for a moment before answering, "Peaches."

"Peaches?" he asked. "You wish to name a male horse Peaches?"

"Don't be silly," she said, shaking her head. "Peaches is a perfect name for a giwl howse. You should name a boy howse Gilbewt, if he is a pwoud howse. A sad howse should be named Sadly." Andrew nodded in agreement with her innocent logic and she seemed pleased to have his approval. "How many howses do you have?" she asked.

"Many," he replied quickly doing a mental count because he knew what her next question would be.

"Exactly how many is that?"

"Eighteen, I believe," he replied.

"That is a gweat many howses," she said approvingly.

"Yes, but none are named Peaches, Gilbert, or Sadly."

"You should talk to youw gwoom about that," she said pensively, petting the horse. "Gwooms know a gweat deal about howses. Maybe he can help you pick out a bettew name fow youw howse next time."

Andrew chuckled to himself, but it seemed the Great Horse Inquiry was over. Garnet the coachman hopped down off the carriage perch and offered the bits of carrots he carried for the horses. Andrew nodded his thanks and showed Mary how to feed the horse so he did not nip her fingers off. She held her hand flat with the carrot in the middle of her palm and laughed as Bentley's whiskers tickled her hand.

Mary turned her chubby face to regard him. "Missus Willis says you awe to be my new papa. Is that twue?"

Andrew shifted her in his arms. "Do you want me to be your new papa?"

"I don't know yet," Mary admitted. "That lady looks like my mamma. Is she going to be my new mamma?"

"That is entirely up to you," Andrew replied honestly.

"You are to come live with us, and there will be great many people who will be excited to meet you, when the time is right. We will do our best to take care of you, make sure you have food and dolls and whatever else little girls need." Andrew frowned. *What* did *little girls need?*

"I don't like dolls," Mary replied, her little arms wrapping around his neck. "Can you tell stowies?"

"I'm sure I could figure it out," Andrew replied.

"I can teach you," Mary replied with a grin. Mary looked so much like Clara that it was startling.

"I think I would like that."

Footsteps crunching on the gravel caught his attention and he turned to see Mrs. Willis returning, Clara tucked under her brother's arm. Clara's gaze met Andrew's, warming at the sight of him holding Mary.

"Mary dear, do get off of the duke, for Heaven's sake," Mrs. Willis chided. As if in defiance Mary leaned in closer to him. Andrew wanted to laugh.

"She's not a bother, Mrs. Willis," he assured the reverend's wife. "Are we ready to be off?"

Nodding, Clara smiled at Mrs. Willis before accepting Garnet's assistance into the carriage. Reverend Willis came out of the house and nodded to Andrew before helping Mary and Mrs. Willis into the post-chaise.

Andrew followed Clara and Patrick into their carriage and settled himself onto the rear facing seat. He rapped his knuckles onto the roof, and a moment later the carriage lurched into motion, conveying them back to Foley Cottage.

Gentle reader, the days have been so boringly unbearable. This author can only hope the Duke of B— returns soon, unattached and ready to choose his bride.

Chapter Twenty-Five

With promises to return soon, the following day Andrew and Clara made their return trip to London, mostly in a comfortable silence. Clara read a bit from the books she had packed for the six-hour journey. After an hour of staring out the window, Andrew had grudgingly accepted *Pride and Prejudice* from Clara's books. She was fairly certain he knew she packed it specifically for him.

Clara hadn't said much about the finality of the death of her sister and was thankful Andrew hadn't pressed her for a reaction. She was not sure if she was upset or not. She had lived the past three years thinking her sister was dead, was there any difference now that she was absolutely certain she was? What would she have done if her sister turned out to be alive, rejoice and embrace her? Christina had given herself to let Clara live, that much she understood and appreciated. She was grateful to Christina for her sacrifice, but that sacrifice had given them both Mary, whose full name was Meredith Clara Baker. It brought tears to Clara's eyes to realize her sister had named her daughter for both Clara and their mother Meredith. It was a relief to discover, after all these years, Christina had still cared about her family. After she ran off with the footman, Clara had assumed it was Christina's last vain and selfish act, and it was liberating to know that it was actually an act of selflessness. The trip to the parsonage had been to seek answers, and while it answered the question of whether or not Christina was still alive, it also answered the question that had plagued Clara for five years: had Christina ever really cared about or loved Clara at all? Clara was sorry she had ever doubted her sister and glad she finally knew the truth. She felt as though she could finally let Christina rest in peace.

Their arrival at Bradstone House was uneventful. Luke, Susanna, Sarah, and Patrick—who had been given rooms at Bradstone House—disappeared into the house to ready for that evening's events. Norah and Nick where holed up in Norah's recovery room deep in a game of chess when Clara poked her head in. Throughout the dinner party, Clara smiled as much as she could, but she was exhausted. She was torn, wanting to be near Mary and yet protect her at the same time. It was harder to leave Mary in West Sussex than Clara had imagined, though she knew Mary was in good hands. Andrew's idea to suggest the reverend and his wife stay at Foley Cottage with Mary was ingenious, but Clara knew he regretted leaving Mary as much she did.

But there were things to take care of in London. Andrew needed to finish out the session of Parliament as well as the social season. Clara intended to hire a nurse or governess and many tutors for Mary, and the best place to interview would be in town. There was also the constant threat of Jonathan and what he may do once he found out about Mary. That alone was motivation for Clara to leave Mary safe and sound in the country.

There was also the matter of their wedding.

The morning of the wedding was dreary and grey,

though that was a common occurrence in London, so Clara paid it no mind.

Martha, who had been permanently promoted as her new lady's maid, woke her early, as Clara was set to be at St. George's Church in Hanover Square by eight o'clock.

After a bath, her hair was brushed and set to dry, and Clara managed to consume part of a biscuit and a cup of tea before she was dressed for the occasion. Her wedding gown was the palest of pink silk, a little more elaborate than she might have chosen, but she felt divine. Sarah gifted her a long strand of pearls to wear.

"They are lovely," Clara breathed, looking to Sarah with affection.

"Fit for a duchess," Sarah replied, leaning to her to buss her cheek. "Shall we be off?"

Clara nodded. "In a moment, if you please."

Sarah nodded understandingly. "We will be downstairs. You are to go in the carriage, and Susanna and I are to follow separately."

Once alone, Clara had a moment to think.

She was about to marry Andrew. Of all the scenarios she'd envisioned when she snuck away to the Macalister Birthday Ball, this, while at the highest point of her dream, was not one she would have bet on for herself.

She knew Andrew loved her, which was a feat in itself, though she still doubted whether his affections had any longevity. Was it irrational to want to wait longer?

A soft knock came from the door. It was Martha reminding her she was expected at the church soon.

Descending the stairs, Clara's mind was racing. Not with anticipation or excitement, but dread. Was she about to make a huge mistake? Could she survive being married to a man who she was not certain she could trust?

More prudently, if she left, could she survive her brother on her own?

Sarah and Susanna awaited her in the front foyer, walking with her to the carriage.

"We will see you at the church, dear," Sarah said, closing the carriage door as Clara settled herself into the front facing bench.

"We will see you there, correct?" Susanna asked as Sarah climbed into the second carriage.

With a determined nod, Clara managed a smile. "Yes, I will be there."

Susanna beamed. "Enjoy your last few moments of *not* being a duchess," she said cheekily.

The carriage rolled into motion, and Clara was careful not to rest her head against the back of the bench so not to mess her hair. Martha had spent so much time curling and pinning, it would be a shame to ruin it. But Clara's eyes fluttered closed as the rocking of the carriage lulled her into relaxing, just a fraction. Everything would be fine. She would make certain her life with Andrew would be happy. She would make him happy. Her life over the past month by his side, as his fiancée, had not been miserable. There was no reason to expect her marriage would be anything different.

The carriage came to a stop, and Clara sighed. Time to put on her best smile and step into her new life. At least Andrew would be there.

But as she descended from the carriage, she realized it was all wrong. This was not St. George's Church. She had no idea where this was, in fact.

Little bells of alarm rang in her head, and she looked back and forth and down the street. The street was frightening normal, though it looked vaguely familiar. Dark bricked home fronts with white framed windows and white stones lining the garden levels, all flanked by black iron fencing. Each house was pressed together in a long row, the bricking varying from house to house. Each street stretched out in a square, a garden park in the middle with bright green grass and tall trees.

The door to the house opened and a man stepped outside. For a brief moment, she stood frozen in shock as she recognized the face sneering down at her.

"I wouldn't run, Clara," Jonathan Masson drawled. "You will not get far in that dress. Do come inside. We've so much to discuss."

Looking down again at both ends of the deserted street, Clara realized she was stuck. The carriage was gone. She had no idea where she was. The area looked well-kept, but she'd been in the carriage for a good fifteen minutes. She could be on the other side of the Thames for all she knew.

With the hope that Andrew would be able to find her, retrace her steps or send out Halcourt's dogs, Clara moved up the front steps and through the doorway, leveling a haughty glare at her brother as she moved past him and into the house.

It was long past what was acceptable to be late to your own wedding.

Andrew knew this, not by a readily available timepiece, because there was none, but by the level of whispers and stirrings that went through the amassed crowd. His family was here, his Macalister aunts, uncles, and cousins as well as his mother's Ralston relations. All had come to support, no matter what the outcome.

The remaining congregated guests, roughly a hundred or so at least, were here to see whether the bride or the bride-groom would fail to show.

As Andrew had been standing before the congregation waiting, it was clear he was not favored.

Where on earth is she? Andrew wondered. Luke was missing too, so that was something, as Luke had been tapped with guarding her until she arrived at the church. If Clara was not here, at least Luke was likely with her.

Andrew frowned as his thoughts strayed to worrisome

territory. Were Clara and Luke together somewhere?

Preposterous, Andrew decided, but the feeling of unease did not lift. Something was wrong, he knew it in his bones. Clara should have been there, he believed she would show at the church. He had trusted her, again.

The doors opened, and Patrick stuck his head out, glancing around nervously before coming through the doors and down the aisle towards him.

Something was definitely wrong, and by the look on Patrick's face, *very* wrong.

Hurrying down the aisle, he met the young man halfway.

"What is wrong?" Andrew asked, but Patrick shook his head, leading Andrew back out of the church.

"What has happened?" Andrew asked once they were out of the sanctuary.

"Clara's missing," Patrick said bluntly. "We don't know where she is."

Andrew swore as the blood rushed from his face. "How is that even possible?" Andrew asked. "Susanna said she saw her this morning."

Patrick shook his head. "Their carriages left together, but only one arrived at the church, and that was nearly an hour ago."

Andrew swore rather loudly as he ran a hand through his hair, fear turning his blood cold. She was supposed to be safe, *he* was supposed to keep her safe.

"What are we to do?" Patrick asked, his eyes darting to the room full of friends and family and inauspicious onlookers.

"Give me a moment," Andrew said, knowing what he had to do. He'd done it once before, after all.

Stepping back into the sanctuary, a hush swept over the room. Speaking loudly, his voice carried over the pews, echoing off the walls before hitting him with the truth of the matter.

"I apologize for the delay," Andrew announced. "There

will be no wedding today."

And he turned and fled the room before he was mobbed by, well, everyone.

Andrew ducked into the carriage outside the church doors, the one set to deliver him and Clara to their wedding breakfast, but it seemed that was not to happen now.

Clara was missing. She's either been delayed by something, or worse, run off.

As soon as the carriage stopped before Bradstone House, Andrew had the carriage door open, jumping down from the footstep and hurrying into the house. Howards opened the door before Andrew got to the front stoop.

"Is Luke here?" Andrew shouted to his butler as he yanked his gloves off, tossing them and his hat angrily to his valet who came rushing into the hall to retrieve them.

"No, your grace," Howards replied and Andrew cursed under his breath. "He has not been seen for at least an hour."

"I saw him here at that time," Bexley said, coming in the door after him, with Connolly and Halcourt. "Just before we left with you for the church."

"I've sent word of her disappearance," Halcourt said, cutting Andrew off with reassurances that he'd done it discreetly.

"I don't need any more scandal," Andrew said warily. "Clara does not need more scandal."

Susanna and Sarah arrived just then, Norah a few footsteps behind them.

"She was in the carriage," Susanna told Andrew before he would even ask. "She said she was going to the church. I believed her, Andrew. Something has happened. She would not leave you like this."

Wouldn't she? Andrew wondered, chastising himself for even thinking it. It was what she planned to do all along.

"She did not return, did she?" Sarah asked Howards and the butler shook his head.

"No, my lady," Howards insisted. "Lady Clara left the house with you. Both carriages left the house, though one returned."

"The carriage carrying Lady Clara, you say it has returned?" Halcourt asked, turning towards the butler.

Howards nodded.

"Allow me to check over the carriage, your grace," Halcourt said, but did not stop for permission.

Andrew strode towards his study, his sisters and friends following, shooting worried glances between each other.

"Redley is out looking for Luke and Clara," Bexley said as they came into the study. No one sat or went for brandy or really knew what to say or do.

Andrew paced the length of the room like a caged lion.

What if she'd actually left him? Would she have left a note? Taken things with her? Or simply disappeared into the dreary London day, never to be heard of again?

His heart clenched at the thought of losing her, of the idea she might have abandoned him and he sank into a plush leather chair.

I trusted her!

"Your grace," came Halcourt's voice as he entered the room, rather hurriedly. As Andrew looked up at one of his oldest friends, he saw a white paper, folded with a wax seal, pinched between Halcourt's fingers. He was offering him the letter.

"This was on the carriage seat," Halcourt replied. "Along with a coachman stuffed into the boot. Alive but concussed."

Andrew snatched the letter, a shred of hope rushing through him. She wouldn't leave without giving explanation.

But as he read through the lines on the paper, the tiny scrawl written was not Clara's elegant loopy handwriting, but someone else's.

"He's taken her," Andrew said quietly, his voice wracked with fear. "Morton, he says he has Clara. I am to pay him five thousand pounds if I want her returned."

"Oh goodness," Sarah said as Susanna gasped. "That is a great deal of money."

"I will pay it," Andrew stated, refolding the letter but Halcourt pulled it from his hands. "A horse, I need a horse. The banks will be open, will he take a bank note you think?"

He went to hurry from the room, his mind refocused on something productive. He knew where Clara was, or at least he knew what had happened. She hadn't run off on him, she'd been abducted. In Andrew's delirious state of mind, that was much better.

Halcourt saw reason and stopped Andrew in his tracks, planted his hands on Andrew's chest and gave him a shove.

"Halcourt, unhand me!" Andrew snapped.

"Your grace, you need to listen to reason here," Halcourt insisted. "This is not the way to go about this."

"He has asked for money, I shall give it to him," Andrew replied, attempting to step around Halcourt but Bexley walked into his path.

"Not like this, Andrew," Bexley said, shaking his head.

"He has Clara," Andrew insisted, glancing between his friends. "What is so complicated about this?"

Sarah stepped into his way next, each one of them making a barrier between him and the door.

"This is Clara we are talking about," Andrew pleaded. "None of you understand, I cannot lose her." He could not lose someone again.

Sarah set a hand on his arm gently. "Andrew, we have all come to love Clara as one of our own. Do not think we do not want her safely returned. But Lord Halcourt is correct. Paying this ridiculous ransom is not the way."

"I would drain every penny to have her back," Andrew replied. "How can you all not see this?"

"We know, Andrew," Susanna said.

"I bet Morton knows it too," Bexley added.

Andrew sank into the chair below him, running his hands through his hair. Damnation, they were all right. If he paid Morton off this time, who was to say he would not come back for another payment? He would not be blackmailed into saving the woman he loved. There had to be a smarter way to go about this.

"What do you suggest?" Andrew asked, his gaze falling on Halcourt.

The door opened just then, and Luke came bursting through the door, panting as if he had run the entire way.

"Luke!" Andrew shouted.

Luke launched into an explanation before Andrew could say another word. "I barely had my eyes off her for a second, Andrew. The carriage with Sarah and Susanna turned, and I did not realize the carriages had been separated until a few blocks had passed. I retraced our path but there was no sign of the carriage."

"I trusted you!" Andrew bellowed at him, glaring. "I trusted you to keep her safe! You were supposed to watch her, and she was abducted! By Morton!"

"We will get her back," Sarah was saying to him.

"I will send for the Runners," Halcourt interjected. "And Lord Kensburg is searching the streets as well."

"What about the friend of yours, the one who helped with the footman?" Andrew asked.

"He's left town, I am afraid," Halcourt replied, pulling on his gloves. "More's the pity, missing fiancées with ransom demands are sort of a hobby of his. I will return within the hour." Halcourt bowed and quickly left the room.

But within the hour there was knocking on the front door and it was not Halcourt, and it certainly was not Clara magically reappeared.

Howards strode hesitantly into the study. "Lady Radcliff, there are some ladies inquiring after Lady Clara. I've put them in the lilac drawing room. Should I send them away?"

Sarah exchanged a glance Susanna before they both rose.

"No, Howards, we will deal with them," Sarah said.

"Make something up, Sarah," Andrew wanted.

"I intended to," Sarah replied.

"The nerve of those harpies, coming to inquire after

Clara after she failed to show at the church," Susanna clucked as they wove their way through the furniture in the study.

"I'm coming too," Norah said rising from her seat. Sarah and Susanna glanced at her in surprise.

Norah's nose lifted in defiance. "Despite what you might think, I do not hate Lady Clara. And she is to be my sister. At the very least, I can run interference where the nosy society ladies are concerned."

"Thank you, Norah," Andrew said. Norah managed a weak smile, still not fully recovered from her poisoning ten days earlier. Her complexion was pale and she seemed exhausted, but she was on her feet. That was saying something.

The morning hours turned towards the afternoon as the grandfather clock chimed twelve times for noon. A tray of sandwiches was sent in for the various occupants coming and going. Halcourt had returned with a stack of papers: everything he had on Morton, he informed. Andrew and Bexley began reading and sorting, trying to find a clue as to where Morton would have taken Clara.

Luke and Redley were in and out, snagging tea and sandwiches as they passed through the doors, both leaving to deal with Halcourt's seedier contacts in the less polite parts of London.

Watching Luke converse with Halcourt before exiting the room, Redley at his heels, Andrew realized something.

"Luke works for you," Andrew said to Halcourt.

His friend did not look up at him. "I do not know what you are talking about."

"Be serious, Halcourt," Andrew said. When Halcourt refused to look at him, Andrew shook his shoulder. "Jeremiah, you cannot lie to me about this. Does my brother work for you?"

Halcourt's head snapped up, his gaze meeting Andrew's. "I do not know what you are talking about," he repeated with a nod, before looking down again at the papers.

Andrew swore under his breath but knew it was not the time to dwell on Luke's nefarious activities with Halcourt. One problem at a time.

Noon turned to one, then to two, then three o'clock in the afternoon chimed in the hall. A constant stream of women were in and out of the first floor drawing rooms, nosy and eager for information about Clara. So far, as best Andrew could tell, her abduction was not known throughout the *ton*, but her absences had been noted. Not only at the church earlier in the day, but now when she failed to appear. Some were calling her cowardly. Some assumed she'd already taken off out of town.

"Most of the gossip focuses on cold feet," Sarah informed him, taking a momentary break from fending off the gossiping hordes. "Since you have not run off towards Scotland in pursuit, people have surmised she did not toss you over for someone else. Though that is the most preferred explanation."

"Thank you, Sarah," Andrew said. "For handling that aspect of this."

Sarah shrugged. "It is no bother. I'd rather the *ton* had the facts straight this time instead of spinning stories to fit their own narrative."

"And what have you told them?"

"That Clara was simply ill," Sarah replied. "Norah was ill last week, so we've told everyone Clara unfortunately has caught the same malady but should recover soon. And is most eager to marry you once she is well."

Andrew nodded and looked away from his sister.

Sarah stepped closer, squeezing his hand. "She is eager to marry you, Andrew. Just you wait and see."

Andrew felt helpless. He had failed miserably, unable to keep her safe from her brother after all. And now, he was unable to do anything to help. Halcourt insisted he remain at Bradstone House in the event another note were to arrive, changing the demands.

Patrick arrived just after four in the afternoon, having done a search of Morton House in Mayfair, and also riding out to a closer estate, both to no avail.

Patrick had joined them perusing through the quantity of information Halcourt had amassed on Jonathan Masson. Titled deeds, bank ledgers, details of acquaintances; Andrew shuddered to think how Halcourt had been privy to these details.

"I say, this sounds familiar," Patrick said, pulling a leaf of parchment out of a file. "This name here, I recognize it. Fredrick Meyers; he was a friend of Jonathan's I believe."

Halcourt was looking over his shoulder. "Yes, that is why it is on the list titled 'Acquaintances.'"

"No, I remember it from somewhere else," Patrick said, his lips dipping into a deep frown, his brows pinched together. "There was a house deed I saw once, years ago. I was leaving for sea and went looking for something in Jonathan's office and came across the deed to a house in Grosvenor Square. This man's name was on the title, I remember because I had a childhood friend named Stewart Meyers so it stuck with me."

The story stuck out to Andrew, as it had a similar ring to a story Clara had told him, about correspondence she had noticed with the same name.

"Morton has a house titled in this man's name?" Halcourt asked, pointing at the name on the paper and Patrick nodded.

"It was a deed and a letter detailing the funds to be released for the house," Patrick explained. "I asked Jonathan about it, and he was furious I'd seen it. Luckily I was leaving the following day.

"He hasn't any property on Grosvenor square," Halcourt said, frowning at the stack of papers and folders, reaching for the one containing a list of property deeds.

"I think it was the house he had for his mistress," Patrick

said, and Halcourt nodded.

"It would make sense for him to hole up nearby," Halcourt replied. "Familiar territory and access to the toll roads out of town."

"And the docks," Patrick added.

"Yes, but we cannot just tear down every house on Grosvenor Square," Andrew said shaking his head, running his hand through his hair in frustration.

"We'll have to stake out the entire square," Halcourt said, glancing at Luke and Redley who had come in part way through Patrick's story.

"Luckily, it is not too large an area," Luke added.

Redley nodded in agreement.

"Then we start at Grosvenor Square," Andrew concluded. "House by house if we must."

"I remember the number from the deed," Patrick interjected.

Andrew, Bexley, Luke, and Redley all turned to look at him. Patrick swallowed hard and blinked as he looked at their astonished and annoyed expressions.

"Number fifteen," he supplied with a shrug.

Andrew went straight to the gun safe beside his decanters of brandy and port. He handed a pistol to Bexley who began slipping bullets into the chamber. Redley shook his head "no," and Luke passed on the pistol as well, claiming he was already armed. This would have been more surprising to Andrew had his mind not been focused on rescuing his fiancée. He loaded his own pistol, snapping the chamber into place.

"Stay here, Patrick," Andrew said to the younger man, who squared his shoulders to argue, but Andrew raised his hand to cut the young man off. "No, I want you out of this. Clara does not need any more tragedy in her life, and to have you involved only augments the destruction Morton has caused."

"Take my horse, at the very least," Patrick insisted.

Andrew nodded to him as they hurried out of the study. Outside, the horses were waiting in the drive, saddled and ready to go. Luke gracefully leapt onto Homer, Redley and Bexley mounting their respective horses. The groom handed Andrew the reins to Patrick's horse and he launched himself into the saddle. Andrew tried not to think of what Clara could be going through. He just wanted her safe in his arms. If he had to kill Jonathan Masson to accomplish that, then so be it.

"Stick around," Andrew said to Patrick as he gained control of the horse, turning him around towards the open gates. "Morton might not make it out of this one alive and you may be the earl before the day is out."

Patrick nodded, a stunned expression racing across his face. Andrew turned the horse and hurried after Bexley, Luke, and Redley.

Chapter Twenty-Six

$\mathcal{C}$lara stood calmly in a ground floor sitting room, watching as her brother paced impatiently across the room, glancing out the curtained windows each time he passed. She carefully surveyed the room, noting the furnishing still covered in white Holland covers. Bright sunlight streamed in through the open window, the bits of dust glinting in the light as Jonathan's movement about the room disturbed the peace that had once resided here. A large ball of twine sat on the table with a knife.

Her calm demeanor hid the fear racing just beneath the surface. She focused on maintaining the evenness of her breathing, keeping the tears from her eyes. She would not let him know how terrified she was.

"I am expected somewhere," she informed, her chin tilting up. Jonathan turned to glare at her, his eyes dark and cruel. He looked a little haggard, his clothes casual and wrinkled like they had been slept in. He hadn't shaved, and his dark hair was falling in his face. But his sneer, a look of pure hated, sent shivers through her.

"Yes, I know just where you are expected," he replied. "Ran off to be Bradstone's whore after all?"

Clara's jaw clenched so tightly she feared her teeth might crack.

"I had hoped to find you dead by now," he said, continuing his pacing. "But I must say this is a much more enjoyable outcome."

"How did I get here?" she asked.

"In a carriage, my dear," he replied flippantly, not looking at her. "Has your time with the duke really addled you that much?"

"How did you convince Bradstone's coachman to drive me here?" she asked, seething.

"Oh I did not," he replied. "Knocked the man out and drove you here myself. No one really looks at the servants, you know. You were certainly too caught up in your nuptials to look twice at me."

Clara frowned. Hopefully Andrew would realize she had not run off.

The idea that she was still in London was comforting. Just like Jonathan to have an evil plan, yet be stupid about it. Did he not know that Andrew would not stop until she was found, even if he had to tear through every house and building in all of London?

Clara's heart sank just a little knowing that was not possible. They hadn't been able to find Jonathan the entire time he had been back in town, what made her think they would find her now?

Clara fought the tears that threatened to spill over. No matter what, she would not give her brother that satisfaction.

"If you are going to kill me, could you simply get on with it?" Clara asked. "This cat and mouse game you've been playing is growing awfully tedious."

Jonathan frowned at her. "I've not been playing any games."

"Yes you have," Clara replied. "Having Andrew shot at, the attempted poisoning. Both failed, you know."

"Those were not attempts to kill you, sister dear," Jonathan sneered. "Merely reminders, that despite what Bradstone thinks, you are not safe with him. You shall never be safe anywhere. That was all merely a build up to encourage you to cooperate."

He came towards her then and Clara quickly scrambled away.

"For Christ's sake, Clara, I'm not going to kill you," he said, binding her hands behind her back with a long strip of twine.

"Your prior behavior suggests otherwise," she argued, struggling against him. Even though he had lost a stone in weight, he was still stronger than her. "You want me dead so you can inherit mother's Patterson money." The twine was wrapped tightly around her wrists as she fought to get free.

"How do you know about that?" he asked, shoving her roughly into a sheet-covered chair.

"It does not matter how I know about it," she spat at him. "Because it will not work. You will not inherit the funds."

"Don't worry about me killing you," Jonathan replied. "Believe me, for my plan, I need you very much alive."

Hauling her to her feet, he practically dragged her from the room and up the flight of stairs, stopping at a bedchamber down a long hallway.

"I am simply going to make sure Bradstone regrets ever looking your direction," Jonathan replied, leering at her. "I am going to make sure you two are miserable together."

Before Clara could wonder what he meant, he had the door opened and she was tossed roughly to the floor.

All the air rushed out of Clara as she gasped to regain the breath that had been knocked from her.

"When he comes for you, and he will come, I have no doubt, he will pay handsomely," Jonathan snapped, bending down to her. He yanked her head back again, leaning in close so she could feel his breath on her neck.

"He will rue the day he thought to cross me," Jonathan whispered harshly in her ear. "Filthy upstarts, the pair of you. Just wait until he takes his lusts somewhere else when he cannot bear the sight of you."

With that he threw her back onto the floor, her head hitting the hardwood, and stomped out of the room.

Black spots appeared in her vision and she struggled to stay conscious. Andrew was coming for her. It was the only comforting thought she had.

Clara did not know how long she lay there, crying onto the hardwood floor. A pounding lower in the house startled her and she snapped her eyes open. She heard it again and sat up, wondering if there was someone else locked in this house with her.

"Morton!" she heard Andrew's muffled voice from below and her heart leapt into her throat. He had found her. Somehow, some miracle had occurred and Andrew had found her.

Clara pulled herself to her feet and glanced wildly about the room, looking for something to help her escape. It was a fairly sparse room with very little furniture—a wash basin with a framed mirror and a nightstand with a chipped vase standing beside a four poster bed. She did not know if there was anyone guarding her door. She pressed her ear against the door listening for some sound but heard none. Her hands were still bound behind her back so she needed to rectify that in order to leave the room.

She closed her eyes and thought, forcing herself to calm down. Andrew was here, he was going to have Jonathan arrested and she would be free. Assuming, that is, if her brother did not kill him first. Even though Jonathan had said he did not want either of them dead, she did not dare believe him.

She sat on the floor, thankful that her wedding dress was more loose fitting. Her hands were bound, but not too horribly tight, and she was able to lie on her back and pull her arms down under her bottom, pulling her arms and hands over her legs. At least with her hands in front of her she could use them, even if there was no way for her to unbind them in the room.

She tried the knob cautiously and slowly, careful not to make a sound, but it was locked, from the outside it would seem, as she saw no sign of a key. She looked back over the room, searching for some sort of weapon, something she could break the door with.

Taking in the contents of the room, she figured only the chamber pot tucked under the bed and the vase were heavy enough to do any damage, and even then, there was no guarantee. She lifted the thankfully clean chamber pot to the door and set the vase beside it.

Maybe, if she could free her hands, she could find a way out of the room. Break down the door with the chamber pot or damage the knob with the vase. If she made enough noise, perhaps Jonathan would come and investigate, and she could knock him out. Perhaps someone would find her.

She took a deep breath, ignoring the pains her head was causing her. Full of determination, she heaved the chamber pot into the air and threw it at the vanity mirror, the glass panes shattering loudly in the still silence.

Andrew lifted the heavy knocker on 15 Grosvenor Square and slammed it down. It had taken him much longer to arrive than he had wanted, having met up with the Bow Street Runners as they left Bradstone House.

"Best to be prepared," Halcourt had iterated and Andrew had grudgingly realized the wisdom in his friend's words.

He pounded again on the massive wooden door, though he was not exactly expecting a butler to appear to whom he would present a calling card. He fought the urge to glance to his left and right where he knew Luke and Redley were waiting to go in after him. Once Jonathan was distracted, his brother and cousin would go in to find Clara. Bexley and Halcourt stood across the street, two Bow Street Runners in the back of the house and Connolly was on horseback, ready to pursue if Morton attempted to escape on horse.

Andrew huffed and impatiently tried the door knob and was surprised when it turned and the door opened with a soft click. Not wasting time, he pushed open the door and went inside.

"Morton!" Andrew bellowed, his voice echoing off the sparse front foyer.

"Ah, your grace!" Morton said, stepping into the hall, grinning at him in a slightly mad way. "I've been expecting you! Please will you not join me for a drink?"

Andrew's eyes narrowed at the earl's wild tone, charging at him, gathering the front of Morton's shirt into his fist.

"Where is Clara?" Andrew demanded.

"If you will release me, I would be happy to tell you," Morton replied, his brows rising. "If we can remain like this. I am quite content either way." Morton's gaze dropped to Andrew's mouth.

With a snarl, Andrew released him, tossing him away.

Morton laughed and straightened his cravat. "Now, let us have that drink, and I will detail how you can buy back your fiancée."

Glaring at Morton's retreating back, Andrew followed him into the study. He would play Morton's game, for a few more moments, if only to allow Luke and Redley to find Clara. Then he would beat Morton to a pulp.

Morton had stepped to a sideboard, one of the few things not draped with white sheets. Pouring a drink, he offered one to Andrew.

Andrew shook his head in refusal and surveyed the earl's ragged look, like he had been on the run for quite some time. He was in need of a bath and a shave and possibly a meal.

"Where is she?" Andrew asked.

"Oh, she is quite safe," Morton replied.

"That did not answer my question," Andrew said, his irritation starting to boil again. "Where is my fiancée?"

"Funny that," Morton said jovially. "I don't seem to remember giving you permission to marry her."

"I don't need your permission," Andrew replied.

"I am her guardian," Morton said, taking a sip of his drink. "I only interfered today out of friendly concern. I'd hate for you to regret marrying the chit. She's rather damaged goods, you know. Been away in Italy. Or was it Prussia? I cannot keep the details straight."

"What is it you want?" Andrew asked impatiently.

"Growing desperate now?" Morton asked, setting his glass down and standing up. "Like maybe your ability to keep her safe isn't as reliable as you had thought? I was able to get to her when she was sequestered in your household. One threat to a maid was all it took. And she proved quite easy to abduct this morning. Apparently your competency should be reexamined."

"What do you want?" Andrew asked again, trying his best to keep him distracted, giving his kin time to search the house. She was here somewhere, he knew it.

"Do you feel helpless? Powerless? Responsible, even? Like you might have felt twelve years ago when your poor brother and father met such a similar fate? It would be such a shame if dear Clara were to wind up on the side of some road left for dead. I cannot imagine you want that kind of scandal attached to your name, again. It would be such a tragedy for you to lose another family member."

There was a crash from somewhere inside the house and Andrew turned in the direction, hopeful.

"Ah, don't mind that," Morton said, shrugging. "You

never know what the servants will be up to."

"I have not seen any servants yet," Andrew replied, antic-ipation racing through him. Had that been Clara? Was she hurt? Was she fighting? He desperately needed to see her, to know she was safe, even if meant he had to tear Morton and this house apart.

"Yes, that is the beauty of servants," Morton said, strid-ing lazily across the carpet. "You don't see them until you need them. Like when I needed that footman to run off with your former fiancée. That was a convenience."

"What do you want from me?" Andrew asked.

"Funny you should word your query that way," the earl drawled. "As a matter of fact, there is something I want from you."

"Five thousand pounds," Andrew answered. "I've a bank note here, if you'd like your money."

"Price has gone up," Jonathan said. "Twenty thousand pounds."

Andrew did not flinch. "Done."

Morton did. "Really? You'd hand over *twenty thousand pounds* sterling for the return of your little bride-to-be. Interesting."

"Now where is she?"

"*She* is right here," Clara's voice said, and he spun around to see her standing in the doorway with Luke behind her. Her hair was messed and her wrists were red, but she looked well enough. She smiled at him, and he closed the distance between them, pulling her into his arms.

"Lovely, now we can have a proper negotiation," Morton said, a mad grin spreading across his face. "I am a very patient man, but now that I know your weakness, you will not be able to sleep well until you pay up. Once I've bled you dry, then I think I will have Clara killed. The Patterson funds, don't forget."

"No," Clara said looking at her brother. "Andrew is not paying you a shilling."

"Then you will never be truly safe," he countered.

"I don't care," she spat at him. "He is not paying you a pound. And you will never get your hands on the Patterson gold. You are missing one key point in this grand scheme of yours. You have failed to locate and eliminate all the remaining heirs."

"I dealt with your twin easily enough," Jonathan snarled at her. "Patrick can easily die at sea. And I will deal with you all the same. Once you are dead and gone, it will be mine. And like I said, I am a very patient man. You could just turn it over to me. That could work too. Though I doubt it would stop the blackmailing."

"I'm not the remaining heir," Clara stated and Jonathan eyed her dubiously, as if she had just told him she was the King of England. At least he thought her as mad. "You did not check your facts as well as you thought. When Christina died, she left behind a child, a *female* child."

"It is not true," Jonathan said, his voice low, his eyes black with hatred. "Christina died without issue. That child died with her."

Clara shook her head. "Her last act was to fool you. I've seen Christina's daughter, and there is no doubt. But you will never get your hands on her. She is so well hidden that you would have to burn England to the ground to find her."

"Tell me where she is!" Morton shouted but Clara stood her ground. Anger raced across Morton's face, his hands trembling.

"Why Jonathan?" Clara asked. "Why do you hate me so?"

Morton's jaw clenched. "I hate you because you always had Bradstone's eye, when I so desperately wanted him to look at me the way he always looked at you."

Clara's eyes grew wide and Andrew realized the meaning behind Morton's words a heartbeat later.

Morton turned to him, glaring. "I loved you," he stated, his voice just above a whisper. "And you only ever had eyes for her. Before you inherited, I thought . . . I thought maybe . . . as a second son, you wouldn't have had any responsibilities, you would be my friend, and maybe you wouldn't care that I loved you. But then you became the duke." Turning his gaze to Clara he continued, "And your face only reminded me of what I had lost. And I hated you for it. And I hated Christina because she looked like you. Now I will take everything from you, like you did to me."

"Jonathan," Andrew said, but stopped when he realized his old friend had tears streaming down his face. "Then, I would have still been your friend, even if I did not have the same feelings as you. But now . . ." Andrew's face hardened as he glared down his former friend. "You've let this hate consume you. Your reasons have become irrelevant, as your actions have far surpassed anything rational. You will be tried for the abduction of my fiancée, the attempted murder of myself and of my sister who was poisoned at your command. You cannot hate me for not reciprocating your feelings. You cannot hate me for falling in love with your sister."

Andrew smiled down at Clara, love and pride flowing through him. But he did not see what Morton was doing until it was too late. A brutal roar ripped out of the earl and he pulled a pistol out of his coat, took aim and a loud gunshot rang throughout the room. Instinctively Andrew threw himself over Clara, pulling them both to the ground, but he knew he was too late.

"Clara, Clara, please be unhurt," Andrew said frantically searching her clothing, and Clara blinked her eyes open. She looked around frantically and her gaze landed on Jonathan's crumpled body. Andrew looked to see what she saw, noting Luke's reflection in one mirror, and Redley standing in an opposite doorway, both holding smoking pistols.

"Andrew, I'm fine," Clara said, choking on a sob. "I have not been shot."

He gathered her to him, holding her tightly against him, grateful for those five words. She buried her face into his neck, hot tears soaking through his neck cloth.

"You don't need to see this, Clara," Andrew said, when she turned her head to observe her brother's crumpled dead form.

"It is all right, Andrew," she said. "I need to see that it is finally over." Leaning away from her, he searched her eyes before nodding and helping her to rise to her feet. She moved closer to Morton, looking sadly onto the face of the brother who hated her so much. His eyes were glossed over in death, a permanent scowl on his face and two bullet holes, one in his forehead and one in his chest.

She turned away and sought comfort in Andrew's arms, which he graciously offered. Luke and Redley were moving into the room, the sound of the footfalls soft on the worn carpet.

"Thank you," he said to Luke and then to Redley. Each one nodded before looking away.

"We will handle this, Andrew," Luke assured him, looking down at Morton's bleeding corpse.

"Let me get you home," Andrew said softly in her ear, and Clara agreed.

Chapter Twenty-Seven

Gentle reader, is today the day? After failing to attend her own wedding the first time, it seems the Duke of B— is willing to give Lady C— another try. One is only left to wonder at his motives, but after all this time, might the Duke of B—have fallen in love with his scandalous bride-to-be? Will Lady C— show at the wedding this time after a bout with a mysterious illness? Or will she jilt him once and for all?

Clara stood outside the doors to St. George's Church, just steps from the doors that would lead her down the aisle to Andrew.

"Patrick," Clara said, her voice wavering. "Am I making the right decision? Andrew loves me, does he not? He will not come to regret this?"

Patrick's eyes practically rolled to the ceiling. "For goodness' sake, Clara, are you still worrying about this?"

Clara glanced at her brother guiltily.

"You've been silly for that man since you were a child," Patrick reminded her. "I was there, I remember. And as much as he came to Morton Park to holiday with Jonathan, his attentions often wandered to you."

"I was a child," Clara scoffed. "He was a sixteen-year-old lord when I was a ten-year-old in braids, running after him like a silly little girl."

"Why are you so quick to deny his love for you?" Patrick asked.

"Because no one else in my life has ever loved me!" Clara whispered furiously. "Father hated me, Jonathan hated me. Christina, for her faults and misguided attempts to protect me still ran off and left me alone. And you, Patrick, you left as well. I don't disparage you for it, I am happy you were away from our brother's hatred, but I was still alone."

"Are you alone now?" Patrick asked.

"No," she whispered.

"His grace has done nothing but champion you since you reconnected last month, correct?"

Clara nodded. "Even after I told him I intended to leave him, he still did not waver."

"He accepted guardianship of Mary, the daughter of the woman who jilted him," Patrick reminded her. "That takes a lot of love and faith to do for someone. He did not do it for Mary, and he did not do it for Christina."

Clara nodded, her eyes filling with tears.

"And when you had disappeared, he was frantic," Patrick continued. "He was ready to give away his entire fortune to have you safely returned. I'd never seen someone so pale and full of worry. Don't you think that should tell you something?"

"Yes," Clara replied with a laugh. "That he loves me."

"Clare-bear, that man loves you in such a way it makes the rest of us wary of being in the same vicinity for fear whatever he is afflicted with might seep out onto us."

Clara laughed lightly again. "I've been a fool, have I not?"

"The biggest," Patrick assured her with a smirk. "But you have time to remedy that. Shall we go into the church? I believe they are waiting for us. *Again*."

Clara glanced at the heavy arched doorway, knowing the rest of her life lay beyond that door. Her gateway to happiness.

"Go and get him, Paddy," Clara asked. "I wish to speak to him first."

Patrick watched her face for a moment before nodding. "Stay here," he instructed. "I'll not have this happen again."

It was like being in a repetitive form of hell, Andrew realized. How many times had he stood up, waiting for a Masson sister to appear at the church doorway?

The murmurs were traveling through the congregation again, wondering where the bride could possibly be. It was a scene he'd lived much too often.

Luke stood beside him, discreetly checking his watch fob. At Andrew's dark glare, Luke quickly slipped it back into his pocket.

There were more people this time, Andrew realized, his eyes moving past the first five or so pews filled with his friends and family, but the remainder of the church had filled nearly to the brim with onlookers and gossipmongers expecting a grand show. Expecting Andrew to be stood up, for the third time.

The door creaked open and a stillness went through the room as each body turned towards the door. Andrew's eyes snapped to the doorway, eager to see his bride, to marry Clara after everything they'd been through.

But it was Patrick who walked down the aisle towards him, rather quickly, and Andrew's stomach dropped.

Again? Could this possible be happening again?

"Pardon the interruption, you grace," Patrick said, leaning close to Andrew to keep his voice from being overheard. "But you are needed outside."

"Where is Clara?" Andrew ground out.

Patrick swallowed. "Please, your grace, come with me."

With a deep sigh, Andrew followed Clara's brother out of the sanctuary.

"I'm sure this cannot be happening again," Luke said loudly to the congregated guests and a tentative laughter carried Andrew through the doors.

Clara was there, beautiful in her pale yellow wedding gown, a different gown than she had previously worn to their wedding. She did not look happy.

"Andrew!" she said, her face brightening when her eyes landed on him.

"I will leave you two alone for a moment," Patrick said before ducking out of the room.

"Clara, what are we doing?" Andrew asked. "You were supposed to be down the aisle nearly half an hour ago."

"Yes, yes, I know," Clara said, wringing her hands together. "And I'm terribly sorry for that. I can only imagine what you must be thinking up there, waiting for me."

"Again," Andrew reminded her. "From Christina leaving with my footman and you being abducted, yes, my mind is racing to every possibly dreadful outcome. But you are here, so why are we not in there? Is everything all right?"

Clara's face softened, reaching out for his hand. "Yes, actually, everything is wonderful."

"Then why—"

"I love you, Andrew," she said with a soft smile.

"Yes, darling, I love you too," Andrew replied. "Now can we—"

"I am sorry for denying your love for me," she continued. "Before we married, I wanted you to know I was doing it for me, I was choosing to be your wife for nothing other than my love for you. Not because I have no other options or because I am in need of protection, but because I want to be with you for the rest of our days."

"Is that all?" he asked, stepping closer to her, tracing a finger along her jaw.

"I've been in love with you since I was a child," Clara told him, her voice soft. "What started as an infatuation, impish kisses and declarations of a silly girl, manifested into something deeper over the years. Despite the setback when you almost married my sister, I am here now and I love you still."

"My darling," Andrew said, cupping his hands around her face and kissing the tip of her nose. "I am so devastatingly in love with you I hardly know how to breathe. It seems illogical my feelings for you could be this deep after a near month's acquaintance, but I suspect my attachment to you goes back years, since you sat atop my horse, grass and pond weeds in your hair and proclaimed you would marry me someday." He set his lips against hers, gentle, but with a promise Clara knew he would not break. "Had our lives not been derailed by the external forces pulling us apart, I suspect I would have returned to Morton Park each summer, not to spend time with your brother, but to see you. I would have courted you properly, and someday I would have married you. Despite the path our story took, this is the ending that was intended all along. Today is that someday, darling. Together, we will determine what happens next, a life of our making."

Clara nodded. "That sounds lovely."

"Now, may we be married?" Andrew asked. "I believe we've waited long enough."

Andrew felt a strange sense of déjà vu as Clara walked down the aisle towards him. Five years ago she had hurried down this aisle towards Andrew, careful not to stumble as she came to deliver the news of her sister's elopement. So much had changed since that day, and he was grateful for it all. He met her gaze as he watched her progress down the aisle, adoration radiating from his bright blue eyes.

Clara squeezed her brother's arm, and Andrew was thankful for Patrick's steady presence at her side, as she looked like she was nearly skipping down the aisle. If only Norah would have let her wear a crown of rose buds in her hair . . .

Three hundred of their closest friends and relations had decided to attend their nuptials, which was strange by society standards. Andrew heard later there was a hefty wager on whether or not Clara would show this time, and he might have overheard Patrick boasting of his winnings later in the day. Clara beamed at Andrew as they repeated the same words countless couples had done before them, and he smiled back in complete devotion. When the priest gave the instruction, Andrew took a step towards her, tipping her chin up and placed a firm kiss on her lips, lingering a moment longer than necessary. He pulled away, a broad grin spread across his face, his blue eyes twinkling with the hint of mischief she had a talent for pulling out of him.

A loud cheer went up in the church as the new Duke and Duchess of Bradstone stood grinning at each other, their eyes melting into a shared heat, and the priest had to nudge Andrew, reminding him to sign the register.

Andrew led her down the aisle, not bothering to wipe the lopsided grin off his face. Clara grinned from ear to ear, and he knew they looked the quintessential love match, but he did not mind.

They were, finally, here together in the end.

They ran through the shower of rice, laughing and holding hands as he lifted her inside the formal ducal carriage, the brilliant Bradstone coat of arms emblazoned on the side.

Andrew's bright grin did not falter as the carriage rolled into motion, completely and utterly in love with her, and Clara grinned in return, her feelings reflected in his heart. The carriage rolled through the streets of Mayfair, carrying them towards their happily ever after.

And oh, what an adventure it would be.

Acknowledgments

Thank you . . .

Mom, for giving the best advice, even bits about handbags and shoes.

Brittany, Kelly, and other medical professionals who I've cornered and peppered with questions, any mistakes are mine alone. You all gave the best medical insight and provided excellent ideas.

Jenny M., for seeing what this book could be before I saw it myself. You are the best editor an author could ask for.

J, I placed my trust in you all those years ago and have never regretted it. Thank you for your unwavering support and for cooking dinner when my mind is stuck in 1813.

About the Author

*E*rica Taylor is a mother of two and military wife married to her high school sweetheart. Raised in the mountains of Colorado, she holds a BA in History from the University of Colorado. Erica has been writing stories as long as she can remember. She picked up her first romance novel while on a beach vacation as a teenager, and fell in love with falling in love, sexy heroes, and the feisty women who challenge their lives.

A self-confessed geek, Erica loves anything *Harry Potter*, *Doctor Who*, or *Star Wars*, can spend hours in Target with a Starbucks, and truly believes a cat makes a home. Currently living in South Africa, Erica can often be found writing during soccer practice or piano lessons and is not afraid to let dinner burn if it means getting the story out of her head.

The story continues in . . .

A Suitable Affair

Now Available

Chapter One

———— ❀ ————

September 1813
London, England

It was not an everyday occurrence that Lady Susanna Macalister was nearly trampled to death in the middle of Hyde Park. The pounding of hooves should have been her first intimation there was something amiss that fine Tuesday afternoon, but her thoughts at the time were scattered, delaying her response to the potential danger. As she turned to see a great, black beast charging straight towards her, Susanna stood helplessly frozen in shock, wondering how the day could have gone so terribly wrong.

Fortunately, her walking companion, Viscount Riverton, managed to keep his wits and push her out of the rider's path, shouting as the great, black horse reared up.

Susanna caught herself against a tree and turned to see her would-be assailant, tilting her head against the afternoon sun to where he was perched atop a very large horse. As the rider pulled sharply on the reins to regain control of his animal, she could see that his very handsome face was highly displeased, his gaze boring into Lord Riverton with something akin to hatred.

She could just barely make out the color of the rider's hair tucked beneath a cap—dark blond, matching the scruff around his mouth, chin, and jaw—but as he narrowed his gaze and focused solely on her, the color of his eyes was inscrutable, which was a shame because Susanna believed everything was in the eyes. She felt warmth rush through her, coloring her cheeks red, more from the heat of anger in the insolent gaze of the rider, than the adrenaline from her near-death rendezvous with the horse's hooves. The beast neighed angrily, clearly unhappy that the slight form of Susanna had curtailed his romp through the park.

"D'Artagnan, will you cease?" the rider cried at the horse, pulling him in a circle, attempting to regain control. The horse did not appreciate his master's tone in his command; he reared up again and spun about. Susanna took a few steps backward again, and Lord Riverton darted out of the way.

"Westcott, contain your cattle!" Lord Riverton exclaimed, grasping his jewel topped cane and waving it at the horse, which only angered the beast further. The rider glared again at Lord Riverton before digging his heels into the horse's flanks and taking off in the direction he had been initially headed.

"Goodness!" came a cry from Susanna's sister-in-law, as she hurried towards them. Clara, the Duchess of Bradstone, was close in age to Susanna, though half a head shorter and remarkably pretty. "What was that?"

"That, your grace, was the Earl of Westcott," Lord Riverton replied with indignation as he replaced the beaver hat that had toppled off his head, tucking his dark hair beneath the brim. He pulled out a handkerchief and dabbed at the perspiration on his neck before replacing it in his pocket. Riverton was a solid fellow, taller than Susanna—but only just—with dark brown hair and eyes. He was decidedly attractive yet not alarmingly so. Not someone you would necessarily notice in a crowd.

Susanna watched as he fiddled with the angle of his hat, expecting more of an explanation. "And *who* is the Earl of Westcott?" she asked impatiently, since he seemed more acquainted with the earl than either she or Clara were.

Lord Riverton did not meet her gaze, but answered her query. "Westcott was once almost my brother-in-law, when I was affianced to his sister, Lady Elizabeth, before she was tragically taken from me."

"How terribly sad for Lord Westcott to have to endure such a terrible loss," Susanna said, and Clara discreetly nudged her with her elbow. "And you too, of course, Lord Riverton," Susanna added.

He nodded sadly and looked away. "I am sorry for his appearance, Lady Susanna."

"No bother," Susanna said dismissively. "You cannot control the comings and goings of the earl."

"Quite right," Lord Riverton said, but he still looked crestfallen and quite shaken by the episode. "I beg for your apology, but I must take my leave. Westcott's appearance has quite thrown me into despondency. I was unaware he had returned to town."

Susanna nodded, though she was less traumatized than the viscount, and she was the one who had been throw into a tree and almost trampled by a horse. "Yes, of course."

"You will be able to find your way safely home, yes?" he asked, and took a few steps backwards, his dark eyes glancing around nervously.

Susanna glanced at her sister-in-law, who looked as bewildered as Susanna felt. "Yes, we will manage," Susanna replied with a roll of her eyes.

Riverton shot her a look that was so brief she almost thought she had imagined it. She stared at him for a moment longer, wondering if the anger that had flashed across his face was intended for her or for the man who almost trampled her. Lord Riverton tipped his hat and walked quickly away.

Susanna shook off the feeling of unease creeping up her back. Having been courted by him for months, Susanna thought she had assessed Lord Riverton's disposition fairly accurately, but she had never seen him agitated or frightened, never anxious, and certainly never hateful. He seemed to be a very calm and even-tempered fellow—steadfast—though almost boring if she was being completely honest. She must have misinterpreted his facial expression.

"Well, what an interesting turn of events," Clara said, raising an eyebrow at the viscount's retreating back.

Susanna couldn't agree more. The day had begun normally enough: her maid, Annette, had laid out a wonderfully pretty, lavender morning dress with a cream, satin sash across the midsection. After dressing, she broke her fast with her sisters in the breakfast room, then did some light reading in the garden. It was a bright day in early September, and Susanna was pleased when Lord Riverton had made a surprise appearance after tea and invited her to go for a walk. She donned her best bonnet and made sure her chaperone was the proper distance behind her as she and her fiancé strolled through the park.

Well, almost fiancé. Susanna had been hoping her suitor's unannounced appearance today would mean there would be a ring on her finger by the end of the afternoon. Apparently she had quite mistaken his intentions. He had merely come to ask for her forgiveness for being unable to attend the house party this coming weekend.

Clara linked her arm through Susanna's, and they turned back toward Bradstone House on the other side of Hyde Park. Riverton had forwardly introduced himself during a mutual friend's house party in July, and while his suit wasn't unwanted, it was surprising. Until then, Susanna had never heard of him. Her brother Andrew, the Duke of Bradstone, had been initially hesitant about him. Lord Riverton was the first to openly approach the stoic family patriarch and ask for permission to court her. Susanna knew her position in society and her family connections opened many doors, but they closed just as many when it came to her marriageable prospects. Not only was she the daughter and sister of the Dukes of Bradstone, but she had four additional brothers, and not many suitors were willing to take on the lot of them in order to pursue her hand. Some proclaimed they were not intimidated by her pack of brothers, but, in the end, she had not been worth the hassle. The fact that Riverton had been willing to brave the Macalister clan had been enough for Susanna to give the viscount a chance.

It had been over two months since Lord Riverton had begun to court her. She was expecting a declaration any day now, but there was something holding him back, and she wasn't certain how to push him along.

"It is curious that Lord Riverton seemed more shaken by seeing someone from his past than you were by almost getting trampled by a horse," Clara commented, slyly glancing at Susanna for a reaction. Careful not to give her one, Susanna nodded in agreement.

"I've not known him to be so skittish," Susanna replied evenly. "Odd, yes, and peculiar in his choice of friends, but perhaps it was the memory of his lost fiancée that bothered him so?"

Clara shrugged. "Either way. At least this gives us a chance to walk by ourselves without a male looming over our shoulders and interfering with our conversation."

"Was there a topic you wanted to discuss in particular?" Clara glanced at her and nodded. "There was, actually."

Susanna sighed. "You've been dancing around this since last week, Clara. Let us have it out and see how we can fix whatever problem you have created."

"It is not I who created this problem," the duchess rectified. "It is you."

"Me? What could I have possibly done?"

"I know Andrew has approved of this match mainly because you asked him to," Clara began. "I want to make certain you know you do not have to engage with him any longer if you truly do not want to. I fear you are agreeing to Riverton's courtship based solely on a desire for a husband and not due to actual affection for the viscount."

Susanna stopped walking and eyed her sister-in-law. "You think I am merely accepting the first man to ask?"

"Of course not," Clara said. "But I must tell you what a bore Lord Riverton is."

"He is not a bore."

"He is quite peculiar, as you have already mentioned," Clara responded. "And his manners are uncouth."

"He was startled," Susanna said in Riverton's defense.

"He left us in the middle of the park with no footman or means to get safely home," Clara replied. "It was quite ungentlemanly."

"But we are home," Susanna said, indicating the large Park Lane mansion just on the other side of the street.

Clara crossed her arms and sighed. "I do not want to quarrel with you. I simply wish you to be as happy as I. You need not settle simply because the viscount showed you some semblance of attention. You deserve a little romance, Susanna, and I do not think Riverton possesses anything of the sort. Yes, he would provide a good, solid household and position, and a reasonable companion, but you should be *wooed*, Susanna, not simply courted. Courting is boring."

"This is coming from the expert on courtships," Susanna said, rolling her eyes. Her brother's courtship of Clara was not exactly the example by which all courtships were expected to follow.

"My courtship may not have been traditional, but the end result was the same," Clara said defensively.

"I know, Duchess Clara," Susanna replied, using the family's pet name for their new duchess. "I do appreciate your concern, but I think the situation with Riverton simply needs to run its course."

Clara nodded. "I am merely a champion for your happiness, dear."

Susanna smiled genuinely at her. In the few short months she had known Clara—through her very unconventional and dramatic courtship to her brother—the duchess had become more than simply a friend. She really felt as though Clara was truly her sister.

"I am famished," Susanna said. "Let's see what Cookie has set up for luncheon."

Clara laughed and linked her arm through Susanna's as they made their way across the cobblestone street, the events of the park pushed to the back of their minds.

Ian Carlisle, the Earl of Westcott, was not pleased.

He had been late to his meeting, and it was all his brother-in-law's fault.

Almost brother-in-law. And it was not *entirely* Viscount Riverton's fault. Had the viscount's dark-haired walking companion not stepped into his path, Ian would not have been forced to give up his course in order to not trample the poor girl to death. Still, Riverton was present and that gave Ian reason enough to blame his almost brother-in-law.

He glanced around the rose tea room he had fashioned into a makeshift study in his father's London home. It had been Beth's favorite room, and while his first instinct had been to board it up upon her death, he found himself unable to do so. It comforted him to be here, to hold onto a piece of his poor, dead sister.

"Problems, cousin?"

Ian was startled out of his brooding thoughts by Lord Rheneas Warren, the Earl of Bexley.

"Same problem as always, Rheneas," Ian answered and watched his cousin as he strode into the room. The earl winced at his Christian name but did not correct him, though Ian was the only person aside from Bexley's mother whom he permitted to call him Rheneas. They had once been boys together at Ashford Hall in Wiltshire. Ian had not been allowed to attend Eton, on his father's orders, and had envied his cousin's time spent there and the friends he had cultivated. As soon as he could muster enough courage, Ian bought himself a commission and left the country, leaving his sister in the care of his senile mother and father. He would never forgive himself for his moment of rebellion.

"I came over as soon as I heard," Bexley said, taking a seat across from Ian's desk. "Heard what?" Ian asked, looking back down at the missive in his hands.

"That you have officially returned to town," Bexley replied, popping off his hat and gloves and setting them aside. "It's been three years, cousin."

Ian looked up at him shrewdly. "I saw you not six months ago at Easter."

"Yes, but Easter was not spent in town."

"So the startling revelation is that I am in London?" Ian asked, placing the parchment in a file. "Nice to know I can still cause a stir. Besides, I have been here many times in the past three years."

Bexley scoffed. "But no one was paying attention then. Your appearance will turn some heads, though not as many had you waited until the regular season. At least now people will not think you are here to look for a wife."

"Gads no," Ian replied, shaking his head. "Last thing on my mind, I assure you."

"However, the fact that you raced hellbent through Hyde Park, almost trampling Lady Susanna Macalister, is bound to cause some commotion."

"Is that who that was?" Ian asked, the surname ringing a bell. Bexley nodded. "I am friends with her brother, you know."

"The duke, right?"

Bexley nodded again. "He was most displeased to hear you were causing quite a dangerous disturbance in the park."

"Is he the Hyde Park Watch now?"

Bexley chuckled. "No, just very protective of his kin."

"I assume you sent my utmost apologies for offending his grace's sensibilities?"

"He demanded a personal apology for himself and his sister," Bexley responded. "The duke is hosting a house party this weekend, and he has issued you an invitation. Or rather, his new duchess has."

"I am honored," Ian replied sarcastically, weary at the thought of having to attend a society function. "I suppose I cannot refuse?" he asked, rubbing his brow.

Bexley shook his head. "No one refuses the Duchess of Bradstone." His cousin stood and retrieved his hat and gloves from the side table. "I will be here at nine sharp Friday morning to collect you."

Ian nodded and Bexley left, leaving Ian alone with his thoughts. As much as he avoided London, he really did not avoid society. Truth be told, he never had a proper season. He left the country just before he was old enough to make his own bows before the King, only doing so when his father forced him while home on a brief leave. Ian was gone again after having only attended a few balls, one musical, and two nights at Almack's Assembly Rooms. He had not returned again until his sister's betrothal three years ago. Since then, the Home Office had kept him busy enough, not allowing him to spend much time in England, much less London.

Ian threw his quill down on the table and sighed, resigning to his fate. His appearance in London this time was only spurred by a summons from his superiors; it was the unfortunate encounter with Lady Susanna that had made him tardy this morning.

He supposed he owed Lady Susanna a sensible explanation and apology. It wasn't very gentlemanly of him to nearly crush a lady of quality with his horse, especially when that lady was the sister of a duke who was a friend of his cousin. Plus, he felt oddly obligated to warn Lady Susanna of his past with Riverton. He knew not of her connection to the viscount, but if she was walking with him in Hyde Park, she should know the sort of character Riverton was. Ian did not think the viscount was fit company for any lady, and he doubted Lady Susanna was aware of that just yet. He could not divulge everything he knew about the viscount, but he would think of something to get Lady Susanna away from Riverton. Ian would be damned if another unsuspecting young lady fell victim to Riverton's whims.